THE ARTIST'S WAR

CLARE FLYNN

Storm

Ebook ISBN: 978-1-80508-725-0
Paperback ISBN: 978-1-80508-726-7

Cover design: Debbie Clement
Cover images: Arcangel, Shutterstock

Published by Storm Publishing.
For further information, visit:
www.stormpublishing.co

ALSO BY CLARE FLYNN

Hearts of Glass

The Artist's Apprentice

The Artist's Wife

The Penang Series

The Pearl of Penang

Prisoner from Penang

A Painter in Penang

Jasmine in Paris

The Chalky Sea

The Alien Corn

The Frozen River

A Greater World

Kurinji Flowers

Letters from a Patchwork Quilt

The Green Ribbons

The Gamekeeper's Wife

Storms Gather Between Us

Sisters at War

In memory of William Joseph Flynn 1890–1937

The highest reward for a person's toil is not what they get for it,
but what they become by it.

John Ruskin

ONE

Little Badgerton, Hampshire, April 1916

Alice Cutler was having a crisis of confidence. She stood by the cottage window, staring out over the meadow to the distant trees which were starting to put on new leaves. She asked herself how she had ever imagined she'd be capable of taking on the running of the glass workshop in her husband's absence.

After all it wasn't as though she had any business experience. She wasn't even a trained artist. Her knowledge of making stained glass was entirely the result of watching and learning from Edmund. He himself had trained at the best specialist school of crafts and design and in the studios of Christopher Whall, the finest living practitioner of the art of stained glass. How could she dare to presume herself capable of taking up the mantle herself?

Alice traced her hand over the cold glass of the window as the pale morning light slipped into the room that served as both kitchen and living room. Outside the window splashes of primroses brought welcome colour after the long dark and barren winter.

It was almost time to move across to the stone-built studio next door and get to work on a different window – one that consisted of small pieces of glass cut ready for her to paint and fire. Her mouth felt dry at the thought of it.

How could she possibly undertake such an important commission as the Latchington window, without Edmund's guiding hand, his quiet advice, his gentle encouragement and his unwavering love?

The responsibility was too great, the burden too heavy. Wouldn't it be better to close up the workshop for the remainder of the war and return to working up at the big house as a VAD? The thought was so tempting. She could cover up the workbenches with sheeting, leave the kiln to grow cold, tidy away the cutting tools, brushes and jars of paint pigment, and close and lock the studio door until her husband's return. Didn't she have more than enough to occupy her in caring for Lottie, her eight-year-old stepdaughter? She could return to working a part-time shift at Bankstone while Lottie was at school.

The Latchington window could wait for the war to end. Lady Lockwood, who had commissioned the work to honour the life of her late son, Bevis, would surely understand that it was far too big a job for Alice to take on her own slender shoulders.

Behind her, the kettle whistled on the hob. Alice went to make a pot of tea. A few minutes later, nursing a cup between cold fingers, she settled in her chair, gazing at the empty armchair on the other side of the fireplace. There was still an indentation in the seat cushion where Edmund had last sat. Alice stared at it, picturing Edmund sitting there enjoying his cup of morning tea beside her.

The pain of loss was worse than a physical one. The wrenching agony of absence. The dull ache of loneliness. The reminders of him were all around her. The coldness of the sheet on the other half of the bed. Unrelenting silence in the cottage once Lottie was asleep or at school. Edmund's heavy-duty work apron hanging on the back of the studio door. A half-finished drawing of an acorn in his sketchbook. All the long, lonely nights when she cried out for him in her sleep, waking to the realisation that he could neither hear nor answer. Most of all, the sheer convulsive terror that he might never come home to her, that she would never see him striding towards her across the meadow, never again run her fingers through his thick wavy hair, pushing it back from his brow, never again know the feeling of those strong arms wrapped around her, nor feel the soft touch of his lips.

Alice's hand jerked, spilling tea into the saucer. She took a sip and thought how everything felt better with a cup of tea. But it had to be piping hot. Once tepid, she couldn't bear to drink it.

She'd promised Edmund to carry on. When he had set off up the hill with his kitbag over his shoulder, he'd asked her to continue the work on the Latchington window. He'd spoken of his belief in her and his conviction that she was more than capable of doing it without him. He'd told her he would always be with her in spirit.

Across the short distance between the cottage and the workshop she heard the snap of the latch and the creak of the heavy oak door opening.

Maurice.

He was another reason Alice had to keep going.

Alice put down her cup, pulled her shoulders back, reached for her studio apron and set off to join him.

Captain Maurice Kynaston had been wounded in the Battle of Loos. It had cost him a leg – and apparently also his fiancée. Refusing the chance to have a prosthesis made and fitted, he'd chosen to manage only with the aid of a crutch – and like many of the limbless war-wounded, he had proved himself remarkably adept at getting around on one leg.

Soon after his arrival at Bankstone, Maurice had begun

assisting in the stained-glass studio. He'd told Alice and Edmund that the work fulfilled a long-term desire to work with his hands – an ambition that had been sidelined by his army career. The Bankstone medical officer had acknowledged that the work appeared to be therapeutic for the captain and was aiding in his recovery from depression, following the loss of his leg.

'Morning, Alice.' Maurice greeted her as she came into the workshop. 'A cold one today. Frost first thing. Shall I light a fire?'

She nodded, grateful. As he set about laying the fire, Alice went to the workbench and tried to decide what to do next. She mustn't think about the magnitude of the project, but instead break it into small manageable tasks that she and Maurice could complete. Small steps. That's what Edmund would say.

She smiled at Maurice as he raised himself up from where he had been sitting on a stool in front of the fireplace, coaxing the fire into life. He never complained about his absent leg, although Alice knew enough from her short nursing training and her service at Bankstone, to appreciate that at times he must experience great pain. Every day, moving around and completing simple tasks such as lighting a fire were logistical challenges for the captain. She remembered the first time she'd met him, when she found him quietly weeping over the memory of a dead comrade, in his bed on the ward at Bankstone. A handsome man in his early thirties, with a neatly clipped moustache, there was nothing arrogant about Maurice and she had increasingly come to depend on him in Edmund's absence.

'What would you like me to do this morning?' he asked.

She handed him a dish with a small mound of dried-up green pigment. 'Can you revive this, please, Maurice? Mix it up well with the knife before adding water gradually. Not too much. Judge the feel as you go. No rush. Keep most of it in a tidy little lump on one side and make a small pond in the middle of the palette to work from. You can add more water as needed. Once you're happy with the mix and the colour, let me know, and I'll show you the pieces I'd like you to work on. I need you to apply a soft green wash to them all.'

Alice felt awkward giving Maurice instructions. Not because he was unreceptive – he wasn't. But because she was barely past the beginner stage herself, constantly consulting the tightly packed notebooks she had filled when Edmund had taught her. She closed her eyes and imagined her husband standing on the other side of the large central table that dominated the workspace. Once she had pictured him at work, it was a case of mirroring his actions as she had done so often before.

Maurice settled himself on a high stool beside the workbench, hanging his crutches from an adjacent hook that Edmund had attached to the wall for the purpose. The captain set about mixing and refreshing the pigments into a loose solution of paint. He was an adept pupil, working quietly and confidently, but never afraid to ask for help when in doubt. Alice enjoyed his reassuring presence. While Maurice lacked the artistic flair essential to a true stained-glass artist, he was a highly competent craftsman, dextrous, diligent and steady-handed. The perfect assistant.

They worked in silence until mid-morning, when Alice suggested she make a pot of tea and they stop for a short break. She returned with a plate of biscuits as well as the tray of tea and they settled in front of the fire on a couple of wooden chairs.

After a few moments of silence, Alice asked, 'Do you see much of my brother? I do worry about him.'

Maurice looked up sharply. 'Yes, I suppose so. Victor and I are still on the same ward.'

'What does he do all day?' Alice frowned. She had tried asking Victor the same question, but he was always evasive.

'He reads a lot. Mostly, the financial newspapers. Writes letters occasionally—'

She interrupted him, curious to understand more about the brother who had changed so much since he'd gone to war. 'Do you know who he writes to? He tells me nothing.'

'The families of men in his platoon, I think. Those who lost their lives. A long job getting through the list. He treats it with great care and diligence.'

'Oh,' she said, surprised. 'I hadn't realised that. I imagine it's quite a responsibility.'

'Victor cared a great deal for his men. I'm sure he was an exemplary officer.' Maurice paused. 'He's never mentioned what he did before the war.'

'He worked as a stockbroker. In the City. Don't ask me about it as I haven't a clue.' Alice hesitated, then added, 'Actually, he worked for my husband's father, Herbert Cutler.'

Maurice raised his eyebrows. 'Ah! The man in prison awaiting trial. Of course.'

'Edmund and his father have been estranged for years. And I don't imagine Victor has much of a relationship with Herbert Cutler now. They fell out when Victor joined up.' Alice paused for a moment then decided to confide in the officer. There was something about him that inspired trust and confidence. 'Victor was going to marry Dora, Edmund's former wife, but that was all off once he announced he was accepting a commission. And I gather Herbert Cutler was furious that Victor walked out of the firm and left him in the lurch.'

'Do you know why he decided to volunteer? It sounds as though it was a sudden decision.'

'It was. A friend of his was killed on the *Lusitania*. After that, he was determined to do his bit to put a stop to the German aggression.'

Maurice sipped his tea, then put it aside as he reached for a log and, leaning forward, placed it carefully onto the fire. 'Last night, Victor told me the War Office wants to talk to him about a new role.' He looked at Alice, pausing momentarily. 'Once he's fit enough.'

Alice froze. Her heart thumped in her chest. She twisted round to look directly at the captain. 'Surely not? He isn't going back into service, is he?'

'Not to the front. Sorry, did I give you a fright?' Maurice smiled apologetically. 'It's working for the War Office. Based in London. He doesn't know any details but I understand it involves some form of statistical work.'

'That sounds the perfect job for Victor. He's used to working with financial matters. It all goes over my head, I'm afraid. But taking a job sounds a marvellous idea. It will give him a sense of purpose again. Keep him busy. Stop him brooding.'

Maurice said nothing, but stared deep into the fire. It crackled as it started to consume the new log.

'I'll go over to Bankstone later. Maybe he'll tell me about it,' Alice said brightly. But she doubted he would. Victor had seemed preoccupied ever since he'd been admitted to Bankstone. He wasn't hostile towards her – there was no sign of the antipathy he had shown to her after the death of her then-fiancé: Edmund's brother, the man Victor had been in love with. When Alice had happened upon their secret relationship it had marked the end of her engagement and the end of Gilbert's life.

Time had brought about a reconciliation between her and Victor, which Alice was grateful for – especially now, with the war causing so much grief and separation – but Alice still wished her brother would confide in her, instead of exhibiting the stiff upper lip the officer class were expected to show.

TWO

Browndown Training Camp, Gosport, Hampshire, April 1916

Since their arrival at the Gosport military training camp, Edmund Cutler was thankful he was able to undertake his training with his friend Robert Fuller. The two men had been called to arms on the same day and left Little Badgerton together to travel the thirty miles or so to the camp. The men at the camp came from all over the country so Edmund counted himself lucky to be with a kindred spirit. Edmund had a feeling their training would not be protracted, and they were likely to be shipped out to France sooner rather than later. He hated the thought of the Channel separating him from Alice.

But in the meantime, the induction into the army was intense. Constant drilling, route marches while carrying heavy packs, hours of practice wielding their bayonets with which they had to charge at and stab sandbags. There were frequent inspections of kit and uniform with punishments if standards weren't met.

Late one afternoon, Edmund and Robert were sitting on their camp beds, polishing their boots with Dubbin. The smell of the Dubbin permeated the cramped space of the hut, where the rest of the platoon were similarly occupied. The strokes of the brushes across the leather formed a steady beat, as the men unthinkingly fell into a collective rhythm as they polished.

'I feel like I'm back at boarding school,' said Edmund. 'Except instead of six of the best if the work didn't pass muster, here it'll be a hundred press-ups. I know which is worse.'

Robert Fuller glanced over at his friend and smiled. 'At my school no one cared enough about the state of our shoes to punish us for them not being shiny.'

'What? They never gave you a hiding? Come on! I don't believe it!'

Robert snorted. 'Oh, trust me, I had many a leathering. Just not for dirty shoes. At least a good thrashing is over in a couple of minutes. The press-ups here are sustained torture.'

'What did you get punished for?'

Robert shrugged. 'Reading books under the desk during mathematics lessons, being late for class, getting in fights, answering back to the master, all the usual stuff.'

Edmund grinned. 'Handing out copies of *Das Kapital* in the playground, were you?'

'Not far off it. That and reading John Stuart Mill when I should have been working on logarithm tables.'

'Logs!' Edmund's face contorted. 'Might as well have been Chinese. Never read either Mill or Marx, I confess. One of my masters used to lend me his copies of *The Hobby Horse* and then *The Yellow Book*. That's what got me so interested in the Arts and Crafts movement. I also read *The Boy's Own Paper* avidly. Loved all those tales of derring-do.'

'Well now we get to live them apparently.' Robert Fuller's voice dripped with sarcasm. 'Plenty of scope for adventure once we get to France.' He snorted in derision, then turned the boot he was polishing to work on it from another angle. 'As far as I can remember from when I was over there, acts of derring-do now consist of shooting rats and staring at the walls of a dugout, accompanied by the constant thrum of shellfire.'

Their conversation was evidently overheard. From the bed opposite a voice called out. 'Some of us can't wait to get over there and give the Hun a good pounding.' The speaker was a young man probably still in his teens, based on the healthy crop of acne on his face and the pitch of his voice.

The older man sitting on the next bed jumped in. 'Aye, the lad's right. You're a real miserable bastard, Fuller. Last thing these boys need before we even get out there is someone telling them rubbish like that.'

Fuller looked up. 'Rubbish, is it? Since I'm the only one who's ever set foot outside England, let alone visited the battle-fields, I happen to know what I'm talking about.'

'Aye, but all the more reason not to put the wind up the lads,' the man persisted.

'Put the wind up them? Don't be daft. What I'm actually saying is that most of the time it's crushingly boring. Waiting. Hour after hour. Day after day. Waiting for something to happen. Waiting for a shell to have your name written on it or a sniper to spot you if you stick your head above the parapet. Not a lot of scope for heroism. Did nobody tell you, Ackroyd, trench warfare's a war of attrition. Day after endless day standing around. Waiting, waiting, waiting. You can't even see the Germans. They're doing the same thing half a mile away in their own trenches.' He put down one boot and picked up the other. 'Besides, I wasn't aware I was addressing the whole hut. I was labouring under the misapprehension I was actually talking to Cutler.'

'Well, mebbes keep yer voice down a bit.' The older man glanced at the spotty-faced teen on the bed beside him. 'Most of us are patriots and don't want to listen to your political nonsense and all those long words as means nowt.'

Fuller was about to respond, but a glance from Edmund

gave him pause and he lowered his head and swept his brush over the tin of Dubbin before spreading it across the boot in his hand.

'Don't waste your breath on Ackroyd. He loves to pick trouble. Spoiling for a fight.' Edmund shook his head and lowered his voice. 'He knows if that happens the sergeant'll take his side since they're old pals. Don't give him reason.'

'You're right of course. But it sickens me when I hear lads like that still believing all the rubbish the papers feed them. I just want them to have a better idea what to expect.'

'Why? What's the point? It won't change anything. We're still going to be sent over there no matter what we think. If it helps the lad to believe he has a chance to become a hero, why disabuse him of that? He'll find out soon enough. The time to warn people that the whole war is an exercise in insanity passed long ago. We're caught up in the machine now. We just have to get on with it.' Edmund held his boot up to examine it in the fading light from the hut window. He gave it a couple more brushstrokes then replaced it with the other. 'You heard from home yet?'

Robert's mouth stretched into a rictus. 'We can't talk here with this lot listening. Let's finish up outside.'

Edmund was about to protest that it was too cold to sit out there but reminded himself they'd soon be exposed to all manner of weathers – there'd be no hut or camp beds once they were at the front. He took the boot and his brush and followed Robert to sit on the step outside the hut.

'I can hardly bear to read her letters,' said Robert. 'The paper she writes on is all crinkled up and smudged from her tears. And we haven't even left Hampshire yet.'

'Viola's taken it bad?'

'You could say that. But it would be an understatement. She acts like the world is about to end. What about Alice?'

'Putting a brave face on. I know she's in bits but she's doing her best to hide it from me. I still feel a cad for not telling her I'd signed the attestation papers.'

'What difference would it have made if you had? Look at me. I certainly never signed up for this and yet here I am. No bloody choice in the matter. Well, I suppose I could have opted for prison and hard labour.'

'Viola must be used to you being away though. All that travelling you did with your writing assignments. Obviously, she's scared about you being in the army but at least, unlike Alice, she's used to you not being at home.'

Fuller snorted. 'You're joking, man. Viola has never got used to my absence. She used to kick up a fuss even if I went to London to see my publisher for lunch. Every time I went abroad there'd be wailing and gnashing of teeth.' He put down his boot and laid the brush aside. 'In the end I stopped telling her in advance. Waited until the last minute then told her as I was walking out the door.'

Edmund frowned. He couldn't imagine such a lack of trust between himself and Alice. 'That's harsh. Didn't she know you did a lot of travelling when you met?'

'Course she did. But she thought she'd get me to change. Couldn't understand why I wouldn't get another job, or even find something else to write about that didn't involve me leaving the house.'

Edmund frowned. It sounded unhealthy. He couldn't imagine Alice behaving like that. He said nothing.

'Viola has never understood that travel writing is more than a job to me. It's a passion. When we met, she was training to be a teacher. We'd talk for hours and hours and I told her about all the places I'd visited. We made plans to travel together. To the Peloponnese. To Asia Minor. To Egypt.'

Robert leant back against the hut door. He rolled a cigarette and lit it. 'Everything changed though. She fell pregnant straight away and from then on all she wanted to do was to keep house. Couldn't even get her to walk in the hills with me anymore.'

Edmund finished polishing his own boots and looked at his friend, curious.

Robert drew on his cigarette. 'I started to feel trapped, suffocated.' He let out a long breath. 'Look, it's not about the children. God knows that's hardly down to her alone. We both knew what we were doing. Crazy for each other. But she changed. I got an offer to write a book about the excavations in Mesopotamia. I wanted us to go together. Our eldest, Molly, was ten months. No reason why we couldn't have gone as a family. There was a house laid on for us. It would have been an adventure. But she wouldn't. We argued. I went anyway.'

He looked up at his friend. 'Hell, Edmund, don't look at me like that! I have to make a living. When I got back eleven months later, she presented me with our second child. She'd never even told me she was pregnant. Wrote to me all the time I was away but never chose to mention that little matter.' He splayed his fingers out and studied them then rubbed away at a spot of polish around one of his knuckles. 'Not that it would have brought me home sooner, I suppose.

'From then on, being at home was like a jail sentence. Viola didn't want us to see anyone else. She wanted me all to herself. I felt like her prisoner so I couldn't wait to get away again. She's never understood that.' He clenched his fists tightly. 'I love the bones of that woman but she's slowly killing me.'

Edmund was lost for words for a few moments. He remembered how Alice had told him that Viola asked her not to call whenever Robert was home – claiming it was his stricture not hers. This was a different side to the story.

Robert looked up at him. 'You think I'm a right bastard, don't you? Going off for months at a time like that and leaving her.'

Edmund raised his eyebrows and shook his head. 'Far be it from me to judge. I made a wreck of my first marriage.'

'I did wonder what the story was about that.'

'Fell for her beauty and didn't take the time to get to know her well enough. I was desperate to have her. Utterly besotted.' Edmund shook his head. It was hard to imagine himself ever feeling that way once. 'We met at art school, and I envisaged a future where we'd work together. Like Alice and I do now. Well – not even like that – Dora was an illustrator and I'd have been happy if she'd pursued her own work, not necessarily assisted with mine. But she stopped. Just like that. The day after we were married, she wanted no more of it. Told me she hated painting. It was like a shaft through my heart. I realised I didn't know her at all.' Edmund closed his eyes for a moment. He hated thinking back to the time when the knowledge he'd made a terrible mistake had grown stronger every day.

'Turned out we had nothing in common at all. Absolutely nothing. She couldn't bear me to touch her. Couldn't stand the sight of me. But I'm making it sound like it was all her fault. That's unfair. I was the one who persuaded her to marry me. I brought it all upon myself.'

Robert gave a dry laugh. 'We're all the architects of our own destiny. There's plenty I'd do differently if I had my time again.'

'You're not married to Viola. Do you ever think of leaving her?' As soon as the words slipped out Edmund regretted them.

But Fuller wasn't perturbed. 'How could I? We've three children together. I love them all. I love Viola too. And there's never been a problem in the bedroom. I love her but I find it impossible to live with her all the time. It would crush the life out of me. Trouble is, I can't even criticise her. It's simply that she loves me too much.'

Edmund wanted to disagree. To tell Robert that a love that completely suffocated someone else was too selfish to be a real love. He tried to imagine Alice behaving that way but couldn't.

He sent up a silent prayer of thanks that he'd found her. Alice always put him before herself. He remembered when they'd lost their baby so late in her pregnancy; how she had put her grief aside to talk to Lady Lockwood on his behalf and save the valuable window commission. She'd agreed to marry him even though it went against her own principles. She'd willingly taken on his child and agreed to bring Lottie up as her own. And how had he repaid her? Signing the Derby Scheme papers without telling her and now finding himself here in this crowded tent, about to put his life and their future at risk.

Edmund thought all this but said nothing.

Robert continued, oblivious to Edmund's silence. 'Maybe I shouldn't be telling you all this. But I've bottled it up for years.'

'I'm sorry.' Edmund didn't know what else to say. Now the dark spells of melancholy Alice had told him Robert suffered periodically, according to Viola, made sense.

But this unexpected confessional from Robert was cut short when Sergeant Lumb appeared round the corner of the hut and stood, arms akimbo, surveying the pair. 'Right, you 'orrible lot. Kit inspection. Get inside. By your beds, now!'

They picked up the boots and brushes and went back into the hut.

THREE

Harriet, Countess of Wallingford, opened the door to her husband's bedroom to find out why he'd been absent at breakfast.

When in London, the earl refused to be woken by his valet, preferring to breakfast with Harriet and the children while still wearing his silk dressing gown – something that was a constant irritation to Jenkins, his valet, and a source of amusement to Harriet.

The bedroom appeared empty, and she was about to look in his study, when she noticed the pair of slippered feet sticking out from the far side of the bed.

Had he passed out? Failed to make it into bed after imbibing too much port the previous evening? Harriet tutted to herself – her husband prided himself on his iron constitution and appeared to tolerate an enormous quantity of alcohol with no apparent ill effect. Irritated, she moved across the room to investigate. 'The children missed you at break—'

The earl was lying on his back, stark naked, eyes wide and glassy, mouth open.

She rushed to his side, knelt beside him and touched his face.

Stone cold. Reaching for his wrist, she felt for a pulse.

Nothing. His skin had taken on a ghostly pallor instead of its usual port-wine red complexion.

Probably dead for some hours.

Harriet glanced at the swollen belly, the varicose veins like grapes on his spindly legs, the shrivelled penis like a sleeping slug. Death had robbed him of any dignity. She pulled the eiderdown off the bed and spread it over his body to cover his nakedness.

Poor old thing, she thought. *I'm actually going to miss you. Never expected to think that. But you weren't such a bad old stick, were you?*

Still kneeling beside the body, she stroked his thin grey hair away from his brow. To her surprise she felt a tear in her eye but quickly brushed it aside. It must be shock, she told herself. Finding one's husband, the father of one's children, dead on the bedroom floor was hardly an everyday occurrence.

The children. How on earth was she going she tell them? They adored their father. Purveyor of sweets and treats. Always willing to let them ride on his back playing horsey. They would be devastated. Crispin and little Poppy anyway – Godfrey was too small to understand.

Should the doctor be summoned? Presumably one would be required to officially pronounce the earl dead. Harriet got to her feet and rang the bell to summon Jenkins. The trusted valet would know what to do.

As Harriet waited, it began to sink in. Widowed at only twenty-seven. When she'd first married the old boy, that would have been a dream come true, but now she felt sad and very alone.

She took several big gulps of air, pulled her shoulders back, and clenched her fists. Time to face the world. There were announcements to be made and a funeral to arrange.

It turned out that the earl's funeral had already been planned. It had been set out in meticulous detail by His Lordship himself, and in line with family tradition. He was to be laid to rest alongside his forebears in the marbled Wallingford vault at their ancestral home in Suffolk.

Harriet had visited Wallingford Hall only once, on the occasion of her short honeymoon, and had had no wish to repeat the experience. She preferred the London townhouse in Portman Square with its proximity to shops, theatres, parks and concert halls. Wallingford Hall was a severe, draughty Palladian mansion, crammed with uncomfortable furniture and ugly portraits of dead earls and their spouses.

Harriet recalled how the odour of manure from the pigs bred on the estate overpowered the dusty smell of the house, when the wind was in the wrong direction – which seemed to be most of the time.

Now, two days after the earl's sudden death, Harriet was sitting in the drawing room at Portman Square with her best friend, Alice Cutler, asking her to accompany her to Norfolk for the funeral.

'I don't think I can cope on my own,' Harriet admitted. 'Please come with me, Alice.'

'Of course I'll come. Since Edmund's away at training camp I'll need to ask Eleanor to look after Lottie but they'll both enjoy that.' She touched her friend on the arm. 'But don't say you won't be able to cope. I've never known you be unable to cope with anything in all the years we've known each other. You're indomitable. Whenever I feel overwhelmed by something, I think of you and ask myself what would Harriet do.'

Harriet gave a little snort. 'I'm far from indomitable when I'm up against Monty's old fossil of a mother. The old crow's barely breathing, yet she manages to scorch me to a cinder with just a look from her evil eye. She will have been sharpening her claws in readiness for seeing for me.'

'Gosh,' said Alice, 'I didn't even realise his mother was still alive.'

'I'm convinced she only carries on because she's fuelled by her loathing of me. She must be well into her eighties or nineties, and she's never made a secret of how much she disapproves of me. Poor old Monty got it from both barrels when he told her he was marrying me.'

'Why? Did you upset her in some way?'

Harriet rolled her eyes. 'I didn't have to. She'd made her mind up before she met me. She was as thick as thieves with Monty's first wife, who was ten years older than him and one of the dowager countess's cronies. As far as the old witch is concerned, I'm a jumped-up little nobody who has usurped her dead friend's memory and presumed to steal away her beloved son. Now that poor Monty's gone, she'll doubtless hold me responsible for his death.'

'Surely, she's happy that you've provided her with grandchildren? There were no children from the first marriage, were there?' Alice couldn't help wondering whether her friend was indulging in some dramatic exaggeration. Alice had never met Monty's mother but surely she couldn't be as monstrous as Harriet was painting her.

'The dowager countess has no problem with the children. They're essential to the perpetuation of the Wallingford line. Her issue isn't with the fact that they exist: Just that she doesn't want to have anything to do with them. She's old school – her philosophy is that they must be seen rarely and not heard at all. And the only child she has any interest in at all is Crispin, being the heir.

'As for me – I'm nothing more than the depository of her son's seed. I've no more status than one of the wretched sows they breed on their awful smelly estate.'

Alice tried not to laugh. Harriet was always so irreverent, so fearless about expressing her opinions. 'The dowager countess sounds terrifying. Of course I'll come with you. It's the least I can do and a fraction of all you've done for me.'

Unsaid, but very much in mind, was the memory of Harriet being with her when Alice had lost the child she was carrying, in a premature stillbirth.

Harriet jumped up and gave Alice a hug. 'We won't even have to spend the night in the ghastly place. You can stay here at Portman Square the night before, then Foster will drive us to the station, and we can take the train to Norfolk first thing in the morning. After the service, there'll be a small reception at the house which I intend to duck out of once I've put in an appearance.' Harriet got up and moved over to stand by the window. 'The family solicitor will be there for the reading of the will.' She gazed through the window at the rain-drenched plane trees in the gardens of the square, bare branches dripping in an anthropomorphic show of misery. She turned to face Alice. 'I'd really like some moral support for that. Not that I expect any surprises, as Monty was always clear that the children and I are the prime beneficiaries. There were no children from his first marriage. He had no siblings and I imagine he thought he'd outlive his mother, who was left a substantial inheritance by Monty's father.'

Harriet moved back and sat down again. 'A friendly face in the room will dilute the impact of the old fire-breathing dragon.'

'What will happen to her? To the dowager countess? Doesn't she live there?'

'Nothing, as far as I'm concerned. She's welcome to live out her miserable days in that ugly old mansion. She'll be long dead before Crispin finishes his education and is ready to take over the estate.' Harriet stuck out her bottom lip. 'Assuming he has the poor judgement to want to do so. Which I fervently hope he won't.'

'And if he doesn't want to live there?'

'There's an estate manager, Mr Troughton. He pretty well runs the whole show anyway. Crispin can live off the income and do what he likes.' Harriet smoothed the fabric of her skirt over her knees and smiled at Alice. 'I've always rather hoped he'll develop a wanderlust and take himself off to see the world before settling down. Like they used to do on the Grand Tours.' She shook her head. 'But that's years away. Whatever he decides will be his choice not mine. Even if it involves being a pig farmer or snoring all day on the benches of the House of Lords.'

As if on cue, the heir apparent burst into the room and hurled himself into his mother's lap. A mop of curls, a chubby face and a slightly too pink complexion made it evident that he was the progeny of the late earl. The seven-year-old had also inherited Harriet's bright blue-grey eyes and the ability to issue forth a rapid flow of excited words like machine-gun fire.

'Mama, Mama, Miss Eccles says I have to stay at home and learn my seven times table while she takes Poppy and the baby to the park. It's not fair!' His eyes welled with tears. 'Miss Eccles says, since Papa has gone to heaven, I am the man of the house and must behave with diggingty and duck-orum until he's laid to rest.' He looked up at his mother, who stroked his mop of hair away from his forehead. 'It's not fair, Mama.'

Harriet looked over the top of his head at Alice and rolled her eyes. 'Darling boy, your mama is talking with your aunty Alice, so you must do as Miss Eccles says and go back to the nursery and study those multiplication tables.' Anticipating the protest, she kissed the top of his head. 'When we've finished talking, you can come for a walk in the park with us.'

The little boy jerked upright, brushing the tears from his eyes. 'Just me. Not Poppy and Godfrey?'

'Just you. Now run along and work on those tables, as Aunty Alice and I will be testing you. If you get them all right, we'll ask Cook for some dry bread and you can feed the ducks later.'

This suggestion evidently met with unqualified approval, as Crispin clambered down from his mother's knee and ran out of the room.

When he'd gone, Harriet turned to Alice and sighed. 'Miss Eccles is very old school. But she came with the best of references, and I'd struggle to cope without her.' She ran her palms over her skirt again, smoothing out the rucks her son had created. 'Soon Crispin will be too big to want to sit on his mother's knee. They grow up so fast.'

'How have the children taken His Lordship's death?'

Harriet shook her head. 'Tears at first but they soon got over it. Monty was away in Norfolk so frequently.'

Harriet bit her lip, clearly wanting to change the subject. She hadn't expected at all to be so saddened by the death of her husband. Yes, it may be down to shock but it was impossible not to feel some warmth toward the man who had fathered her three beautiful children. She paused, leaning forward. 'I haven't even asked you how you're getting on with Lottie. I can't wait to meet the child.'

Alice breathed out slowly. 'It's early days and the poor child has lost first her maternal grandfather, then her mother and now Edmund has disappeared into the army, and she must feel that is a betrayal of some kind. How can a little girl be expected to understand the necessity of conscription? How can she even understand the concept of war? All she knows is that everyone who has ever meant anything to her is absent – even Edmund's awful father. While we may all see him for the monster he is, to a little girl he was the kind man who bought her toys.'

'Does she know Mr Cutler's in prison?'

'Lord, no! How could I explain that? It would mean telling her that her daddy's father murdered her mother. Besides, Cutler hasn't been tried yet. He could still get off. I can't tarnish his name if he's proved to be innocent of the crime.'

Harriet snorted. 'You've read the papers, Alice. That poor woman was brutally murdered. She couldn't possibly have tripped and fallen when she was so badly bruised all over. And even if she had, the fall would hardly have killed her. She was a fit and healthy young woman, not an old lady with a weak heart and brittle bones.'

'It was a marble fireplace and there was broken glass in the grate.'

'And who put it there?'

'He admitted he threw a tumbler at the fire in anger but that hardly constitutes a murder weapon.'

Harriet leant back in her chair and frowned. 'Why are you defending him, Alice? He's never done you any favours and he has been utterly cruel towards Edmund. We both know he's a thoroughly rotten man.'

'I know. I know. He's loathsome. But that doesn't make him a murderer.'

'Well, we'll find out soon enough. When's the trial?'

'It keeps getting delayed. Shortage of barristers. Everyone's been called to arms.' Alice let out a long sigh. 'If only this dreadful war were over.'

'I'll drink to that. Now it's time we rescued that little rascal from the tedium of the multiplication tables and took a stroll to Hyde Park.'

FOUR

Apart from the usual snoring, the ward was silent, the scratching of the night nurse's pen had stopped, and she had temporarily left her post at the nurses' station. Victor Dalton, wide awake, was conscious of movement from the bed beside his.

'Where are you going?' he whispered, as the man in the next bed swung himself upright and got out of bed with the aid of his crutches. Captain Maurice Kynaston paused and looked back at Victor. 'Can't sleep. I'm going to go and sit in the day room for a while.'

'If they catch you, they'll have you back in bed in a trice. That night sister's a stickler.'

'I'll stuff the pillow under the blanket, so they won't notice. Nurse Tipton's always half asleep. And she's in the scullery washing out bedpans. I've got five minutes to get away.'

'In that case, mind if I join you?' Without waiting for an answer, Victor pushed his covers aside and got to his feet unsteadily. He stuffed his own pillow under the bedclothes and fluffed up the counterpane, then followed the captain out of the ward.

A few moments later, they were sitting side-by-side, woollen rugs spread across them, in the basketweave chairs that lined one side of the room. It overlooked what had been a beautifully curated ornamental garden, arranged around a central water well feature, when Mrs Bowyer had been in residence. Since the house had been repurposed to serve as a military convalescent hospital for the duration of the war, the garden was neglected and choked with weeds.

'You don't mind me joining you?' Victor asked.

The captain smiled and shook his head. 'Not at all.'

'It's the first time I've felt like leaving my bed. Doing it on my own when I'm not supposed to has more appeal than being dragooned by those bossy VADs.'

Maurice stroked his chin. 'Until recently your sister was one of them. But in her case, not at all bossy. She was the first person here I ever felt inclined to talk to.' He brushed a finger over his neatly trimmed moustache and turned to face Victor. 'I say – I hope you don't think it a bit rum that I'm working with her every day in the studio. I'd like to assure you nothing untoward happens. Edmund Cutler himself asked me to continue to help out there while he's away at the front. And the MO reckons the work is therapeutic for me.'

'I'm not my sister's keeper.' Victor drew his blanket up over his chest and softened his voice. 'No, Captain, I'm glad working there helps you. And I'm sure it's a great help to Alice. In fact, if you don't mind, I may stroll over there and have a look at what you've both been doing. I've never actually seen what they get up to in that workshop.'

'Call me Maurice, please. We're no longer at the front. As soon as I can find somewhere to live and receive my discharge, I'll be coming out of uniform.'

'Aren't you intending to go home?' Victor was curious. He

had a vague recollection of Alice mentioning there had been a fiancée. Past tense.

'Nothing there for me. The thought of all that pity in people's eyes...' His voice trailed away. 'At least here at Bankstone, people have only known me like this.' He indicated the flat space under the crocheted rug where his left leg should have been.

'What's the appeal of stained glass? You don't strike me as the arty type.' Victor stared ahead through the window to the deserted moonlit garden beyond. A shaft of light from the moon lit up one side of Maurice's face. Quite a handsome face, Victor realised for the first time.

'It's working with my hands. When I'm painting or cutting glass – even sweeping up the floor – it stops me thinking about the war and everything that happened over there. It's as though I'm transported into another world where all that matters is the task in hand.' Maurice splayed his fingers out in front of him. 'Now my leg's gone, it makes me feel at least one bit of my body can be physically useful. There's not an artistic bone in me but I'm pretty dextrous, though I say it myself.'

'Dextrous, eh?' Victor chuckled, then realised it was the first time he'd laughed since leaving the peninsula of Gallipoli – and there'd been precious little reason to laugh there.

The two men lapsed into a companionable silence for a few minutes then Victor said, 'So would you mind if I dropped in on you? Maybe later this week, once I've got enough strength up to walk across the meadow.' He swallowed, suppressing the rather alarming sense that this was starting to feel like a courtship.

'I'd be delighted. Of course I'm only the hired help. It's up to your sister. But I'm sure she'd like nothing more.'

From behind a curtain hanging over the doorway at the far end of the room, the night nurse emerged. She stood, legs astride and arms folded under her ample bosom. 'So there you are, you naughty boys. It's the middle of the night and you're not supposed to be out of bed.'

'We're neither naughty nor boys,' said Victor then realised he sounded pompous, when the nurse was only teasing them. But he hated being infantilised, even in jest.

The nurse bustled over to them. 'You two are trying to get me into trouble with Sister, aren't you?'

'The last thing we'd want to do.' Maurice was being conciliatory. 'I suppose you're going to order us back to bed?'

She unfolded her arms and smiled. 'What's the harm as long as you're warm and comfortable and not disturbing the other patients?' She tucked the knitted rugs around them more securely.

Victor felt as though he was wrapped in a papoose.

'Would you boys like a cup of tea?'

Victor smiled. 'If you make us tea, I'll even overlook your repeated refusal to grant we're grown men.'

'You're all boys to me.' Nurse Tipton, who was long past the first flush of youth herself and with a maternal demeanour, smiled. 'Charming ones too. Righty-ho. I'll be back in two shakes of a lamb's tail.'

When she'd gone, Victor sighed. 'I shouldn't be so crabby, but I hate the way they infantilise us.'

Maurice shrugged. 'To be honest, it doesn't bother me. A spot of mothering doesn't go amiss after all I've seen.' He ran a hand through his hair. 'I lost ninety per cent of the men in my unit at Loos. Utter chaos. It was like a slaughterhouse. Lying in that shell hole for days I'd have welcomed a bit of mothering. I just lay there, staring up at the sky, broken and waiting to die. I owe my life to the stretcher bearers who found me. Too late to save the leg, alas, but they managed to save my life.'

His voice was so quiet that Victor had to strain to hear.

'Sorry,' Maurice said more audibly. 'Didn't mean to drag all that up. You'll have seen things as bad or worse at Gallipoli I imagine.'

'If it helps to talk about it, I'll listen.' Victor turned his head to look at Maurice.

'Not sure it does really. It doesn't change anything. But you're the only person I've felt able to talk to. So, thank you.'

Victor felt a rush of tenderness. He wanted to reach out and take the captain's hand, but he clasped his own hands together instead.

Maurice closed his eyes for a moment. 'I reckon the Germans had it worse than we did. I came across a couple of dead ones in a machine-gun emplacement. One of them had been chained to his gun. Literally chained like a dog to its kennel. Can you imagine. The savagery of that.' As he spoke his voice broke.

Victor couldn't help himself. He reached out and grasped Maurice's hand, squeezing it gently in his own. The captain returned the pressure but pulled away as Nurse Tipton returned bearing their tea.

'Do you miss it?' Victor asked when they were alone again. 'I know that seems an odd question but, despite all the horrors, doesn't it feel as though life had more meaning out there?'

Maurice shook his head and sighed. 'I hated every miserable minute. But I do miss my men.' He sighed again and it seemed to come from deep inside him. 'I miss all those who died and I feel I've let down those who are still living, by abandoning them there.'

'You didn't abandon them.'

'It feels that way. I'm ashamed that I made it out of there when most of them didn't, and I worry constantly about those that are left behind. I lie awake at night seeing their faces and saying their names. Forcing myself not to forget them.'

Victor felt momentarily ashamed of his own self-pity. His misery had been less about those dead or still fighting and more about his own physical damage. He took a gulp of tea. She'd put too much sugar in. Probably thought she was doing them a favour. He drank it down quickly, wincing at the sickly sweetness that masked the slightly bitter taste that he loved about tea.

He put down the cup and turned to look at Maurice. Something about the man made Victor trust him enough to lay his bitterness bare, to expose his resentment and anger – even his self-pity. 'I don't feel the way you do. I think of the dead as fortunate. I've been asking myself all the time why I didn't die out there. Why did God, if he exists, decide to send me back here with a medal, minus an eye and with chronic pain, when I'd have been better off dying. I feel bitter. But you're telling me I ought to feel ashamed.'

'I didn't say that. We all react in different ways. But I do believe you and I are the fortunate ones. We still have lives to live even if they're not the ones we envisaged.'

'Disfigured? Pain-ridden? What kind of life is that?' Victor's voice was flat.

Maurice stared out at the night-dark garden. 'I heard the MO tell you the pain will ease with time. And yes, we're all damaged. We'll all have to learn to live with missing parts, life-long injuries, shattered nerves, nightmares. But at least we're all in the same boat. A generation of broken men.' He looked thoughtful for a moment. 'Maybe it's the women we should feel sorry for. They're also having to adjust to how their men now are. Imagine how it must feel to wave your husband off to the front only to have him return as a vegetable, or broken in pieces, or disfigured to the point where he is repulsive to you. Men with half their faces blasted off. Completely limbless. Totally blind. Or like a lad in my unit, newly married, who had his manhood sheared off by a piece of shrapnel.'

He drained his teacup and put it down on the small table next to his chair. 'I had a letter from a woman last week. Her husband had been sent home on leave. He was all smiles and hugs, ate a huge plate of bacon and eggs, told her he was going to lie down for a while, then went upstairs and blew his brains out.' Maurice made a choking noise. 'I'm sorry. I don't know why I'm telling you all this. But it's because of what happened to them that I feel I have to find a way to carry on.'

Victor wanted to kneel beside Maurice's rattan chair and hold him in his arms to comfort him.

But he didn't. He couldn't.

What was happening to him? He barely knew the man. Victor bit his lip and struggled to find something bland to say that wouldn't betray the confusion of his growing feelings.

Where had these emotions come from? Victor hadn't felt so drawn towards another man since Gilbert died. He'd experienced lust and physical attraction, but it had been a brief bodily desire lacking any true feeling. Even with the American film actor Max Stieglitz, Victor had enjoyed his company, relished his body and been shocked and saddened by his death. But it had gone no deeper.

Yet here he was on a moonlit night in a cold conservatory, listening while a virtual stranger opened his soul and told him his innermost secrets. Above all else, as he looked at the silhouette of the man sitting beside him, Victor was consumed by an overwhelming tenderness and a longing for closeness that he couldn't recall experiencing with anyone before. Perhaps not even with Gilbert.

FIVE

The parish church of the village of Wallingford Magna was packed for the earl's funeral. It was apparent that Harriet's late husband had been highly regarded among the local gentry, the villagers, his servants and the farmhands on the Wallingford estate.

Alice sat beside her friend in the front pew. Harriet was holding herself bolt upright and looked serene and dignified in her elegant mourning apparel. But Alice could sense the tension her friend was disguising so well.

As they waited for the service to begin, Alice looked about her discreetly. Across the aisle from them a small shrivelled old lady sat beside a middle-aged companion, both dressed head to toe in floor-sweeping black bombazine, more fitting for the previous century. The diminutive old woman was evidently the late earl's mother. She resembled the Grim Reaper, lacking only the sickle, her eyes riveted on the coffin of her son. But she shed not a tear. Alice began to understand Harriet's antipathy towards her mother-in-law, whose appearance and countenance seemed to send out a message that no one should approach. The Dowager Lady Wallingford's face was carved with deep lines, indicating that her frowning was not a temporary state occasioned by mourning but part of her character. She did not appear to be the kind of woman who would be sympathetic or welcoming to any daughter-in-law.

The church service was blessedly brief. When the pallbearers carried out the coffin, the dowager countess claimed unspoken precedence over her son's widow by walking in front of her immediately behind the coffin, aided by a stick and her female companion, who hovered close at hand.

Only Harriet, her mother-in-law and the latter's companion, along with the officiating clergyman, witnessed the interment of Monty in the family vault. The vault was housed in a mausoleum in the grounds of Wallingford Hall and held generations of his ancestors. The space was too small to accommodate any other mourners.

Alice, along with the other guests, was shown into a gloomy wood-panelled drawing room that looked as though it needed a good dusting.

Knowing nobody, she positioned herself by one of the windows and stood alone, gazing out over the rainswept parterre towards a distant haha and fields beyond. The latter were dotted with small wooden huts to house the ancient rare breed of pigs which were the estate's speciality. Alice could see no sign of the pigs themselves and assumed they must be sheltering inside the huts. She hadn't noticed the noxious smells Harriet had warned her about either.

It was hard to believe that the avuncular earl was lying cold in his coffin. Alice gave an involuntary shiver. She'd never understood how her dear friend had agreed to marry an ugly old man simply because he had a title and a fortune. Harriet herself had joked about it, claiming that love played no part in marriage and she had been right to put her future security first. And now she was free of him anyway. So maybe her pragmatism had been justified.

Alice ran a finger down the windowpane, tracing the runnels of rain on the other side of the glass. Suitably depressing weather for a funeral. At least they didn't have to stand in a muddy graveyard watching as the coffin was lowered into the ground. But how depressing that here was another death to add to the many – her own stillborn son, Edmund's brother and her fiancé, Gilbert, Edmund's first wife, Dora, and his mother, Susan, and young Bevis Lockwood, the object of the Latchington window – not to mention the growing list of names of war dead recorded daily in the newspapers. Alice shuddered, trying not to imagine Edmund's name appearing there.

After about fifteen minutes, Harriet, following behind the old lady and her rather sinister-looking companion, emerged from the stone mausoleum. When they arrived in the drawing room the dowager countess held court from a stiff-backed chair as the invited guests filed by to offer their condolences.

As soon as the formalities were completed, Harriet handed Alice a glass of sherry. 'Dutch courage,' she said. 'Mr Forsyth, the family solicitor, is waiting in the library to read the will.'

Alice was reluctant. 'Shouldn't it be family only?'

'Certainly not. I'm not facing the old crow on my own. She'll have that creepy companion woman with her so I must have you. I've already told Mr Forsyth you'll be there.'

So Alice dutifully followed her friend into the library, where the elderly bespectacled solicitor was installed behind a heavy oak table with what must have been the earl's Last Will and Testament set out before him. Four chairs were arranged in two pairs, set in a semicircle with a wide gap in the middle. The two of them slipped into their seats on the left and waited for Lady Wallingford to take her place on the other side of what felt like an uncrossable divide. As far as Alice could tell, the old woman hadn't spoken a word to her daughter-in-law since they'd arrived from London.

After much adjustment of her old-fashioned gown,

performed by the companion, the elderly countess settled. Alice stole a sideways glance at her stern profile. In her all-black apparel and with a prominent nose, she did indeed resemble a malevolent crow.

The solicitor cleared his throat and began to read. There were several small bequests, mostly to household servants, including Jenkins, the earl's valet.

There was no mention of the dowager countess. Alice assumed it must be because she had already been provided for by her late husband.

Everything else, after the bequests – the Wallingford estate, the London house and all remaining assets – were to pass to Harriet and the children. No surprises there then. Alice realised that little Crispin had already become the Earl of Wallingford.

'Thank you, Mr Forsyth,' said the dowager. Her voice was sharp and clipped. 'I will now leave you to explain the details of her inheritance to *her*.' The tone was acerbic. Assisted by her equally sour-faced companion, the elderly woman rose to leave. Alice presumed she was angry that Harriet had inherited everything. But there was the ghost of a smile on her craggy face as she left.

Mr Forsyth cleared his throat again and peered at the two remaining women over the top of his spectacles. 'I have something of importance to tell you, Your Ladyship, and I'm afraid it's not good news.'

'You're doubtless going to say that my mother-in-law wishes to remain here in the main house. I want you to know that I have no objection.'

The solicitor removed his glasses and polished them on a handkerchief he withdrew from his top pocket. 'Er, no. In fact, Her Ladyship has already removed to the Dower House. She inherited that upon the death of her late husband, the thirty-first earl.'

Harriet raised her eyebrows and glanced at Alice.

'I'm not aware how much the late earl told you about his financial affairs,' he began, avoiding looking at Harriet.

'Absolutely nothing. He never discussed them, and I never asked. He was always a most generous man.' Harriet folded her hands on her lap.

Mr Forsyth shuffled his papers, clearly embarrassed. 'Then I am sorry to be the bearer of bad news. It seems Lord Wallingford made some rather poor investment decisions as well as feeding an, er... somewhat extravagant gambling habit. Horse racing, I understand.' The man appeared to be extremely uncomfortable, and Alice had the impression he'd rather be anywhere than here in this room.

'And?' Harriet prompted him.

Alice glanced at Harriet, concerned. She could see her friend's hands were trembling, but Harriet's face remained calm.

'His Lordship had raised hefty mortgages against Wallingford Hall and a few weeks ago the bank informed him of their intent to foreclose. The Dower House is of course in Her Ladyship's name and hence not affected, but I'm afraid everything else: this house, the farmlands, the tenanted properties, the piggery, is now the property of the bank. I'm very sorry.'

Alice reached for Harriet's hand. Her friend looked pale as a ghost, but calm.

'So, there'll be no income from the estate?'

'Nothing. There will be no estate. I understand from the farm manager, Mr Troughton, that the swine were sold at the Ipswich livestock market a week ago.' The man lowered his eyes and studied the back of his hands.

'The London house?'

'Yours. And you will be glad to know not mortgaged. But I'm afraid without any income you will be unable to afford the upkeep.'

'My children?' Harriet spoke softly. 'What of them?' Her fingers were now tightly curled, and Alice saw her knuckles were white.

'There is a longstanding provision – an endowment – to provide for the education of both boys at Harrow School. The late earl and his father before him had been generous benefactors of the school... in happier times.'

He picked up the papers from the desk, tapped them into a neat pile and stowed them inside a leather briefcase. 'Obviously it's not my place to advise you, Your Ladyship, but you would be wise to consider selling the house in Portman Square. The running costs are substantial and there's a large staff. Were you to sell, then buy somewhere more modest and try to manage with fewer servants, you should be able to support yourself on the income from the capital. But I'd urge you to seek solid financial advice.' He paused. 'And maybe, eventually, another husband.'

He tightened the strap on the leather case and rose to his feet. 'Once again, my condolences on the death of the earl and I wish I had been able to offer you more favourable news. Now I must bid you good day.' He nodded and left.

Alice turned to face a shocked Harriet. 'I don't know what to say, dear friend, but you must talk to Victor immediately. He'll know what to do. He's an absolute wizard with financial matters.' She wrapped her hands around Harriet's fingers, noting how cold they felt. 'Come on. Let's get back to London. I can see now why you didn't like this place.'

As the two women were leaving, the old lady's companion passed them in the large marble-floored entrance hall.

She stopped and addressed Harriet in what was an unmistakable French accent. '*Hélas!* What is it your English playwright said? "Hoist by your own petard". Goodbye, little gold digger. You must be so sad that your plans did not work out.'

With a smile that would curdle milk, she turned on her

heels and swept away towards the drawing room to rejoin her mistress.

'What on earth brought that on?' Alice, astonished, turned to see Harriet's reaction.

Her friend was open-mouthed. 'I've absolutely no idea. Before today I'd never met the woman.' With a shake of the head, Harriet pushed open the front door and Alice followed.

SIX

Life at the Browndown training camp near Gosport was an unrelenting series of arduous tests, mostly conducted outdoors – sometimes during the night.

Edmund, accustomed to working quietly and cerebrally in his own studio beside his beloved Alice, was unused to responding to barked orders and life amidst the hurly-burly of the barrack room. He knew the same was true of Robert, who, having worked as a travel writer, was used to being totally independent, and resistant and resentful about taking orders.

There was no gentle easing in of the men. The army was determined to give all the new recruits a thorough training, albeit in an extremely short time frame that offered little or no opportunity for rest.

The barrack huts were draughty and often damp, the camp-beds uncomfortable and the food both repetitive and unappetising, but the kindness and camaraderie among the men made it tolerable for most of the recruits – although not for either Edmund or Robert, both of whom craved some solitude.

While the aim was to get the men ready for the front as rapidly as possible, the training was thorough and covered all the basic fundamentals. It mainly consisted of assembling, and carrying heavy kitbags, keeping the contents pristine and polished, square-bashing and route marching, bayonet practice using sand-filled sacks, simple map-reading, and instruction and practice in the handling and firing of service rifles.

The camp was sited between the shingle shore of the Solent on one side and several acres of heathland on the other, where a mock battlefield had already been constructed. The land there was surrounded by rough bracken and gorse and earlier contingents of troops had built a network of trenches within which the men were to be introduced to the principles of trench warfare. The site was evidently a replica of what they could expect to find over in France – zigzags of frontline, communication, and reserve trenches, including those of the enemy – all too visible at less than two hundred yards away.

The corporal in charge of their section explained that the front-line trench followed a zigzag formation along its entire length so that the enemy would be prevented from getting a clear line of sight, were they to break out of their own line. These trenches were intersected by communication trenches for the safe evacuation of the wounded and to allow for more men to be rapidly deployed into forward positions.

As well as practising firing from these ready-made trenches, Edmund and the others were required to dig further small trenches of their own – so-called slit trenches, just big enough to offer cover to one or two men. The kit they were expected to carry included small trench tools which Edmund considered inadequate for the task, but contributed to the weight.

The main trenches were already equipped with artillery and machine guns where the men practised, sometimes with live ammunition. The overall intent was to give these raw recruits a swift immersion into the realities of trench warfare within the safety of the British Isles. This included nightlong exercises, sleeping in the trenches in rotating shifts to snatch spells of rest, as well as living off the kind of rations they could expect in the field of battle.

As soon as he had a rifle in his hands, the reality of what lay ahead became stark to Edmund. Until now, the war had been an abstract concept. Something going on across the Channel in a foreign country. Now as he raced along the beachfront in a bayonet charge, it was all too easy to imagine plunging the bayonet into the body of a German soldier rather than a sandbag hanging on a rope from a frame. He felt sick at the thought.

Later, sitting on a heap of shingle beside the shoreline next to his friend, in a rare ten-minute break granted by the platoon corporal, he asked Robert whether he thought he would be able to repeat this for real.

'You mean could I run a German through?' Robert lit a Woodbine and drew the smoke into his lungs. 'Of course. If it's him or me, no contest. I intend to survive.'

'Yet you did everything you could to avoid conscription. I still don't understand it.' Edmund rummaged in the pocket of his greatcoat and pulled out the small sketchpad he kept there along with a pencil.

'It's simple. I think this entire war is a waste of lives. We're in it for all the wrong reasons. The Germans have done nothing to us. They invaded Belgium and France but they'd no quarrel with Britain.' He stared out at the gunmetal grey waters of the Solent towards the Isle of Wight. 'There's been no attempt to negotiate a settlement. That's what I have against it. The politicians are too lazy and too arrogant to sit around a table and thrash this out, so we're sent as lambs to the slaughter. But that doesn't make me a pacifist. If I have to go out there, I intend to do my utmost to stay alive.' He plucked a stray strand of tobacco from his lip.

Edmund stared at the beach in front of him. 'I'm not going to argue with that. But I wish I could be as sanguine as you are about killing people. Those Germans are probably just like us. Young men with wives and sweethearts at home. Lads like him.' Edmund jerked his head in the direction of the callow youth with the bad skin who was skimming stones onto the water. 'O'Connor's barely out of school. I bet his mother cries her eyes out every night worrying about him.' Edmund bent his head and began drawing a seagull wading in the shallows.

'What are you doing?' Robert leant forward and looked across at his friend. 'Not drawing?'

'Just a quick sketch.' He nodded in the direction of the seagull waddling along beside the water's edge.

'Is that even allowed?' Robert drew again on his cigarette before grinding it into his shoe and kicking shingle over it. 'If the Corporal sees you drawing pictures of an official military establishment, he's likely to put you on charge for spying for the enemy.'

'Don't be daft. What does the Kaiser care about a blooming seagull?'

'It's a giveaway that we're on the coast.'

Edmund frowned then laughed. 'You're ribbing me, Fuller. I think the Kaiser knows all too well that Britain is an island and everywhere's close to the coast.' He elbowed his friend in the ribs but closed the book and put it back in his pocket.

They sat in silence for a few moments then Edmund spoke again. 'I don't think I can do it, you know.'

'Do what?' Robert was staring out at the dull grey waters.

'Kill someone.'

'I doubt you'll get near enough to get a chance to use your bayonet.'

'Come on. Why else are they training us to use them? You heard the drill sergeant when he said they're building our offensive spirit ready to engage with the enemy at close quarters. But anyway, I don't just mean bayoneting them, I mean killing in general, whether with my Lee-Enfield or operating a machine gun or an artillery battery.'

'You'll have no choice. Once you're out there your misgivings will vanish and you'll be desperate for scalps. As soon as you see what the bastards are doing to us, all sentiment will go out of the window.'

'It's not sentiment.'

'What is it then. Religious misgivings?'

Edmund shook his head. 'No. It's as you said just now. I've no quarrel with any of those men, so why would I want to kill them? Take a man's life. Just think about it.' He stretched his lips taut. 'The only German I ever met was a chap at school and he was a good fellow. I don't want to think that I might unknowingly be responsible for Wolfgang's death.'

'Do you know how many men are out there? Millions. You're being fanciful now. Sounds like sentimentality.' Robert picked up a handful of shingle and let it run through his fingers. 'You'd better get past it quickly. Once we're over there it will be kill or be killed. You want to go home to your wife, don't you?'

'Of course I do.'

'Well then.'

The corporal blew his whistle to summon them back for the next bout of jousting with the sandbags. As they moved back along the shore to join the rest of their section, Robert added, 'You might as well forget about the bayonet practice, as far worse things await us tomorrow.'

'What? And how do you know?'

'Willis overheard the sergeant talking to the corporals in the mess this morning. We have a cross-country run fully laden with kit, then an assault course. Once you've crawled through mud and gorse on your belly you might be glad to be over in France with a rifle in your hand. That's supposing we survive the ordeal.'

. . .

Robert was correct about the following day. The men were put through an intensive day of endurance. A two-mile run carrying a full kitbag, packed tightly with equipment so it weighed a ton. A lengthy session of physical exercises followed, then marching and drilling in the exercise yard.

The run proved too much for some of the men, who were forced to revert to walking pace after a few hundred yards staggering along with their heavy loads. Edmund had been used to cross country runs at school and both he and Robert were relatively fit from all the walking they did. He much preferred it to the savagery of bayonet practice. There was something primeval about a troop of men running along a beach, making bloodcurdling cries as they plunged their weapons into soft yielding sandbags.

Edmund thought of the strange woman who'd tucked a white feather in his lapel in Hyde Park when he'd been enjoying an afternoon with his young daughter. A rush of anger coursed through him that people such as her could shame men like those around him at the camp into thinking themselves inadequate or cowardly. He thought too of Leonard Fitzwarren and his elderly uncle, a retired colonel, back in Hampshire, who had both claimed status and rank from the army and their inherited wealth, but had never seen active service. That men like the Fitzwarrens could apply pressure to young men to 'do their duty' and sit in judgement on others in the recruitment tribunals made Edmund enraged – but all too aware that he was powerless to do anything about it.

SEVEN

Alice's stay with Harriet meant Victor's plan to visit Maurice in the studio had to be postponed.

He found himself avoiding Maurice during the day, fearful of the emotions the other man had roused in him. But he was able to watch him through the windows of the day room. During Alice's absence from the stained-glass studio, Maurice had joined a small working party of officers who were restoring the ornamental garden. Originally created by the renowned garden designer Miss Gertrude Jekyll, when the Lutyens house was built for Commander and Mrs Bowyer, the garden was a formal one. A pattern of pale stone pathways intersected and centred on a water well and the plantings had been mainly in tones of white and silver with swathes of Miss Jekyll's favourite lavender next to the box hedges that marked its perimeter.

Maurice's missing leg prevented him from digging, but he shuffled along on his backside supported by an old cushion as he weeded or sat at a small wooden table on the paved patio while he potted seedlings. The two other officers who worked alongside him chatted and joked with each other, but Maurice worked apart and in silence.

Victor felt furtive watching him like this. After shutting himself away to write letters in the small study that had become a quiet room, he'd gone to the day room, where he could pretend to snooze in one of the cushioned rattan chairs while gazing at Maurice through the windows.

What was he thinking of? It was foolish to even entertain the idea of that kind of friendship with Captain Kynaston. Victor told himself that their intense talk during the small hours had been the natural consequence of the lateness of the hour and the traumas both men had endured. The near-death experiences on the Western Front and in the Eastern Mediterranean had been so removed from everyday life that it was understandable that those who went through them would share a special bond. He remembered the way he had held a man while he died on the arid slopes of a godforsaken Turkish hillside. The intensity of moments like that were a direct consequence of war and not a normal state. Holding the captain's hand as they'd sat side-by-side in the dark had been natural in the circumstances and Victor mustn't let his own unnatural tendencies impinge on their friendship – or he risked both alienating Maurice and bringing shame upon himself.

Besides, hadn't Maurice been engaged to be married until the war intervened? His fiancée, shocked by his loss of a leg, had asked to be released from her promise in order to marry a man exempted from active service. Victor told himself to get a grip, and stop entertaining any illusions about Captain Kynaston.

One morning, after breakfast, Victor was on his way to the study, where he planned to read the financial newspapers, when he came across Maurice in the corridor.

'Have you been avoiding me, Lieutenant Cutler?' Maurice's tone was light and the use of his military title ironic. 'I've barely seen you these past days.'

'I've been catching up on my reading. I thought you were busy working in the garden. I still plan to call on you and my sister when she returns from London and you start work again. Assuming you don't mind?' Victor realised he sounded like a shy boy speaking to a much-admired school prefect.

'Of course not. I was worried I'd offended you – or bored you with all my melancholic musings the other night.' Maurice's eyes were fixed on him as he waited for him to reply. To his surprise, Victor realised the captain was nervous too.

'Certainly not.' Victor looked away, anxious to conceal his awkwardness from Maurice. 'I'm honoured you were able to share a confidence with me.'

Now it was Maurice's turn to look away. He adjusted his crutches and started to move away, pausing after a couple of steps. 'I say, Victor, have you ever seen the window here that Alice and Edmund created for the owner of the house?'

Victor shook his head.

'It's meant to be off limits to us inmates, but Alice showed me one day. Come – it's magnificent.' Maurice looked along the passage, checking there were no nurses or orderlies around, before pushing open a nail-embossed oak door that bore a STAFF ONLY sign. Victor followed him into a wood-panelled hallway with a broad stairway leading up to a landing area. The focal point of the landing was a huge, mullioned window containing three stained-glass panels. They depicted a ship at sea, a lighthouse, the rear view of a uniformed naval man gazing through a telescope at sea nymphs frolicking with dolphins. The morning light poured through the window spreading a myriad of colours over the parquet tiled floor of the hallway.

Maurice was already starting to negotiate the stairs, an oper-ation at which he was surprisingly adept, wielding his crutches as though born with them. 'Come and look closer.'

Victor followed him. Once on the landing, he moved up to the window and inspected it. It was indeed a magnificent work. Bright, vibrant, intricate. It was composed of numerous pieces of glass of varying sizes and colours, all hand-painted with the most delicate brushwork. He shook his head. 'It's marvellous. I'd no idea. You say Alice and Edmund did all this?'

'Designed it, cut every piece of glass, painted them and fired them in their kiln. They even mixed their own paints.' He pointed to the brilliant sunset in the top right corner – a myriad of shades of red, yellow and orange. 'To get these hues they had to etch the glass with acid. Dangerous stuff.' He shook his head. 'I am in awe of their talent.'

Victor was amazed. 'I can't believe my little sister did this. I'm so proud. Edmund too. It's breathtaking.'

'There's another in the village church. The old girl who owns this place wanted to create a lasting memorial to her late husband, who served in the navy. The church one is of Biblical scenes with a nautical theme.'

'I'm absolutely staggered. I'll have to take a walk into Little Badgerton and have a look.' Victor stroked his chin. 'Honestly, Maurice, I didn't take this stained-glass window lark seriously. I thought it was little more than a hobby.'

'They're a talented pair. Apparently, Edmund learnt his craft from the best teachers and it seems your sister has a natural aptitude.'

'I knew she was artistic. Always with her paintbox. But I'm ashamed to say I didn't take much interest. Thought it was just what girls do. You know – something to occupy her until she got married. What an idiot I am.'

Maurice laughed. 'Alice told me she was merely dabbling at art until she began working with Edmund. Stained glass has turned out to be her vocation.'

'I'll say!' Victor put his hands on his hips and studied the window again. 'I will most definitely have to pay you both a visit at that studio.'

· · ·

A few days later, Victor accompanied Maurice across the meadow to the stone structure in the Bankstone grounds that housed the stained-glass studio.

Alice had returned to Bankstone the previous evening, after accompanying Harriet to the funeral.

Maurice pushed open the door with one of his crutches and called out to her. 'I've brought a visitor with me. Your brother has come to check what we get up to over here.'

Alice gasped and, grinning widely, flung her arms around Victor. 'Just the person I want to see. I've so much to tell you. And I'm utterly delighted you are out and about on your feet again.' She pulled back to allow herself to see her brother's face. 'How was it walking over here? Much pain?'

Victor realised he hadn't even thought about the pain. Yes, it was always there and now with her mentioning it, became apparent again. But negotiating the pathway over the field alongside Maurice had been a pleasure. Victor was finding any time spent with the other man was a source of a deep sense of calm and well-being.

'I have so much to tell you, Victor. First, I'm going to make us all a pot of tea.'

'Would you like me to leave you alone?' Maurice edged towards the doorway.

'No, not at all, Maurice. It's nothing you can't hear too.' She seized Victor's hands between hers and squeezed them. 'I'm so happy you've come.' Turning to the captain, she said, 'Thank you for bringing him, Maurice.' With that she disappeared into the scullery to prepare the tea.

While she was gone, Maurice showed Victor around the studio, pointing out the full-sized cartoon of one section of the Latchington window that was attached to an easel at one end of the room. He showed him the neatly sorted collection of cut pieces of glass which were ready for painting. 'My job is to prepare a paint solution and then apply a base coat to these. A kind of wash. It gives a good surface onto which Alice will apply the various paints.'

Moving across to the workbench, he showed Victor the range of tools used for cutting the glass, the jars and tins of pigments, gum arabic and other ingredients.

'Complicated stuff,' said Victor. 'And you enjoy doing this?'

'I love it.'

Victor shrugged. 'Wouldn't be my cup of tea at all but I'm hugely impressed by the complexity of the operation and the skill involved.'

'Don't tell *me*,' said Maurice. 'Tell *her* that.' He kept his voice low. 'She needs to know. Her confidence has taken a bit of bashing since Edmund left.'

When Alice returned and served the tea, Victor told her he'd seen the Bankstone window. 'Honestly, Alice, it took my breath away. I had absolutely no idea of the quality and beauty of the work you and Edmund have produced.' He waved a hand around the studio. 'I'd barely understood what all this involved. Hadn't given it so much as a look when I was here before. But Maurice has been telling me all about the process. I'm very proud of you.'

Alice blushed. 'Really? That means so much to me, Victor.'

He saw her eyes were misting with unshed tears and he felt a rush of guilt that he'd been intolerant and unkind towards her so often in the past. He smiled at her and patted her hand. '*Really*. And I'm glad you have Maurice here to support the work while Edmund's away.'

Alice bit her lip at the mention of her husband's name. 'Maurice is a godsend. Now, enough of me, I need to tell you what's happened to poor Harriet.'

'I heard about the earl passing away. That was unexpected.' Victor gave a shrug. 'But I seem to think there was no love lost between her and her husband, was there? Pretty much a convenient arrangement.' He picked up his teacup and took a sip of tea. 'Harriet's a resilient woman. I'm sure she'll thrive in widowhood. I'd always got the impression she was looking forward to it.'

'Victor!' Alice frowned. 'He was the father of her children. And as it happens, she'd become rather fond of him. But that's not the news. It's that there's nothing left.'

Victor's head went back in puzzlement. 'Nothing left?' He echoed her words. He glanced towards Maurice, who had refused a cup of tea and was busy assembling brushes and cutting tools on the workbench.

'The earl had mortgaged the Wallingford estate and failed to make the repayments. The bank owns it all. Harriet has been left with only the house in Portman Square but barely anything to keep it running. It will have to go, along with the servants, the motorcar, everything.' Alice grabbed her brother's hand. 'I told her you'd help her, Victor. You will help, won't you?'

Alice described the funeral in Norfolk, the hostile behaviour of the dowager countess and her French lady companion as well as the implications of the will.

'The solicitor's right,' said Victor at last. 'She'll have to sell the London house and buy somewhere more modest. Trouble is, with the war, the property market isn't exactly buoyant.' He thought for a moment. 'Maybe her best option is to rent it. There's demand for large central London buildings, but to rent not buy. The War Office and various government departments, clinics and convalescent homes are all looking for space. She could let it out for the duration of the war, rent a smaller place outside London and live on the difference. Assuming she gets rid of most of the staff, she ought to be able to manage. But I'd need to look at the books and do more homework on the lettings market.'

'Would you do that?' Alice's tone was eager. 'You've always

liked Harriet. And she adores you.' She paused. 'She'll be here on Friday. I've persuaded her to come down and stay at the vicarage for a couple of days. She and Eleanor have become friends. And I was hoping you'd have a chat with her and look at some of the paperwork.' She turned to Maurice. 'And you must meet her too. She's a delightful woman.'

'It would be a pleasure.' Maurice smiled politely.

Victor felt a stab of resentment at Alice. Was she planning to do some matchmaking between her friend and the captain? He pushed the thought away. What if she was? It was no concern of his. He nodded at his sister. 'Of course. I'll be happy to do what I can to help Harriet. What rotten luck. I'd no idea Monty Wallingford was a gambling man. And the bad investments. He sounds even worse than Papa.'

'Much as it pains me to say it, all that has kept Papa from ruin is Herbert Cutler. I can't deny my father-in-law has a talent for managing money.' She patted Victor's hand. 'But you, Victor, are his match in financial matters and vastly his superior as a human being. Harriet will be in very safe hands.'

EIGHT

Edmund stood on the shoreline watching the clouds towering above the Channel. They appeared frozen, unmoving, their multi-toned layers an artist's dream, looking as if they had been painted on a stuccoed chapel ceiling by a long-dead Renaissance master. The water below was a peppermint green and the sky above the cloud mass an unseasonal celestial blue.

He moved back across the shingle beach and sat on a low wall where he took out his sketchbook and began to draw, using rapid pencil strokes and soft hatching to build up an impression of the cloud formation. Edmund tried to take advantage of every precious minute away from the heavily timetabled training to do some drawing. But time was scarce and any officer or NCO who saw a man malingering would be even harsher in his judgements when inspecting kit, beds and drills.

Edmund had adapted to army life better than he'd expected. Better in some ways than Robert Fuller. Robert constantly bucked against authority, trying to reassert his individuality in the face of the army's attempts to turn its recruits into interchangeable fighting men, obeying orders without question or hesitation. Edmund now felt that he had resigned himself to that aspect of military life, recognising resistance was futile and would eventually be crushed – so why fight it?

He didn't mind the physical drilling. Strong and fit, he welcomed the opportunity to walk and run – even to parade around the drill yard – after his years confined to the studio for most of the day. It was exhilarating to be out in the fresh air although the landscape of flat, rough scrubland was dull in comparison to the hills and woodland around Little Badgerton.

What he loathed was the munitions training. Constant practice wasn't changing his attitude. The machine guns filled him with horror, rifle target practice worried him as he had a good eye and didn't want to be singled out as a marksman and trained to become a sniper – so he deliberately aimed slightly off target. But worst of all was the feeling of his steel bayonet plunging into those sandbags knowing that on the battlefield it would be human flesh.

Edmund was in a dilemma. Should he ask to speak to his company commander and confess his serious misgivings about man-to-man combat? If he were to do so he risked being branded a coward, a Nancy boy and a conchie. But he wasn't a coward. He had no fear for his own safety. It was a deep-rooted reluctance to take another human life. Before he'd come to the camp it hadn't been apparent. It had never occurred to him to declare himself a conscientious objector as Robert had unsuccessfully attempted to do. Yet as soon as he'd attached the bayonet to the top of his Lee-Enfield and hurled himself at his target the reality had struck him and it was repugnant. He was desperate to know if there was any way he could avoid it. Was it too late?

Listening to the barrack room talk and the conversations in the mess it had become clear to Edmund that his views were not shared by the majority. Some men exhibited a blood lust he found chilling, relishing the prospect of skewering 'the Hun'. Others saw proficiency with weapons as the essential means of self-protection. Some hated the route marches and discipline. But no one appeared to share his visceral revulsion at the thought of killing the enemy.

He wondered whether this reluctance traced to the haunting memory of the death of Dan Southerton. Edmund still harboured a lingering sense of guilt over the young man's suicide from drinking etching acid stolen from the Bankstone studio. Every time Edmund thought of taking a German life, he reminded himself of the culpability and responsibility he had felt about Dan's death – with far less justification.

The anxiety grew on a daily basis and manifested itself in his consistent failure to hit the target on the shooting range. This infuriated the NCOs who were training the unit, as in all other respects Edmund excelled. He was strong. He was quick. He was nimble over obstacles. But the more they screamed at him the worse he performed at shooting.

Now, sketching on the deserted shore, he longed to be back in Little Badgerton. Back to the days before the war when the future held no threat, and life had seemed uncomplicated. He felt the absence of Alice and his daughter, Lottie, like a missing limb. The pain was unrelenting.

One afternoon, at the end of an exercise which involved the unit of men running through the shallows along the shore, instead of returning with the other men to the barracks to dry off and clean up his kit, he'd lingered here on the beach, letting his puttees and boots dry in the sun. He told himself that these stolen fifteen minutes could easily be made up if he was quick once he returned to base. And if he got hauled up for it, surely it was worth it?

A stentorian voice cut though the quiet contemplation that always accompanied his drawing. 'What the dickens are you doing, Private?' It was the drill sergeant, a short stocky man with a permanent scowl.

Edmund groaned inwardly. Punishment was now an inevitability. Sergeant Hoddle sought any excuse to knock the recruits down a peg or two.

As he got to his feet and prepared to make his futile excuses to the sergeant, he heard the rhythmic crunch of a horse's hooves cantering across the shingle towards them.

The rider reined his mount in and came to a halt beside Edmund and the sergeant.

'Good Lord, is that you, Cutler?' The voice was polished, patrician. The rider was wearing an officer's uniform, with the rank of a lieutenant.

Edmund looked up at the horseman. He had become habit- uated in the short time he'd been at Browndown to reading the uniform and the insignia not the man. He raised his hand to shade his vision from the surprisingly bright spring sunshine. The rider looked familiar. Edmund realised he'd known him at Harrow but hadn't seen him in years. 'Cloverbrook,' he said. 'Tristram Cloverbrook.'

Lieutenant Cloverbrook swung himself out of the saddle and landed with a scrunch on the shingled beach. 'I say, old boy, what on earth are you doing as a private?'

Edmund felt himself bristle. Cloverbrook had been in the year below him at Harrow.

The drill sergeant looked between one and the other, his expression a mixture of annoyance and mystification. Eventu- ally he saluted the lieutenant. 'Apologies, sir. This man should not be outside the camp. I will ensure he is properly disciplined.'

'You most certainly won't.' The officer patted his horse on the neck and turned to face Edmund. 'Good God, man, why in heaven's name haven't you taken a commission?'

The sergeant was shuffling his feet, uncertain what to do or say. Eventually Lieutenant Cloverbrook solved his problem by dismissing him. 'You can leave us, Sergeant, Private Cutler and I are old school chums. We have some catching up to do.'

With a face like a wilted lettuce, Sergeant Hoddle shook his head and strode away towards the camp, his feet sounding loudly as he crossed the shingle beach.

'So?' Cloverbrook stood beside his horse, studying Edmund, still with an expression of disbelief. 'What the blazes are you doing as a Tommy?'

'I enlisted as a soldier.'

'That's crazy. You must apply for a commission.'

'I don't want one.' Edmund hated having to explain himself. 'Look, Cloverbrook, it's good to see you after so long, but I think it would be better for both of us if we shook hands now and then forget we've ever known each other.'

'Don't be like that. We're old pals. Same school. That counts for a lot. You seriously intend to go out to France as a private?'

Edmund didn't feel the need to answer that.

'What are you doing here on the beach? Looked to me like I turned up at just the right moment or that sergeant would have had you on a charge.'

'Yes. Thank you for that. I was doing some sketching. We don't get a lot of free time. I like to spend mine drawing.' He jerked his head towards the sky. 'Wanted to capture those clouds.'

'Let's have a look.' Cloverbrook flipped over the pages, glancing at the various drawings Edmund had made of the landscape, the ships passing along the Solent, the men at rest in the billet.

'I remember now. You were always a bit of a whizz at the old art classes. Went to art school, didn't you? I remember there was a bit of a stink about that at the time. Seem to remember your pater wasn't too thrilled.'

'No, he wasn't.'

'These sketches are awfully good, old boy. Is that what you do now? Or did – before the war? Paint pictures?'

'I make stained-glass windows actually.'

'I say. That's rather splendid.' Lieutenant Cloverbrook swung himself back into the saddle. 'Churches and things?' He appeared to have exhausted potential topics of conversation. 'Well then... Damn good to see you, Cutler. Let me know if you change your mind about that commission.' He looked down at Edmund from his elevated position on his mount. 'Any bother with that sergeant, ask him to talk to me. I'll tell him I asked you to meet me here on the shore.' With that he squeezed the heels of his polished leather boots into the flank of his horse and took off up the beach, a hail of shingle showering up behind him.

Later, after the evening meal in the mess, the drill sergeant accosted Edmund as he was leaving with Robert. 'So you're pals with Lieutenant Cloverbrook, eh, Cutler? Went to the same posh school, did you?' Sergeant Hoddle appeared to be genuinely curious rather than bawling him out as usual. 'Interesting. Very interesting. Why didn't you apply for a commission?'

'I didn't think I'd be good officer material, Sergeant.'

'Not for you to decide though, is it, Cutler? You think you know better than the recruiting officers, do you?'

'No, Sergeant.' Edmund felt humiliated, belittled, diminished. Being put on a charge right away would have been better than this slow torture that would likely end up with one anyway. He certainly wasn't going to do as Cloverbrook had suggested and call on their past acquaintance to get himself off the hook.

The man narrowed his eyes. 'I've had a conversation with the lieutenant. He tells me you're an artist. Is that so, Cutler?'

Edmund nodded, wishing he'd returned from the beach with the other men and had never encountered Cloverbrook. Knowing an officer socially wasn't likely to win him any favours among the other men.

'If you're an artist you must have good eyesight and steady hands. So why are you such a lousy shot?'

Edmund felt a chill creep through him. 'I don't know, Sergeant.'

'You're one of the fittest, strongest men in your unit, yet one of the poorest once there's a weapon in your hands.'

Here it comes, thought Edmund. The abuse and accusations that he was somehow lacking in manhood.

To his surprise, the outcome was different.

'I don't think you're cut out for the infantry, Cutler. But with your speed, strength and ability to draw there could well be another role for you. I had a conversation with the lieutenant, and he has asked to see you in his office. Right now.'

Edmund looked at Robert, who scratched his head but offered no comment.

'What are you waiting for?' Sergeant Lamb's voice rose. 'Get over there. Don't keep the officer waiting.'

A few minutes later, Edmund was admitted to Lieutenant Cloverbrook's office. He was nervous about why the officer wanted to see him again. Strange how that could be the case with a man who had been junior to him at school. But that was the army for you.

'Good show, Cutler. At ease.' He indicated a chair in front of the desk.

Edmund sat, wondering what the reason for the summons was. He hoped he wasn't going to be coerced into applying for a commission.

'I've been reading your reports, Cutler. Had an interesting conversation with the drill sergeant and your unit corporal as well as the firearms trainers. They all find you a bit of an enigma. Top of the class at strength, endurance, running and exercise but a bloody disaster when it comes to anything involving weaponry.'

Edmund said nothing.

'I was put in charge of training here after the Battle of Loos. I've a bit of a dodgy lung and the gas attacks didn't help. I was banged up in the casualty clearing station until they sent me back to Blighty and told me I was no longer deemed fit for active service. Can't say I was disappointed.'

Edmund was wondering where this was leading. Surely his former schoolmate hadn't summoned him here to review his own army career.

'I owe my life to three brave men. Stretcher bearers. The wind was meant to be westerly to blow the gas into the German lines. Meant to make up for our lack of artillery but it didn't get much further than No Man's Land and some of it blew back over our lines. I got caught in it and ended up poisoned by chlorine and lying in a flooded trench. Dashed lucky those chaps found me there. Carried me for hours to get me to safety. One thing I learnt while I was out there was those men are the real heroes of the Western Front.'

Edmund couldn't imagine how painful being poisoned by gas must be. He hoped he'd never find out. Poor Cloverbrook.

Cloverbrook continued. 'At the beginning of the war, the army made bandsmen stretcher bearers. They hadn't the kind of battle training the infantry had. But there's a big difference between carrying a trombone on a parade ground and carrying a comatose man on a stretcher over rough ground in the middle of shellfire and explosions. Most of those poor devils have copped it by now. Since the beginning of last year, the medics out there have been insisting on the recruitment of a different type of men. Strength and endurance are the prime requirements. Strong enough to carry a dead weight for long distances, able to endure the risks of rescuing wounded men under heavy fire, and intelligent enough to be able to administer first aid right there on the battlefield. I think you'd be a perfect candidate, Cutler. I'd like to put you forward.'

Edmund was dumbfounded.

'Well? What do you think?' Cloverbrook didn't wait for a reply but carried on his monologue. 'I believe you'd make an excellent stretcher bearer. Of course, once you get out there to the front, it will be up to the regimental medical officer whether he accepts you. But I'm going to make a recommendation to the camp CO that you're put forward. It's a noncombat post. We've been told to keep an eye out for suitable candidates. Not an easy position to fill as most men can't wait to have a gun in their hands. You'll remain with the regiment but you won't be issued weapons.'

Edmund felt a surge of relief and gratitude. A non-combative role where he might actually do some good. A chance to save lives instead of killing people. He gulped, hardly daring to breathe. 'I'd like to do it, sir, if they'll have me.'

'We'll see. Now get back and get those boots shining or Sergeant Hoddle will be happy to have a reason to put you on a charge.' As Edmund turned to leave, Cloverbrook added, 'You being able to draw is an added advantage. Apparently it's useful to draw maps to identify landmarks so all the bearers know where they are. Not essential but desirable according to the brief.'

Edmund felt euphoric. He saluted the lieutenant and left the office before the man could change his mind. Outside, he ran back to his barrack hut, heart thumping and eager to share the good news with Robert.

Later, in the mess while most of the other men were gathered around the piano singing, he told Robert what the lieutenant had told him. Robert drew on his Woodbine and shrugged. 'Rather you than me, but if it's what you want.'

'It is. Trouble is, if the RMO doesn't agree, it won't happen.'

'He'll agree. If they're right about the job requirements you're the perfect man for it. But seriously, Edmund, do you have any idea what you'll be letting yourself in for? Those poor bastards are in the thick of it, out carrying wounded men in the worst conditions. Do you honestly want to be used like a carthorse – and while risking your life?'

'I want to have a chance to do a job that actually might help people. I'd rather be a carthorse than a killer.'

Robert shook his head. 'I hope you won't come to regret it, my friend.'

NINE

Alice stood in the studio doorway, watching her stepdaughter, Lottie, cross the daisy-splashed meadow to catch up with the group of children walking together to the village school. There was a chill in the air today and she had called Lottie back to put her scarf on.

There was no eagerness in the girl's movement along the path through the field. No happy rush to join the other children. Just a slow steady walk with shoulders slumped, and then a falling in behind the others as they made their way along the lane towards the school.

Superficially, the little girl had settled into her new life in Little Badgerton, and according to Miss Trimble, was doing well at her lessons. Yet Alice couldn't help worrying. At home, Lottie was quiet, withdrawn and outside school didn't play with the other children, preferring to sit at the table in the cottage and draw with her pencils and crayons. It was clear that she had inherited the artistic talents of her parents – Alice hoped that Lottie would continue to enjoy drawing and not turn her back on it as Dora, her mother, had done.

She worried whether the child missed the comfort and

space of her grandfather's town house in Grosvenor Square and her frequent trips to Hamleys for expensive toys, as well as to the zoological gardens. Even more, she'd worried that Lottie was struggling to get over the death of her mother. But if she was, she concealed it from Alice.

Keen to draw the child out, Alice asked about her drawings, enquired each day what she'd done at school, and who her friends were. Lottie was always polite but noncommittal. Alice encouraged her to play with the few dolls she had brought from the London house, but Lottie showed no interest in them. There was only one pastime other than drawing that the little girl showed any inclination for. Before he'd left, Edmund had constructed a swing from a length of rope and a piece of timber he'd found in one of the outbuildings and hung it from the oak tree which stood a few yards from the cottage. Lottie spent hours swinging back and forth, never seeming to tire of it. Eschewing all offers of assistance, she pushed herself off with her feet, jerking her legs forward and backward with a relentless energy that made Alice think of the pendulum on the long case clock at Dalton Hall that had always fascinated her as a child. Watching her from the cottage window, it seemed to her that the little girl used the swing as a kind of talisman, as though it had magical powers and might transport her to some other place. The expression on her face was one of intense concentration – but with a hint of sadness. Was she thinking of Dora? Alice bit her lip and wished she could find a way to get Lottie to tell her.

When Alice and Edmund had married, she had invited Lottie to be her bridesmaid. The child had been delighted to the point of joyfulness, but what Alice had thought to be a breakthrough proved short-lived. Once Edmund went away to join the army, Lottie, while never complaining or showing any signs of distress, had detached herself and retreated to her own closed world.

But it wasn't only Lottie's distance from her that was making Alice feel low. She stood by the large table in the centre of the studio and looked at the work she had done so far. Doubts rose in her. Had she got the balance right between the colours in the floral border? Had she overdone the staining on the sheaves of corn making the yellow tones too brassy? She frowned, bent over the table to look closer, then took a few steps back and looked again at a distance. Why, oh why wasn't Edmund here to advise her, to offer a practised opinion? She doubted her own judgement. Much as she loved her stained-glass work, her heart had gone out of it. Without Edmund beside her in the studio, leading the process, it seemed too great a responsibility. Working to make stained glass felt removed from the more important concerns and worries of life since the war had begun – unlike the work she'd been doing at Bankstone as a VAD. Yet she had no choice but to continue. Were she to stop she would be letting Lady Lockwood down, as well as Edmund. But she was now an apprentice without a master.

Edmund's letters were full of questions on how she was progressing. So she couldn't stop. Couldn't give in to the doubts and fears. She simply had to press on.

Were Maurice Kynaston not there working alongside her, she wondered whether she might have succumbed to the temptation to give up.

A week later, Alice was working with Maurice in the studio when her brother appeared in the doorway. When he had accompanied Maurice the previous week, she'd assumed Victor was merely showing a polite interest in her work and the visit wouldn't be repeated, yet here he was, making himself at home in the only comfortable chair, a rather battered threadbare cast-off from the big house. He was apparently content to sit there in silence and didn't try to watch the progress of the work she and Maurice were doing.

He did however watch Maurice. Alice realised with a sudden flash of insight that her brother appeared to be smitten with the quiet man from Shropshire. His attention barely left Maurice, even though the captain had his back to him, intent on his work mixing pigments and applying washes to the pieces of cut glass.

Alice realised it wasn't out of any curiosity to see the nature of the work Maurice was doing, but rather, a need to be close to him. While she had gradually come to accept Victor's attraction to members of his own sex, she found it puzzling and unnatural. She was anxious that Victor could be treading on dangerous ground if he was developing feelings for Captain Kynaston. Victor was still an army officer and risked a court martial and imprisonment should he be found out.

She had never fully got over her own feelings of guilt for the part she'd played in the death of her then fiancé, Edmund's brother Gilbert, and the all-consuming grief it had occasioned in Victor. She glanced at Maurice and wondered whether he was aware of Victor's feelings and whether he reciprocated them. She remembered that before the war he had been engaged to be married. There was no indication that his feelings lay in the same direction as Victor's and Alice fervently hoped Maurice would not be shocked were he to discover them – and that Victor wouldn't get hurt in the process.

The three of them were silent, Alice and Maurice exchanging only the occasional word pertinent to the tasks they were working on, and Victor feigning to read the newspaper.

'Have you heard from Harriet?' Victor eventually broke the silence. 'I wrote to offer her my help but explained I'm not yet up to making the trip into town.'

'Hasn't she replied yet? You'll hear from her this week, I'm sure. Harriet's frightfully grateful and told me she's already started to put your suggestions into place to reduce the size of the household.' She turned to face her brother. 'The earl's valet decided to retire, so she was saved from having to dismiss him. He got a legacy from His Lordship and plans to return to his village to live with his elderly mother and grow vegetables. Harriet was hugely relieved as he'd been in service with the earl since boyhood.' Alice held a piece of green glass up to the light, before laying it down and selecting another one. 'The children's nanny has had to go too. Although as Miss Eccles was a bit of a tartar, I doubt Harriet lost much sleep over that decision.'

Alice went across to the workbench and chose a paintbrush. She turned to go back to the table but stopped dead. 'I've just had a splendid idea, Victor. Thinking of tartars, there's a woman who lives in the Queen Anne house just down from the vicarage. Very crotchety. Always complaining about the noise of the church bells. Apparently, she's leaving Little Badgerton to move in with her daughter while her son-in-law is at the front. She's put a sign up in the post office looking for a tenant. It's quite a spacious house with a nice garden. Perfect for Harriet and her children.' Alice put her paintbrush down, tore off her apron and reached for her coat and hat. 'No time like the present. I'm going to see the place now. She's left the keys with the postmistress.'

'What if it doesn't suit Harriet?' Victor folded his newspaper.

'I'll know at once when I see it. Obviously, I can't commit on her behalf, but if it's suitable I'll send her a telegram.' She buttoned her coat up, her face wreathed in smiles. 'I feel good about this. It would be absolutely wonderful to have Harriet here in Little Badgerton. I'll be back within the hour, Maurice. You've got plenty to be getting on with.' With that, she swept out of the studio.

.   .   .

When Alice had left them alone, Victor picked up his newspaper again and pretended to read it while continuing to sneak covert glances at Maurice Kynaston from behind the safety of its pages.

What was the matter with him? What was it about Maurice that provoked these feelings in him? Feelings of tenderness, of warmth – and yes, he wouldn't deny it, of desire too. Maurice was a quiet unassuming chap. On the surface he seemed interchangeable with so many men Victor had met in the army, in the City, and before that at school. What was it about him that set Victor's heart pounding inside his chest, that made his hands tremble and caused him to forget the chronic pain in his legs and head caused by his shrapnel injuries?

He was musing over this when he realised Maurice had spoken. 'Sorry, what was that? I didn't catch what you said.'

'I was asking whether you'd thought any more about that job with the War Office. You sounded quite keen to find out more when you mentioned it before.'

Victor sighed. 'I'm not sure I'm ready to return to work yet. Even travelling up to town for the day for the interview feels like a step too great at the moment. As for actually taking on the work...' He rubbed his temple. 'I don't seem to be able to concentrate. My mind's racing all the time. I struggle to focus.' As he spoke, he wondered what it was about Maurice that enabled him to voice his innermost thoughts.

Maurice continued his work. He was painting a kind of undercoat on the cut sections of glass, steadily and patiently working through a pile, carefully setting the pieces on one side to dry afterwards. He held each one by its side edges, working with deliberation and concentration. 'You never know, Victor, you might find it beneficial. I certainly do. Working here in the studio has given me a sense of purpose and helps calm me.'

'Calm you?'

'Calms all the thoughts in my head. Sometimes it's like a

kind of madness. Replaying the war repeatedly. My mind recreating it endlessly, even with my eyes shut. As though I'm still there and it's happening in front of me but I'm powerless to do anything but watch. Over and over again. Men dying again and again.' He edged into place the wooden bridge that supported his wrist and prevented him smudging the paint on the glass surface. 'Do you think they'll ever completely stop? The visions. The memories. The nightmares.'

Victor put down the newspaper. 'Surely, they must. Given time. It's still all horribly fresh to us now. But as time passes, who knows?' He sat back in the chair and stretched. 'But by God, I hope it does.' He got up and moved over to the fireplace where he put another log in the grate, before turning back to look at Maurice. 'Do you honestly think taking a job with the War Office is the way to do that? To help stop the madness. Surely it will make it worse.'

'A desk job in London? Not exactly the frontline, is it? Have they said what's involved?'

Victor shook his head. 'Probably compiling lists of casualties or analysing statistics on deaths by age or education status. The kind of nonsense those Whitehall types dream up.' He sighed. 'Oh, what's the point? I think I'll write to them today and decline.'

'Why not at least go and find out what it's about?'

Victor looked down. He didn't want to admit the real reason. That he couldn't bear to show his face among the wider public since his injuries. The thought of walking – no, limping – down Whitehall with that ugly black eyepatch and the long scar that now cut through his cheek was horrifying. What if he met someone he knew? What if the pain proved too much? What if he was overcome with fear? But he couldn't voice these foolish doubts to Maurice.

'Why don't I come with you,' said Maurice. 'Alice mentioned needing some new pigments. I could go and buy them while you're at your interview. Then maybe we could have a spot of lunch. Make a day of it. It would be a change of scene for us both.'

Victor knew he'd like nothing more than to spend time alone with Maurice. But something made him hesitate. 'Are you up to it?' he asked – then immediately regretted it. 'I mean London can be exhausting at the best of times, but you have to get around on crutches.'

'They still have cabs, don't they? Or even trams and buses? It'll do me good. If I get tired, I'll stop in a café for a rest.'

Victor grinned. The idea was growing in appeal. 'I suppose I could call on the countess as well – and I need to look in on my set. It's been empty since I left for Gallipoli. My valet joined up as soon as the war started. The place no doubt needs an airing.'

Maurice had put down his paintbrush and was looking puzzled. 'Your set?'

'My rooms at Albany. On Piccadilly. Bachelor apartments are called sets there. I lived in one before the war. The sets are much in demand, but an old school pal passed his on to me when he left to live overseas. Damned lucky for me as it's very convenient. Bang in the centre of town. I miss the place. But then I miss so much about life before the war.'

'Well then, that's settled. It seems we both have good reason to make the trip to London. When shall we go? Have they suggested a date for the interview?'

'Asked me to telegraph them when I felt up to travelling.'

'How about next week then?'

Victor smiled. 'I'll ask the MO to give me a supply of painkillers.'

Maurice picked up his brush, ran it over the watery green solution he had made on his palette and began painting again. 'Have they given you any indication of what they want you to do?'

'The letter from the War Office said it was with the

Ministry of Munitions. They seemed to think my experience as a stockbroker would be useful. That's why I suspect it will be compiling tables of statistics.'

'You won't know until you meet them, will you? Do you have to take it if you don't want it? I mean are you obliged to stay in the army?'

'Yes. My commission stands for the duration of the war. The other option is training, but I haven't the stomach for that. I hate the thought of drilling more young men to send to their deaths.'

'I'm able to cut the ties completely as my service predated the war. I suppose I could offer to do a desk job, but I can't imagine doing anything I'd like as much as this.' He bent his head again over his task, completely absorbed in it.

Victor watched him working, noticing Maurice's smooth hands with their long fingers, as the captain held the paintbrush, sweeping it in even confident strokes over the surface of the glass. Maurice was seated on a high stool, his remaining leg providing steadying balance. He was wearing a heavy linen apron over his army uniform and Victor could see the outline of his broad back and shoulders beneath the wool serge. He remembered Maurice had told him he'd competed as a sprinter before the war, winning county championships and narrowly missing qualification for the London Olympics in 1908. Maurice's head was in profile and Victor could see the concentration in his eyes, the way he bit his lip as he worked, the lock of hair that fell across his brow.

A deep longing gripped Victor, an almost uncontrollable desire to move across the room and take the captain in his arms. He looked away, gazing into the fire, squeezing his hands into tight fists in his pockets.

TEN

'It's perfect. I love it.' Harriet Wallingford spun round on her heels and executed a twirl as she swept an arm out in an extravagant sweep of the room. 'You're my guardian angel, dear Alice, and I can't tell you how wonderful it will be to live just a few hundred yards from you and be able to see you whenever I want.'

They were standing in the wide hallway of The Hawthorns, the brick-built villa next door to the Little Badgerton vicarage. Light streamed in through the floor-to-ceiling windows at the far end of the hall which overlooked the rear garden. 'And to be next door to your aunt and uncle. I adore Eleanor and Walter.'

'You really like the place?'

'I told you; I *love* it. The house is perfect. Plenty of room for us all. The children will think they're in paradise with that beautiful garden and the apple orchard.' She clasped her hands together. 'I think we must keep chickens and maybe a couple of sheep.'

Alice gave a little snort of amusement. 'You? Keeping sheep and chickens? I'll believe that when I see it.'

'There's a war on. We all have to do our bit. I shall enjoy playing the country gentlewoman. Besides, the children will help.'

Alice was still sceptical but she was relieved that Harriet was approaching the idea of moving so positively.

'And the village school is so close. Honestly, Alice, I can't believe it. You clever old thing.'

'You won't find it too small after that huge house in Portman Square?'

'Good Lord, no! I was never that keen on the town house, just on being in the heart of London. But I can't think of anything I'd like more than being here in this delightful village with plenty of fresh air and beautiful scenery.'

'Won't you get bored?'

'Certainly not. I'll learn to make jam. Maybe help Eleanor with some of the church activities. Feed the sheep and chickens.' She grinned at Alice.

'I think the idea with sheep is you don't have to feed them. They keep the grass down. But they'll probably end up eating the contents of your garden too.'

'Well, that's no good. Cancel the sheep. I shall become a pillar of the community instead. Perhaps a rather crumbling pillar. Can't really see myself running the Mothers' Union. And since I haven't a clue about cooking, I doubt I'll be much good at the jam making. But the children will keep me busy.' She clapped her hands together. 'I intend to manage with as little help as possible. Just a couple of girls from the village to do the heavy work and of course a cook. But I've no intention of having a nanny again. I want to enjoy having Crispin around for the few years before he's whisked away to Harrow and becomes all moody and distant.' She chuckled. 'Remember how you said Victor was when he went to Eton?'

'The moody phase didn't last long. After he'd been there a while, he began to appreciate his little sister again.' Alice smiled, remembering. She gave her friend a hug. 'I'll be thrilled to have you here, Harriet.' Alice was delighted that she had been able to help her friend. 'If your mind's made up, let's go and hand back the keys and tell Mrs Mayhew at the post office that you're going to take it. Afterwards we can have a cup of tea with Eleanor and give her the good news – then the school will be finishing so you can meet Lottie and we can show you around the place and let Miss Trimble know she can expect a new pupil.'

'Don't mention to her that Crispin is the Earl of Walling-ford. I don't want him getting teased or being treated any differently from anyone else. Just plain old Crispin Wallingford will do. I'm beginning to think titles are more trouble than they're worth.'

'You won't get any disagreement from me. I'm more than happy to be Mrs Alice Cutler now and not the Honourable Alice Dalton.'

Harriet smiled. 'Have you heard anything from Dalton Hall? Any news of your mother softening her attitude now you're married?'

'Nothing. Victor hasn't even told them he's here at Bank-stone. Just that he was injured and will be in touch when he's ready. I've explained to him that Papa and I have reconciled but he's reluctant to speak to either of them.'

'Surely as his next-of-kin won't they have been informed that he was injured and is in hospital here?'

'Apparently not. They were told when he was wounded at Gallipoli. Then later that he was being repatriated. But once he got to England, he refused to contact them. Said he couldn't stomach seeing them. I suspect it's because he lost the eye. He knows Mama will make a dreadful fuss about it.' Alice bit her lip. 'You know what she's like. So, I've decided it's best to give him time. After all, I have no room to talk, after years with no contact with them. It's only thanks to Eleanor that Papa came to my wedding.'

Arm-in-arm the two friends left The Hawthorns and walked past the church of St Margaret to the vicarage, where Eleanor greeted them with freshly baked scones and tea. She was as delighted as they were that Harriet was going to take on the rental of the adjacent property and join the small community of Little Badgerton.

After Alice and Harriet's visit to inspect the village school, Eleanor offered the vicarage pony and trap to transport Harriet to the station. Alice and Lottie accompanied Harriet there and saw her off on the London train. It had been agreed that she and her children would be moving to their new home in two weeks' time.

Back in Little Badgerton, Alice unhitched the pony, stabled him, brushed him down and filled his water bucket, watched by a solemn-faced Lottie. She'd tried to get the little girl interested in helping care for the animal, but Lottie preferred to watch from a distance. Perhaps when the Wallingfords arrived Lottie might enjoy taking little Poppy under her wing. Alice hoped so, as she was beginning to despair of ever seeing the child animated by anything.

When they returned to the cottage at Bankstone, she gave Lottie her tea, and washed the dishes while her stepdaughter, as usual, occupied herself by drawing pictures. Alice looked over her shoulder and saw she had drawn a picture of a woman holding the hand of a small child. A self-portrait with Dora?

She was about to admire the picture, hoping she might be able to get Lottie to open up. But too late. Lottie noticed and closed the drawing book. She tidied up her crayons and got to her feet. 'I'm tired, I think I'll go to bed now. Do you mind?'

Alice wanted to hold the little girl in her arms and ask her what was wrong, but she sensed this would be unwelcome. She gave Lottie a sad smile and told her that of course it was all right. 'I'll come and kiss you goodnight shortly.'

What was she doing wrong? She removed her apron, dried her hands and sat down at the table to write to Edmund. She longed to tell him about Lottie's behaviour and ask his advice but knew it would cause him to worry. Instead, she wrote about Harriet's imminent arrival and how she hoped Lottie would become friends with Crispin and Poppy.

Edmund's letters were frequent and usually contained sketches he'd made of seabirds, flowers and occasionally of other men in the camp. He wrote of the tedium and discipline of military life, the constant kit cleaning, the endless square bashing and how the route marches and physical exercises were making him fitter. She closed her eyes, imagining, as she so often did, that he was here with her, trying to recapture how it felt to be held in his arms and to feel his soft lips upon hers.

Her reverie was disturbed by a knock at the door. She opened it to find Victor standing there, wearing his army great-coat, a solemn expression on his face.

'Sorry to disturb you, Alice, only I wanted to catch you after Charlotte was asleep.'

Victor persisted in calling her stepdaughter by her full given name. She assumed this was because of knowing the child first when she was with Dora, who'd had a deep-seated aversion to the more informal name Edmund preferred.

Victor brandished a letter in a brown envelope with some kind of official stamp on the back. The front face was filled with a series of redirects. 'This came today. From Pentonville Prison. Cutler wants to see me.'

'Come in, come in. I'm about to make a pot of tea.' Alice filled the kettle and placed it on the hob. 'What on earth does he want with you?'

'Well for a start he wrote it a couple of months ago. It had been all over the place before it reached me here at Bankstone. He appears to have chosen to forget how he damned me from here to eternity when I told him I was taking a commission.'

Alice set out the cups and saucers. 'He asked Edmund to visit him in that jail.'

'Did he go?'

'Yes. But I think he wished he hadn't. His father showed not a sign of remorse about poor Dora. Said he wouldn't plead manslaughter as he's not guilty of anything since Dora fell and hit her head while in a state of inebriation.'

Alice put a tea cosy on the teapot, before sitting down again opposite her brother.

'He claimed she was drunk?' Victor jerked back in his seat. 'The woman barely touched alcohol. That's a ridiculous claim to make. And wasn't it the other way round? Captain Kynaston filled me in on what the papers said at the time he was arrested. He'd been drinking heavily at his club and according to his butler had carried on drinking when he returned to Grosvenor Square.'

'The butler said as much to us when we arrived there the next day. In a fit of anger Cutler had even thrown his whisky tumbler into the fireplace – the shards of broken glass may have contributed to Dora's death. And the butler and housekeeper said he'd raised his voice to her. It seems he was angry because she'd allowed Edmund to see Lottie when he'd expressly forbidden it.'

Alice poured the tea and held a cup out to her brother.

'What kind of man denies his own son access to his only child?' Victor shook his head. He accepted the cup of tea his sister handed him. 'Well.' He brandished the letter. 'He wants me to keep the brokerage going. Says he'll be back after the trial acquits him. He's hired the best defence lawyer in London. He's determined to fight this.'

'Why does he need you then?'

'He wrote this months ago. I imagine he'd heard I'd been injured out of the army. I suppose he wanted me to pick up the reins. But most of his clients will have found a new brokerage by now. He doubtless wanted me to run around London drumming up new ones. Clearly has no idea that I haven't been discharged even though I'm no longer on active service.'

'What are you going to do?'

'As it happens, I'm going to London the day after tomorrow for that interview at the Ministry of Munitions. Did Maurice tell you he's decided to come too? Says he has materials to purchase for the studio.'

'Yes, he did. But I'm not sure it's a good idea for either of you to be dashing around London until you're completely recovered.'

He gave her a long steady look. 'We're never going to be completely recovered, Alice.' He took a sip of tea. 'We've decided to go and that's that.'

Alice knew better than to argue.

Victor continued. 'I'll call in at the brokerage while I'm in town. Talk to the clerks. Find out what the state of the client ledger is. If I don't take the war office position, I might as well go back and pick up the pieces of what's left. I read the financial papers every day anyway. And I need to look at the situation with Papa, since Cutler's not been around to manage his finances.'

'Do you really think there'll be much business left in the brokerage? Cutler's arrest was a terrific scandal and in all the papers.' Alice didn't know much about the workings of the stock exchange – but enough to know that it was very much based on a system of trust and the old boys' network.

'Only what I'd describe as "inertia business". You'd be surprised though how many people fall into that category. Failing to react even when events call for it. Trusting the status quo. Lots of wealthy widows who never trouble themselves to

check on their own portfolios. And of course, people like Papa. I
bet he hasn't done anything with his holdings since Herbert was
arrested. Either that or he's withdrawn all his funds and placed
them on the four o'clock at Kempton Park.'

'The racecourses are mostly closed because of the war so I
doubt he's done that,' said Alice, keen to defend her father.

'Didn't stop old Monty Wallingford, did it?' Victor had
never liked to be bested by his younger sister.

'I imagine the earl lost most of his money before the war.
And it wasn't just horses. It was gambling in general.'

Victor sighed. 'Actually, Alice, Wallingford was living a life-
style out of all proportion to his income. Hence the mortgaged
estate. Seems he was pretty clueless. I also suspect he wasn't
wise in his choice of estate manager. The piggery had been
losing money for decades.'

Alice put down her cup. 'So, you'll help Herbert Cutler?'

'I'll help myself. Papa too. And the reputation of the firm.
But don't worry, I'll extract my price. It will be my name over
the door. I'd been asking for it to be Cutler and Dalton, but
maybe Dalton Associates makes more sense. Should Herbert be
found innocent then perhaps Dalton and Cutler could be
considered.'

'I'm glad I don't have to do business with you, dear brother.
You drive a hard bargain.'

'No more than that man deserves.'

'I won't disagree with that.' Alice finished her cup of tea and
tightened her lips. The idea of Victor getting involved with
Herbert Cutler again made her nervous. She told herself there
was nothing Cutler could do to harm Victor from inside
Pentonville, but that didn't stop her feeling anxious. Her
brother was still recovering from his injuries. He was advising
Harriet and now it looked like he would be adding oversight of
their father's portfolio too, as well as a possible role in the
Ministry of Munitions. How could he take on Cutler's

brokerage business on top of all that? But most of all she was fearful that Cutler would try to enlist Victor in his efforts to prove his innocence.

Alice knew better than to voice her misgivings to her brother, so she bit her tongue and began to clear away the tea things.

ELEVEN

The orders for mobilisation came suddenly. The men had been doing a gruelling cross-country run. Edmund was one of the first back at the barracks, where he saw the orders pinned up on the noticeboard. They were to leave camp at dawn the following day.

So this was it. Soon the English Channel would be between him and Alice, not just thirty miles or so of road. He tried to swallow, but his throat constricted, and a bitter taste filled his mouth. Tonight's letter would probably be the last he would write to her from English soil.

Later that evening, he sat on his camp bed, pillow stuffed behind him, writing pad propped on his knees, and his back resting against the wall of the wooden hut as he struggled to find the right words. Everyone else in the usually noisy barrack room was doing the same. The scratching of pens and the occasional sigh reflected their universal concentration on their loved ones.

Edmund tried to shape his thoughts into a coherent flow, but his mind was racing. Should he write about meeting Cloverbrook and the offer of the role with the RAMC? While Alice would no doubt share his relief that he wouldn't be wielding a gun and taking lives, he was sure the risks of venturing out as a stretcher bearer into No Man's Land, often under fire, would be apparent to her. Perhaps it would be better to frame the role more broadly. He could simply tell her that he was going to serve with the medical corps and be engaged in the battle to save lives rather than take them. He could leave it vague enough for her to assume he'd be deployed as an orderly at a casualty clearing station or as an ambulance driver. He hated to obfuscate, but causing Alice pain and anxiety would be worse. He told himself that until he got to France, he wouldn't know exactly what he'd be doing anyway. The regimental medical officer might even deem him unsuitable. He could be sent to a post away from the front. Or on a hospital train. And the mobilisation orders referred only to a training camp over there – they could be stuck there for months. In the end, he decided to opt for a positive tone and stress the strong possibility of being given a non-combative position.

He devoted the rest of the letter to enquiring about her and Lottie's well-being, Victor's recovery, and progress on the Latchington window. He included some sketches he'd made of seabirds and a drawing of Robert for her to give to Robert's wife, Viola. He read the letter through and decided it would have to do. Who knew when he'd have another opportunity to write?

The following day, they left the camp before dawn, travelling by lorry to London, where at Victoria station they were herded onto a waiting train. There were far more men than the train's capacity, hence a rush to grab the available seats. Edmund and Robert had to settle for perching on their kitbags in the corridor. The weather was unseasonably hot, so by the time they reached Folkestone the conscripts were tired, sweaty and uncomfortable in their woollen uniforms.

They embarked for France on a two-funnelled former

passenger ferry. While the decks were crowded, the breeze over the Channel provided a welcome respite after the heat of London and the train. When they landed at Boulogne, they were ordered onto another train to be transported to the enormous British Expeditionary Force camp at Étaples, about twenty miles south of Boulogne.

After about fifteen minutes, the slow-moving train stopped in a siding to allow another train to pass in the opposite direction, heading back towards Boulogne. Edmund and his comrades gazed through the windows and saw nurses and orderlies moving along the central aisle between two tiers of beds. As the train passed at a snail's pace they stared across at the haggard faces of the men in the lower tiered beds, many with bandages covering part of their heads and faces, some almost like Egyptian mummies. Where their eyes were visible the patients stared back at them, expressions blank, hollow and wretched, despite the fact that they were now heading home. As the locomotive slid slowly by, Edmund counted nine ward cars as well as another car packed with walking wounded. The chatter among the men around him died away as they all absorbed this evidence of the toll the war was taking on the British army. Edmund glanced at Robert, who shrugged and gave him a knowing look. Edmund realised Robert had seen it all before when he'd been out at the front the previous year as a civilian writer covering the war for *The New Statesman*.

After the hospital train had moved away, the atmosphere remained subdued. All the banter, singing and joking that had characterised the crossing over the Channel stopped. Now they were close to the theatre of war. Perhaps still distant from the front – but close enough to witness its output – a stream of seriously wounded men, many of whom would face a future with bodies, minds or both damaged irrevocably.

As well as untested new recruits, their train carried a number of men returning to the front, having recovered from injuries back in Britain. These men were sent first to Étaples to be reintegrated into the army and seemed to be dreading the return to the camp more than their eventual return to the front.

'It's an 'orrible place is Eat Apples,' said one veteran, sitting on the floor near Edmund. 'The instructors are a vicious lot. Right bunch of bastards.'

Edmund glanced at Robert, who was listening intently.

'We call them Canaries cos of them yellow bands they wear on their caps and their sleeves. None of 'em have a bleeding clue what it's like at the front. Cowards they are. Vicious bloody cowards. Take it out on us poor buggers.' The man, a stocky fellow with a ruddy complexion, rubbed at his legs to get the circulation going as there was so little space in the cramped compartment.

'How? How will they take it out on us?' Robert leaned forward.

'Exercise us till we're nearly dead on our feet in the Bull Ring. Punish us for the slightest thing.'

Another glance passed between Edmund and Robert.

Seeing their bemusement, the man said, 'The Bull Ring's what they call the training ground in the sand dunes. Bastards keep us there till we're half dead. And even though us lot have already seen active service at the front they let the Canaries loose on us before they send us back there. Call it "reintegration". Reintegration, my arse! It's state-sanctioned torture.'

Another returning soldier interjected. 'I reckon the idea is we'll have such a bad time there that we'll be begging to get back to the trenches. I'd rather face the Hun than those mean bastards any day.'

After stopping again in several railway sidings, this time to allow goods trains laden with armaments to overtake them, their train eventually pulled into the camp at Étaples. A journey that should have taken about forty minutes to an hour from the dockside had taken over three.

The green unripened rye in the fields they passed on the trip from Boulogne had made it hard to believe the front was only about sixty miles to the east of them. Here on the plains of northern France farmers were still planting and harvesting. Edmund didn't know why that should surprise him – after all, the population, including the French army, needed to be fed. Life had to go on here despite the fact that just a matter of tens of miles away, tracts of farmland, towns and villages were now devastated ruins. While Edmund was yet to see the front, he'd read enough to know of the carnage that was taking place there. He shuddered, imagining how he would feel if that was happening to Little Badgerton.

The Étaples camp was vast. It was a tented city spread out along the northern bank of the River Canche. The men filed off the train to be confronted by an ocean of tents stretching as far as the eye could see. The tents were shaped like the wigwams Edmund remembered from books about the American West he'd read in childhood. A network of roads cut through the camp and, as well as the tented troop accommodation, there were hospital buildings, storage warehouses, quartermasters' stores, segregation areas for infectious diseases, women's quarters for nurses and, ominously, an extensive cemetery.

There was no mention of the promised transfer into the medical corps for Edmund. He asked whether he could have a meeting with the regimental medical officer but was told to wait until he was summoned. He hoped this delay didn't mean he'd been forgotten or that the RMO had rejected him.

He and the rest of his unit were immediately subjected to the draconian training regime at Étaples under the brutal Canaries. If he'd baulked at bayonet practice before in Browndown, there was no escaping it now. The first morning in the camp, Edmund, despite his misgivings, found himself with rifle and bayonet in hand charging across the Bull Ring towards the suspended sandbag target. The exercise he hated most.

Conscious of the need to smash the bayonet into the waiting sandbag, he gripped his rifle firmly.

Not firmly enough.

He had anticipated the clear run onto the target that he had been accustomed to at Browndown. But here at Étaples nothing was straightforward. As he drew close to the target and readied himself to plunge the bayonet into the hanging bag of sand, one of the sergeants rushed at him sideways and knocked his bayonet out of his hand just as he was about to strike.

Edmund bent down to retrieve the bayonet. That was when he felt the pain of the sergeant's boot. Burning, searing, slicing through him. At first he thought he'd fallen on the bayonet and the blade had cut through him. He fell forward onto the slippery ground of the sand dune. Another boot made contact with his ribs. He struggled to get up. Sand up his nose and his mouth. Ears ringing. Choking. Burning. Pain, pain, pain.

Then the angry voices.

'Bloody idiot! You feeble excuse for a man! If you're going to stick a blade in the Hun then you have to mean it. Stab the bastard! Stab him!' The sergeant's voice was rasping like sandpaper but shrill and loud.

Another voice from the other side of him: 'Wake the bastard up!' Then another searing pain, this time on his right side. Edmund struggled to breathe. He felt the rough scrape of the sand grains and the sharp razor blade cuts of marram grass slicing across his face. His collar was jerked backwards so that the front of it dug into his throat, choking him.

'Get up, you snivelling little bastard.'

As he was staggering back onto his feet he felt another blow to his lower back.

The anger rose inside him like a volcano. Heat from the pain in his kidneys where they'd kicked him. Heat from the anger in his heart. He roared upwards and was about to strike out when he realised the two Canaries who'd struck him were

no longer there. One was lying on the sand, a bloodied brow
and an already swelling eye socket indicating where he'd been
punched. The other was crawling away, a look of fear on his
face as Robert Fuller advanced towards him.

Edmund shouted, 'No! Don't!'

Before he could do anything to intervene, one of the other
Browndown men flung himself forward, grabbed Fuller by the
ankles and brought him to the ground. Then the dozens of other
men who had been waiting their turns for the bayonetting exercise all hurled themselves into the mêlée in a vain effort to
prevent the two Canary sergeants establishing who had been
responsible for the counterattack.

'Less than twenty-four hours in France and you've already
brought disgrace upon yourself and your regiment.' The officer's
eyes drilled into Robert. 'We will not tolerate this behaviour. It's
despicable.' He slapped his swagger stick across his palm and
glared out at the assembled men. 'This was a cowardly attack
upon Sergeants Gosling and Bottomley. I intend for the entire
unit to be punished by restricting rations for the next fourteen
days. And for Private Fuller, I sentence him to Field Punishment Number One. Bear in mind, all of you, I will not tolerate
attacks on my NCOs. That kind of behaviour merits the death
penalty. Only because this is your first day here have I decided
to be lenient.'

Edmund looked at his friend then stepped forward. 'Permission to speak, sir?'

'Not granted.' The officer narrowed his eyes and focused on
Edmund. 'If you have more than one or two brain cells, I'd
suggest you keep your mouth shut, Private, until invited.'

Edmund gritted his teeth. Why had Robert intervened to
help him? Grateful for his loyalty, he still wished he hadn't.

What was Field Punishment Number One? He felt the bile rise in his throat.

All too soon Edmund and his comrades discovered what the punishment was. Fuller was taken to the perimeter of the Bull Ring and tied by the ankles and wrists to a fence post in full view of the training ground. There he was to stand, rain or shine, for two hours each day for the following fourteen days.

Fuller himself was defiant. He made no complaint, even though the weather was hot, and he was forced to wear full uniform. Unable to wipe away the sweat, scratch, relieve himself, or talk to anyone, he stood pinioned, burning under the heat of the midday sun.

The torture was almost as great for Edmund. He felt responsible. If he'd gripped his rifle more tightly the sergeant couldn't have knocked it out of his hands. If he'd stood firmer, they wouldn't have been able to knock him off his feet and Robert wouldn't have felt obliged to intervene. It should be he who was tied to the fence posts, even though he couldn't help but feel grateful it wasn't. He still bore dark bruises from the kicking the Canaries had given him, like crushed blackberries across the skin of his sides and lower back. He still felt the dull ache even days after their vicious attack.

All the men from Browndown were now wise to the Canaries and on their guard.

'We should get one of them buggers on his own and do him over,' said Ackroyd one evening when they were all lying on their camp beds about to sleep. 'That ugly bruiser what kicked the 'ell out of Cutler.'

'Don't be daft,' said another. 'Unless we take the whole bloody lot of them out, we'll all cop it. And we can't take on the whole campful.'

'Aye, and it's not only whatever charge the officer puts us on when we're court-martialled, it's them beating the crap out of us on the way there. Fuller had had a good kicking before he even got in front of that captain. It ain't worth it.'

'But it's not right that Fuller has to be punished for doing what the rest of us should have done.'

'Much as I appreciate the sentiments, chaps, I don't need you boys to play the hero for me,' said Fuller. 'Ginger's right – it's not worth it. At least while I'm tied to the bloody fence I'm not having to run up and down those sand dunes with a bayonet pointing up my arse like the rest of you do.' He wiped a hand over his brow which was burnt red from the sun. 'I reckon I've got it light, boys.'

While none of them believed him, they were all grateful that he was letting them off the hook.

Edmund lay in the dark of the tent and cursed his own reluctance in combat practice. If he'd been more enthusiastic with the bayonet and a little less hesitant, Robert wouldn't be strapped to a post and grilled in the heat like a piece of steak. 'I'm sorry, Robert,' he whispered into the dark space between their camp beds.

'Don't apologise, pal. If it hadn't been you, it would've been me, or any one of us. Those men are out-and-out bastards and nothing's going to change that. Remember what the fellow on the train said. Now get to sleep.'

TWELVE

Alice took the long way round to Viola Fuller's cottage, climbing up through the beech woods and walking along the top of the escarpment before descending on an ancient pathway to the little house nestled within trees. It was a relief to see a thin curl of woodsmoke rising from the chimney. Viola must be up and about and not, as Alice had feared, lying in bed, her pillow sodden with tears.

Taking to her bed and crying was a not infrequent occurrence as Viola continued to struggle with being separated from Robert by the war. At first, Alice had been sympathetic but recently Viola's victimhood had begun to be wearisome. Alice herself was grieving over Edmund's absence. So too were half the women of Little Badgerton over husbands, sons and brothers at the front, and worse. But life had to go on.

Throughout the Fullers' common-law marriage, the couple had experienced long periods apart because of Robert's work as a travel writer. Viola should by now be accustomed to his long absences. But she seemed determined to be wedded to her sorrow, elevating her pain to heroic proportions, like Penelope's

endless cycle of weeping and sleeping during the years of
Odysseus's absence. There was a self-indulgence about it that
bordered on vanity and tested Alice's patience and empathy.

As she came down the hill, the ground underfoot was soft
and springy, and the air smelt of damp moss and decaying
leaves. Cowslips were growing on the lower slopes, in splashes
of buttery yellow. In the distance, she saw Viola emerge from
the cottage with a laundry basket under her arm. She began to
hang out the washing on a line hung between an apple tree and
the side of the house. Her back was to Alice, so she didn't see
her approach and jumped out of her skin when Alice called out
in greeting.

'You gave me a fright.' Her voice sounded tetchy, rather
than pleased to see her friend. 'Help me finish hanging out the
washing and I'll put the kettle on. I'm afraid there's no cake as I
didn't get round to baking yesterday.' Viola released a long sigh.

Alice took a pair of pillowcases from the basket and began
to peg them on the line. 'A nice breeze and plenty of sunshine.
They'll be dry in no time.' She smiled at her friend then added,
'How are the children?'

'Same as ever. Under my feet all the time. The baby's
crawling now.'

They finished the task and went inside the cottage. The
kitchen was tidier than usual – Viola tended to let the house-
work pile up during her bouts of misery then went at it with a
frenzy. Alice still found it strange that her friend claimed
Robert suffered from depression when the only sign of melan-
cholia Alice had ever witnessed in the Fuller couple was in
Viola herself. Perhaps it was a form of transference whereby
Viola refused to confront her own distress and grafted it onto
her husband instead.

But today Viola was functioning and if not cheerful, was at
least placid.

'I've brought you something.' Alice rummaged in her pocket as they sat down to share a cup of tea. She pulled out a piece of folded paper and handed it to Viola, hoping it would cheer her up. 'It's from Edmund.'

Frowning, Viola took it. 'From Edmund? For me?'

'Go on,' Alice coaxed. 'Look at it.'

Viola unfolded the sheet to reveal the pencil drawing of Robert. It was an excellent likeness. Edmund had captured him, unawares, as he leant against the wall of the practice trench, in a rare break between the relentless drilling at Browndown Camp.

Alice watched her friend as she studied the drawing in silence. Then the tears started.

Through sobs, Viola said, 'This drawing will be all I'll have left of him. I'll never see him again.' She pushed the paper away. 'What good is a picture to me? I want him here. Now.'

Alice sighed inwardly. She'd hoped the portrait would have raised Viola's spirits, offering her a glimpse of her husband as he had been recently, providing a reassurance that he was hale and hearty. When it had arrived Alice had felt a twinge of disappointment that it wasn't a self-portrait but had believed it would be a boon to Viola and had lost no time in bringing it to her. She said nothing, waiting for Viola to calm herself.

After a while, the sobbing subsided in strength and turned into soft sniffles. Viola looked up with watery eyes. 'It's a struggle financially too. The separation allowance is only twenty-three shillings a week and I've the rent to pay, not to mention feeding and clothing the children. Now that Molly's at school she's growing so fast that I can't keep up with it. I make her clothes but it's the shoes. They last only a couple of months and she's bursting out of them. At least *you* can work. I'm stuck at home with a baby. I can't get a job like so many women are doing now the war's on.'

'Have you considered doing childcare? Lots of women are

working in the factories – you might be able to make a few shillings by looking after their children.'

'Who round here could afford to pay me to do that? Besides, don't you think I've enough on my plate here already? It's all right for you. There's just Edmund's child. None of your own.'

Alice felt the sting in Viola's words. The stillbirth of her son had been devastating to her and to Edmund and the pain remained visceral. But Viola appeared oblivious to the effect of her words.

Alice trembled and bit down on her lip to stop the threatening tears. It was bad enough Viola giving rein to her emotions without Alice joining her.

There was a whimpering sound from the next room. Viola wiped the back of her hand across her eyes and got up. 'The baby's awake so Francis will wake from his afternoon nap any minute now.' She disappeared into the other room and returned with the ten-month-old baby held against her. The child was gurgling happily.

Viola sat down and reached for a bowl of puréed vegetables that had been cooling on the table. She began to spoon-feed the baby. 'So, they'll be in France by now. That's it then.'

'Edmund says they're being posted to a training camp and could be there for months.'

'Believe that if you want to.' Viola's lip curled. 'I'm not so gullible.'

'At least they're together. It must help having a friend out there.' Alice was determined to be cheerful.

'I don't know whether I'm relieved or more anxious that Robert and your husband are together,' said Viola eventually. 'If something happens to one of them then how will it feel if the other is unharmed?' She dragged the teaspoon under the baby's chin, scraping up the residual food and feeding it back to the child. 'It may sound awful but I'm going say it anyway. If they were in different regiments, or battalions, or in different parts of the world, I think I'd be able to accept it more if something should happen. But if they're together and something happens to one of them, won't we each think *why him*? Why me? Why not you?' She put down the spoon, wiped the baby's mouth with a bib then ran a hand through her loose uncombed hair. 'You're looking at me as though it's a dreadful thing to say. But I'd be less than honest if I didn't say it, Alice. I can't help but think I'd resent you if Edmund survived an attack that Robert died in – and I think you'd feel the same too. Wouldn't you?'

Alice stared at her friend, unsure what to say. Bewildered by her convoluted train of thought.

Viola pressed on. 'Perhaps you prefer a more romantic view of things. Our men going into battle together. Brave pals, side-by-side.' Her voice had a sarcastic tone.

'Actually, yes. I do rather take comfort from the thought that Edmund and Robert will be supporting each other.' She felt herself bristle. 'Why are you saying this, Viola? Why?'

'I just want us to get some things straight while we're able to think clearly. If one of them should die, we won't be able to. It'll be too late. I'd like to sort it out now, while we can. So we can support each other. You do see that, don't you?'

Alice didn't. 'I'm sorry, Viola. I do take comfort that my husband is with someone he knows and from the thought that if either is wounded the other will do their level best to help them. I'm happy that they're not alone, that they have become good friends. So no, I don't see that at all, Viola.'

Suddenly she wanted to get out of what now felt like the claustrophobic atmosphere of the cottage. She stood up. 'I must go. Lottie will be home from school in an hour or so and I need to get her tea ready.'

Viola wiped her baby's hands as the child had been dipping them into the bowl of puréed vegetables. She looked up at Alice. 'You're offended. But you shouldn't be. I'm merely being honest. Better now than later.'

The drawing of Robert still lay on the table and now had a little green splash of baby food on it. Alice gritted her teeth and bit back the temptation to say something else. Anything said now could not be unsaid.

Muttering only goodbye, she pushed open the door of the cottage and stepped outside. It felt like a blessed release.

THIRTEEN

During the train journey up to London, Victor stared out of the window, unseeing, deeply aware of Maurice Kynaston's presence opposite him. The other seats were occupied, so Victor felt tongue-tied and constrained from talking to his friend.

But his reticence wasn't only because they were in a crowded space where their conversation would be overheard. It was also because he was in turmoil. Why did Maurice have this effect on him? The man wasn't particularly handsome and certainly had given no indication of reciprocating the attraction, but it was as though an invisible thread ran between them, attaching them together. It was more than a physical attraction – Victor could only describe his emotions as being a kind of tenderness, a warmth that enveloped him whenever he was in Maurice's company.

He thought of the last relationship he'd had. Max Stieglitz had been an American moving-picture actor, as classically handsome as a Greek statue. But Max had inspired lust, not love, in Victor. His death in the sinking of the *Lusitania* had been the trigger for Victor to volunteer. But the feelings that inspired him enlisting had been anger at Germany about what

happened and sadness at Max's untimely death, not the grief
that had possessed him when Edmund Cutler's brother,
Gilbert, had taken his own life. Victor had believed the love he'd
felt for Gilbert would never be matched, that a hole had been
hollowed out of his heart that could never be filled. Yet here he
was, so powerfully drawn to the man in the seat opposite that he
was afraid to look at him for fear of giving himself away.

For the first time in his adult life Victor felt insecure and
lacking confidence. With the scars on his face, the cloth patch
where he'd lost an eye, and his slight limp, he considered
himself disfigured, ugly, undesirable. Regardless of that, it was
foolish to think of Maurice as a potential lover when the man
had given no indication of being queer.

The train drew into Clapham Junction and people got on
and off. Victor turned his head and realised Maurice was
looking at him. Their eyes met and Maurice smiled. A frisson
went through Victor. He smiled back.

A young couple took the seats next to Maurice and two
bowler-hatted City businessmen occupied those next to Victor.
The couple were talking in whispers and holding hands.
Maurice glanced at them and smiled again at Victor. Still
Victor's powers of speech had abandoned him, but it felt as
though there had been something in that little exchange of
glances that was different, that marked a slight shift in their relationship. He allowed his gaze to drift back to the captain and
found it was met and returned. His heart skipped a beat.
Maurice *did* feel something for him. Victor wasn't imagining it.
How was he going to get through the morning's business
knowing that later there might be an opportunity to test this –
without burning his bridges of course. It would be too risky to
play his full hand until he was certain Maurice felt the
same way.

Parting at Waterloo was a wrench. Victor was heading to
Whitehall for his interview and Maurice to a pigment supplier

in Covent Garden. He settled into his seat in the taxi and took several gulps of air. Then he bent forward and twisted in his seat to look back for a glimpse of Maurice, climbing into another taxi. He felt heady, excited, unable to think straight. He told himself to snap out of it or he'd muff up the interview. That would be a mistake that could lose him a desk job – and force him into a posting in officer training.

As the cab wove through the streets of London, Victor tried not to get distracted by these errant thoughts about Captain Kynaston. He took slow breaths, seeking to calm his racing pulse. He needed to focus on the task in hand. But how could he when he didn't even know what job he was about to be interviewed for?

Victor's visit to the War Office was brief. He was ushered into a sparsely furnished meeting room where he was quizzed about his war record, his education and his position with Cutler & Son in the City and previously in New York. The uniformed officer conducting the interview apparently had a full résumé and was merely checking the listed information against Victor's own account. After ten minutes, the man said, 'Very well, Lieutenant. It all seems to be in order. You need to go now to the Ministry of Munitions. They're expecting you at eleven thirty.'

'Where is it?' Victor felt he should have known, but the man didn't seem perturbed by the question.

'Five minutes from here. Over in Charing Cross Buildings.'

Victor knew the place but had never been inside. It stood in the gardens beside the Embankment and was next door to the Cecil Hotel where Max Stieglitz and his unhappy wife, Florence, had stayed when in London. That now seemed a lifetime ago. Both Max and Florence were dead, and Victor was missing an eye, badly scarred and wearing uniform. He would never have predicted that when he'd been drinking cocktails in the Cecil's bar while the Romanian band played czardas for the entertainment of the mostly American guests. Florence had got drunk and gone to bed while he and Max had escaped to enjoy a night of pleasure in Victor's set at Albany. The memory wasn't a happy one – Victor felt sad thinking about the death of his friends.

Arriving at the ministry, Victor was shown into an office overlooking the gardens, where two men were seated behind a large table. One was in uniform with the rank of major and the other was soberly dressed in the manner of a senior officer in the civil service. They introduced themselves as Major Rothbury-Harris and Mr Pointer. Victor took a seat facing them across the polished table.

All Victor knew of the Ministry of Munitions was that it had been established the previous year to address the disastrous shortage of shells and ammunition and had already achieved great success under the leadership of the Liberal politician David Lloyd George. Beyond that he was in the dark.

Mr Pointer did most of the talking, explaining that the production of munitions had been transformed by a series of changes in procurement, production, recruitment, cost control and oversight. As the civil servant spoke, going into details about factory locations, inventory levels and quality control, Victor was increasingly puzzled as to why he had been selected as a suitable candidate for a position there.

Observing his perplexity, Major Rothbury-Harris interjected. 'I expect you're wondering, Lieutenant, why we are talking to you.'

'I confess I am, sir. My war experience has been limited to leading a unit in Gallipoli and before the war I was employed as a stockbroker. Neither role seems adequate preparation for this.'

'*Au contraire.* Your experience is the perfect combination for our requirements.' The army officer tapped a manila folder in front of him. 'Mentioned in dispatches, DSO. Good show,

Lieutenant Dalton. But it's your experience in business that will be most valuable to the task we have in mind for you.'

'I'd be very surprised if that's the case, sir. My experience is confined to selecting and trading stocks on the London and New York exchanges. I have no knowledge of procurement, of factory management or such.'

'This job will require the utmost discretion, Lieutenant.' The speaker was now Mr Pointer. 'We have reason to believe your former employer, Mr Herbert Cutler, may have been involved in illegal profiteering as an arms trader, and worse.'

'And worse?' Victor caught his breath. Not in surprise that Herbert had been profiteering, but that he'd been found out. Herbert was a wily character and Victor thought that as his former boss had harboured ambitions to enter Parliament, he would be unlikely to take what would surely be dangerous risks.

'Until we instituted stronger quality and operational controls as part of this ministry's radical overhaul of munitions supply, significant quantities of defective materials were produced. As a result, shells frequently exploded prematurely as they were being loaded, killing many of our own men. Dud shells, defective fuses, that kind of thing.' He waved a hand dismissively, as though the means by which war was waged were details too trivial for him to concern himself with.

Major Rothbury-Harris relit his pipe and took up the story. 'The initial assumption was that these bad quality arms were destroyed and any reaching the front was the result of human error. However, we now have reason to suspect that Herbert Cutler may have diverted large quantities of these defective munitions before they could be disposed of. We believe he supplied them at full cost knowing them to be faulty.'

'But that means...'

'Yes, that means he knowingly allowed our own men to be put in peril on the field of battle. You know as well as anyone, Lieutenant, that there is peril enough out there without this. Of course, at this stage we have no substantive evidence. It's entirely based on hunches, and this is where you come in. We need you to audit Cutler's arms transactions and establish whether this is the case.'

Victor blew out a breath. 'You know of course he's in prison awaiting trial for the murder of his daughter-in-law.'

'Likely to be reduced to manslaughter.'

'That's still a lengthy sentence with hard labour.'

'Assuming he doesn't get off.' The major and Mr Pointer exchanged knowing glances before the civil servant continued. 'And that must be a possibility. The trial has already been delayed by two months, but it won't be put off much longer. Cutler is represented by the best KC in the realm. Soon he could be a free man again.'

Victor allowed this to percolate through his brain. Cutler exonerated of killing Dora. Something he hadn't expected. He felt sick at the thought.

The major drew on his pipe before removing it and setting it on the desk in front of him. 'That's why you're the man for this job.' He folded his arms and leant forward, skewering Victor with his eyes. 'We need you to examine those transactions forensically. We can't have an outsider doing it as that would arouse Cutler's suspicion, but if you return to your employment in his brokerage, you'll be perfectly placed to undertake the necessary research. You'll need to come out of uniform. Tell him the army discharged you on compassionate grounds because of the extent of your injuries.' He tapped the manilla folder again. 'All the paperwork is prepared already.'

Victor was stunned but filled with a new sense of purpose. He hadn't expected to be handed a chance to unmask Herbert Cutler. But then neither had he suspected Cutler of going so far as betraying his country.

Major Rothbury-Harris got to his feet. He walked around the desk and stood beside Victor, who was unsure whether to remain seated or to stand. In the end he stayed put as the major walked across to stand at the window. 'Pointer will take you through all the necessary protocols. I just want to stress the absolute imperative for complete secrecy. No one, I repeat, no one, must be told of your investigation. This is a matter of national security.'

'Are you implying that Cutler did this to aid Germany?'

Major Rothbury-Harris raised a hand in a chopping motion. 'I'm implying nothing. He could be a German agent. He could be a profiteer. He could be both. It will be your job to find out.'

'What do I tell people my job is? I've mentioned I might be working for the ministry.'

'Tell them you were unsuitable for the role and have been deemed unfit to continue in service.'

Victor was uneasy. 'If I'm to investigate this properly I'll need to inspect paperwork at the munitions factories and depots, establish the paper trail. How can I do that if I'm working as a City broker?'

'Good point.' The major exchanged glances with Mr Pointer. They clearly hadn't thought this through.

'Might I make a suggestion?' Victor interlocked his fingers and placed his hands on the desk.

The two men nodded. It was as though they had some form of telepathic communication.

'Why don't I continue in uniform as an employee of the ministry, but in view of Cutler's present and possibly future incarceration, you grant me leave to work two days a week in the brokerage to restore the business and protect the assets under management. I can fabricate some story that I'm undertaking statistical analysis.' He waved a hand in the air. 'Work rates, staff turnover, productivity, inventory levels. That kind of thing. I'll make it sound suitably boring. You know, Mr Pointer. The kind of things you civil servants are always producing to keep the wheels of government turning.'

Mr Pointer looked affronted, but before he could protest, the major strode back across the room and picked up his manilla folder. 'Excellent. That's just the ticket. You're a natural at this game, Dalton. I knew we'd chosen well.'

It was drizzling slightly when Victor emerged from Charing Cross Buildings. Before he'd entered the ministry office, he'd expected to be offered a straightforward administrative position. Instead, he'd been given the chance to bring his old employer to justice. And to do so while still having the opportunity to revitalise the brokerage. In his wildest dreams he couldn't have imagined a better assignment. He would relish the challenge – unearthing the evidence of Cutler's wrongdoing wouldn't be easy but he couldn't wait to tackle it.

He walked over to Trafalgar Square intending to pass the time until he had arranged to meet Maurice by strolling around the National Portrait Gallery – only to find it was closed to the public and in use by the War Office for the administration of spousal separation payments. The war had encroached on everything.

He thought of dropping into Ciro's, round the back of the gallery but it would be shut until the evening. Since he'd arranged to meet Maurice for lunch in the Café Royal, he decided he might as well go straight there. He could pass the time with a drink and mull over what had happened at Charing Cross Buildings.

To his surprise and delight, he found Maurice was already there. The captain started to get up to greet him, but mindful of the missing leg, Victor gestured to him to stay seated.

'How was your morning?' he asked as he pulled out a chair opposite Maurice. He was rewarded by a large smile as the captain indicated the pile of parcels wrapped in brown paper on the banquette beside him.

'Productive. I obtained everything Alice needed, from gum arabic to iron oxide.'

Victor frowned and gave a little shake of his head, amused. 'How on earth have you managed to understand all that stuff so quickly?'

'I don't. I was furnished with a detailed list. I'm merely the humble servant eager to do your sister's bidding.' He waved a piece of paper on which Alice had neatly listed all her requirements and Maurice had ticked off each one with his fountain pen. 'You must understand, Victor, I'm no artist, nor will I ever be. I simply like to work with my hands. I haven't a creative bone in my body.' He smiled. 'Without instruction I'd be completely clueless. Yet I flatter myself that once I know what's required of me, I can do what I'm bid accurately and efficiently. Just don't ask me what colour would go with another, whether to stain a piece of glass or leave it be. I haven't a clue.'

'And you like working that way? Under my sister's directions?'

'She's a hugely talented artist. Even I can see that. And yes, I do like it. I find the work satisfying, very calming, almost meditative. About as far from the hell of fighting as you can imagine.' He stretched his lips into a tight mirthless smile.

'I feel like that about horse-riding. But I won't be doing much of that until the war's over unless I take the vicar's old nag out for a sedate walk round the village.' Victor moved his head, his eye still on his companion. 'I suppose my escape from the hell of war is in numbers. I've always liked mathematics. Taking a set of figures and making sense of it. And usually that means making money from it.' He gave a dry laugh.

A waiter came and took their lunch order. Both men settled for cold cuts with salad.

'I don't seem to have much appetite today,' said Victor, all too aware that being near Maurice might have something to do with that.

'Dash it. You must think me awful. I haven't even asked you how the interview went.' Maurice looked mortified.

Victor waved a hand dismissively. 'Well enough.' He paused then added, 'Exceptionally well actually. They only need me for three days a week and I'm free to pick up the pieces at the brokerage again for the rest of the time. That's good news, as I can sort out my family's affairs, as well as the countess's. Not to mention find out what state the firm's in with both Cutler and I being absent.'

'What kind of work do they want you to do?'

'Just as I suspected. Statistics. Analysis of production rates, costs, that kind of thing. Frightfully tedious – but like your work for Alice I think I'll find it a pleasant distraction after active service.'

'And did you have time to check on your flat? What did you call it? Your set, wasn't it?'

The blood rushed to Victor's neck, and he felt hot under his collar. 'No time. I rather hoped you wouldn't mind tagging along with me after lunch.'

Maurice's broad smile reached his eyes. 'I'd love to. It's only round the corner, isn't it?'

'Yes. Just off Piccadilly. Next to the Royal Academy.'

'Then if I won't be in the way, I'd be delighted to accompany you.'

In the way? Victor could think of nothing he'd like more than being alone with Maurice Kynaston in his own private place. 'You won't be in the way, Maurice.' Their eyes met and again Victor felt the same frisson he'd experienced on the train. His appetite for cold beef had entirely dissipated and he put down his knife and fork.

Maurice did the same and Victor called for the bill.

They walked the short distance to Albany in silence, grateful that the drizzly rain had now stopped, and the day had brightened. As they turned into the courtyard at the front of the buildings, Victor said, 'I no longer have a manservant. Milton didn't want to serve in the army so when I took my commission he decided to retire. I won't even be able to offer you tea.' He pointed a finger. 'However I'd laid down several cases of champagne before the war, so we can drink to your successful purchases and my new job.'

'Better and better,' said Maurice.

The set was in darkness when they entered, all the curtains drawn. Victor showed Maurice into the drawing room and threw open the curtains, letting the afternoon light flood into the room. 'Make yourself at home. I'll nip down to the cellar and find that bubbly.'

Maurice stood, leaning on his crutches as he surveyed the room. 'It's quite a place. A gem, hidden away here. I must have walked past many times and had no idea it was here.'

Victor told himself that Maurice's readiness to accept the invitation to come to Albany was a good sign. He went to fetch the bottle and a pair of champagne flutes. There was something innately decadent about drinking champagne in the late afternoon. Uncharacteristically, Victor was nervous about what lay ahead as he opened the door to the wine cellar.

When he returned, Maurice was sitting on the sofa. He'd removed his uniform jacket and tie. Victor swallowed, desire sweeping through him. He turned away, conscious that his feelings must be written all over his face, and set about opening the bottle. He was all fingers and thumbs, and his hands were shaking.

'Bring that over here,' said Maurice. 'You'll be more comfortable sitting down.'

Victor hesitated, surprised.

'I do outrank you, Lieutenant Dalton. At least for now. So that's an order.'

Victor needed no further encouragement. In his hurry to move across to join Maurice, he left the bottle on the sideboard.

·   ·   ·

It was more than an hour later that they remembered the champagne. By now they were in bed and Victor, naked, returned to the drawing room to retrieve it. This time he had no difficulty uncorking it.

'Afraid it's a little warm now.' He handed a glass to Maurice, who took a sip.

'Best I've ever tasted. But that's down to the company.'

Victor climbed back into the bed and rested his body against Maurice's as they sat side-by-side, propped up by pillows. He reached for his friend's hand. 'I didn't know, you know. Whether this would be what you wanted. I wasn't sure if you were like me. You were engaged to be married. Of course I hoped. But I was afraid. I mean, have you ever done this before?'

'No. At least not since boarding school when everyone messed about.' Maurice's lips formed a tight line. And he hesitated before giving the rest of his answer. 'But I was in love once. We just never had a chance to make love.'

'The man who died in the shell hole with you?'

'How did you know?'

'The way you spoke about him. Made me hope that perhaps you might be like me.'

'I was worried you might not be that way. Your sister told me you'd had plans to marry Edmund's estranged wife, so naturally I assumed—'

'A marriage of convenience. At the behest of her father-in-law, my employer.'

'I see. What about you? Have ever done this before?'

Victor sighed. 'Oh yes. Rather more times than I care to remember. I've never had any doubt about my preference for men.' He stroked the palm and inner wrist of Maurice's hand and took another sip of champagne. It was making him feel light-headed. Or perhaps that was the lovemaking. 'But I've only once been in love. He died too.'

'Gallipoli?'

'No. He shot himself. His name was Gilbert, and he was engaged to be married to Alice. She found us together and was understandably shocked. She called the engagement off and he, mindful of scandal and shame, shot himself. He was Edmund's older brother.'

Maurice gave a little gasp of surprise then wove his fingers through Victor's and turned to face him. 'We have so much in common, you and I. Both of us have bodies broken by the war. Both with painful memories and haunted by nightmares. And we've each lost someone we loved.'

Victor felt a surge of emotion course through him. 'But now we've found each other.' He put down his glass. Maurice did the same. And they turned to embrace.

FOURTEEN

By the time Robert had served his fourteen days of Field Punishment Number One, Edmund's morale had plummeted. It was as though his own guilt had drained the spirit out of him.

The punishment had been intended as a humiliation, but Fuller had remained defiant, brushing off what must have been severe physical pain. As well as this degrading punishment he had been forced to undergo hard labour, mostly breaking rocks for road laying, or carrying and loading heavy sandbags for transportation to the front. These trials were conducted without pauses for breaks, until the point of utter exhaustion. All under the scrutiny of the Canaries and accompanied by their jibes and insults.

Back in the barracks each night, Edmund asked Robert how he was capable of such stoicism.

'Those bastards will never get the better of me. Besides, I've got off lightly. I met a couple of Kiwis. They're conchies who refuse to hold a weapon. They're now on their second consecutive twenty-eight-day sentence.'

'Consecutive? But that's not allowed. Twenty-eight days is the maximum according to army regulations.'

Robert gave a dry laugh. 'They ignore the rules. Some of the officers here are as bad as the NCOs. They'd be happier if we all dropped dead. That fellow on the train was right. They hate us because they've never served at the front themselves. But they hate the conchies even more because they know they're the bravest of the lot of us. The Canaries call him them cowards but they've ten times the courage of those bastards. You've no idea how much punishment they've been forced to take. It's beyond cruel.'

Getting ready to turn in one evening, Robert pulled off his shirt and Edmund noticed his wrists were red-raw where the handcuffs had bitten in. Another shaft of guilt ripped through him. It was his fault Robert had felt obliged to defend him. He hoped the Canaries wouldn't single Robert out and pick on him in the future now that his punishment was over – but he feared they would. He'd be a marked man as long as they were at Étaples. The Canaries took pleasure in breaking men.

The two friends sat in the mess-tent eating tasteless bully-beef stew. Fuller ate with relish, this being the first proper meal he'd eaten in the past fortnight when he'd been fed only on bread and water.

'Thank God, it's over,' said Edmund. 'I'm sorry you had to go through that.'

'For Pete's sake, stop apologising, my friend. I did what I had to do and what I wanted to do. No need to fret about me.'

Edmund didn't know what to say. But nothing he could say would ever make up for what Robert had suffered.

'Being strapped to a fence post is a rare opportunity for some quiet thinking time. I could watch you lot running up and down sand dunes carrying sandbags.'

'Ackroyd said you had to carry sandbags too as part of your hard labour.'

Fuller grinned. 'A damn sight easier loading bags onto a parked lorry than having to run up and down steep sand dunes while those bastards blow their whistles at you.' He chuckled. 'As for breaking rocks, I just imagined I was swinging the pickaxe into the head of that fat sergeant with the moustache like a dead ferret. Very satisfying it was too.'

'I'm trying to picture my father having to do hard labour if he escapes the noose. Can't imagine it.' Edmund tried to think about his father as little as possible but inevitably at some point he would have to confront the fact that Herbert Cutler was to be tried for the murder of Edmund's estranged wife.

'You think he'll get off with manslaughter then? I thought he was likely to swing for it.' Realising what he'd just said, Fuller hastily apologised.

'No need to say sorry. He deserves to suffer for what he did to Dora.' Edmund accepted a cigarette – he rarely smoked. 'There was never any affection between me and my father. Even when I was a boy. He's a bully and a monster.' Edmund exhaled a puff of smoke. 'He used to beat my mother until she became so terrified that she did his bidding without question. He and I finally fell out completely when I married Dora. He said she was like a costermonger – to her face. Suggested I'd have been better off using her as prostitute and there was never a need to marry a girl like her. Then once she and I separated, he took her in and treated her like a duchess.'

'Was he sleeping with her?'

Edmund snorted. 'No. Dora would never have agreed to that. She disliked the physical side of marriage. Besides, he's the coldest of fish. His only interest in Dora was knowing it would anger me. That and enabling him to prevent me seeing my own daughter.'

'Sounds a right bastard. But how will you feel if they hang him?' Robert's voice was quiet, and his eyes showed concern.

'I despise him but he's still my father. No one wants to know their parent is going to be executed. But neither did I want to have face the knowledge that he'd murdered my wife.

Our marriage was over but Dora was the mother of my daughter and she wasn't a bad person. It was hardly her fault that our marriage failed. I must bear the brunt of that myself.'

'You're always too ready to shoulder the blame, my friend. You need to cut yourself some slack.'

Edmund shrugged and ground out the butt of his cigarette. 'Remind me that I don't actually like smoking next time you offer me a cigarette and I've a mind to take it.' He grinned at Robert.

They had been in the camp at Étaples almost three weeks when Edmund was finally summoned to meet the regimental medical officer.

Edmund was shown into a large tent next to the casualty clearing station. The RMO looked haggard: his hair was dull, matted and long overdue for a wash, and his eyes were bloodshot. He was sitting behind a camp table and had a stack of paperwork in front of him. 'Take a seat, Private Cutler,' he said. 'I'm sorry it's taken so long for us to meet. I was up the line and delayed in getting back here. Bit of a show. All hands on deck. You know how it is.'

Edmund didn't but he could imagine that the RMO had had quite a time of it, judging by the dark rings under his eyes.

'Sorry, I should introduce myself. I'm Dr Fountwell. Captain Fountwell. But I'll happily answer to Doc.' He picked up some of the papers in front of him and read. Tapping the edge of the sheets he put them down again. 'You've been recommended for a position as a stretcher bearer. Your report says you're physically very strong.'

Edmund said nothing, waiting, anxious to find out whether he would be accepted as a bearer or forced into the infantry.

'What did you do as a civilian?'

'I'm an artist. In stained glass.'

The doctor removed his glasses and rubbed his eyes. 'You mean people still do that as a profession? I thought it was all medieval. Old churches and stuff.'

'There's a fair few of us who do it still.'

'How do you make a living though? Do the churches pay you?'

'Sometimes. But it can be libraries, town halls, private homes, all kinds of places.'

The doctor nodded, his lower lip protruding. 'Well, I live and learn. And how did you end up doing that?' He shuffled the pages again and bent his head to read. 'Says here you're an Old Harrovian.'

'Yes, sir. But I've always loved art. I went to the Central School of Arts & Crafts. I was apprenticed to Mr Christopher Whall, the finest stained-glass artist of our times.'

Fountwell shrugged. 'Never heard of him. But I'm not exactly an authority on art. Harrow, eh? So why are you enlisted as a private? You could have taken a commission.'

Edmund decided it was better to tell the truth. 'To be honest I didn't much enjoy my time at Harrow. And I think there's something wrong in the assumption that only those who went to public school are capable of leadership. There's a deep-rooted snobbery about it all. The way the army refers to men promoted from outside into the officer class as temporary gentlemen infuriates me. I have a friend here at the camp. We joined up together. He'd make a far better leader than me but comes from the wrong class. Sorry... I didn't, er...' His voice trailed away and he looked down.

'Actually, I quite agree. Went to the local grammar school myself. But we doctors automatically get commissioned. Short of the government turning communist I don't think there's much you or I can do about the class system.' Captain Fountwell took off his spectacles again and rubbed them absently with his handkerchief. 'And what's the appeal of being a stretcher bearer? Most chaps can't wait to have a gun in their hands and take a pop at the Hun.'

'I'm not like most chaps then. I'll do my duty if required but I'll never relish it. If it's possible I'd rather help save lives than take them.'

'Even German ones?'

'I've nothing personally against them. I doubt most of them know any more than I do why we're fighting.'

'You're a conscientious objector?' The doctor's brow furrowed.

'No. As I said, I'll do my duty. I just happen to think that there might have been better ways to resolve matters than digging ourselves into ditches and hurling shells at each other.'

The RMO leant back in his chair and tilted his head on one side. 'Like what?'

'Like getting round a table and talking for a start. Or if it has to be a fight, how about a duel between the Kaiser and the King?'

Fountwell narrowed his eyes but seemed to be suppressing a chuckle. 'I'd buy a ticket for that one. You *are* a communist then?'

'Afraid not. I've not even read Mr Marx's book. I'm a patriotic Englishman who happens to believe war should be a last resort not a first option.' As he spoke, he realised he was sounding like Robert Fuller.

'What do you know about battlefield medicine?'

'Virtually nothing, sir. My wife worked as a VAD so she told me one or two things. But she was dealing with convalescent cases, not acute ones.'

'Things are very different here. We have to act fast and make some tough decisions. That means giving priority to those who have the best chance of surviving. It's not for the faint hearted. And it's not just the medics who have to make those life and death decisions. As a stretcher bearer, you may have to leave behind some men in favour of others. You might only be able to make one trip from the battlefield to the nearest aid post or from there to the casualty clearing station. That means choosing to carry the man who is most likely to benefit from medical care and leaving the others.'

He lit a cigarette and offered the packet to Edmund, who declined. 'It can be bloody awful. Having to leave a man to die. Like playing God. Make sure you always carry plenty of cigarettes and matches. If there's no hope, at least you can hold a hand and offer a last smoke.'

Edmund swallowed. The prospect of being out there was increasingly scary. Would he have the strength of mind to make those life-or-death decisions? To be able to abandon a dying man to his fate? To be able to assess the survival chances between badly wounded men?

'You're not the sort to go all queasy at the sight of blood?'

'I doubt anyone has the luxury to be queasy about blood from what I've heard about the front.'

'You'd be surprised.' Fountwell drew on his cigarette. 'Think you could cope with a man whose bowels are hanging out, without throwing up?'

Edmund tried to swallow again but his mouth felt dry. 'I don't know, but I hope I'd do whatever I could to help anyone needing it.'

The RMO rubbed a hand over the back of his neck and studied Edmund for a moment. 'So, what do you think, Private Cutler? Reckon you'll be up to it?'

'I'm prepared to do my best, Captain, if you'll have me.'

'We can't ask more than that, I suppose. I'd hazard a bet you'll do well enough, Private. And a darn sight better than some of the poor sods we had as bearers when the war started. Not that I'm blaming them. No. I blame the army for thinking any old fool could do it and putting the least competent men into the job. Everyone out here now knows when you're wounded you want someone with a calm demeanour, a strong body and quick wits. Never mind what the old fools back in the War Office think. We've taken the decision out of their hands.' He ground out his cigarette into the improvised ashtray in front of him – an old sardine tin – and fixed his gaze on Edmund. 'I think you'll do well, Cutler. Welcome to the RAMC.'

FIFTEEN

Alice stood at the window, staring out across the fields. The weather that afternoon was grim; the treetops on the distant wooded hills were dull shadows against a pale dirty sky. Their lower parts were blotted and smudged by misty rain, which crept slowly and horizontally across the valley, like a grey sheet billowing on a washing line.

She glanced at the carriage clock – a wedding present from her father. Time for Lottie to get ready for school. Then Alice remembered it was Saturday. She moved across to the sink and filled the kettle, deciding to enjoy a cup of tea before waking her stepdaughter. She returned to the dismal view through the window. It summed up exactly how she felt.

The kettle whistled and Alice took it off the hob. As she did so she heard a soft whimpering sound from the adjoining room. She opened the door, looked in and saw Lottie was weeping quietly into her pillow.

A rush of tenderness took hold of Alice. Without stopping to think, she moved to the bed and lay down beside the little girl, wrapping her arms around the small thin body. 'My darling girl, what's the matter? Did you have a bad dream?'

Through the sobs a tremulous voice answered. 'I'm frightened.'

Alice kissed the child's head, torn between hating seeing the little girl suffering this way, and relief that finally the suppressed emotion was surfacing. 'There's nothing to be afraid of, Lottie. I'm here and you're safe.' She stroked a few damp strands of hair away from her daughter's hot brow.

'I don't want to live in an orphanage.'

Alice's head jerked in surprise. She sat upright, continuing to stroke Lottie's hair and try to soothe her. 'Of course you don't. You live here. With me. And with Daddy too when he comes home from the war.'

'But he won't come home. Molly Fuller says when daddies go to war they get killed by the Germans and they never come home. There are lots of children in my class whose daddies have died in France. And since you're not my proper mummy you won't want me then and I'll have to go and live in an orphanage.'

Instinctively, Alice gathered up the little girl and cradled her against her. 'Oh, my poor sweet darling, that's not true! Molly is talking nonsense. It's true that some daddies don't come home from war and that's very sad. Then they go to heaven like your mummy. But most will come home as soon as the war is over.' She paused, choosing her words carefully. 'I'm sure Daddy will come home to us before too long. But even if he has to be away for a long time or...' She choked back a tear. 'Or... or even if God decides he wants him in heaven, I will *never* send you away to the orphanage. I love you, Lottie, and I love being your new mummy. I would be very, very sad if you weren't here with me. So you don't have to worry. I won't ever let you go.'

'You promise?'

'I promise.' Alice reached into the pocket of her apron, pulled out a clean handkerchief and dried her child's eyes. 'And don't listen anymore to Molly Fuller.' Alice seethed with anger at Viola's daughter – but was all too aware where the child was getting this nonsense from. It wasn't fair to blame Molly, who was younger than Lottie and surely only parroting her mother's miserable words.

She stroked Lottie's cheek. 'Is that why you've been so quiet and sad for a while?'

Lottie nodded. 'I wanted to be quiet so I wouldn't disturb you and get in the way and you wouldn't send me away to the orphanage.'

'I will never, never, *never* send you away, my beautiful girl. I'm so happy that you live here with me. Having you here is wonderful. Otherwise, I'd be very lonely without Daddy.'

She bent and kissed the seven-year-old. 'No school today, so you and I can do something together. Why don't I make some pancakes for breakfast while you get washed and dressed? We can have them with the honey Mrs Collins gave us yesterday.'

'Yes, please.' Lottie rewarded her with a rare smile.

Alice picked up a hairbrush and began to brush the little girl's hair, smoothing out the knots and letting it fall in the thick glossy waves she had inherited from her mother, Dora. 'Since there's no school you can keep it loose today.' Alice went over to the chest of drawers, opened a small wooden box and took out a tortoiseshell hair clasp. 'This was a gift to me from your daddy. I'd like you to have it.'

Alice swept back a lock of the child's hair and pinned the clasp in place. She held a hand mirror for Lottie to inspect the result. 'You look beautiful.'

'Can I really have it? To keep?' Lottie's expression was eager.

'Of course, my love.' She dropped a kiss on the girl's brow. 'The weather's bad so we could bake a cake together then tomorrow after church, take it as a gift to my friend Mrs Wallingford and her children. They moved into The

Hawthorns yesterday and tomorrow they will have had some time to unpack and settle in so we can go and say hello. It'll be a chance for you to meet the children. Crispin will be in your class. Poppy's a little younger.' She hesitated then added, 'And I hope you'll be very kind to them as their daddy went to heaven recently.'

'Did he die in the war?'

'No. He wasn't well.'

'What was wrong with him? Did he fall and bang his head like my mummy?'

'No. I think there was something wrong with his heart.'

'I'll say a prayer for him when I say my prayers for Mummy and Grandpa Fisher. And for Daddy to be safe in the war.'

'That would be very thoughtful of you, Lottie.'

Baking together proved to be a satisfying time for both Alice and her stepdaughter. Lottie helped stir the cake batter and to her great delight was permitted to lick the spoon afterwards.

Alice enjoyed having a helper – she'd never particularly relished baking but doing it with the child was fun. As they prepared the mixture and Alice explained each step, they chatted happily. Now Lottie had received the necessary reassurance, all the silent brooding was gone and the sunny little girl had returned. It was an enormous relief to Alice that she wouldn't have to seek Edmund's advice and hence cause him worry.

Later that afternoon, stepmother and daughter sat together at the large deal table and each wrote to Edmund. Lottie needed no encouragement to do a drawing for her father to include in the envelope. She did a picture of herself beating the cake mixture, with Alice greasing the tin.

'That's perfect!' Alice studied the drawing. 'You are so good at drawing, my darling. Your father will be very proud when he sees that. I'm sure he'll want to keep that in his pocket so it's with him all the time.'

Lottie's lip trembled. 'So, he can look at it if he forgets what we look like?'

'Your daddy won't ever forget what we look like. And remember he has this picture too.' She moved to the dresser and picked up a framed photograph of the three of them taken at a studio in Petersfield just before Edmund left for training camp. 'He told me in his last letter he looks at it every night before he goes to sleep.'

'Then I will look at it too before I go to bed.' Lottie looked sheepish. 'Do you think then I'll dream he's coming home?'

'You might do. If you look at it and think of him as you go to sleep. After you've said your prayers of course.'

The little girl smiled.

The following day, after the morning service at St Margaret's, Alice and Harriet drank tea and enjoyed the cake baked by Alice and Lottie. In the nursery room above, the children were playing, their activity marked by a series of bumps and crashes.

Harriet rolled her eyes. 'It's like a herd of elephants up there.'

'I'm afraid Lottie's adding to it.' Alice gave her friend an apologetic smile. She wiped a crumb from her mouth with a napkin. 'Actually, despite the racket, I'm jolly relieved that they're all getting on so well as Lottie has been like a little ghost. Turns out she was worried her father would die and I'd send her packing to an orphanage.'

Harriet gave a gasp of horror. 'What on earth gave her that idea?'

'One of the children at school. Actually, the daughter of my friend, Viola. You know, the one whose husband joined up with Edmund and is in the same regiment.'

'Why would the child say something so cruel?'

'I can only imagine her mother said as much.'

'And she's supposed to be your friend?' Harriet's eyebrows shot upwards. 'Some friend.'

'She's depressed. To put it mildly. Does nothing but weep all day. She can't cope with Robert being away. She's convinced herself, and seems set on convincing her children, that Robert is doomed to be killed at the front.' Alice took a gulp of tea. 'I've tried hard to sympathise with her, to be kind to her, but I'm finding her company draining.' She released a long heartfelt sigh. 'You probably think I'm terrible to speak this way about a friend, but I work so hard to try and stay cheerful for Lottie's sake and I can't understand why Viola weeps openly in front of her children and takes to her bed at every opportunity.' She wove her fingers together. 'It seems wrong and feels to me that she's letting the side down. Surely, it's our duty to soldier on. Isn't it the least we can do while our menfolk are risking their lives?'

'I couldn't agree more. Of course, it's easy for me to say that as a widow who managed to rub along well enough with her husband but never for a moment felt anything remotely like love for him.'

'Do you miss him at all?'

'To be honest I barely knew the man. He spent most of his time in the countryside. I miss him on the children's behalf. He was a wonderful father to them when he was around. They loved him dearly. And yes, I did grow to be quite fond of him. But frankly, once I found out about the money, I've been very cross with him. If it's possible to be cross with someone who's dead.'

She rolled her eyes. 'Don't look at me like that, Alice. It's different for you. You're madly in love with your husband. Imagine if instead you were married to that old man you pointed out to me in church this morning. I bet if he'd been your husband and had died, you'd be heaving a sigh of relief and planning to redecorate the house.'

Alice couldn't help smiling. The thought was preposterous. Harriet was referring to Colonel Fitzwarren, local magistrate, chair of the local military service tribunal and Alice's former employer.

'There was not the remotest possibility of me ever marrying the crusty old colonel. He hates women with a passion. He employed me as a last resort having scoured the county for a man prepared to work for him. Then dismissed me the moment his nephew returned from India and agreed to work for him.' She smiled. 'Besides, I was determined to remain unmarried, until Edmund came along and swept me off my feet.' She laughed. 'Same goes for the colonel's awful nephew, Leonard Fitzwarren. I caused him a lot of pain with the sharp application of my knee to an unmentionable place when he tried to kiss me in his uncle's conservatory when in his cups.'

Harriet snorted her tea through her nose and had to mop it up with her napkin. 'That pompous-looking chap with the heavily oiled hair and the ebony walking stick sitting next to the colonel in church?' She grinned at her friend. 'I'm proud of you, dear Alice. I hope he learnt his lesson.'

'He's never been near me since.' Then Alice's expression changed. 'But he got his revenge in the end.'

'How?' Harriet looked concerned.

'He was instrumental in Edmund attesting and having to leave sooner than would have been the case if he'd waited to be conscripted.' She bit her lip. 'In fact, Edmund might still have been here now.'

'Did Edmund know the Fitzwarren chap was fresh with you?'

'More than fresh. If I hadn't applied my knee to his groin he'd have forced himself on me. It was beyond flirtation. I was actually frightened.' Then Alice smiled. 'But yes. I told

Edmund what happened. That's what brought us together. He was so angry he couldn't hide his emotions and that's when everything changed between us.'

'If I believed in that kind of nonsense I'd say "how romantic".'

'Perhaps you'll meet someone who'll change your mind and convince you it isn't nonsense.'

Harriet chortled. 'No chance of that. I've no interest whatsoever in men. I've got my children. There's nothing else a man can give me. I married for money and look where that got me.'

'So next time, marry for love.'

'I don't believe in love.' Then seeing her friend's face, she quickly added, 'I don't deny that you love Edmund but that's a rare thing and is not something that will ever happen to me. It's a lot of poppycock. You'll never convince me otherwise.'

'I know *I* won't but one day a man might do so.'

'Assuming there are any left after this dreadful war.'

Alice started to answer but felt a rush of emotion. She was caught between Viola, who was moping and miserable, and Harriet, who was cynical and pessimistic. It was hard to keep her own spirits up. Then she told herself to be grateful for Harriet and for the fact that their children were evidently getting on well. Her friend had lost her husband, her home and her future, so surely Alice could afford to be a little more generous than she might otherwise be.

SIXTEEN

The prospect of visiting his former employer in prison was distasteful to Victor. His natural instinct was to refuse, as he had no wish to be associated with Herbert in any way. But investigating Cutler's business dealings required him to win back his confidence. Nothing in his life so far had led him to believe he'd ever have cause to enter a prison. Yet, if he were to fulfil the mission set him by his superiors at the ministry, he had no alternative but to accept Herbert Cutler's request and visit him in Pentonville.

As soon as he entered the visiting room, Victor wished he hadn't come. The place had an unpleasant institutional smell – unwashed bodies and unappetising food, underpinned by disinfectant. He sniffed with distaste. How was Cutler, accustomed to fine food and wine, managing to bear the place? But of course, he had no choice in the matter.

Victor sat down at the table which the guard had indicated and looked around. There were a couple of other occupied tables but no sign yet of his employer. Then a door at the far end of the room opened and Cutler walked in between a pair of prison guards.

Victor watched him as he approached. Herbert Cutler's normally tall and upright figure was slightly stooped and his hair looked thinner and greyer than Victor remembered. He rose to greet him.

Cutler pulled out the chair opposite and sat. 'Thank you for coming, Dalton. Still in uniform I see. What happened to your face? Missing an eye? Didn't I tell you it was a mistake getting involved in the war.'

There was a note of mockery, but Victor chose to ignore the remarks. 'Why did you want to see me?'

'I need you to come back into the business. There's only a couple of clerks left and I've no idea of the state of the client list.'

'You told me never to darken your door again when I was commissioned. Why do you want me back now?'

Herbert Cutler avoided Victor's steady gaze. 'I have lawyers to pay, and I need to ensure my affairs are in good order. And looking at the state of you, it would seem you can't be too choosy – I may be your only chance of rebuilding your career.'

Victor snorted. Being back in Herbert Cutler's presence was unsettling. The man exuded a kind of raw malevolence like the villain in a Victorian 'penny dreadful'. But having murdered his daughter-in-law he was exactly that. It was tempting to stand up and walk out of the room, but if Victor was to do what the War Office expected of him, he had to get back in Herbert's good books.

Cutler's fingers were loosely linked together on the table and Victor noticed how the usually perfectly manicured nails were chipped and dirty.

The older man stretched his lips into a hard line then spoke again. 'You know what's required, Victor.' His tone was now conciliatory, almost pleading. 'I can trust you. We've lost a lot of clients. Probably most of them.'

'*We*? I thought you'd dismissed me?'

'Perhaps I was a little hasty. I was upset at losing you.' Cutler paused and Victor recognised the old flash of cunning in his eyes. 'Especially as I was about to make you a partner. It came as a shock when you joined up. I never imagined you as the patriotic type.'

'You were wrong about that.'

'And the war hasn't changed that?'

'If anything, it's made me more determined to defeat the enemy.'

Cutler sneered. 'Losing an eye not enough? Are you trying to say you plan to go back there?'

'I can't go back to Gallipoli. Even in here you must be aware of the news. The whole operation was evacuated earlier this year. A lost cause. And I wouldn't be much use on the Western Front with my injuries.'

'You're still in uniform though.'

'I'm working for the War Office. Part time.'

Cutler raised his eyebrows, a spark of interest in his eyes. 'Doing what?'

'Statistical analysis. Preparing reports for Parliamentary committees. All very dull. It's in the Ministry of Munitions.'

'Interesting!' Cutler leant forward, his hands now clasped tightly in front of him.

Victor realised the man was already calculating how he could put this to his advantage.

'Before I was wrongfully shut up in here, I was doing some nice business in munitions. Highly profitable. With your contacts we might be able to revive that. Could be a lucrative sideline for you.'

Victor kept his expression impassive. 'How so?'

'You could come back to the brokerage, salvage what's left, bring in some new clients, and using your connections in the War Office eventually revive some of the munitions contracts I was handling. I told you when the war started that wars are always excellent times to make money.'

Victor pursed his lips. This was better than he'd expected. But he knew he mustn't agree too readily, or it would arouse Cutler's suspicions. 'I see little incentive for me to come back to the firm. You've disgraced the name.'

Cutler banged a fist on the table. 'I'll be out of here next month. They'll never provide conclusive proof of murder.'

'Manslaughter may stop you hanging but it will still mean a long sentence and a ruined reputation.'

'I'm not pleading manslaughter. I'm innocent. I'll walk out of court a free man.'

'You can't assume that. It's up to the jury.'

A contemptuous snort.

Victor pressed on. 'And if it's all so easy, what do you want me for?'

Cutler sighed. 'You're right. I can't assume things. But if I'm to win, it carries a large price tag. My KC is the most expensive in the country. I need you to get things back on an even keel at the brokerage. Restore the cash flow. Reassure those clients that remain. Get out and win back some of those who left and charm some new ones into investing.'

'I've told you the Cutler name is mud. If you want me to get out there and bring in business, it can't be under your name. If you're eventually exonerated by the court things will be different but until then your name is poison. No one wants to hand over their investments to a murderer. Particularly to a man who brutally murdered a young woman while her small child was sleeping upstairs.'

Cutler smashed his fist down hard on the table again, this time attracting the attention of the guard, who approached and delivered a warning that the interview would be cut short if there was another outburst.

'Very well, Dalton,' Cutler said when the guard had retreated. 'What do you want?'

'That partnership you mentioned a few minutes ago.'

'Done.'

'And my name over the door.'

'Cutler and Dalton. Done.'

'No. I told you. The Cutler name is poison. The firm will be called Dalton Associates. Should you be exonerated we can restore your name and reinstate you as senior partner.'

Cutler bent forward on the edge of his chair, hands on the table, and let out a long weary sigh. Dalton could see he was defeated.

'Get the papers drawn up and I'll sign.'

Now that he had what he'd come for, Victor rose to his feet. He couldn't wait to get out of this place. He felt contaminated by proximity to Cutler. What was the old adage? *He who sups with the devil should have a long spoon.*

On leaving Pentonville, Victor went straight to the Cutler offices in Cornhill. After the period of closure when war broke out in 1914, the stock exchange had reopened more than a year ago, although the numbers of men moving in and out of the exchange and doing business in the area had reduced markedly with so many either volunteering or being conscripted.

The premises of Cutler & Son were quiet when Victor entered and went up the stairs. The firm's nomenclature had been more of an aspiration than a statement of fact. Gilbert Cutler had worked for his father briefly before his death back in 1908. Edmund Cutler had flatly refused to have anything to do with the business, thus incurring his father's wrath. Victor, after building his knowledge of the markets while based in the New York branch of Cutler & Son, had returned to England at his employer's request not long before the war broke out.

Standing now in his boss's old office, he looked out of the window at the street below. It seemed decades ago that he had stood here beside Cutler when war was declared. He remembered it had been on the Tuesday after a bank holiday, and there had been a celebratory atmosphere in the streets of London. The stock exchange had closed several days before that in an effort to calm the markets. At that time, Victor like so many others had assumed the war would be over by Christmas. Herbert Cutler had maintained it was likely to last much longer and that Germany should not be underestimated. How right he had been about that.

Now, Victor wondered whether Cutler had been right too about his other claim – that where there was war there always plenty of money to be made. He was determined to find out how far Cutler had gone to fulfil that prophecy. Were Major Rothbury-Harris and Mr Pointer correct in their suspicions that Cutler had been knowingly trading defective armaments? If he was, then he would have more than Dora's blood on his hands – he would be culpable for the loss of life of countless men on the field of battle.

Victor removed a cigarette from its silver holder, lit it, then summoned the chief clerk. Time to start work. His first task would be to establish how much of the stockbroking business was salvageable, then it was time to pay his parents a visit.

SEVENTEEN

Robert was perched on the edge of his camp bed, reading. He looked up as Edmund entered their tent. 'How did it go?'

'I'm in. From now on I'll be training with the medical corps.' He told his friend about the interview with Captain Fountwell.

'Congratulations.' Robert raised his arms and stretched. 'Lord, I'm still stiff as hell from being tied to that bloody post. At least it sounds like he's not one of those public-school types.'

'I suppose you include me in that sweeping judgement.' Edmund stood, hands on hips, glaring at his friend.

'Not at all. You've always been one of us. You never took a commission and as far as I can tell you're not exactly rolling in money. Or airs and graces.' Robert gave him a sly grin. 'So, what's involved?'

Appeased, Edmund said, 'I have to attend special training. Apart from the odd run I won't be training with you lot and the blasted Canaries – no more weapons drilling and I can say goodbye to the bayonet. Apparently, most of the training is focused on lifting and carrying safely. We're also to attend a weekly lecture on medical matters from one of the medics.' He tried to conceal his eagerness.

'I thought you were just expected to carry the wounded to safety as fast as possible. Why the medical stuff? They've got doctors or nurses for that haven't they?'

Happy to share what he'd learnt that day with his friend, Edmund sat down on his camp bed and started to adjust his puttees. 'They're trying new approaches to treating the wounded. Unlike the way the French do it – getting the injured away from the field of battle and into hospitals as fast as possible – we'll be giving some treatment almost immediately, where they lie.'

'You say *we*, but you're not qualified.'

Edmund shrugged, impatient at his friend's pedantry. 'I know. But they reckon it's best to do some preliminary dressing of wounds before we even attempt to stretcher them off. Apparently, the numbers bear that out.'

'What? You're expected to start bandaging men up in the middle of No Man's Land?'

'I'm not clear on the details yet, but the principle is that as soon as a wounded man is found and before he's put on a stretcher, the bearers do what they can to improve his chances of surviving the carry.'

'The carry?'

Edmund was starting to be irritated by the barrage of questioning. Was Robert resentful that he was still subject to the brutal regime of the Canaries while Edmund had escaped it? He decided to give Robert the benefit of the doubt. 'It's how they describe transporting men by stretcher. No point in even trying if they bleed out before you've got them as far as an aid post, let alone as far as a casualty clearing station.'

Fuller shook his head. 'You've already got all the jargon, eh? But how the hell can you do that when you're not medically trained? I thought doctors spent years learning how.'

Edmund shook his head. 'It's terrifying, frankly. Apparently, we'll pick most of it up with experience. There's only limited formal training – the doc says the bearers have mostly learnt by trial and error and then they pass it on to each other. He reckons the survival rates from fractures and shrapnel wounds have increased dramatically.' He bent down to tie a trailing bootlace. 'Anyway, I won't be performing operations. Just applying dressings. But done in the right way they reckon it can improve survival chances.'

'Rather you than me, pal.' Robert grinned. 'I'm not sure I'd be too happy knowing someone else's life depended on me. And I'm bloody certain I wouldn't want to be out there with my hands full carrying a stretcher without a gun to defend myself.'

Edmund shrugged but was relieved that Robert wasn't resentful. 'I may come to regret it. But right now, I can assure you I'm immensely relieved.' Edmund held out a hand and pulled his friend up from the camp bed. 'Time to take our seats in the finest restaurant in northern France.' He bowed and made an extravagant flourish like a maître d'. Referencing the ubiquitous brand of stew he said, 'I hear there's *boeuf à la mode de Maconochie* on the menu tonight. I even heard a rumour there may be a couple of morsels of meat in there among the beans and carrots.'

'What? Real meat?'

'Come on, pal. If we're lucky we may even find the odd potato too.'

The following day, Edmund met his fellow stretcher bearers. A sizeable contingent of them turned out to be conscientious objectors. The assumption was that he was one too.

'I'm not,' he told one of the men. 'I agreed to serve in the infantry. But I admit I hated the weapons drilling, especially bayonet practice. It churns my stomach imagining that the sandbag might be a living human.'

'So, you *are* one of us.'

'No. If I had to kill, I'd do it. At least I *think* I would. I have no religious convictions. I suppose you could say my reluctance is squeamishness on my part.' He looked at his new colleagues. 'I doubt there are many men who genuinely enjoy killing others. Most of them just get on with it – as I would have done if the opportunity to join the medical corps hadn't come up.'

Another man spoke up. 'Most of us are like you. We don't have moral objections. More a case of being picked out as we had the necessary qualities. I'm certainly no conchie myself but I've no problem with these lads.' He indicated a group of men who appeared to stick together. 'Anyone saying these boys are cowards is plain wrong.' He held out a hand to shake Edmund's. 'Johnny Ivans. This is my second stint at Eat Apples. I had twelve weeks back in Blighty with a shoulder injury.'

'Pleased to meet you. I'm Edmund Cutler.'

The day began with an anatomy lesson given not by a doctor – apparently there was no one available. Instead, a jovial RAMC sergeant stood at a chalk board where he had drawn a badly proportioned stick man. He turned to face the class – about forty men – and said, 'Before you start taking pot shots at me, I'll admit I'm no draughtsman. But as the anatomical charts are locked in the RMO's quarters and his batman didn't think to retrieve them before they left this morning, you'll have to make do with this.'

It was ludicrous. How could the class understand the three-dimensionality of the human body from a disproportionately sized stick drawing?

Although reluctant to draw attention to himself, Edmund raised a hand. 'Excuse me, Sergeant, but I'm a trained artist. Years of life drawing. If it would help, I can draw you a body that's more anatomically correct.'

The sergeant seemed hesitant to hand over the chalk –

particularly to a non-ranking newcomer. But Edmund's offer had provoked curiosity among the men. So, with a shrug, the sergeant conceded the blackboard to him. Keen not to be perceived as undermining the man's authority, he worked rapidly then handed the chalk back to his superior. As he stepped aside, there were a couple of admiring whistles.

'Sit there,' said the sergeant, indicating a seat near the front of the class. 'I may need you again, Rembrandt.' The remark earned a ripple of laughter. Edmund hoped the name wouldn't stick but feared that it would.

The lesson in rudimentary anatomy included a simple explanation of the circulation of the blood, the difference between arteries and veins and a practical exercise in the taking of pulses. The sergeant, significantly more affable than the Canaries Edmund had been used to, told the class that they'd get more details from the RMO when he gave his weekly lecture.

When the anatomy lesson had finished, the sergeant divided the men into groups of five for some practical training in lifting and carrying. 'The assumption is four men to a stretcher but so far that's proved a luxury we rarely experience on the battlefield. There are never enough of us and always too many wounded, so we'll start with four but by the time you leave the camp for the front I'll need to be sure you can all manage with two per stretcher.'

'What's the fifth man for?' one of the men asked.

'He's the patient. No good using dummies or sandbags. We need to be certain you know exactly how to lift and carry a live man. You'll rotate so you'll each have a chance as patient and carrying in front and at the back, on the left and on the right.' He gripped his hands behind his back and surveyed the rows of men in front of him.

The class went out into the Bull Ring where they undertook

an arduous series of movements in response to the sergeant's commands.

'Open out stretchers.'

'Take up stretchers.'

'Forward march.'

'Right about turn.'

'Halt!'

'Down stretchers.'

On and on, in an endless succession of manoeuvres as the sergeant bawled at them.

The stretchers themselves were heavy, made of thick canvas with leather straps that chafed and cut into the bearers' shoulders. By the end of an hour's drilling Edmund's hands were calloused and his back aching.

As the days passed, Edmund and his fellow bearers received further instruction in the art of the carry, learning how to get up and down hill and over rough terrain. Patients feet first going down. Headfirst going up. They were told to avoid use of morphine except in the most extreme pain, as an unconscious body was a dead weight and made the carry significantly more onerous.

They learnt how to use their field dressings and how to apply pressure dressings. The sergeant had volunteered for the St John Ambulance in peacetime and hence was well-versed in first aid. Under his instructions they learnt the importance of applying pressure to staunch a bleed.

Edmund found the classes interesting, the carry exercises exhausting, and particularly enjoyed the weekly lecture given by one of the MOs, usually Captain Fountwell. During these sessions, which some of the men found tedious and irrelevant, they were told of the latest developments in field medicine, including surgery and anaesthesia. It helped Edmund understand the importance of making the carry as smooth and comfortable as possible to reduce stress in the patient and enhance his chances of survival.

Fountwell, a tall thin man with heavy horn-rimmed spectacles and a neatly trimmed moustache, constantly stressed how essential the bearers' contribution was to the survival of the wounded. 'If I can emphasise just one thing above all others, it's to staunch the bleeding with pressure,' he said. 'Until recently, the majority of men with femoral fractures died either before reaching the casualty stations or soon after. Since we started doing this, it's all changed.'

His eyes swept the room. 'Thanks to bearers we're significantly improving the chances of survival.' He turned to the chalkboard and taking a piece of chalk underlined what was written there. 'Stopping haemorrhaging by careful use of pressure dressings. Keeping fractured limbs supported and stable.' He waved an arm in the air using a dramatic gesture. 'Use what you can. Make a splint from a tree branch or the wounded man's bayonet. By being resourceful and keeping your wits about you, you can save lives.' He folded his arms, his face serious. 'The chance of me and the other doctors being able to do work on men with positive outcomes is in your hands. We can only do our magic if you chaps can deliver them to us in the best possible state. We depend on you, gentlemen.'

As he listened to the captain, Edmund felt for the first time since leaving Little Badgerton that his life had some purpose.

Over the ubiquitous stew in the canteen, Edmund compared notes with Robert. His friend was having a hard time of it, with the Canaries constantly picking on him and looking for any excuse to punish him. Robert himself said nothing of this. It was Ackroyd who told Edmund.

When Edmund asked his friend about it, Robert shrugged it off.

'Look,' said Edmund, 'I could ask the RMO if there's a chance of getting you transferred to the bearer corps.'

'No thanks, pal.'

'It's hard graft but at least it's interesting.'

Robert's tone was tetchy. 'I told you, no. I can handle a few extra drills and the odd kick in the pants. Those bastards won't get the better of me.'

Edmund took a spoonful of stew and chewed silently through the gristle, trying not to gag. He needed as much nutrition as he could get, no matter how unpalatable. He knew Robert Fuller well enough by now to realise that there was no changing his mind. The man was stubborn, but he was also brave.

Robert finished eating and clattered his spoon back onto the tin plate. 'So, what did you learn in school today, my friend?'

'Gas drill.'

'Surely we all know by now how to put a bloody mask on and off.'

Edmund gave him a wry smile. 'Try putting one on a wounded man who's crying out in agony, suffering from panic and trying to tear the blasted thing off.'

'Fair enough,' Robert conceded. 'That stew was particularly revolting today. All gristle. No meat.'

'I'm asking Alice to send some more tins of sardines. A couple of tins of biscuits too.'

'I'll do the same. I could murder some shortbread.'

Edmund nodded. 'Anything's better than those dry old army biscuits they give us. So hard I could repair the roof of my cottage with them.'

'Mr Huntley and Mr Palmer have a lot to answer for.'

EIGHTEEN

Alice had a dilemma. Her progress on the creation of the Latchington window had been slower since Edmund's departure but she had now reached a critical point where she needed to decide how to handle the lead work. She was anxious about doing it – or overseeing Maurice doing it – without Edmund's guiding hand.

She felt compelled to fulfil the promise she'd made to Edmund to finish the window. Neither she nor the captain were skilled in the process of leading-up. She still had much to do to complete the detail painting, staining, acid etching and firing, and was confident about tackling that, but the leading was like a dark cloud hovering above her and filling her with anxiety. Alice picked up a strip of lead and laid it tentatively over two pieces of glass. When Edmund had done the leading the process had looked so straightforward and logical but now her hand shook as she picked up the strip of lead again and flexed it between her fingers. She was paralysed with fear of messing up the window.

There was also the fact that Maurice had completed the shape cutting and base coat painting so now she must either dispense with his services or find a way for him to gain the necessary skills to undertake the leading. She had watched Edmund do it on other windows but had not been directly involved herself and lacked both the confidence and the inclination to undertake what she feared would be an intricate and complicated task. She still had a lot of painting to complete – and limited time as she had a rule of not working when Lottie was home from school.

Alice contemplated writing to Edmund and asking him to set down a detailed step-by-step set of instructions but dismissed that idea quickly. It would take more time than he would have available, occupied as he seemed to be morning until night with training exercises for his new role in the RAMC. Besides, she had his treasured, much-thumbed copy of Christopher Whall's excellent illustrated manual on making stained glass. But it was one thing to read and understand the directions and quite another to put them into practice without any expert oversight.

Picking up the book, she turned to Chapter Ten and read it through for the second time. There were illustrations of the set-up of the workbench, of the tools required and a clear explanation of how to go about the lead work. She moved over to the easel and consulted the cut-line Edmund had prepared before he left for the front. This was his master plan for the window. It had guided them in the cutting of every piece so far; it numbered every section to ensure the individual pieces that would make up the window were worked on in the right order. It contained a key to the colours involved in every piece of glass; and finally, it showed the position of the lead lines. All in all a comprehensive blueprint for the window.

Yet despite all this, Alice still hesitated. She had faith in Maurice but it was unreasonable to expect him to undertake the leading without more guidance.

Pacing up and down the studio, she chewed over the problem. What would Edmund do?

The answer to that was clear.

He'd show the captain exactly how to do the leading work, just as he had shown him how to use the tools to cut the glass – and how before that he had taught her too: patiently explaining, demonstrating, watching, encouraging. How desperately she missed him. She swallowed, forcing back the incipient tears.

As she picked up Whall's book again, an idea formed in her head. Christopher Whall had helped her once before, when she had been anxious about Edmund's withdrawal into despair after the suicide of a former colleague. At Alice's invitation, the master artist had visited them in Little Badgerton and convinced Edmund he had no reason for recriminations over Southerton's tragic death.

Might he help her again now, were she to ask him? She couldn't expect him to come down to Hampshire, but perhaps he'd be willing to accept Maurice Kynaston as an unpaid pupil in his Hammersmith studio. Or failing that, he might suggest another glassworks where Maurice could learn the requisite skills.

The more she thought about it, the more Alice was convinced this was a solid plan. Maurice was a quick learner and a dextrous pair of hands. Mr Whall's workshop could probably do with some help, as she imagined most of his apprentices would have been conscripted into the armed forces. She wondered whether she ought to check with Edmund first but decided that would merely delay matters and might be a source of anxiety to him and a sign that she wasn't coping. Her mind made up, she took up pen and paper and wrote to Mr Whall.

Alice didn't have long to wait for an answer. The stained-glass artist replied by return, expressing his willingness to host Captain

Kynaston in his studio, provided the officer could find his own accommodation while in London. Now all she needed to do was persuade the captain himself that this was a good idea. There was also the need for approval from the medical officer at Bankstone. The doctor had been supportive of Maurice working in the studio, but would he be as willing were that work to be in London and possibly for several weeks? And where could Maurice stay? Alice didn't pay him any wages, at his insistence, but she could hardly expect him to stump up for lodgings from his own purse.

There was only one way to find out. She bit her lip, took a deep breath and approached the captain as he was tidying away the cutting instruments.

'We've reached a critical point in making this window, Maurice.' Her voice was hesitant, desperate not to offend him. 'All the cutting and base-coat painting is complete now.'

His face fell. 'You don't need me anymore.'

'On the contrary. I'd like you to do the leading work. The placement of the lead lines is all marked out on Edmund's cutline. The problem is I don't feel confident enough to show you how.' She picked up Christopher Whall's manual and tapped it against her other hand. 'There's a detailed explanation in here but I know there's no substitute for watching someone else and trying it out under supervision.'

'I see. You want to wait until Edmund returns.'

Alice stretched her lips into a grim line. 'Heaven knows when that might be. No, I'm wondering if you'd be prepared to spend a few weeks in London working under the tuition of Christopher Whall or one of his assistants.'

'He's willing to take me on?'

'He is. He replied to my enquiry today.'

'What a marvellous opportunity.' Maurice's usually serious expression broke into a grin. Then he added, 'I'm indebted to you and Edmund for all you've taught me. I shall do my utmost not to let you down.'

Alice allowed herself a smile of relief, then remembered the proviso. 'The only drawback is accommodation. Mr Whall is unable to offer lodgings and I have no funds to pay for them.' She twisted the fabric of her apron in her hands.

Maurice Kynaston grinned broadly. 'Alice, don't worry. I have friends in London who will be only too happy to put me up while I'm there. Or failing that, there's the officers' club.' He took her hand in his. 'Did you mention my disability to Mr Whall?'

Alice told him she hadn't. 'But that's because I never even think of it as you make so light of it yourself. To be honest, I barely notice as you're so agile on those crutches.'

'When does Mr Whall want me to start?'

'As soon as you're ready.'

'I'll need to clear it with the MO. He's been trying to talk me into wearing the prosthetic limb and I've been resisting. I find it dashed uncomfortable. Maybe if I promise to start using it for a few hours each day as he suggests, he may look more favourably on the request.'

'We'll work it out somehow. I can't tell you how grateful I am that you're prepared to do this. Thank you, Maurice.'

When Maurice had left, eager to make the necessary arrangements with the Bankstone medical officer, Alice picked up a piece of glass. She had a couple of hours before Lottie came home from school. Today's task was to paint the plumage of the giant eagle that formed the centrepiece of the Latch-ington window. The work required steady hands and much patience as she painstakingly delineated each individual feather in a complex pattern of shadows and stippling. She fell into an almost trance-like state as she concentrated on the different sizes and shapes of the feathers, creating texture so that the bird, although a mythical creature, seemed to be three-dimensional and real. As she worked, she constantly stepped back to view the effect from varying distances. She wanted it to look real and convincing from several feet away and delicate and painterly when close.

So absorbed in the task was she that it was only a softening of the light that made her realise it was time to cross the meadow and meet Lottie, who would be returning along the lane with a group of other schoolchildren. The ritual of meeting her by the roadside was something Alice treasured, even though Lottie had assured her she was perfectly happy to cross the field on her own.

To her surprise, when the child appeared at the brow of the hill from the village, she was alone. Usually there were about half a dozen children, including Viola's daughter Molly. Alice realised her stepdaughter was running.

Heart pounding, she hurried forward to meet her.

As Alice reached her stepdaughter, she noticed her face was streaked with tears. Lottie brushed a hand over her cheek to remove the evidence.

'What happened, Lottie? Where are the others?'

Lottie glanced back over her shoulder but said nothing. She started to walk across the meadow towards the cottage. Alice walked beside her, uncertain whether to press the child to tell her what was wrong. She decided to wait until the little girl was ready to tell her.

Safely inside the cottage, she poured a cup of milk for the child and watched as Lottie drank it, leaving a small white moustache on her upper lip.

'Why were you on your own just now, sweetheart?'

'I ran ahead.' Lottie looked down at her lap and Alice saw her lip was quivering.

'Please tell me what's wrong. I promise you won't be in any trouble.'

Lottie hesitated, then raised her left hand which had been

lying across her lap. She opened her fingers to show Alice what she'd been clutching. Resting on her palm was a clump of what was unmistakably Lottie's own hair. Alice gasped.

'How did that happen?' She moved close and stood beside the child and inspected the top of her head. There was a bald patch from where the lock of hair had been wrenched. Alice felt a rush of anger and sorrow. 'Who did this to you?'

Lottie said nothing but her lip continued to tremble. Alice's love for the child mingled with protective anger. The hair had clearly been pulled out. How could anyone hurt her like this? Instinctively, she wrapped her arms around the little girl and drew her against her breast.

After a few moments, Lottie spoke. 'May I have my tea now? I'm hungry.'

Alice suppressed the urge to keep questioning the little girl. Better to find out when Lottie felt ready to tell her – much as she was desperate to know now. 'Of course, my love. Bread and jam? And there's some seed cake I made this morning.'

Lottie nodded but remained silent.

As Alice prepared the child's meal, she felt a rising tide of fury. Who had done this to Lottie and why? Was all the progress she'd made to win the little girl's trust about to be undone? She decided to give her some time and not press the subject immediately.

Later that evening, when she went to kiss Lottie goodnight in bed, she stroked the child's forehead and asked whether her head was hurting.

'Just a bit. Not very much now.'

'It'll be better in the morning, my love.'

'But there'll be a bald patch, won't there?'

Alice bit her lip. 'It will grow back quickly, I'm sure.'

'But everyone will see.'

'I have some pretty ribbon in the drawer. Tomorrow, I'll make you a bow and we'll cover it up completely.' She lowered her head and kissed the child. Taking a deep breath she added, 'But if you won't tell me who did it, I'll have to go up to the school and ask Miss Trimble.'

Lottie's eyes widened and her brow furrowed. 'No! Please. I don't want the whole school to know. Promise me you won't tell Miss Trimble as Molly will get into trouble and she'll pick on me again.'

Molly. Of course it was Molly.

'Very well. I won't tell Miss Trimble but only if you tell me why Molly tore a chunk of your hair out.'

The realisation that she'd given away who the culprit was dawned on Lottie and she hesitated before answering. Eventually she said, 'When I told her you said you won't send me to the orphanage, she said I was a liar so I'll probably end up in prison like my grandfather.'

Alice clasped a hand to her mouth.

Lottie looked up at her. 'Is it true what she says? That my grandfather is a murderer? And he killed my mummy?'

Alice swallowed. How on earth was she going to answer that? What would Edmund have said? It was so hard being a lone parent and the responsibility felt all the greater because she wasn't even Lottie's natural mother. Alice was desperate not to let her absent husband down and to do the right thing by this little girl.

'Your mummy had an accident and hit her head. The police are trying to find out how it happened. Your grandfather says she slipped and hit the marble fireplace.'

'But he's in prison so they must think he did it.' Lottie's chin was trembling.

Alice bit her lip. How to explain that to a child... 'He's not a proper prisoner. He's just being kept there until they find out exactly what happened.' She squeezed Lottie's hand. 'Now go to sleep, my love, so you're fresh for school tomorrow.'

'You won't tell Miss Trimble?'

'No. I won't tell her.'

'Promise?'

'I promise.'

Alice left the room, decision made. She'd keep her word and say nothing to the teacher but tomorrow she was going to pay a visit to Viola Fuller.

NINETEEN

In the ward at Bankstone, under cover of darkness Victor stretched an arm out across the space between the beds and reached for Maurice's hand. Their fingers interlocked. 'Thank heavens for Alice,' Victor whispered in response to the news his friend had imparted. 'The plan's perfect. You can work with this chap in Hammersmith all day then come to me at Albany each evening.' He squeezed Maurice's fingers. 'I'll give you a key.'

Maurice's voice was a soft murmur in the silence of the ward. 'It depends on the MO giving it the go-ahead.' He sat up in bed. 'Quick! The nurse has just gone to make a cup of tea. It's that dozy one. If we do the pillow trick, she won't notice we're gone.'

The two men got out of bed, rearranged the bedding and moved quietly between the ranks of sleeping officers, Victor supporting his friend to lessen his reliance on the crutches so they could move more quietly. They headed for the conservatory.

Victor wrapped his arms around Maurice and held him, drawing him into a kiss. Such moments were all the sweeter for being rare. Maurice pulled away first. 'We have to be careful. You know what will happen if we're discovered.'

'Happiness makes me reckless. Right now, I feel as though I can face anything as long as I'm with you.'

'I was saying just now I have to get the doc's permission before I can start work with Whall.'

'No reason why he shouldn't give it.' Victor stroked the back of Maurice's hand then turned it over, bent his head and kissed the captain's open palm. 'After all, he wants us out in the world as soon as possible. He's given me the green light to start work at the ministry with the proviso that I come back here for a check-up in a month. It's likely he'll discharge me then. They're desperate to free up beds.'

Victor stood up and looked through the window towards the formal garden beyond. The moon was a waxing crescent, a thin sliver of white like the tip of a fingernail. His one good eye struggled to see in the pale light, making out the dark bulk of the ornamental water well and the narrow spikes of flowers in the herbaceous border. He opened the glass door. 'Let's go outside.'

Maurice looked around him then reached for his crutches and followed Victor out onto the lawn. As soon as they closed the door behind them the two men stopped to breathe in the night air after the stuffiness of the ward. The smell of newly mown grass and, as they passed the herbaceous border, the sweetness of night-scented stock. They made their way to a bench under an oak tree, where they'd be out of sight from the house. As soon as they sat, they fell upon each other, passionately yet tenderly.

'It's torture,' said Victor at last. 'Being so near to you and unable to touch you. I can't tell you how happy you've made me that soon we'll be alone every night.'

'It'll only be for a couple of weeks then I'll have to come back here to help Alice finish the window.'

Victor gave a groan. 'If only I were my sister. Having you all to herself day after day.'

'If that were the case, we'd never get any work done.'

'You're right.' Victor ran his fingers down the side of Maurice's face, feeling the growth of stubble rough against his skin. 'What will we do? I mean how will we manage when we are apart? I doubt I'll be able to bear it. When will the window be finished?'

'I don't know for sure. Don't forget I'm the beginner there. Once Alice has finished the painting and firing, we'll do the leadwork then we'll install the window. After that she has no other work lined up.'

'Ask Alice then. We need to make plans, Maurice.'

'First and foremost, I need to find somewhere to stay here in Little Badgerton. If I'm well enough to go and work in Mr Whall's studio they won't let me stay on in Bankstone when I come back.'

'Then come to Albany!'

Maurice sighed. 'I meant while Alice and I finish the window. I'll have to find lodgings locally.'

'After that what?'

'I'll apply for my army discharge. Then I'll need to find a job.'

'You can come and work in the City.'

'And do what?' Maurice was dubious. 'I love using my hands. As soon as I get into the studio, I feel calm, grounded. Happy even.'

Victor was impatient. He couldn't understand the appeal for Maurice of working as Alice's dogsbody. 'Maybe I can get you a job in the ministry.'

Maurice took both Victor's hands between his. 'My dear boy, I can't think of anything I'd hate more. I'm done with all that. I've told you I want to do manual work. Preferably skilled. Once Alice finishes Lady Lockwood's memorial window I may train as a carpenter. Or a frame-maker. Or find work in one of the glass studios in London.'

Victor wrapped his arms around Maurice and rested his head on his chest. 'Imagine. Both of us working in London. We can live together at Albany.'

'How could I possibly live there full-time with you? They're bachelor apartments. People would ask questions.'

'I'll say you're my valet. Since Milton left, I've no one. We can pretend it's you.'

Maurice laughed. 'I ought to be insulted by that suggestion but anyway it's wholly impractical. You'll need to find a real manservant – then people will wonder why you have two.'

'I'll manage without. I'll get a housekeeper to come in each day.'

'She'd notice immediately there were two of us.'

'Then I'll pay her lots of money. Look, Maurice, we'll find a way. Let's take each day as it comes. Meanwhile, I'm overjoyed that I'll have you all to myself while you're doing this training business in Hammersmith.' He leant forward and kissed Maurice slowly. 'We'll find a way to be together all the time. Now I've found you I couldn't bear to let you go.'

Even though it was too dark to see his face clearly, Victor knew Maurice was smiling. He decided to ask him a question that had been preying on his mind. 'Did you always know, Maurice. That you preferred men?'

'I suppose deep inside I did but I wouldn't let myself accept it. I just didn't allow myself to think about it, wouldn't confront the question.' He gave a sigh. 'I'm the only son of older parents and it was always expected I'd follow my father into the army. We lived in a small country town, very conventional. It had been assumed since boyhood that I'd marry Penelope Stanton. I'd known her since we were children. Our parents were best friends. They played bridge and golf together. We became engaged but somehow the question of naming the day was always avoided. I found reasons for delay. She was patient but I could tell she was unhappy.'

'So when you lost your leg, she used that as an excuse to break off the engagement?'

'No. I wasn't truthful when I told you that. Penelope would never have abandoned me because I was injured. She's a compassionate woman. I feel ashamed that I said it – even though she'll never know I did.'

'So why then? Did you break it off yourself?'

Maurice turned his head away. 'No. I was too big a coward to do that. I just let it drift on and on. Then finally she put me to the test. We went for a picnic just before I left for France. She wanted to send me off with a special day. We were beside a lake.' Maurice's voice had a tremor. 'We drank champagne, and she swam. Took off most of her clothes and went into the water.' He paused, as though searching for the right words. 'It was so out of character. Maybe down to the champagne. She kept calling for me to join her, but I didn't want to.' He took a cigarette from his pocket and lit it.

Victor waited for him to continue his story.

'Eventually, she came out of the water. She was dripping wet, the few undergarments she was wearing clinging to her. I should have been excited, but I felt nothing.'

He paused again to draw on his cigarette, the smell of the tobacco heavy in the air. 'She took off her underwear and lay down on the grass beside me. Stark naked. I didn't know what to do. I froze. So she took my hand and placed it on her breast.' He put his head in his hands. 'It was dreadful. I pulled it away. I knew she was suffering. I knew I was causing her pain. But I couldn't help it. Penelope wasn't a girl with low morals. I'm certain she would have preferred to wait until marriage, but the poor girl was at her wits' end. I was leaving for France, and I think she thought it would be her gift to me. A sign of commitment. A promise. Something for me to remember while I was at the front. That and a means of testing whether I cared for her enough.'

He drew again on his cigarette, releasing a long plume of smoke from deep in his lungs. 'God, reliving all this is bloody hard... I failed that test. I didn't want her sacrifice. I didn't value her gift. I humiliated the poor woman. If I'd said I found her repulsive I couldn't have been clearer. I'll never forget the look on her face. The hurt. The sadness. The utter mortification.'

'I'm sorry.' Victor squeezed Maurice's hand.

'So that was that. I suppose she worried she'd be left on the shelf, as within a few months she'd married the local bank manager. A widower fifteen years older than her.'

He ground out the butt of his cigarette under the heel of his slipper.

'Have you heard from her since?'

'No and I never will. It's why I won't ever go back to Shropshire. When we broke off the engagement my parents told me I'd disgraced the family name, and they were ashamed of me. I don't think they'll ever forgive me.'

'Do they know you're...'

'I don't know. Perhaps they suspect. But that kind of thing is never mentioned. We're not the kind of family who airs our feelings. As far as my parents are concerned, I've failed in the most basic of duties – marrying a respectable woman and starting a family.'

In the pale light Maurice's face was a picture of misery. Victor reached up and brushed a lock of hair back from his brow and held the palm of his hand against Maurice's cheek.

'I'm sorry. I didn't mean to blurt all that out.' Maurice looked away.

'Thank you for trusting me enough to tell me.'

'Did your parents ever try to push you into marriage?'

Victor sniffed. 'Fortunately not. Their priority was trying to get Alice married off. First to Gilbert and then, apparently, while I was out of the country, to Edmund. But Edmund went off and married poor old Dora. Alice had had enough by then so she left home and came here. She's never been back to Dalton Hall.' He shook his head. 'No, the nearest I got to matrimony was when Herbert Cutler came up with a scheme for Dora to divorce Edmund and marry me. I almost went along with it. A beautiful spouse would have been an asset and removed any gossip about my being "a confirmed bachelor". But I went to Gallipoli instead.'

The silence of the garden was interrupted by the throaty warble of a bird, trilling and chirruping into the darkness of the night. It was coming from a thicket of shrubs. Maurice placed a hand on Victor's arm. 'Listen.'

They sat side-by-side on the wooden bench as the bird continued its song.

Maurice spoke softly. '*My heart aches, and a drowsy numbness pains My sense, as though of hemlock I had drunk.* I can't remember the rest.'

Victor listened. 'It's stopped. What bird was it?'

'A nightingale. Didn't you learn "Ode to a Nightingale" when you were at school?'

Victor shrugged. 'I never paid much attention in English lessons. Not one for poetry. I preferred mathematics and science.'

'Not a romantic then.'

Victor laughed out loud. 'I think you'll find I am. It takes a lot to bring it out in me, but——'

Maurice interrupted. 'We need to get back to the ward before the nurse sees we're missing. We have to be careful, or we'll jeopardise your job with the ministry and your position in the City.' He turned to face Victor in the darkness. 'We're still in the army. We could still be court-martialled.' He stood up and Victor followed, the spell broken.

As they walked back across the garden towards the conservatory, Victor had an idea. 'You were planning to come to London to start at Whall's on Monday. Come a day earlier. With me. I'm lunching at Dalton Hall with my parents on Sunday. I want you to join us.'

'I couldn't possibly. You haven't seen them since you came back from Egypt. They won't want me tagging along.'

Victor gave a dry laugh. 'You don't know my parents. Especially my mother. She's about as affectionate as a viper.' He put an arm around Maurice's shoulder. 'Seriously. I want you to come. I've been dreading seeing them. You'll make it bearable.'

'As it happens, I've already met your father.'

Victor spun round. 'When?'

'At Alice's wedding. Lord Dalton gave her away.'

'Gosh. I'd forgotten you would have been there. So, all the more reason to come.' They stood on the threshold to the conservatory. 'Say you'll come, Maurice. Please say you'll come.'

'How can I refuse you?'

The two men embraced, clinging to each other as though their lives depended on it. When they broke apart Victor pushed open the door and went to sit on one of the basketweave chairs. 'You go ahead. I'll wait here for ten minutes so if the nurse sees one of us, she won't realise we were together. I'll tell her I couldn't sleep and went outside for some air.'

Together, they took the train to Richmond the following Sunday.

'We'll get a taxi from the station to Dalton Hall. We can go back to Albany later in my motor,' said Victor, 'assuming Papa hasn't sold it.' He laid his hand on Maurice's in the otherwise empty first-class compartment. 'I don't know how I'll get through the rest of today. I can't stop thinking about being alone with you at last.'

'Me too.' Changing the subject, Maurice smiled, squeezed

his hand and said, 'Tell me about your visit to Pentonville. You've said nothing yet. How was it?'

'Grim. Horrible place. The smell alone is enough to put anyone off a life of crime. As for Herbert Cutler, I can't believe I once looked up to him.'

'So, he's not like Edmund?'

'Couldn't be more different. Edmund and Gilbert took after their mother, thank goodness.'

'I'm interested to discover how much you and Alice take after your parents. I thought your father was a good fellow, but I didn't spend much time with him and I'd no particular reason to pay much attention to him. I was barely aware Alice even had a brother then, let alone how much you'd come to mean to me.'

Victor felt a surge of joy. He knew by now he was falling in love with Maurice but was reluctant to ask him if he felt the same, in case he didn't. Besides, he wanted him to say it without prompting. Then he realised Maurice could be thinking the same – waiting for him to speak first. Victor told himself he would. Not now, but tonight. At Albany. In bed. It was always easier to speak of feelings when they were physically close. He glanced at Maurice's profile beside him and longed to speed up time.

'What did Cutler want?'

Victor gave him a brief summary of the conversation. 'At least I managed to get his agreement to my name over the door.' It was tempting to tell Maurice everything, including the ministry's concerns that Cutler had been both profiteering and dealing in faulty armaments before his arrest for Dora's murder, but he'd given his word to the men from Charing Cross Buildings to keep his mission secret.

'And you think you can restore the business to health?'

Victor grinned. 'I'll have a damned good try. And I can tell you one thing, I'm a dashed good businessman.'

'I've no doubt of that.'

'Of course, Cutler's name is mud in London, but people have no reason to doubt me.'

'Working for the Ministry of Munitions, still in uniform and with a DSO, they'll be flocking to your door.'

'Not quite. But I'm confident I can get back some of our lost clients. I have a charm offensive planned. But first there's my father. According to the chief clerk, Papa has been trying to regain control of his finances. That would be an unmitigated disaster – for my parents, for the future of Dalton Hall and not least for me and Alice.' Victor explained to Maurice that his father had a profligate streak and an inability to resist the next shiny investment opportunity mentioned to him. His losses, pursuing pie-in-the-sky ideas had cost Lord Dalton dearly, until Herbert Cutler had taken a grip on his finances. At the time Victor had been working for Cutler in New York and hence in no position to object. Now was another matter.

The taxi passed through the stone gateway and started up the long tree-lined driveway. The road bent sharply after a hundred yards and the house came into view. Dalton Hall consisted of two wings: the original Jacobean and a later Palladian one with a fine stone portico. Victor experienced a sudden unexpected nostalgia for his family home and remembered that one day it would be his.

He glanced at Maurice beside him and made a silent prayer that he would find a way by then to have Maurice with him. Victor rarely felt unhappy with his lot and never regretful that he wasn't like other men, married with a family. Since early childhood he had known his feelings were directed only towards his own gender and while he'd always been discreet, he had never felt shame about being what others described as queer. At school, it hadn't attracted attention, as most of the boys experimented with each other or were experimented upon by older boys or abusive masters. But in society, in the world in general and the army in particular, homosexuality was a crime, an offence, an outrage. Victor knew all too well that it could cost him his reputation, his commission, and his future. Society was so unfair. His feelings were entirely natural, inescapable, innate. Why did he have to hide them away and live his life as a secret?

As though reading his mind, Maurice discreetly pressed his leg against Victor's and smiled.

The taxicab pulled up in front of the building and the two men got out and ascended the stairs to the front entrance.

TWENTY

There was a sense of mounting excitement and movement at Étaples as the month of June drew to a close. After a long period of seemingly endless drilling, Edmund and Robert's unit had received the orders to mobilise. They were in the reserve troops, set back behind the lines, ready to be deployed if and when needed during what was to be known as a 'big push' to open up the Western Front.

When they arrived at the reserve trenches, the excitement and impatience among the men of the unit was palpable. For a full week, the British and French artillery had subjected the German lines to constant bombardment. Day after day, the men became accustomed to the booming of the guns, like a violent thunderstorm, only louder, denser, with no promise of cooling rain, only the rain of lead and fire.

Edmund thought how much worse, louder, more terrifying it must be on the receiving end in the German trenches. From behind the British artillery lines the noise was a whistling, swooshing sound as the shells were fired, followed by crackling, crashing, booming as they exploded far away. The thump of artillery was enough to send men mad. No escape. Endless, monotonous, deafening, terrifying. Even though they were some distance from the frontline, Edmund felt the earth shake under him. It was as though the hard solid ground had turned to something quivering and unstable beneath his feet. He looked around him at the previously confident men, Robert included. Now there was no laughter, no comradely grins, no feeble jokes or banter.

He readied his saddlebag, checking he had everything he needed: a bottle of iodine, packages of field dressings, a leather pouch with cigarettes and matches to comfort those in pain or dying, blue morphine tablets, a map carefully folded inside oilcloth to indicate where aid posts were and the position behind the lines of the CCS. Then he prepared to wait. They'd been told the offensive was to begin at dawn on the first of July, once the heavy bombardment had worn down the enemy.

How could anyone survive being the target of that relentless pummelling? Yet, later, they were to discover that the week-long barrage had failed to obliterate the heavy thicket of barbed wire and to penetrate the deep solid defences of the German trench system. Amongst the shells used many proved to be duds – faulty munitions that should never have reached the front. Others were shrapnel shells, deadly to soft flesh but unsuited to breaking through solidly built defences. The round-the-clock pounding of the German lines proved to be as futile as trying to hammer a nail with a feather.

Edmund and his cadre of stretcher bearers were told they were to be held in reserve and would participate alongside their unit in the later stages of the upcoming attack on the Somme. In the meantime they would be required to support the evacuation of wounded from the earlier waves. They were separated from the other men in their unit and moved behind the lines to a CCS – a casualty clearing station – ready to help receive the wounded.

The men looked at each other. While they wouldn't be

going out into the field of battle until the rest of their unit did, unlike their comrades who would have time for rest and reflection, they'd likely be on their feet from the beginning of the offensive.

Captain Fountwell told them they would be working alongside orderlies to receive wounded men brought in by the bearers supporting the first day's push.

'You'll only be out in the field once your unit is up. The plan is for that to be in a week or so, but you'll need to be ready in case it's sooner. Maybe even in a couple of days if things don't go to plan.' His grim expression indicated he thought that was likely.

'Do exactly what your sergeants tell you. But once the battle starts, you'll all have to think on your feet. Your job will be to keep any wounded men alive until the medical team can get to them. The bearers will drop them here and return to the field of battle to retrieve more wounded.' He stared into the distance. 'If the advance goes well, you won't be needed at all and will be rejoining your unit in reserve. But if not, it'll be all hands on deck... I have full confidence in you all.' He nodded, his lips stretched into a tight line, then he turned away and went back inside his tent.

Edmund recalled what he had learnt in the classroom at Étaples. Any men stretchered in without hope of recovery were to be moved by the orderlies immediately to what was termed the moribund ward. There, instead of doctors, they would receive the ministrations of a clergyman. When their suffering was over the orderlies would then shuttle the dead from there for burial. Meanwhile, for those with a chance of survival, Edmund and his colleagues were to assist the orderlies in readying them for treatment by the doctors.

Dirt and mud were to be washed off the patients, clothing around wounds cut away, wounds cleaned and 'tickets' checked and completed where these had not already been done by the bearers bringing them in. The tickets carried names and serial numbers from the men's tags, time and date and nature and location of injuries.

When Edmund and his colleagues arrived, the CCS had been cleared of patients in readiness for a surge of new ones. Most men had been transferred to hospital trains to be moved further away from the lines or back across the Channel to be nursed in England. Empty beds lined the tents. Blankets, basins and bandages were at the ready. Doctors, nurses, orderlies and the seconded bearers were all poised, ready to leap into action.

The barrage guns quietened after dawn. There was a deathly stillness for a few moments, then at seven thirty a.m. over the distance Edmund heard the synchronised screech of whistles signalling the men in the frontline to go over the top. The first day of the Battle of the Somme had begun. This was to be the biggest attack the British had undertaken so far in the war.

Then they waited. And waited. And waited.

At first Edmund thought this must be good news. So few men wounded that none had reached the CCS. But he doubted this could be the case. There ought to be a steady flow of bearers bringing wounded in for treatment. He looked around him. Johnny Ivans whispered, 'Why's it so quiet? The whistles went hours ago.'

Edmund shook his head. But inside he feared the worst. Was it so bad that even the stretcher bearers and ambulances couldn't get through?

Rumours began to circulate that the soldiers in the first wave had been mown down like ripe wheat under scythes. Listening to the reports, Edmund felt sick to the pit of his stomach. As soon as the artillery barrage had ended, the German gunners had emerged intact from their trenches to meet the oncoming British and French with a heavy curtain of machine-gun fire. Wave after wave of men, all moved forward slowly to certain death. Falling and falling, like sheaves of corn, on and on, throughout the day until darkness fell.

In the CCS they waited. Nothing. An eery silence. The following days still no one arrived at the temporary hospital. Inside the tents were lines of empty beds, piles of stretchers and blankets, at the ready. Edmund's colleagues sat around playing cards to pass the time, with a mounting sense of dread. To keep his growing anxiety at bay, Edmund himself sketched – little pencil portraits of the other bearers talking, drinking tea, eating the usual indigestible bully beef stews.

Eventually word reached them. The carnage was so utterly devastating that the entire evacuation process had broken down. The sheer number of casualties had completely overwhelmed the system. Edmund felt numb. For the whole operation to seize up, the loss of life must have been devastating. The nerves gnawed away at him as they continued to wait.

On the seventh of July it was as though a dam had burst and the clearing station was overwhelmed with hundreds of wounded men arriving in an endless procession of ambulances. Edmund watched as the long train of vehicles edged closer. On and on, a never-ending snake. His anxiety gave way to anger. How could they let this happen? How could they have messed it up so badly? Who was responsible? Why were the generals in charge so utterly incompetent?

Outside the tents, the ground was churned by wheels, the hooves of horses and the to and fro of bearers and orderlies shifting the wounded into the CCS. By now, the wounded men were close to death, dressings filthy and unchanged, many of them starving, having lain on the battlefield in pain for days.

Forcing back his anger, Edmund helped to unload the first of a long stream of ambulances, backed up all the way to the front. He was overcome by the worst stench he'd ever experienced, when the doors to the vehicle opened. Two men had died where they lay inside, others had soiled themselves, someone had vomited. They lay in agony, their wounds dire – some practically torn apart and barely alive. He reeled back, covering his mouth and nose with his hand. But he couldn't walk away. Some of these men could be saved and it was his duty to give his all.

As he worked in silence, he thought back to a day he had spent in Hyde Park with Lottie, when a woman had tried to pin a white feather on his jacket. How he wished that woman could witness what was happening today. All the platitudes about bravery and service to King and country uttered by people like her, rang hollow here amid the stench and filth and death of the Somme. There was no honour and glory in a war like this one.

The surgeons worked around the clock, often asking the orderlies to administer the anaesthesia. Like stretcher bearers, the orderlies had learnt skills far beyond the basic fetching and carrying that their roles officially required.

By the time the queue had cleared Edmund was barely able to stand. Physically and emotionally exhausted, he had witnessed sights more terrible than he had ever imagined and hoped he would never see again. Men sobbed for their mothers, prayed, shouted, died. Edmund tried to block out the screams of the dying, but they were all around him. Relentless. He felt as though he had stepped inside a Hieronymus Bosch painting – no, worse – as a painting couldn't convey the sounds and smells he had witnessed that day.

After hours of miserable showery rain, that evening it began to rain heavily. Edmund stood in the doorway of the moribund ward, his back to the dying men there. They would all be in the ground before morning. Sooner, he hoped, for their sakes. He stared out through the pouring rain and reflected that it had been the worst day of his life.

. . .

Whilst there had been some limited successes during that fatal first day of the Somme, it proved to be the bloodiest battle in British military history with more than fifty-seven thousand casualties of which nearly twenty thousand were killed in just one day.

The British army wasn't prepared for the carnage of that first day. It had come too soon, before the troops, many, like Edmund and Robert, recent recruits to Kitchener's army, were seasoned, battle-hardened soldiers.

The following day more men arrived from Étaples and Edmund and his colleagues finally received the orders to rejoin their unit and prepare for the next advance.

After the bloodbath of that dreadful first day, the Battle of the Somme settled into the usual pattern of small advances and retreats. Ground was gained, sometimes to be lost again. The British, French and colonial forces pressed on but in a more measured way than in that terrible, disastrous first day, constantly learning, experimenting tactically, pushing forward, grabbing what land they could. The all-out big push had failed – small, steady steps were to be the order of the next phase of the long battle.

Edmund was back with his unit, hunkered down in their trenches, playing the waiting game that would characterise much of this terrible war.

Beyond the trenches lay No Man's Land. Hard to believe that this was once fertile farmland, with houses, villages, hamlets, churches. Now there was no colour left in the land-scape. Just greys, browns, sludge. Everything else had leached away. Edmund's palette of paints would be wasted here. But all those monochromatic shades were ripe for pencil sketching. And there was so much time for that. Time to devote to intricate hatching to create the delicate nuances between shadow and texture, plenty of time to turn the page and hatch in a different direction, light lines and heavier, sharp and soft.

He wondered what this place had been like before it was carved up by trenches and blasted by shells. Not so different from Little Badgerton, he imagined. Flatter, but with similar green fields, trees, country lanes, children's voices, the bright colours of flowers. Now a ravaged wasteland.

With pencils and paper Edmund worked to capture the texture of the grain on the wooden pit props that supported the trench walls, the pale light reflecting on the surface of puddles under their feet, the scuffed fur of a dead rat, lying where it had been felled by someone with a stone. Pointless killing it really. They were the rats of Hamelin. So many that they were beyond counting. And there was no Pied Piper to lead them away.

Here, between the brown walls of the trenches it was almost impossible to believe that other world existed. The one they'd all left behind in England, perhaps never to see again. The world of hot baths, melting butter on warm-from-the-oven scones, the scent of freshly picked flowers, the laughter of village children, the crackle of wood on a fire in winter, the pop of balls against tennis rackets or leather against willow. For Edmund most of all it was the touch of Alice, her body curled around his in their narrow bed each night. Her hair tousled across the pillow. The soft whisper kisses of little Lottie.

His heart clenched. Had that ever been real? Could it ever be again? Here amidst this nightmare of screaming shells, the stomach-clenching fear of gas attacks, the throbbing thud of guns, it was hard to imagine ever escaping.

And even were it possible to return to the old world, there was a crippling fear inside him that no one who hadn't been here would ever be able to understand and relate to what they were going through day after day, night after night, in an endless threnody of hellfire.

. . .

That night Edmund and three other RAMC men including
Johnny Ivans were summoned by their sergeant.

'Go and get some sleep. You report for duty here tomorrow
at five a.m.' The sergeant seemed to be avoiding their eyes.
Edmund's stomach clenched. Were they about to go over the
top tomorrow? Might this be his last night alive?

The sergeant cleared his throat. 'You're needed to assist at
an execution.'

There was a gasp from Johnny, and Edmund felt the blood
drain from his face. 'What?'

'You heard me.'

Edmund's throat closed. 'Assist? How?'

'Tying him to the post. Removing the body afterwards.
Burying him. Just do as you're told.'

'Who's being executed? And why?' Edmund couldn't rein
in his horrified curiosity. He was a stretcher bearer, here to help
men, not assist in killing them.

The sergeant hesitated then decided to answer. 'Look,
Private, no one likes it. If you feel bad, imagine how the poor
bastard tied to the post will feel, or the buggers who have to
shoot him.'

'What's he done?' Edmund wanted to ask so much more.
Why they were executing one of their own? Who the man was?
How was his crime so terrible that it merited putting him to
death?

'The usual. Desertion. Or refusal to go over the top.' The
sergeant's face was expressionless. 'Got the wind up I suppose,
poor devil. Too daft to realise that no matter how frightening it
might be, it's better to take your chances out there against the
enemy than to face a firing squad from your own side.' He
stared into the distance. 'But some lads just can't think straight
out here. All those guns pounding away. Enough to turn anyone

crazy.' He shook his head, then walked away.

With a heavy heart Edmund tried to sleep that night but it was elusive. He couldn't help wondering who the man was and why the court martial had decided to take his life. What was the point?

The following morning, Edmund and his chosen fellow bearers marched back behind the lines to join the execution party. They kept their heads bowed, not wanting to look at the face of the weeping young soldier as they tied him to a wooden post and fixed a blindfold, so his features were partially covered. Edmund felt sick to the pit of his stomach.

Not a man – just a boy. Under the band tied around his eyes his pale skin was peppered with pimples. Through the silence of the early morning, he whimpered and called for his mother. It was clear he was one of the many boys who had volunteered to serve King and country. He had *chosen* to come to war. Only to lose his life for changing his mind once the reality bit.

Glancing sideways, Edmund saw the faces of the chosen firing squad, grim, jaws set as though willing themselves not to run away. One thing to cross a ruined landscape and fire at an anonymous German. Quite another to put one of your own to death.

Edmund closed his eyes. It was all too easy to imagine himself standing there, tied to that post. If he hadn't had the chance to serve in the RAMC might he too have been tempted to run away from the lines rather than march over the empty ground to fire upon strangers? And this boy had been a volunteer. No coercion. One of the Pals, eager to serve, until the stark cruel reality of war struck home.

Fortunately, there wasn't long to wait. Edmund watched as a chaplain, white cassock billowing in the breeze, said a final prayer and commended the boy's soul to God. The clergyman stepped back, and the guns cracked out. The young private crumpled, head lolling forward, a red stain seeping through the patch that had been attached to his tunic as a target.

The firing squad and the chaplain left, and Edmund and the other bearers moved to the now dead soldier. In silence they untied his bonds and laid him gently on the stretcher. Before they carried him away to bury him they took off his blindfold. The lad's eyes were squeezed tightly shut as though in the moment of death he had been wincing. Edmund touched his still warm forehead and fought back his own tears. What a waste of a young life. What a cruel ending for a boy who had probably set out to volunteer believing he was embarking on a great adventure.

Later, back in the trench with his unit, Edmund found Robert where he was leaning against a pit prop, smoking a cigarette, while nursing a tin mug of tea. The guns were silent.

'Where did you get to?' Robert's eyes narrowed as he looked intently at Edmund. 'I saw you leaving with some of your bearer buddies. They've been back for ages, but I didn't see you.'

'I wasn't good company.'

Robert snorted. 'We need to stick together, pal. Going off and brooding is a shortcut to hell. Everyone here is missing home. We need to keep each other's minds off it.'

Edmund looked up. 'I witnessed an execution today.' He sensed rather than saw Robert's reaction. A short intake of breath. A suppressed gasp. 'He was only a lad. Probably lied about his age in order to join up.'

'Bloody hell.'

'Apparently desertion or refusal to obey orders. Not sure which.' Edmund took the cigarette Robert proffered, grateful. 'He was calling for his mother and weeping. He wouldn't have been able to stand if he hadn't been tied to a post.' He drew on the cigarette, for once welcoming the bitter taste. 'And the poor bastards who had to do it. They tell them most of them have blanks. But you and I know the difference between firing a blank and the real thing. Anyone can tell.' He drew more smoke deep into his lungs and then expelled it slowly, watching it curl up in front of his eyes. 'How do you live with yourself after that?'

'You live with yourself, my friend, because otherwise you'd end up tied to a post like that waiting for another bunch of men to do the same to you. What choice do we have?' Robert took a gulp of tea then spat it out. 'Bloody petrol cans. Why the hell don't they clean them out properly before putting water in them? I'll never get used to the taste.' He wiped his hand across his mouth. 'How did you come to witness the execution?'

'Had to dispose of the body.'

'Christ. You poor devil.'

'Not as poor a devil as that lad.'

'Aye,' said Robert. 'Poor sod. And his poor mother.'

'I'm going to try and grab a couple of hours' shut-eye.' Edmund didn't want to talk anymore. He needed to be alone. Removing his helmet, he climbed into the dugout in the side of their trench. His mouth was dry and he could still taste the cigarette he'd just smoked. Every time he closed his eyes he knew he'd see again that boy's pimpled skin beneath his mask, see the thin shaking body as they tied him to the post and hear the anguished call for his mother.

TWENTY-ONE

Alice stood in the doorway of the cottage waving as Lottie turned into the lane and headed for school. Alice's heart ached for her stepdaughter. She slipped her hand in her pocket and felt for the piece of hair which she'd carefully wrapped in her handkerchief. Having promised the child not to involve Miss Trimble and the village school, Alice set off to speak to Viola Fuller.

As she walked, instead of her anger dissipating, it intensified. She dreaded confronting Viola but was enraged at what Molly had done and how Viola's loose talk had evidently fuelled the little girl's bullying.

It was starting to rain as she came in sight of the Fullers' cottage, so Alice was relieved to see smoke rising from the chimney. At least it wouldn't be a wasted journey.

There was no answer when she knocked on the door, so she lifted the latch and went inside.

The place was a mess. Dishes were piled in the sink, more dirty crockery sat on the table, where a cat was happily licking the remains of what looked like porridge from one of three bowls abandoned on the table. Alice looked around her, immediately thinking of Goldilocks and the Three Bears. She called out Viola's name.

The door to the bedroom opened and Viola emerged wearing a grubby-looking dressing gown, the baby in her arms, and the middle child, who by rights ought to have been at school, following behind.

'Oh, it's you, Alice,' she said. 'I thought I heard a knock at the door.'

'Are you unwell?' Alice looked around her at the mess. 'Can I help?'

Viola released a long sigh. 'I'm as well as I can expect to be with barely a penny to my name and a husband I'll likely never see again.' She glanced down at her attire and shrugged. 'What did you want, Alice?' Then forcing a smile she added, 'I'll put the kettle on if you can take the baby for a while.'

Viola handed over the child and moved towards the table where the cat was still lapping at the remains of breakfast. She grabbed it around the middle and swept it off onto the floor. 'Scoot!' The cat scuttled away into the bedroom.

Alice dandled the baby while watching Viola clear the dishes from the table to join the pile in the sink. Eventually she said, 'Is this a common occurrence? Not getting dressed I mean?'

'I told you. There's no point. I never go anywhere. Never see anyone.'

'You're seeing me now.' Alice tried to rein in her impatience.

Viola made a little snorting noise. 'I think you know me well enough not to be shocked by a dressing gown.'

'I'm not shocked by the dressing gown, but I'm worried that you don't see fit to put your clothes on. What about the children?'

'These two are too small to notice and Molly's at school.'

Alice drew a breath. 'Actually, Molly is the reason for me calling today.'

There. It was out.

Viola set the teapot on the table and signalled to Alice to sit down opposite her. 'What about her?' Her tone was concerned.

'She's been bullying Lottie.' No going back now.

Another snort from Viola. 'Molly's a *child*. She's not a bully.'

'Her age is irrelevant. Lottie's new to Little Badgerton and the school. She's lost her mother. Her father's at war and she's trying to find her feet. I was hoping Molly would be kind and help her settle in.' The baby wriggled on her lap and a noxious waft from a dirty nappy rose up. Viola seemed to be as sloppy in changing her baby as she was in changing her own clothes.

Viola was tight-lipped. 'For heaven's sake, children will be children.'

Alice had tried to hold back her own anger, but she could no longer hold her tongue. 'It's our responsibility as parents to show our children an example and teach them right from wrong. Not tell them rank untruths.'

'What the hell are you talking about? How dare you?' Viola reached out and snatched her baby back from Alice.

'Look, you need to know exactly what happened. There are two separate incidents.'

Viola turned to look at her. 'What incidents?'

'Molly told Lottie her father was going to die and that when that happens, I intend to send her away to an orphanage. There's only one person who could have suggested that to her.'

'And who might that be?'

'The same person who told her daughter that all men die when they are sent to France to serve their country.'

Viola folded her arms. 'I need to prepare Molly that her father might never come home.' She adjusted the bodice of her gown and put the baby to her breast. 'I'm certain Robert will be killed.' Her voice shook. 'But I never said anything about your husband. How many men from Little Badgerton are already dead? The postman tells me he delivers bad news nearly every day.' She looked straight at Alice. 'But I swear to God, Alice, I never mentioned an orphanage or the idea of you sending Lottie away.'

Alice wasn't convinced. Where else would Lottie have even heard the word orphanage? Certainly not from her. 'Lottie also mentioned that her grandfather murdered her mother. I'd been protecting her from finding that out. At least until the trial's over.'

'You think Molly heard that from me?' Viola's jaw dropped. 'Why in heaven's name would I tell my child that? Like you, I want to protect her from such dreadful things. I swear to God, Alice, I never said a word.'

'Might she have overheard you talking to someone else?'

'Gossiping, you mean? I never see anyone, other than you and the postman and I certainly don't have that kind of relationship with him.'

Alice still wasn't convinced but she didn't want to argue.

'Look, Viola, you and I have been friends for ages. Since I first came to Little Badgerton, and that's about eight years ago. I don't want to fall out. But I can't stand by while your daughter attacks mine. Pulling a hunk out of her hair.' She reached into her coat pocket and took out a piece of cloth which she unwrapped to reveal the dark glossy clump of Lottie's hair. 'This happened yesterday. I've chosen to handle this privately with you rather than involving Miss Trimble, but I need you to talk to Molly and put a stop to this aggressive behaviour.'

Viola looked at the lock of hair in horror. 'Did you see it happen? No, of course you didn't! You can't just come in here throwing accusations around. It could have been any of the children. Lottie probably accused Molly to be spiteful.'

'There's nothing spiteful about Lottie. And she didn't

accuse her. It slipped out.' She swallowed. This was proving to be harder than she'd expected. She was about to say something else then decided to stay silent and let Viola take it all in. She was bound to be defensive.

'I can't believe it,' said Viola at last. 'Molly isn't like that. She's a sweet child.' Then she squeezed her eyes shut and Alice saw she was crying.

Alice got up. 'Let me make that tea while you finish feeding the baby.' She moved over to the stove where the kettle had failed to boil. The fire was almost dying so she put in more wood and stoked it, returning the kettle to the hob. Behind her, Viola was sobbing. The woman was a veritable waterworks. Ever since Robert had left for military service, she had been a broken wreck. Alice suppressed her impatience and tried to summon up some compassion.

Viola looked up, a hand clutching her forehead. 'There's no milk! I meant to go over to the farm to get some, but I couldn't face it. The children had the last drops at breakfast.'

Later, when they sat opposite each other with milk-less tea in front of them, Alice broached the subject again.

'You won't like what I've to say but I'm going to say it anyway. You have to pull yourself together, Viola. You owe it to your children to do so.' She shook her head. 'What happened to my dear friend? The capable woman who kept a spotless home, who baked cakes for her children, who always had a smile on her face? I know you desperately miss Robert but that's true for all of us women whose husbands are at war. It's rotten. It's unfair. But we must go on. We need to for the sake of our children.'

Viola said nothing, but it was clear she was listening.

'It's not normal for a little girl to pull a chunk of hair out of another child's scalp. I'm not blaming Molly, because I think she only did it because she's unhappy. She must miss her daddy and you spending your days in bed weeping while the dishes pile up in the sink isn't helping.' Alice hated nagging her friend but willed herself to carry on. 'And the milk. You have to think of the little ones. It's no good saying you couldn't face going to the farm.' She bent forwards. 'Our men can't turn round and say they can't face it. They have no choice. Don't you see that?'

There was a muffled sob.

Alice wasn't going to give up. 'We've had this conversation before and you took no notice but please, listen to me now. Not for me. Not for Lottie. But for Molly. And for that little one.' She couldn't remember the baby's name. She looked across the room to where the small boy was curled up in an armchair, sucking his thumb. 'And for little Georgie there. Those children need their mother to be a safe harbour in a storm. They need food in their bellies and a clean home. They need smiles and encouragement. And most of all, Viola, they need hope. Hope that one day their father will come home. *You* must give them that hope. And yes, there will be days and nights when you feel desperate and hopeless – I have those too. But wait until you're alone. Cry into your pillow if you need to. But not in front of the children.'

'Have you finished?'

Alice blushed. 'Yes.' Had she gone too far?

Viola sighed. 'Gosh, the baby stinks. Time for a nappy change.' She gave Alice a wry smile. 'Assuming I can find a clean one. You're right. I need to do the washing today. And yes, I'll go over to the farm and pick up some milk.' She leant forward and touched the lock of Lottie's hair where it still lay on the table. 'I'm sorry about that. Lottie has such pretty hair. Poor Molly's needs washing. It's dull and matted. I expect she was jealous. I'm going to wash it for her tonight. Now I think about it, there's definitely something the matter with her. She's been silent and moody. Not her usual happy self.' She choked back a little sob. 'It's all my fault. You're right, Alice. Thank you. I needed someone to shake me up. But I promise you, I never mentioned an orphanage, nor did I mention that Lottie's grand-father is accused of murdering her mother.'

As Alice walked home, she decided she believed Viola. But if it wasn't Molly parroting her mother, who had put those ideas in her head and what had made a usually happy and placid child tear a hunk of hair out of another child's head?

TWENTY-TWO

'Victor! You're alive!' Lady Dalton fanned herself with her hand, before slumping into an armchair.

'Don't over-dramatise, Lavinia. We knew he was alive and recuperating in a military hospital.' Lord Dalton moved across the drawing room and pumped his son's hand. 'Welcome home, Victor.'

Lady Dalton wasn't appeased. 'Yes, but they said he refused to see us. He might as well have been dead for all he cares about us.'

Lord Dalton rolled his eyes and turned to be introduced to Maurice, who was hovering behind Victor.

'Maurice Kynaston, sir. We met briefly before. At your daughter's wedding.'

'Of course, Captain Kynaston. Forgive me.'

'What?' Lady Dalton's voice was a shriek. 'You went to her wedding, Neville?' Her eyes flashed anger as she turned on her husband. 'I told you it was out of the question. Behind my back! How could you?'

'You're neglecting our guest,' said her husband, ignoring the question.

There was a delicate cough from the rear of the room and the butler appeared at the doorway. 'Coffee for four, Your Ladyship?'

The baroness nodded, her expression still angry. Ignoring Maurice and her husband, she turned to face Victor again, when the butler had left. She patted the sofa beside her. 'I don't want to talk about your sister. Her disgraceful behaviour and failure to apologise for it renders her beneath my contempt.' She grasped her son by the sleeves of his uniform. 'Look at you. You look terrible, Victor. Why are you wearing a patch over one eye? And what's happened to your face? All those ugly scars.'

Victor glanced across to the armchair opposite where Maurice was now sitting near to Lord Dalton. He sensed the captain stiffen as his mother burst out so tactlessly.

'It may have escaped your attention, Mama, but we are at war. I sustained shrapnel injuries and among other things I lost the sight of one eye.'

She gasped. 'And the scars? Are you permanently disfig-ured? My beautiful boy! Oh, how am I to bear it?' She clutched a lace handkerchief against her mouth and gazed across at her husband. 'Neville! Say something.'

'What is there to say? Other than that we have a son we should be proud of.' He bent forward, looking keenly at Victor. 'And if he can bear to have lost an eye, I'm sure you ought to be able to do so.' Ignoring the tongue click from his wife, he addressed his son. 'I hear you've been decorated for gallantry. The Distinguished Service Order, no less.' His mouth set in a straight line. 'Was it very bloody for you, dear boy? Out there, I mean. We read the papers and Gallipoli must have been grim.'

'It was.'

The butler returned, bearing a tray of coffee and biscuits which he dispensed to each of them before leaving the room discreetly. Suddenly remembering her manners, Lady Dalton turned to address Maurice. 'Did you meet Victor out in Gallipoli, Captain? Is that where you lost your leg?'

Maurice smiled politely. 'We met in hospital. At Bankstone. I was injured at Loos.' Then pointedly, he added, 'I now assist your daughter, Mrs Cutler, in her work in stained glass. I couldn't wish for a better teacher.' Ignoring the curled lip of his hostess, he pressed on. 'Your son-in-law was kind enough to take me on as an assistant and now that he's serving in France, he asked me to continue to help Alice – I mean Mrs Cutler.'

Lady Dalton's mouth formed a tight bud. 'We don't speak of her in this house.'

Maurice looked down, clearly embarrassed. He brushed at the sleeve of his jacket nervously as if to remove a piece of non-existent fluff.

Victor turned to face his mother. 'Enough of this nonsense, Mama. It's time you got over your childish petulance towards Alice. After all, you schemed for her to marry Edmund Cutler, so you've finally got your way.'

'Not in front of a guest, Victor.' She looked pointedly across at Maurice.

Victor, angered that Maurice had been embarrassed this way, got up and strode to the fireplace. He leaned against the mantel. 'Unless you want to lose a son as well as a daughter, you'd better stop this. Alice doesn't deserve it.'

Lady Dalton pushed out her ample bosom and looked down her nose at her son. 'If you insist on airing all this in front of a stranger––'

'Maurice isn't a stranger. He's a dear friend.' Victor felt the anger bubbling inside him. It had been a mistake bringing Maurice here to this first visit. He'd hoped his friend's presence might have caused his mother to tone down her usual acerbity but he should have known better. He looked at his father. 'Why don't you speak up, Papa? Not only were you present at Alice's wedding, but I understand you gave her away.'

'What?' Lady Dalton's voice was shrill, almost a shriek. 'You did what, Neville?'

Lord Dalton sighed wearily and looked up at the ceiling. 'I don't speak up, Victor, as life would be unbearable if I did. Long ago I realised that taking the line of least resistance was the only way to live amicably with your mother.' He drew himself up in his seat. 'But since you seem intent on airing all our dirty linen, Lavinia, I admit it. I walked our daughter up the aisle and I've never felt prouder in my life. While I was there, I saw how happy she was. I was happy for her too but also for myself. I'd finally got my dear daughter back.'

Lady Dalton was about to interrupt but her husband shushed her.

'Not only that, I was also reconciled with my sister.' As though his own words were giving him courage, he pressed on. 'I've long felt ashamed about the estrangement from Eleanor. I was delighted to meet the Reverend Walter Hargreaves, Eleanor's beloved husband. The only sorrow I feel about this is down to my own shortcomings. I promised Alice and my sister that I would do my utmost to effect a reconciliation with you, but instead I've lacked the courage to stand up to you, Lavinia. And I feel deeply ashamed of myself as a result.'

As he spoke, Lady Dalton rose from the sofa and went towards the door. As she passed Maurice, she said, 'Forgive me, Captain Kynaston, but I have a nasty headache coming on.' She swept out of the room.

'I shouldn't have come,' said Maurice once she was gone. Turning to His Lordship, he added, 'I apologise for embarrassing you by mentioning we'd met at Alice's wedding.'

'Not at all. I'm glad it's out. She'll calm down soon enough.' Lord Dalton raised his hands palm out, in resignation. 'Once she realises she's on her own in this foolish vendetta she'll think again. Lavinia is ultimately a practical woman.' He rubbed his hands together. 'Now, Victor, tell me everything. I want to hear all about your war. But first what are your plans for the future? Not going back out there I hope.'

Victor glanced across at Maurice and tried to meet his eyes, to reassure him, but Maurice was looking the other way. Victor turned then to answer his father. 'I've taken a job with the Ministry of Munitions. Preparing reports. Statistics. Analysis. That kind of thing. It's part-time so I'll also be taking control of the brokerage. Talking of which, Papa, I'm restructuring your investment portfolio. It will be in safe hands again.'

Lord Dalton sighed. 'Marvellous news, but maybe over lunch we might discuss a little tip I received. A chap at my club told me about a marvellous new opportunity in self-lighting cigarettes. Says there's a fortune to be made if we get in quickly.'

Keen to scotch his father's worst financial excesses, Victor wanted to steer the conversation in a different direction. 'Let me have the details and I'll take a look, but generally speaking I'm going to take a cautious approach until the war's over.'

'Caution? Nothing was ever gained by being cautious, dear boy.'

'Herbert Cutler had that attitude I recall and look where it got him. Still behind bars awaiting trial while I'm now running the business.'

'Running the business?' his father echoed.

'Herbert asked me to take over until he's out of prison. I agreed as long as it's my name not his over the door.'

'Good show! But surely Herbert won't agree to that.'

'He doesn't have a lot of choice, Papa. He may well be dangling from the end of a rope after his case finally comes to trial. He needs the money to pay his very expensive barrister and I suspect also to delay the proceedings. He told me the trial was delayed because the war has slowed everything down but that doesn't seem to apply to your average murderer if there is such a thing.'

Lord Dalton looked bewildered. 'Is there? Such a thing?'

'If there is, it certainly isn't Herbert. Most murderers are husbands doing away with their wives and mostly with a cut-throat razor. Herbert will argue he had little or no reason to kill his daughter-in-law, and the fact that she hit her head allows him to argue it was a horrible accident.'

'Good Lord! You mean the bounder might get off?'

'I thought he was your friend, Papa.'

'Strictly business. And your mother never liked the man. Thought he was common. Not one of us.'

Victor refrained from pointing out that not so long ago Cutler had been a regular guest at Dalton Hall and Lord Neville Dalton and his wife had been all too eager for their only daughter to marry one of the Cutler sons. He looked over at Maurice and knew he couldn't put him through the protracted torture of lunching with his parents. The prospect of enduring more time with his mean-minded mother and his spineless father was too much. Far better to head back to town, grab something to eat at one of his favourite haunts then spend the rest of the day and the night in bed with Maurice.

Within half an hour they were in Victor's Morris Oxford heading into central London. He'd been relieved to find that his father hadn't sold the motor during his absence, and it was well polished, with a full tank of petrol.

'Sorry,' he said, squeezing Maurice's hand. 'The parents aren't easy at the best of times but that was particularly bloody. If I'd realised it would be that bad, I'd never have put you through the ordeal. But I genuinely thought they'd be pleased to see me and would have saved all their vitriol until an occasion when a guest wasn't present. I suppose all the time I've been away I'd forgotten how appalling my own parents could be.'

'No apologies needed. We're not our parents.' Maurice smiled at Victor and placed his hand on his knee.

It was like a bolt of electricity. Victor gave a sigh from deep inside. 'Let's skip lunch,' he said, his voice throaty with desire. 'Can you wait to eat tonight instead?'

'There's nothing I'd like more.'

Later the two men were lying in each other's arms.

'I've fallen in love with you,' Victor said at last, tangling his fingers in the captain's hair. 'There. I've admitted it.' He held his breath and waited for Maurice to reply.

'Was that hard to say?' Maurice rolled onto his side and fixed his gaze on Victor.

'I've never said it before. Not even to Gilbert.' He paused, heart pounding. 'I did love Gilbert. But I never told him so. Perhaps I was afraid. Then it was too late. I don't want to make that mistake again.' He kept his eyes fixed on Maurice, waiting. Never had Victor been laid so bare, so exposed, so vulnerable. He'd always had the upper hand. But now, as the silence between them stretched out like a chasm, Victor felt raw, as though his skin had been shed leaving nerves exposed.

Then Maurice spoke. 'I've loved you since the first time we spoke. I just didn't want to let myself believe that you might come to love me too. A man with one leg. A cripple. I've worried you might be toying with me. That I might just be a passing fancy for you.'

Victor gasped and pulled Maurice closer. 'Never! You're the love of my life. And as for your missing leg, I've never known you any other way.' He realised he was shaking. 'I'd do anything for you, Maurice. I want to be with you all the time. I hate that we have to live our private life in secret but when we're together I want you to know that I love you and I can't imagine being without you.'

Maurice gave a deep sigh. 'I love you too, my darling boy.'

.   .   .

The following morning, Victor reported for duty at the ministry
building near Charing Cross. He was given a private office,
sadly not overlooking the Embankment Gardens but with a
window onto an enclosed area populated only by ranks of
rubbish bins and numerous pigeons. Still, at least the office was
his alone. Mr Pointer issued him with a key and told him to lock
the door every time he went out since he was to be handling
material of a highly confidential nature, all of which must be
signed for and returned. As soon as the civil servant left, a clerk
knocked and entered, bearing a pile of brown folders, each with
a little card stapled to the top bearing the legend *Top Secret,
Classified Information. Not to be removed from the premises.*

Victor pulled out a chair, sat down behind the large wooden
desk and opened the first folder. Production statistics. Pages and
pages of them, each detailing individual items with columns
showing daily output rates. He ran a finger down the left-hand
column: shells of different types and specifications, bullets, a
series of numbered identifiers. Victor closed the folder and
pulled the next one towards him. It contained similar documents but for a different factory. He opened another file and
turned over the pages. More sheets indicating rates of rejects by
individual factory. He shuffled the three folders to the other
side of the desk and glanced through the rest of the tall stack.
More of the same. This cursory inspection showed only that
different factories produced different items and at variable rates
with varying levels of faulty products. There were also statistics
for each location that enumerated numbers of staff, rates of
absenteeism, costs of raw materials, labour costs and more.
Another folder appeared to list finished products, raw materials
and their costs by individual production facility and by date.
The list of customers and suppliers included Herbert Cutler.
But this was no surprise as the two men that had hired him had

made it clear he had been a significant player in the munitions market. How to make sense of all of this? It was like completing a giant jigsaw puzzle with entirely blank pieces. His job was to wrangle these numbers into order, find patterns and look for discrepancies. As he pondered the enormity of the task, the clerk returned bearing another pile and wordlessly set them down on the desk.

'I hope that's it?' Victor was starting to feel daunted – particularly as it was less than clear at this stage what he was looking for.

The clerk shook his head. 'There're two more boxfuls. You want them now, Lieutenant?'

His heart sinking, he said he did. As the clerk disappeared back into the bowels of the building Victor looked around him. At least there was plenty of floorspace. He decided the best way forward was to go through each folder, then once he knew all the various types of data and sources he was dealing with he'd lay them out on the floor and work through them systematically until the pattern emerged. This was going to be a long hard job. Yet he felt an eagerness to grapple with it. Somewhere in all these rows and columns of numbers was the evidence that would show whether and how Herbert Cutler had betrayed his country by deliberately buying and selling faulty arms.

Today was going to be the first of many long days. But Victor relished the challenge.

TWENTY-THREE

Alice left Viola's cottage feeling deflated. She was relieved that her friend had acknowledged the need for change but dispirited that Viola still maintained she had not been responsible for the nasty suggestion that Lottie was destined for an orphanage. Alice wanted to believe her. But how else had Lottie come up with the idea? And why had Molly torn a chunk out of her hair? Somehow Viola's claim that it was Molly's envy of Lottie's beautiful hair didn't ring true. Molly had never previously struck Alice as the type to do something so vicious for such a petty reason as her own hair looking scruffy. She hoped that at least it might prove to be a warning to Viola that her daughter needed her attention.

As she reached the top of the ridge, she turned her head to look in the direction of the coast. This morning was hazy so she couldn't see the English Channel. She paused, conscious of a sound she hadn't noticed before. Not birdsong. Not machinery. A soft distant noise, faint but constant. She strained her hearing to discern what it was. Then the realisation dawned. It was the sound of artillery.

How was that possible? How far away from the French

battlefields was she standing? How could that sound be so loud that it carried across the Channel? She felt her legs weaken and she sat, slumped against a tree trunk. Alice closed her eyes, wishing she could close her ears too. The sound she had strained to hear at first now seemed unavoidable. A faint thrum, incessant, almost an echo of a sound. Like a memory.

Instead of heading back to the studio, Alice had planned to call on Harriet but changed her mind and decided to go to see her aunt, rather than face the risk of Harriet being flippant about what had happened. She needed Eleanor's warmth and affection as well as her advice about Lottie.

There was a motorcar on the narrow, gravelled drive. Well-polished but with several scratches around the chassis, she recognised it as Colonel Fitzwarren's. She was about to turn around and return to the cottage, but Eleanor appeared at the landing window, banged on the glass and signalled for Alice to come in. The maid showed her into the drawing room. Eleanor came clattering down the stairs, gave her niece a radiant smile and embraced her. 'What a treat! I was just thinking how little I've seen of you lately, my dear.' She turned to the maid. 'Ivy, will you bring us a pot of coffee in the morning room, please. And some of that delicious shortbread you made yesterday.'

She grinned at Alice. 'I presume you saw Walter's new pride and joy on the driveway.'

'You mean the colonel's car? I was about to turn round and leave until you banged on the window.'

'It's not his anymore. He sold it to Walter for a song. It's a bit scratched as the old boy's eyesight's too poor to be driving and he's now got something much grander, along with a military chauffeur. He persuaded the army that his role as the head of the service tribunal merited him having a staff car. Ridiculous really. But Walter's pleased as Punch.'

Shortly after, fortified with refreshments, they shared news with each other. Eleanor, as the vicar's wife, was well informed as

to all the comings and goings in Little Badgerton. They spoke of
the latest efforts of the knitting circle who were producing socks
and scarves for the men at the front at a prodigious rate. Eleanor
mentioned the tensions between Miss Trimble, the schoolteacher,
and Miss Pendleton, who played the organ at St Margaret's. Both
had been stalwarts of the local women's suffrage group and while
Miss Trimble had thrown herself wholeheartedly into the war
effort, Miss Pendleton harboured resentment over Mrs
Pankhurst's suspension of activities for the duration of the war.

'Miss Pendleton doesn't support Mrs Pankhurst's belief that
women should assume jobs previously done by men in order to
free them up to serve in the army.'

'Why not?'

'She claims that rather than demonstrating that women are
just as capable as men and hence incontrovertibly should be
given equal rights, it will cause resentment when men return.
Women will have been taken advantage of only to return to
their previous state of servitude and none of this will bring the
vote nearer.' Eleanor finished eating a piece of shortbread then
wiped the crumbs from her mouth. 'Whereas Miss Trimble
maintains that Miss Pendleton has no desire to do work of any
nature so is seeing the suspension of action as merely an excuse
for delay.'

Alice shook her head. 'Miss Pendleton wasn't exactly an
activist before the war. She only joined the group when Walter
encouraged her to do so.' Putting down her coffee cup, she
grinned. 'I've always suspected Miss Pendleton nurses a secret
crush on your husband, Eleanor.'

Eleanor smiled. 'You're probably right. She's a terrible
organist but refuses to relinquish her position to anyone else.
I'm sure it's just so she can enjoy a few minutes alone with
Walter each week to discuss the choice of hymns. It's unchari-
table of me but she plays everything at a funereal pace. She

even makes "All Things Bright and Beautiful" sound like a dirge.'

As the two women chatted, the rain drummed against the windows. Alice thought of Edmund and wondered whether it was raining in France. She was unsettled by what she was certain had been the sound of distant guns. Where was he now? Was he in danger? Was he wounded? Afraid? Or – she tried to push this thought away – already dead? For the sound of bombardment to travel such a distance it must be truly thunderous and terrifying over there. She shuddered.

'What's wrong, Alice?' Eleanor's face was full of concern.

'Perhaps it's my imagination. But I was up on the Hangers – there's a viewpoint up there where I like to go – and I thought I could hear it.'

'Hear what?' Eleanor frowned.

'The sound of battle. Gunfire, cannon or whatever it is, explosions. It was very faint, like the rumble of faraway thunder. Do you think I was imagining it?'

Eleanor shook her head. 'Sadly, I don't.' She hesitated. 'Walter was speaking on the telephone this morning to a colleague. This chap, another clergyman who was at Oxford with him, happened to mention that while walking his dog on Hampstead Heath he'd heard it too. In fact, he said he felt the ground vibrate under him.'

Alice made a little choking sound. 'How is that possible?'

'The Heath is high ground, like the Hangers. I asked Walter, and he said something about atmospheric conditions. The chap claimed to have heard it clearly – a low rumble. But his dog must have heard it more clearly as it got quite upset and was running around in circles barking.'

'Oh, God!' Alice sucked in her lips. She could barely breathe. What must Edmund be going through?

The telephone in the hall rang out and Eleanor excused

herself and went through to answer it. She left the door open so Alice couldn't help hearing.

'Yes, my name is Eleanor Hargreaves. Yes, I am His Lordship's sister. Oh no. When? How? Thank you, Thornton.'

There was a pause and Alice's skin began to crawl.

'Does Mr Victor know? Where is he? I'm so sorry—' Eleanor's voice was shaky.

Unable to sit waiting, Alice jumped up and rushed into the hallway where she wrenched the earpiece from her aunt's hands. She bent forward and spoke into the tube. 'Thornton, is that you? What's happened? Tell me.'

The butler was hesitant, evidently searching for appropriate words to break the news, but Alice knew at once her father was dead. It was too cruel. After the years of estrangement, he had been taken from her too soon. She'd spent so little time with him and now there would be no more.

'Where's Lady Dalton? Can you put her on the telephone?' Alice tried to keep her voice steady. She took a breath, drawing the air deep into her lungs. She had to keep calm. She mustn't give way to sorrow. Not yet.

The butler told her that her mother was unable to speak. 'Her Ladyship is very distressed, Miss Alice. Sorry, I mean, Mrs Cutler. I am unable to reach Mr Victor. I telephoned his residence at Albany but there was no reply. I've tried to reach him in the office in the City but the clerk informed me he's not there.'

'Send for the doctor, Thornton. It sounds as though Her Ladyship is in shock and needs a sedative. My brother has a new job with the Ministry of Munitions so no doubt he will be there. Leave it with me. I'll find him.' She clutched at this opportunity for action – she didn't want to think about her father's death.

'The doctor's already here. I sent for him as soon as I found His Lordship. He's preparing the death certificate.'

'Put him on the telephone please, Thornton.' Alice was surprisingly calm. When the doctor came on the line he told her Lord Dalton had suffered a massive heart attack and had died immediately. 'At least he didn't suffer, Miss Dalton.'

'It's Mrs Cutler,' she said, then asked him about a bromide for her mother. 'I'll be there as soon as I can.'

When she had hung the earpiece back on the stand, she turned to Eleanor. 'I need to go at once.' As she spoke, she realised she was shaking.

'I'll come with you. Neville is my brother.'

'Thank you, Eleanor.' She flung her arms around her aunt. 'I need to run next door and ask Harriet to look after Lottie.'

'While you do that, I'll ask Walter to drive us to the station. What about Victor?'

Alice didn't know where exactly he worked or how to get hold of him. 'We could send a telegram to the War Office, but I've no idea which department. They're spread across a lot of buildings.' Then something occurred to her. 'May I use the telephone again?'

Alice waited impatiently for the operator to connect her. She knew she might be making erroneous assumptions, but she had a feeling that one person would know where Victor was.

'Mr Whall? Thank goodness. This is Alice Cutler, Edmund's wife. Is Captain Kynaston there? I need to find my brother urgently to inform him of the death of our father.' She paused for a moment as Whall expressed his condolences, before interrupting. 'I'm hoping the captain will know his whereabouts as they travelled up to London together a couple of days ago.'

The next hours passed in a blur for Alice as she and Eleanor travelled to Richmond on the train. It hadn't sunk in properly that Papa was dead. That no longer would she see the twinkle in his eye as he spoke of some crazy and inevitably loss-making financial scheme. Never again would she have cause to be annoyed at his frequent failure to stand up to her mother. But she sent up a silent prayer of gratitude that they had been reconciled and he had walked her up the aisle at her wedding – the happiest day of her life.

Alice stared out of the train window. Drizzle. The rear view of ugly brick terraced houses stained black by coal smoke, warehouses, factories, chimney stacks, gas holders. The urban landscape reflected the darkness of her mood, the rising sense of despair and hopelessness. As the train thrummed along, she remembered the sound she'd heard at the top of the Hangers that morning. The faint auditory trace of heavy bombardment. Alice felt caught in a limbo between her husband on those distant battlefields and her father now lying dead at the end of this journey.

As though sensing her desire for silence, Eleanor said nothing. As his sister, she too would be grieving Neville Dalton's death. Alice's wedding had marked a reconciliation for her as well – after many years. And now poor Eleanor would have to face Alice's mother for the first time since she'd left Dalton Hall as a young pregnant girl, decades ago, estranged from her brother and banished by Her Ladyship. Would the passage of time and the shared loss of Lord Dalton finally effect a rapprochement? And would it do so also for Alice herself? She didn't want to remember the last time she'd set eyes on her mother – when Lady Dalton had spoken cruelly about Alice's ill-fated pregnancy. Surely now, united in grief, mother and daughter could be reconciled.

It was late afternoon when they arrived at Dalton Hall. Maurice must have succeeded in his mission, as Victor was drinking coffee in the drawing room. There was no sign of Lady Dalton.

Alice rushed over to embrace her brother. 'Thank goodness you're here. I had a feeling Maurice would know where you were.'

Victor looked at her guardedly but said nothing. He put down his cup and rose to greet his aunt.

They discussed what had happened. Victor had established that Lord Dalton had eaten a hearty breakfast, announced he was going to read the morning papers in the library and an hour later Thornton had discovered him slumped in his armchair, already dead, when he'd arrived with a tray of mid-morning coffee. According to the butler Lady Dalton had become hysterical.

'Where is Mama now?' Alice asked.

'Lying down in her room. She refused the sedative the doctor offered.' Victor sighed. 'Clearly, she's in shock but I suspect the histrionics are Mama being Mama. I've always felt she missed her vocation as a stage actress.'

'What happens next?' Eleanor unpinned her hat, removed it and placed it beside her on the sofa. 'I'd like to be useful.'

Victor nodded and crossed his legs. 'Thank you. I think we should arrange the funeral for as soon as possible. Papa will be interred here in the family mausoleum of course. The undertakers are due in half an hour to measure for the coffin and discuss the arrangements. I was thinking we could organise it for three to four days' time. Thornton is pulling together a list of names from Papa's address book.' He looked at Eleanor. 'Perhaps you could organise the announcement in *The Times*.'

Eleanor looked up at him. 'Walter has offered to conduct the service. But of course, I'll understand if—'

'That would be perfect. If you agree, Alice?'

Alice, surprised and glad that he was seeking her view, nodded. 'Perfect. And most thoughtful of Walter to offer. I know Papa would have liked that. He and Walter got on so well at my wedding.' She felt her lip quiver, then swallowed and pulled herself together.

Victor continued. 'There's his club to be informed. And the House of Lords. I'll deal with them both.'

'Gosh, Victor, you're the baron now. The new Lord Dalton.' Alice made a grimace. It was hard to believe that so much could change in just a few hours. 'Dalton Hall will be yours.'

'Let's not rush ahead of ourselves. We'll wait until the will's read.' Victor ran a hand through his hair.

'The will won't change anything as far as the barony is concerned. Primogeniture.'

Before her brother could answer, the door was flung open, and Lady Dalton swept into the room. She was wearing black – a full length day dress with a high neckline encrusted with tiny jet pearls. Her hair was immaculately coiffed. There was no sign of the hysteria she had apparently shown earlier. Victor was right. Already Lavinia Dalton had assumed a new role.

She pulled up short, taking in Alice and Eleanor. 'What are you doing here?' She turned to Victor. 'Thank heavens you've come, Victor. But who told them? They're not welcome here.'

Victor got up from the armchair he was occupying and went to stand in front of the fireplace. 'Stop that immediately, Mama. Alice and Aunt Eleanor have every right to be here. They are grieving a father and brother.' He narrowed his eyes and fixed his gaze on his mother. 'As Alice has just reminded me, I'm now the head of this house and they are both welcome. Indeed, it's thanks to Alice that I'm here at all. She managed to track me down.' He turned and smiled at his sister. And, unobserved by their mother, winked in reassurance.

Lady Dalton's face was like a gorgon's, capable of turning the objects of her gaze to stone. She went to sit in her habitual high-backed armchair and glared at Alice and Eleanor. 'I acknowledge that it is now your right to invite who you please into my home, Victor, but don't expect me to be pleased at that.' She adjusted the parramatta silk of her skirt and sat bolt upright, her hands crossed in her lap, the picture of the grieving widow.

Alice remembered the last time she'd seen her mother, when she'd been pregnant with Edmund's child, the baby whose stillbirth was still an open wound to Alice.

Evidently her mother's thoughts were of the same occasion, as she said, 'I heard you lost the child. Just as well since you weren't married then.'

The cruelty was shocking. Even Alice had expected her mother to show some compassion for her at losing a child – and now for losing a father.

No one said anything. The three of them, stunned, stared in disbelief at Lady Dalton.

Alice and Eleanor exchanged glances. But it was Victor who spoke in response. 'If you ever say anything so vicious and unfeeling to Alice again you will no longer remain under my roof, even though you're my mother. It's time you started acting like one.'

Alice wanted to cheer. She hadn't expected such definitive support from her brother. He had once disowned her himself and blamed her for the death of Gilbert Cutler, but now he reached out his hand to Alice and took hers as she stood beside him at the fireplace.

Lady Dalton's face was disfigured by the ugliness of her scowl.

Eventually Alice, exasperated, spoke. 'It's been a long time, Mama. We need to let bygones be bygones. Now, of all times, we ought to heal the wounds of the past.' She sensed her voice quavering and paused to steady it with a lungful of air. 'I'm thankful that Papa and I were reconciled before he died. He and Aunt Eleanor too. I was deeply sorry that you weren't present to share the joy of my wedding day, but I would like us all to stand together as a family as we lay Papa to rest. It's what he would have wanted.'

'How do you know what he wanted? He barely knew himself if I didn't tell him.'

Alice felt Victor squeeze her hand and was grateful he was still holding it. She saw he was about to speak but instead gave her a nod to continue. 'Perhaps if you'd listened to him more, he might have had a chance to tell you, Mama. He told me that nothing would make him happier than that we were a united family once more.'

Victor nodded in agreement. 'You were here in this very room, Mama, when Papa said how he felt about all this. He told you he'd never felt prouder than the day he walked up the aisle with Alice on his arm.'

Alice could barely breathe.

Victor looked at his aunt. 'Eleanor too. Alice is right. It's time to let bygones be bygones. It's years since Aunt Eleanor left Dalton Hall. Or more accurately was banished by you. You have a simple choice now. Either accept that this is how things will be or leave here and take your misery elsewhere. I can make sure you have a small allowance to make that possible. What will it be, Mama?'

Lady Dalton declined to answer. Instead, she rose imperiously from her chair, threw a venomous look at her sister-in-law and sailed out of the room.

When the door had closed behind her there was a universal sigh of relief. 'That went well,' said Victor in an attempt at levity.

Alice released her brother's hand and went to join her aunt. 'I'm sorry you had to endure that, Eleanor.'

The older woman gave her a weak smile. 'I hoped for a better reception, but I can't say I'm surprised, sadly.'

'Give her time,' said Victor. 'She's just lost her husband. Or rather she's lost her identity. She needs to find another role to play.'

Later that evening, Alice swallowed her pride and went to talk to her mother, who had been absent at dinner. Alice knocked tentatively on the bedroom door.

Inside, she found her mother sitting up in bed reading *The Tatler*. Lady Dalton removed her spectacles, lowered the magazine and pinioned Alice with narrowed eyes. 'Yes?'

'I thought it was time we talked, Mama. Especially now that we're together in such sad circumstances.'

Her mother said nothing, continuing to subject Alice to a gimlet gaze.

'Isn't it time to let bygones be bygones? After all, we fell out in the first place when your efforts to marry me off to Edmund failed. Since he and I found each other in the end, surely you should be pleased that your hopes for us finally came to pass.'

She was standing awkwardly at the side of the bed and when her mother failed to offer her a seat she decided to perch on the edge. Lady Dalton pointedly shuffled sideways increasing the distance between them.

Her Ladyship answered in a frosty tone. 'My hopes were for you to make a good marriage. That involved Edmund Cutler joining his father's brokerage firm and eventually inheriting the Cutler fortune. Instead, he is now a common artisan. What's more, rather than benefiting from his father's wealth, he has linked this noble family to that of a murderer.'

'You can't blame Edmund for what his father may or may not have done. And the man has yet to come to trial.'

Her mother visibly shuddered. 'You have been my greatest disappointment in life, Alice.'

Her mother's cruelty hurt, but she decided not to rise to it – she knew she was baiting her. 'I'm sorry to hear that. I never set out deliberately to disappoint you, Mama. I've followed my heart and I have no regrets. I married a man I admire and love deeply. I never imagined I would feel this way about another person. But I love him with a passion.'

'Don't be vulgar, Alice.'

'What do you mean? Vulgar?'

'Only the lower orders indulge in such nonsense. Marriage is a contract. A business arrangement. It has nothing to do with *passion*.' Her face contorted in distaste as she spoke the last word.

'I'm sad that you feel that way.' As she said this, Alice realised she did indeed feel sad for her mother. Lady Dalton had never known the soaring joy of falling in love and of being loved in return. 'I feel truly blessed. Not only with my darling Edmund but thanks to him I now have a stepdaughter I adore.'

Her mother sniffed. 'Victor told me you lost the illegitimate baby.'

Alice swallowed, hating to hear the beloved son, who'd never so much as breathed, described in that way. 'When my son was stillborn, it broke my heart. Every day I think of him. Every day I feel the pain. But every day I also thank God for the happiness I get from Edmund and Lottie. Do you begrudge me that, Mama? Do you really?'

She looked at her mother, who was now avoiding her eyes. 'The happiest day of my life was the day I married Edmund, and it was made even happier by the wonderful surprise gift of Papa's presence. I would have loved you to be there too, Mama.' She felt the tears rising. 'For Papa's sake, can't you find it in your heart to accept me?'

Alice swallowed. It was hard to be a supplicant when her mother was so unbending. Her pride stuck in her throat, but she swallowed again, thinking of her father, of Edmund, of Victor. 'I'm sorry for running away all those years ago without saying goodbye. I was young. I was headstrong. I ask your forgiveness now.' She wanted to make a plea on behalf of Eleanor too, but that was perhaps a step too far. It was up to Lady Dalton herself now to show some leeway, to bend a little. Eleanor was her sister-in-law, and any perceived wrongs were lost now in the passage of the years.

Lady Dalton looked away, then said, 'Dear heavens. It's going to be such a bore wearing black all the time. Do you think I need to? Obviously for the funeral, of course. But I understand these days it's no longer *de rigueur* to observe mourning dress for a year.' She picked up her copy of *The Tatler*. 'There's a piece in here that says since the war began it's positively unpatriotic to wear black. What do you think, Alice?'

Alice breathed. It seemed mother-daughter business had been resumed. 'I never thought black was your best colour, Mama. And Papa wasn't terribly keen on it. If *The Tatler* says it's acceptable to wear other colours, then I think you should. I'm sure Papa would have approved.'

'You think so?'

'I do.'

'Splendid. Now I need to rest. Tomorrow will be a long day.'

TWENTY-FOUR

He remembered how back at Browndown Robert had warned him that the waiting was a huge part of this war. Edmund occupied his time sketching the other men, capturing scenes from all around him in the hinterland of the Somme battlefield.

For many, the boredom was worse than the gut-clenching fear of an attack. Edmund sat on a pile of sandbags sketching the men alongside him, a sea of khaki, the domes of helmets, dirty stubbled faces, big, frightened eyes or the blank stares of men dreaming of the unreality of home. Among them were men who had survived earlier forward sallies, some whose hands shook, spilling tea from metal mugs or failing to connect their cigarettes with matches. Around them lamps flickered, voices whispered, candles stuttered.

It was a calm night, clouded. The kind of moonless night that made a mission forward under cover of darkness more likely. Somewhere in the distance Edmund saw the bright green flash of a flare shoot upwards. It was ominously quiet.

There was no avoiding the stink though. A heady mix of stale odour from bodies encased in unwashed khaki, the lingering smell of cordite, the waft from the latrines, horse manure, the gut-churning reek of the dead, decaying out in No Man's Land, the more welcome aroma of brewing coffee and the sharp tang of petrol and engine oil.

Edmund put away his pencil and notepad, tucking them safely inside his first aid bag, and accepted a mug of tea from Robert Fuller, who squatted down beside him to share a sandbag. 'Quiet tonight.' Robert's voice sounded unnaturally loud amidst the silence of the trench.

'Eerily so.'

Robert tapped a finger against Edmund's drawing pad. 'Don't you ever run out of things to draw? There's nothing here.' Robert looked around him. 'Everything's the same colour. Dirty brown. Uniforms, sandbags, wooden props, canvas. I don't get how you want to keep on drawing.' He shook his head and reached into his pocket and pulled out a pack of Woodbines. Lighting one, he grinned. 'I finally heard from Viola today. Was beginning to think it'd never happen.'

'What? She hadn't written at all until now?'

'That could be a slight exaggeration,' he acknowledged. 'But she certainly hasn't made much effort. If I didn't know her better, I'd have thought she'd found another man.' He gave a dry laugh.

'I'm glad you heard today. That must lift your spirits.'

'A parcel too.' Robert lowered his voice. 'I don't want all these gannets to know, but you and I, my friend, will be sharing tinned sardines, a jar of Bovril, a couple of chocolate bars and a can of condensed milk.' He licked his lips. 'There's also a pair of socks which I'm saving as a treat. How about you?'

'Alice writes all the time, but she's warned me she may be a bit slow with the parcels of comforts for a while as her father's died.'

'That's rough. For her I mean. Losing her father. Well, for you too if it means the parcel deliveries slowing down.' Robert blew a smoke ring. 'It's queer, isn't it? Imagining them back there, doing the same old things, in the same old places. Ordinary things like going to the grocers, cooking food, dressing and bathing the children, reading the papers. What would you do if you could be back there now?' He grinned and made a mildly lewd gesture. 'Apart from the obvious, that is.'

'I'd walk in the woods. Climb up to my favourite viewpoint up in the Hangers.' Edmund leant back against the wall of the trench, legs stretched out before him. 'Alice mentioned the strangest thing in her letter today. She reckons she could hear the guns. I worked out it must have been on the thirtieth of June, the day before they went over the top. The bloody awful sound of the bombardment. Can you imagine? All the way to Hampshire. She says someone her uncle knows even heard it up on Hampstead Heath.'

'The power of imagination. Sound can't travel that far.'

'I asked one of the medics. He says it can if the conditions are right. And you must agree, my friend, it was loud enough to herald Armageddon.'

'True.' Robert removed his tin hat and scratched his head. 'You pick up any rumours about us going over?'

'Only that they're unlikely to repeat what happened back on day one. No more Big Pushes. The idea now is to confuse the enemy by varying the tactics. Focusing the attack on different places. Keeping them on their toes.'

Robert gave a derisive snort. 'They really think they know what they're doing, don't they? Bunch of deluded idiots.'

'Maybe. But at least they've realised sending us like lemmings over a clifftop is never going to work.' He gave a resigned sigh. 'These days I'm thankful for small mercies.'

'Every day I don't have to climb up that ladder and walk into a rain of death I'm thankful.' Robert lit up another cigarette.

'Anyone told you that you smoke too much?'

'No, but it seems you are.'

'Only because I care for your well-being, my friend.'

'So thoughtful of you to worry about me getting a sore throat when oddly enough all I care about is having my head blown off and my guts strewn like bunting on the barbed wire.' He screwed his eyes tightly closed. 'Oh, God, I'm so bored.'

As soon as the words were out, they noticed a young man resting against the top of the trench ladder, looking out over No Man's Land, protected by the cover of darkness. In a moment of inattention or bravado, or a complacent lapse of memory, the lad struck a match for a cigarette. Before they could shout a warning there was a whistling sound and his head exploded in front of them, covering their faces in fragments of skull and brain tissue and blood.

Edmund gagged. Just a moment ago the chap had been alert, aware, a sentient being, with a future. But that future had been fractions of a second. The horror of what had happened sank in, the sticky feel of the contents of the lad's skull plastered across his face, when there was an explosive sound and a shower of soil burst upwards, covering Edmund's eyes and blinding him. He lurched backwards and more earth and sand from burst sandbags poured over him like lava from a volcano, as the dugout behind them collapsed. Was this it? Was this how it would end? Still blind, he was a mole, burrowing in darkness, eyes on fire, body numb, disorientated. Panic set in. Was he dead? Dying? Where was up and where was down? No breath. Crushed under the weight of the ballast. Throat closed, nose blocked. Mouth desert dry. Choking. Coughing. Darkness.

Just as he thought it was over and he was done for, desperately sending mental messages to Alice, wishing he'd spent more time on his letters to her and less on his sketching, he was aware of a chink of light, the sensation of scraping. Something blunt and heavy sent a shaft of pain through his leg. Then the weight lifted and he realised he was lying on his back under a black sky with a light shining into his eyes.

Hands pulled at him, heaving him upright, freeing him from suffocation under the collapsed dugout. Faces looked down at him. He turned his head and spat, clearing his mouth of the soil and sand mixture. He gagged then coughed up more debris. As he was raised upright into a sitting position the coughing got worse, so there was no time to breathe between the fits. His lungs were on fire. Someone thumped him on the back. Instinctively his hands swept across his face which was sticky with blood. Then he realised it wasn't his own, but what remained of the young soldier. Squinting through stinging eyes he saw the blood and tissue smeared over his fingers where he'd brushed his face. He gagged again. Someone wiped the mess off with a damp cloth and he was thankful. It would have felt wrong to rub away what were the remains of a man he'd been speaking to just a matter of minutes ago, even if it had been only a short exchange of greetings. As he started to reorientate to his surroundings, he pressed his fists again into his eyes, rubbing the debris away. Where was Robert?

He knelt, trying to dig with his hands blindly through the collapsed heap of earth that was the exploded dugout. Was Robert trapped? Hands gripped his shoulders, holding him back.

'Have to find him.' Like a badger digging his sett, he scrabbled in the ground sending loose soil in every direction. He was hauled back, still struggling. 'He's under there. We've got to get him out!'

'He's dead. Lad didn't stand a chance. Smoking at the top of a fire step. Poor wee fool.' The voice had a faint Scottish burr. One of the corporals.

'Not him. I mean Fuller. My pal. He must be buried under the dugout.' Edmund fought against the arms that were holding him. 'Hurry! He could be alive.'

'Very much alive.' A familiar voice. Coming from behind

him. Edmund realised one of the men restraining him was Robert himself. 'You took the brunt of it, Edmund.'

A wave of relief mixed with anger swept through him. Then he passed out.

'Gave me quite a scare, pal. But the MO's had a look at you and reckons you'll live.'

'Where am I?' Edmund was lying on his back on a camp bed. There was a canvas roof above him, and he could sense it was now daylight. He turned his head and saw Robert at the bedside.

'You're in an aid post. Just behind the lines. How are you feeling?'

Edmund gave the question some thought, then said, 'Relieved. I thought I'd died.'

'You remember what happened?' Robert looked concerned.

'That lad on the fire step lit a cigarette and a sniper blew his head off. Then not much else. I thought I was drowning but there was no water.'

'A shell blew up the dugout near where we were sitting. You took the brunt of the collapse. Swallowed a ton of soil and sand. And you had that poor bastard's brains in your eyes as well. But they've given you a good clean-up and washed your eyes out.' Robert patted him on the arm. 'You had a lucky escape, my friend.'

Edmund tried to sit upright and swing his legs off the bed.

'Steady on there. You're not going anywhere yet. The doc wants to keep an eye on you till tomorrow. Then I'm afraid it's back to the rats and wet feet with the rest of us.' Robert got up from where he had been squatting on his haunches beside the canvas bed. 'See you tomorrow.' He raised his thumb to Edmund then ducked through the low opening in the tent and disappeared.

TWENTY-FIVE

Victor was feeling overwhelmed. After his father's funeral, the will reading confirmed that the entirety of his father's estate was to pass to him. There was provision for Lady Dalton to remain at Dalton Hall but beyond that, the assumption was that she would now be dependent on her son. This detail did not appear to make any difference to Her Ladyship, who continued to behave with an imperious manner and clearly saw herself as mistress of Dalton Hall.

Now that he had full access to the estate accounts, it was apparent to Victor that since Herbert Cutler's remand to prison, the late Lord Dalton's financial affairs had received no expert attention. Oddly, the war had not had an entirely negative impact on the investments. Indeed, many British industries were doing well out of the conflict. The armaments business was of course booming due to the insatiable demand for munitions for the Western Front, but many other industries were also benefiting from the war. Victor had been amused by a cartoon in *Punch* satirising the way companies were advertising their products as essential to every man on the front. An infantryman was depicted in front of a vast pile of products, from hair cream and bloater paste to gramophone players and toffee. The caption declared that this was an average Tommy with the goods that advertisers claimed were indispensable to a soldier at the front. Now, as Victor ran through the list of his father's shares, it included many of those featured products – and the dividends indicated they were proving sound investments. Whatever else he thought of Herbert Cutler, he knew how to pick a strong stock.

The administration of Dalton Hall was no small matter. As he perused the accounts, Victor realised that despite his late father's air of idleness, he had done a solid job as far as oversight of the estate was concerned. Rents had been collected on time, debtors pursued, and the sale of some former grazing land for housing development had generated a healthy injection of capital. There was also an arable farm in Essex that, despite some challenges with labour shortages at the start of the war, was now delivering a steady income, thanks to the influx of land girls and a constant demand for grain to feed the troops.

But when Victor had agreed to take on the job with the Ministry of Munitions in addition to revitalising what was now Dalton Associates, he hadn't anticipated his father's demise and the consequent significant increase in his own workload. He felt submerged by the enormity of the tasks in front of him.

There was Maurice to think of too. The few precious nights they had shared at Albany, until his father's death, had cemented his feelings for the captain. As the new Lord Dalton, Victor would be expected to spend some of his time in residence here at Dalton Hall. How could he incorporate Maurice, the work for the War Office and the brokerage into that arrangement? He certainly wouldn't have time to take up his seat in the House of Lords among the slumbering old peers and bishops.

Soon Captain Kynaston would be returning to rejoin Alice in Little Badgerton. The dream of him then finding employment in a London glass studio or learning carpentry and living secretly with Victor at Albany felt increasingly unattainable. It was maddening for Victor to have finally found love only for life to get in the way.

The morning after the funeral, Victor decided to talk to his sister. They met in what had been their father's study, with its Chinese wallpaper, oversized oak desk and windows looking onto the herb garden.

He couldn't possibly tell Alice about his feelings for Maurice – although he sensed she may have her suspicions – but he could unburden himself about his other concerns. Could he persuade her to give up the Bankstone studio and relocate to Dalton Hall where she could assist him with the oversight of the estate?

Alice was unequivocal. 'I wish I could help you, Victor, but I promised Edmund I'd complete the commission we're working on. I can't walk away from it now. It would feel like a betrayal.' She clutched her hands together and looked up at Victor as though appealing for his understanding. 'Then there's Lottie too. She's already been unsettled. Losing her mother so tragically. Edmund going away. Adapting to the local school. I can't uproot her again. Children at that age need stability – and Lottie in particular, given what she's been through. Not to mention that I persuaded Harriet to move to Little Badgerton. It would be cruel to abandon her there just as she and her children are adjusting to their new circumstances.'

Harriet. Her financial position was another thing to add to the long list of Victor's responsibilities. Why had he agreed to look at her affairs and put them in order? He'd advised her regarding the London property but he'd yet to take a proper look at her income and how to manage it. He ran his fingers through his hair and closed his eyes in despair.

Alice stretched out her hand and squeezed his wrist gently.

'I'm sorry, Victor, but I'm sure you'll manage to sort this all out. You're so capable. Couldn't you sell the brokerage as a going concern and concentrate on the War Office job and the Dalton estate? I'm sure Herbert Cutler would welcome the money if you're right about him spending a fortune on his defence costs.' She bit her lip and said, 'Besides, it looks a pretty cut and dried case that he killed poor Dora. At best he may be able to get the charges reduced to manslaughter, but Edmund told me that means a long custodial sentence. He could well die in prison.'

'I don't trust the man an inch.' Victor got up and walked over to the window. He looked out over the herb garden, neglected since the gardeners had volunteered for the army. Beyond the redbrick wall of the kitchen garden, he could see the roof of the garden shed. It was where he'd had his last tryst with Gilbert Cutler before Alice had walked in on them and triggered Gilbert's suicide. Now that he was in charge of the estate, one of the first things he intended to do was get that shed torn down.

He turned back to face Alice. 'I visited Herbert in Pentonville and he appeared confident he'll get off the charges. He intends to plead not guilty.' Victor joined his sister on the sofa. Taking her hand in his, he said, 'Please, Alice. I need your help.'

'I have to finish the Latchington window. The end is in sight. Once that's done, I'll think it over. When Lottie's more settled and assuming Edmund agrees, I'll consider moving back here to Dalton Hall.' She removed her hand from his grip. 'But no promises, Victor.'

Rather than take the train back to Hampshire, Alice and Eleanor accompanied Walter, who, to Lady Dalton's ill-concealed disgust, had officiated at Lord Dalton's funeral. The baroness had assumed the part of the grieving widow with

aplomb, standing ramrod straight to receive the line of mourners, projecting an air of tragic dignity. She studiously avoided
her sister-in-law but was not overtly rude. One day at a time,
thought Alice.

The party from Little Badgerton travelled home in the
vicar's Standard car. Alice would have preferred the train to the
squashed conditions and the bone-rattling ride but knew it
would have been ungracious to refuse her uncle's offer of
transport.

As they drove through the countryside, Alice thought about
Victor's request that she move back to Dalton Hall. She'd tried
to fob him off but knew Victor would gnaw away at her like a
dog chewing a bone, trying to wear her down until she agreed.
The more she thought about it the less she wanted to do it. Not
only was living under the same roof as her mother a difficult
prospect but leaving Little Badgerton would be a terrible
wrench. She loved their little cottage. The place was steeped in
memories. How could she possibly leave it while Edmund was
at the front? Even worse – how could she leave it if, God forbid,
he were never to return? It would be like tearing a limb off. It
was their home. It was the place she felt happiest. How could
she leave Eleanor and Walter? Eleanor was more of a mother to
her than her own. And how could she leave, knowing her stillborn son was buried in the churchyard of St Margaret's? It was
impossible. There had to be a way to make Victor understand.

The journey home was via Winchester, as Walter had an
appointment there with the bishop. While Eleanor did some
shopping, Alice decided to pay a visit to the cathedral. She'd
never been before and hoped that perhaps she might find some
inspiration for her remaining work on the Latchington window.

As soon as she entered the building, Alice was awed. The
enormous nave stretched before her towards the towering stone-
carved high altar. As there was no service in progress, she
wandered up and down the aisles, stopping to look at whatever

caught her eye. She found herself in the north transept, where in a small chapel she found a series of stained-glass windows with episodes from the life of the Virgin Mary designed by Burne-Jones. Each had a central scene, with the upper and lower sections of the windows devoted to a mass of green-leaved briars, which reminded her of the William Morris-designed wallpaper in her mother's bedroom. As she gazed at each window in turn, she was struck by how the vibrant primary colours of the central scene – especially the rich blue of Mary's robes – contrasted with the simple border of vine leaves and the tangle of briars, all in muted shades of green.

She asked herself whether the Latchington window design was too complicated. Had she overdone it? Her borders featured a series of Lady Lockwood's favourite plants and shrubs, as well as sheaves of wheat and poppies. Might it have been better to do as Burne-Jones had done and stick to one plant, using it as a repeating motif? She stood, studying the windows then decided that no, the Latchington window's purpose was to honour and celebrate the brief life of Lady Lockwood's son, Bevis, and the priority had been to create something that every time Lady Lockwood looked at it would remind her of him. Besides, the design had been mostly Edmund's. She trusted his judgement more than anyone's. And that included Sir Edward Burne-Jones.

Tearing herself away from the side chapel, Alice walked back down the nave towards the Great West Window. She caught her breath. It was vast. Light and colour poured down into the nave from the soaring multi-lanceted windows. She moved closer, staring dumbstruck at the scale and beauty of it. Pieces of plain clear glass intermingled with colours, like jewels scattered from a broken necklace. It was an abstract mosaic but with the odd fragment where she could discern a painted face, a part of a building, or a section of a saint's halo. Edmund had once told her that, under the regime of Oliver Cromwell, Roundheads had desecrated the cathedral, smashing the magnificent medieval windows, ransacking the tombs of dead bishops and monarchs and scattering their bones. The people of Winchester, proud of their cathedral, had gathered up the glass fragments, collected the bones and hidden them away in their homes and outbuildings until the eventual restoration of the monarchy. The result was this window, a mad mosaic made from the salvaged pieces, with clear glass filling in the gaps. Alice gazed upon it, enraptured.

This abstract window was dramatically different from the usual portrayal of saints and Bible stories. It struck her as a metaphor for life. The war had shattered so many lives, including hers and Edmund's, damaged the bodies of Victor, Maurice and others, but Alice told herself that, like this window, the broken pieces of their lives could be put back together. When this terrible war was over it would be a markedly different world to the one they had known before. But somehow now she felt certain that it would in its own way be beautiful.

In the car, Alice noticed at once that Walter seemed out of sorts. It was hard, if not impossible, to sustain a conversation above the noise of the Standard's engine but there was something about his demeanour that signalled he was despondent.

Back in Little Badgerton, Alice refused the offer of a cup of tea and rushed at once to Harriet's house, next door to the vicarage, to be reunited with Lottie. To her immense relief, the little girl was beaming and had evidently enjoyed her stay with the Wallingfords. Even more convinced that staying in Little Badgerton was the right thing to do for Lottie as well as herself, she grasped her little girl's hand and walked with her down the lane, across the meadow and into the little cottage that was home.

.   .   .

The following morning Alice found out why Walter's spirits had been low.

She was at the central worktable in the glass studio, writing a letter to the iron foundry, providing the measurements for an order she was placing. It was for the *ferramenta*, the metal frame that would be fixed to the masonry of the window aperture to hold the panel of stained glass. She looked up as the door opened.

Eleanor walked inside, calling, 'Only me. Can you spare some time to talk?'

Alice folded the paper and slipped it inside the envelope. 'Give me a moment to write the address, then I'll walk back to the village with you, and I can post this letter.'

'As long as you're sure I'm not spoiling your plans.'

'You could never do that.' Alice leant towards her aunt and dropped a kiss on her cheek.

She slipped a jacket on, pinned her hat on her head, and followed Eleanor out of the workshop. 'Am I right in guessing this is about Walter?'

Eleanor looked sharply at her. 'How did you know? No, don't answer that. He was like a bear with a sore head on the way back from Winchester, wasn't he?'

'Well, certainly not his usual cheery self.'

Eleanor sighed. 'My darling Walter has taken it into his head that at the age of fifty-five it's his duty to abandon his parish and his wife in order to serve on the Western Front as a chaplain.'

Alice opened her mouth, aghast.

'Exactly!' Eleanor buried her hands in the deep pockets of her silk summer coat. 'He's lost his mind.'

'What brought this on? Has he mentioned it before?'

'No! Never. He hadn't even told me that was why he was meeting the bishop.'

'Oh Lord! What did the bishop say?'

'A resounding no, obviously. That's why Walter was down in the dumps. He argued with him but to no avail, thank goodness.'

'What brought this on?' Alice couldn't imagine why anyone would want to go out to the front if they didn't have to.

Eleanor shrugged. 'A general sense that he ought to be doing his bit, I suppose. That and hearing the stories of the officers at Bankstone and what they've gone through. He thinks he can make a difference.' She sighed with undisguised frustration. 'One of the chaps last week said he owed his life to a padre.'

'The power of prayer?'

Eleanor shook her head. 'Apparently some of the padres make themselves useful by helping out the medical teams.'

'Edmund mentioned that. He said the chaplain attached to their unit goes to all the medical lectures and follows the stretcher bearers. If they can cope, he walks alongside and comforts the patient. If they're down a man, he helps them carry.'

'There's a young man at Bankstone. A lieutenant. He told Walter he'd been left for dead. He was under some bodies in a shell hole, and no one heard him calling out over the noise of shellfire.' Eleanor spoke quickly. 'But a chaplain climbed down into the hole to say prayers over the dead. He heard the poor fellow calling, got him out from under the bodies, dragged him from the hole, then lifted him onto his shoulders and carried him a mile to a dressing station. All while under fire.'

Alice frowned. 'Walter wouldn't have the strength to carry a man all that way.'

'I know, but it's made him believe that the chaplain was directed by God. He thinks he's wasted here holding parish services. He doesn't want to fight but he does want to help.' By now they'd reached the post office. 'But there's more. Go and buy your stamp then I'll tell you the rest. In fact, if you can spare the time, we can do it at the vicarage over a cup of coffee. Walter's out doing his parish rounds.'

Twenty minutes later, the two women were drinking coffee in the morning room.

'You said there was more,' said Alice. She had a feeling she wouldn't like what she heard.

'Walter's taken it into his head that he can get himself attached to Edmund's battalion and tag along with him and the other stretcher bearers.'

Alice, taken aback, stared open-mouthed at her aunt. 'What did the bishop say?'

'He gave him short shrift, thank goodness. Said firstly he's far too old. Secondly, no one can pick and choose where they're sent. And thirdly, there's more need for fighting men than clergy out there and he's needed here to comfort the mothers, widows and orphans.'

Alice swallowed, trying not to picture Walter comforting her and Lottie. She put down her coffee cup, unable to speak.

Eleanor carried on. 'Instead of accepting what the bishop says with good grace, Walter is frustrated and angry. He spent last night talking about how he was determined to change his mind. Oh, Alice, I don't know what's got into him.'

'Do you think he'll keep trying?'

'I'm sure of it. And the bishop could crack under the pressure. You know what Walter's like when he has a bee in his bonnet. He gets obsessed about something and won't let go. Remember the book he wrote about Gilbert White? He talked of nothing else for years and as soon as it was published, he lost all interest.' She gave a deep sigh. 'If only he could find another Gilbert White to obsess about and leave the Western Front to the army and younger members of the clergy.'

'Is there a shortage of clergymen out there?'

'Apparently not. If anything, there's a shortage of them back here. Honestly, Alice, I wish he could see that saying prayers over the dead or dying is no more worthy than comforting those who are grieving them here – or like yourself coping with being apart from their dear ones.'

Alice had a sudden realisation of what was coming.

Eleanor continued. 'I was wondering, dear girl, if you might be good enough to have a word or two with Walter and stress that point. I know how self-sufficient and independent you are, but if you could show the smallest chink in your armour I think he might think again.' She stretched out her hand and took Alice's. 'All it takes is for you to impress upon him that he's desperately needed here in Little Badgerton. Needed by all his parishioners, and also by those poor officers recovering at Bankstone. If he wants to minister to soldiers, there's plenty of them there.'

Alice set her jaw. She owed it to Eleanor to do this. Eleanor and Walter had been her port in a storm when she fled from Dalton Hall eight years ago. They'd welcomed her into their home, helped her find work, first with Colonel Fitzwarren, then later and blessedly with Edmund. Now it was time to help them.

'When I was working at Bankstone as a VAD, some of the men were desperately unhappy. They were coming to terms with disfigurement, losing limbs, or eyes. Some of them thought of themselves as failures for being injured, for letting down their comrades at the front. Their troubles are complex. Even those who put on a brave face often weep into their pillows when the lights are out. Some like Captain Kynaston have been abandoned by their sweethearts because of their injuries. There was one lad who was terrified to go home as he was convinced he'd let his family down and brought shame upon them by being wounded and unfit to return to duty. All those men need comforting, advising, being listened to. In other words, they need Walter. He's one of the kindest, most caring and under-standing men I've ever known. It's here he can make the biggest difference. Not out in France.'

It wasn't Eleanor who replied but Walter himself. Unobserved by the two women he had been standing just outside the open doorway in the hall and heard everything.

'Thank you for that, Alice,' he said, his voice quiet.

'Heavens!' cried Eleanor. 'How long have you been standing there?'

'Long enough to hear a few home truths. It's starting to rain, and I went out without my brolly so I came back to fetch it. They say eavesdroppers never hear any good of themselves, but I've just heard some kind remarks that I'm too modest to believe justified.' He came into the room and sat down in a wing chair near the empty fireplace. 'You've given me much food for thought, Alice. You too, my darling.' He smiled at his wife. 'Listening to you both, I realise now I've been driven by my own vanity. My desire to make a difference is more about my wish to defy age as well as a childish longing to play the hero.'

Eleanor got up from her seat and rushed over to fling her arms around Walter. 'Thank goodness. My dearest love.'

Alice slipped out of the room and made her way back to the cottage, her eyes filled with tears. If only she could so easily find the words that would place her own husband safe by her side here in Little Badgerton. She let the tears flow freely as she walked across the meadow. But as soon as she crossed the threshold of the studio, she swept them away with the back of her hand. She had work to do.

TWENTY-SIX

Against his better judgement, Victor was at Pentonville prison again. He wished he didn't have to see Herbert Cutler again but if he were to fulfil the mission he'd been set by the men at the ministry he had to grit his teeth and get on with it.

This time, Herbert Cutler was already sitting at one of the tables when Victor arrived. Herbert was not alone. A woman who had been seated opposite him got to her feet, nodded to Cutler and moved towards the visitors' door. Victor watched her approach, trying to establish whether he'd seen her before. Dressed in a black skirt, a high-necked white blouse and a bolero-style jacket with an old-fashioned veiled hat with the veil pushed back, she was tall, slim, with a sharp pointy nose, heavily plucked eyebrows, and lips so thin they were almost invisible. Passing Victor without a glance, she left a waft of strong perfume in her wake. Violets, he decided, wrinkling his nose.

Joining Cutler at the table, Victor jerked his head in the direction of the exit, where a warder was now standing. 'Who was that woman?'

'A business acquaintance.'

'A client? Shouldn't you have introduced us?'

Cutler folded his arms, the subject clearly closed. 'So? What do you have for me?'

'First of all, I need your signature on the paperwork to confirm the change of name for the business and my appointment as director.' He reached in his breast pocket and took out his fountain pen to hand to Cutler.

'Is that really necessary?' The older man sounded tetchy.

'Of course it is. We discussed it last time.'

Cutler accepted the pen and signed his name. 'Remember this arrangement is temporary only. Once the court clears me my name will go back over the door.'

'*Our* names.'

'What else?' Cutler drummed his fingers on the table.

'I've been through the books and met with the chief clerk. We're about twenty per cent down on last year. The client numbers are worse than I'd hoped.' Victor took some pleasure in seeing Cutler wince. 'It appears there was a mass exodus when you were arrested.'

'I could have told you that myself,' Cutler snapped back.

'But that's compensated to some extent by an increase in funds under management from some of those remaining, as well as excellent returns. It seems you were right, Herbert, war is indeed good for business.'

'Alas accusations of murder are not. Even false ones.' Cutler leant forward. 'Did you bring those cigars I asked for?'

Victor opened his briefcase and took out a box. 'Just as you asked. Partagás No. 4. From Robert Lewis in St James's Street.'

Cutler took up the wooden box and raised it to his nose, breathing in the aroma appreciatively. 'I'll light up the first of these as I walk out of the court as a free man. Meanwhile it's enough to breathe in the aroma of them.'

Victor cleared his throat. 'There is one lost client whose departure has nothing to do with your situation.'

'Who? And why?' Cutler's brow furrowed.

'My father. He died a week ago. The funeral was on Wednesday.'

Cutler grunted. 'Sorry to hear that,' he said begrudgingly. 'Even though he let me down.'

'How so?' Victor jerked his head back in surprise. This was news to him.

'Promised to ease my way into a safe Conservative seat. But he didn't deliver.'

Victor chose not to comment, secretly pleased that his father had failed to give Cutler a leg up.

'So, you're the new Lord Dalton?' Herbert pushed out his bottom lip, nodding. 'Won't do any harm to have a peer of the realm in the firm.'

Victor wanted to correct him by saying 'running the firm' but bit it back. He'd discovered long ago that it was best not to antagonise Herbert Cutler.

The two men discussed the business of the brokerage until the guard warned them they had only ten minutes left. Cutler lowered his voice to ensure they were not overheard. 'I'd hoped to be out of here in time to complete a large and important transaction but it's not going to be possible. I need you to make it happen.'

Victor felt a rush of anticipation. Might this be linked to the questionable arms deals Herbert was believed to have been involved with? So far the pages of data he'd trawled through in Charing Cross Buildings had yielded nothing to incriminate Cutler.

'The woman you saw leaving just now, Madame Renard, will contact you shortly at the office at Cornhill. She will act as my go-between for a stock purchase I prefer not to put through the firm's books. She will not make an appointment, so you need to instruct the clerk to admit her, and I want you to see her immediately.'

Victor interrupted. 'Who is she? I've never seen her before. What's her relationship to the business?'

'None. Yet. That's the point. She will make a small deposit to open a client account with Cutler & Son—'

'Dalton Associates.'

Cutler waved a hand in the air dismissively. 'Whatever. I need you to liquidate the stocks in my personal account and transfer the proceeds to a bank account for which Madame Renard will provide the details.'

Victor jerked backwards in his seat. 'You expect me to liquidate your own stocks and pay the proceeds over to a woman I've never met, when I have no idea who she is, where she's from and why she should receive the money?' He made an exasperated sound. 'Herbert, that's insane and probably breaks every rule of the exchange.'

'You're acting under my instructions as your client, not as your partner. You need to know nothing more about the lady. It's to your own protection not to know.'

'That's preposterous. How do I know she can be trusted?'

'You don't. But as it's my money not yours you needn't worry. Besides once the money has been transferred it is no longer your concern nor is it a managed asset of the fund.'

Victor knew how much of the stock managed by the firm was in Herbert's name. If this were to be transferred out into Madame Renard's bank account, it would have a significant impact on their balance sheet.

'It's suspicious, Herbert. A shady deal if ever I heard one. For God's sake, man, tell me who she is and what is her connection to you or the firm.'

Victor felt a hand on his shoulder and the warder told him his time was up. He started to protest, but Herbert Cutler was already on his feet. He walked away towards the prisoners' door, without another word. Victor had no choice but to leave himself.

.   .   .

Arriving back at Albany that evening, Victor was disappointed not to find Maurice waiting for him there. He'd given the captain a set of keys.

He poured himself a large Scotch and sat down to mull over his conversation with Herbert Cutler. Was the mysterious Madame Renard Herbert's mistress? Was she blackmailing him? He found both of those possibilities unlikely. Herbert had never struck him as a ladies' man. He wouldn't be surprised if he used the services of the occasional prostitute, but he was far too canny to reveal his identity or expose himself to blackmail. Could she be a relative? As far as Victor was aware Herbert had none – apart from Edmund and Charlotte. He supposed he must have parents somewhere – although they could be dead – and were highly unlikely to be French. But perhaps Madame Renard was English, with a French husband? Or it could be an assumed name?

He took another slug of Scotch and tried to tell himself it was pointless to speculate. He was exhausted. It felt as though he had the weight of the world on his shoulders. The shrapnel still buried in his leg and shoulder caused him more pain when he was tired. He took another slug of whisky to numb the pain.

The door opened and a smiling Maurice walked in and all thoughts of Madame Renard, Herbert Cutler and his painful injuries vanished.

They went to Ciro's, the nightclub that was Victor's favourite – his first visit since his return from Gallipoli. The private club was tucked away in Orange Street, behind the National Gallery, just a few minutes' walk from Albany. There was a jazz band playing quietly for the early evening crowd. The two men sat at a table in the American bar and grill room with its chintz curtains and framed caricatures of famous guests. The bar was presided over by a Scotsman, Harry, who greeted Victor warmly before preparing his customary Old Fashioned, along with a simple gin and bitters for Maurice. To eat, they ordered filet mignon accompanied by a bottle of claret.

'How was your day in darkest Hammersmith?' Victor asked his friend. 'Smash any glass today?'

Maurice chuckled. 'No more breakages. Thank goodness. I'm actually getting the hang of the leading.' He explained how he'd been leading up a small window for a newly built house.

Victor shook his head and smiled. 'You and I are so different. About the only part of what you've just told me that I'd even want to do, let alone be able to, is the accurate measuring. Give me a column of numbers and I'm happy.'

Maurice grimaced. 'Yes. We're chalk and cheese. I've never got on with numbers. Give me a volume of poetry any day.'

'Perhaps that's why I love you so much.' Victor took advantage of the half-light to place a hand on the captain's leg, where the limb ended just above the knee. 'How are you getting on with the prosthetic? You're not wearing it.'

'I have it on for a couple of hours while I'm in the workshop. But it chafes. I'd rather get about with my crutches.'

'But aren't they uncomfortable too?'

'Only when I put my weight on them to move about. The prosthetic rubs all the time, even when I'm sitting, and it's heavy.'

'Unless you wear it, you'll never get used to it.' Victor took a sip of his cocktail.

'Does it bother you? The missing leg?'

Victor reached for Maurice's hand under the table, and gave it a squeeze. 'How can you even ask that? Does it bother you that I've lost an eye?'

'Of course not.'

'The point is, my dearest, you and I have never known each

other any other way. We fell in love as we are, complete with scars and missing limbs. We're a pair of pirates, you with the missing leg and me with the black eyepatch.'

Their steaks arrived and the two men tucked in with relish.

'One thing I don't miss is the food at the frontline,' said Maurice. 'But I can't help feeling bad enjoying this when I think of those men out there on small rations and eating such awful fare.'

'And the flies. That was the worst thing about Gallipoli. You couldn't keep them away. They got in the tea and the food. The moment you opened a can they'd be all over it. Foul.' Victor chewed a piece of steak. 'Mind you the prices have shot up everywhere. What with all the labour shortages and delays at the docks.' He sighed. 'We didn't appreciate just how good life was before the war.'

'How's it going at the ministry?' Maurice dabbed his mouth with his napkin.

'I'm hidden away in an office overlooking the dustbins. Apart from going in and out I barely see anyone.'

'What exactly are you doing there?' Maurice leant forward, curious.

Conscious that he was bound by silence, Victor waved a hand vaguely. 'You'd find it tedious stuff. I just go through endless folders each containing pages of figures. I try to find patterns.'

'Patterns?'

'I mean trends.'

'What kind of trends?'

Victor grinned. 'Why are you so interested? I'm not supposed to talk about it. Top Secret and all that.'

'I'm just curious. That they're interested in trends. I thought if anything was already clear in this war it'd be trends. Deaths and injuries up. Production of munitions up. Prices up.

Women working up. Unemployment down. Surely, they don't need you to tell them that.'

Victor refilled their wine glasses. He hated having secrets from Maurice. He trusted him totally. It was so tempting to tell him about Herbert Cutler and the question marks about his arms dealing, but that could cost him his job. His dilemma was resolved by the band walking on stage for the next set. The singer broke into 'Hello! Ma Baby' making conversation difficult. By the time she finished the song the subject was forgotten.

The arrangement Victor had reached with the Ministry of Munitions was that he would work in Charing Cross Buildings each morning and at Dalton Associates in the afternoons.

So far, he was having more success in restoring the health of the brokerage than he was with unearthing any inappropriate dealings in Cutler's trade in munitions. Most of Cutler's deals appeared to have been direct with the War Office and all shipments were accounted for. There was no evidence of either his buying up arms that were intended to be scrapped or diverting consignments to the German front. It was frustrating. Something had led Pointer and Rothbury-Harris to believe that Cutler's hands were dirty. When he'd asked them exactly what, they'd refused to elaborate, saying they wanted a fresh pair of eyes on it. Victor had resisted reminding them that he was one eye short of a pair.

Every morning, he went through the tables of data, cross-referencing them, laying the papers out on the floor of his gloomy office. No matter how he looked at the numbers he could find no errors or inconsistencies. The production numbers tallied exactly with the shipment numbers plus the quantities that had failed quality control and hence were due to be scrapped.

With a sinking feeling Victor concluded that the only way

to establish if there was anything irregular happening was to visit each ordnance factory and try to sniff out if there was anything untoward. But there were so many factories. How could he possibly visit them all? And what would he look for? It was an impossible task.

If the two men were correct and Herbert Cutler was behind this, Victor might have more luck approaching the problem from the other end – by examining Cutler's private financial transactions through the brokerage.

A few days later, Victor was working on the Countess of Wallingford's finances, completing a budget breakdown for Harriet to review that afternoon when she was due to meet him at the office.

Her substantial town house in Portman Square had been requisitioned under the Defence of the Realm Act which gave the government wide-ranging powers, including the conversion and rebuilding of property to render it suitable for the purpose for which it was required. The fine eighteenth-century building with its elegantly proportioned rooms was to be partitioned into offices to house staff from the Ministry of Works. The rental was more than sufficient to cover Harriet's rent in Little Badgerton as well as provide for her household expenses.

Victor was relieved. There was a small surplus which he planned to invest on Harriet's behalf. Although there was no possibility of restoring the fortunes she might have expected as the widow of a major landowning aristocrat, she should at least be able to live comfortably in her new more modest circumstances. He wished he had been able to intervene and advise the earl while he'd been alive. Then there would have been the possibility of preserving ownership of Wallingford Hall for Crispin to inherit along with the earldom.

Victor had just put aside the folder with his budget for

Harriet, ready for their meeting later that afternoon, when the chief clerk informed him that there was a lady who wanted to see him. Victor frowned. Harriet was early.

'I told her you have an appointment at two p.m. and suggested she return later but she insists on seeing you immediately. Then I remembered you mentioned that a French lady would call without an appointment.'

The mysterious Madame Renard.

Victor nodded. 'Thank you, Mr Lucas. I'll see her at once.'

Moments later, Lucas ushered the woman into the room.

Wearing the same severe black and white ensemble she had worn when visiting Pentonville, Madame Renard carried herself with a ramrod-straight back. Victor tried to estimate her age but found it impossible. Her hair showed no signs of greying, and her face was unwrinkled, but there was something about the eyes and the set of the mouth that indicated experience and world-weariness.

He showed her to a chair, and she settled into it, holding a small leather case like a music case, protectively on her lap.

'Madame Renard, I believe?' Victor took his own seat behind the large oak desk he had inherited from the absent Herbert.

The woman nodded but said nothing. She opened the case and took out an envelope which she handed to him.

When she spoke, it was with a heavy French accent. 'Inside you will find the details of an account at Banque de crédit coloniale de France. I understand that Monsieur Cutler has told you that you must arrange the transfer of monies to this account.'

'It will take a few days. We have to liquidate all the stock.'

'It must be done by Monday next.' Her eyes bored into him, and Victor felt uncomfortable.

'I'll do my best.'

'No. I must have the funds by then.' The woman raised her gloved hands palms forward in a gesture of refusal.

'There will be some costs for currency exchange and bank charges.' Victor was increasingly uneasy. Herbert hadn't mentioned that the account would be in France. Out of the jurisdiction of the British authorities.

'The money is to be transferred in sterling. The conversion will be made *en France*.'

'Very well,' he said. 'Mr Cutler also mentioned you would require the establishment of a client account here.'

'*Bien entendu*,' she said. 'Of course.' Reaching once more into the briefcase she handed him a cheque for ten pounds. It was already signed C. Renard.

Victor was surprised that the sum was such a modest one for the opening of a client account, but he made no comment.

The woman stood up. '*Tout est fait.* We are done.'

'May we call you a cab, Madame Renard?'

'That won't be necessary. I will expect the funds to be in the account on Monday, the seventeenth of July.' Without so much as a word of farewell she left the office.

When she was gone, Victor puzzled over the brief meeting. Perhaps Herbert intended to backdate the transfer of the stock in his own account into this one in Madame Renard's name so it would appear she had requested liquidation of her own assets and the transfer of the proceeds to her French bank account. But if Herbert wasn't cleared of the killing of Dora Cutler he'd be hanged or at best be subject to a lengthy sentence for manslaughter and wouldn't be able to make such a retrospective adjustment.

One thing was clear. Victor himself would have no part in such a fraud. As things stood, he was merely following Herbert's instructions to sell his own holdings and pay this woman. That in itself was not a crime. It was however worthy of further investigation and reporting to Victor's superiors at the

Ministry of Munitions. But first he needed to find out more about the mysterious Madame Renard. How? He didn't even know where she lived.

As Victor was musing over this problem, the door opened, and the clerk peered round it. 'Her Ladyship the Countess of Wallingford has arrived, sir. May I show her in?'

Victor nodded and a moment later Harriet came into the office, a puzzled look on her face. 'The woman who was in here just now. I'm sure I've seen her before. And I'm certain she recognised me as she pulled the veil down over her hat when she saw me. It was obvious she didn't want me to recognise her.' Harriet frowned as she racked her brains. 'I'm sure I'll place her in a moment.'

'She's a client of Herbert Cutler. I've never met her before myself. Very abrupt. French.'

'Good gracious! Of course! The French woman. Alice and I saw her at Monty's funeral. She's the dowager countess's companion. Thoroughly unpleasant. She accused me of being a gold digger and said she was pleased my plans hadn't worked out.' Harriet sank into the chair Madame Renard had recently vacated.

'You're sure?' Victor felt his heart racing.

'Absolutely certain. When someone insults you like that at your husband's funeral you don't forget it. Why was she here? Is it to do with Monty?' Harriet looked pale.

Victor shook his head. 'I don't know. Herbert told me to expect her. She was here to open a client account. That's all I can say. I'm bound by client confidentiality.'

'There must be a link. Surely, Victor? Why would a French lady's companion be opening an account at a prestigious City stock brokerage? Hers is not exactly a well-paid job I imagine.' She placed the flat of her palm above her chest. 'My goodness. Was Herbert Cutler advising Monty? Did he play a part in the disastrous mismanagement of the Wallingford estate?'

Victor got up and came around to Harriet's side of the desk where he perched close to her. 'Don't let your imagination carry you away. If Herbert had been running His Lordship's affairs they'd be in a much better state. Whatever else I'd say about Herbert Cutler, I'd never accuse him of poor financial management. It's thanks to him that my father didn't burn his way through the Dalton estate. He's always been an astute financier.'

'Then what? It's too much of a coincidence.' Harriet frowned.

Victor had to acknowledge she had a point. 'Look, Harriet, will you leave this with me? I'll take a closer look at the late earl's financial transactions and see if I can find anything suspicious and if I can establish any link between him and Herbert. I'd like to know how this Madame Renard met him. How long was she the dowager countess's companion?'

'Certainly as long as I was married to Monty. But I avoided going to Norfolk. Her Ladyship scared the wits out of me and I never so much as spoke to the creepy companion. I didn't even know she was French until she insulted me in the hallway as Alice and I were leaving.' She raised her hands, palms up.

'Do I have your permission to dig a little more into your late husband's finances?'

'Of course. Not that I expect there'll be much to find. Everything seems to have been poured into the estate. Setting up the pig farm appears to have been a massive drain.'

'I can't promise to find anything that will benefit you and the children but there's no harm in taking a look.' Victor tapped the folder on his desk. 'Now I'd like to run through the budget I've pulled together for you.' He returned to the other side of the desk, sat down, then opened the manila file and went through the sheet of figures.

When he'd finished explaining the financial picture, he smiled. 'You won't be able to afford a villa in the South of

France when the war's over, but you will be able to get by quite comfortably.'

'As long as I can keep a roof over my children's heads and pay the bills I'll be happy.' She sighed. 'I married poor Monty for his money. In fact, I spent quite a lot of it in the early days, but as soon as Crispin was born everything changed for me. My greatest joy is my children. And I'm happier than ever living in Little Badgerton. I don't miss the social whirl at all. Nor do I miss the things I thought mattered to me like fine clothes.' She gave him a sad smile. 'If I think of my life, apart from the children, my other great satisfaction has been my involvement in the women's suffrage movement. Having a sense of purpose, enjoying the camaraderie of like-minded women. I miss that since the war. But I am loving being near to your darling sister.' She pulled on her gloves and turned to face him. 'Dear Victor, you can't imagine how grateful I am. You're my guardian angel.'

'Not at all. It's my pleasure.' He grinned. 'I wish all my clients were as agreeable to deal with as you.'

Victor showed her out, summoning her a taxi to take her to Waterloo. As she stepped into the cab, she leant through the window and said, 'Madame Renard, eh? You know *renard* is French for fox. Better be wary, Victor.' Her taxi pulled away into the traffic.

What fortuitous timing. Now he knew where to find Madame Renard and had a valuable line of enquiry to follow.

TWENTY-SEVEN

A few days after Alice had returned from her father's funeral, Viola paid her a visit. She was neatly turned out, her hair secured in a bun and the baby in her arms looked clean and content.

'I heard about your father. I'm sorry, Alice.' She gave her a sad smile. 'When I met him at your wedding, he seemed such a nice man. Not at all scary for someone who's a lord. Please accept my condolences.'

'Thank you, Viola. It was kind of you to come.'

'It's not the only reason.' Viola pulled out a chair and sat at the table. Alice was filling the kettle, but her friend told her to wait a moment. 'Sit down. I have to tell you this before I lose my nerve. Then we can decide what to do about it over a cup of tea.' Viola looked anxious. Almost jittery.

Alice sat down opposite her.

'This is going to be hard for me to say, but I must tell you. Then I'll need your advice as to what to do about it.' Alice noticed Viola's hands were shaking.

'Go on.' Alice couldn't help feeling nervous herself.

'I mentioned that Molly was out of sorts. Moody and silent.

At first, I thought you were right, and it was because of me neglecting her. But it wasn't that. After you told me what happened, I asked her about pulling Lottie's hair and she denied it. She shouted at me and ran away. It took me two hours to find her. She was hiding in the woodshed, crying.'

Alice gasped and stretched a hand out to touch Viola's arm.

'Even after that she still wouldn't tell me what was wrong. I thought it was because she didn't like being found out about the hair pulling. Then her behaviour got worse. Much worse. She stopped speaking altogether. Alice, I've been at my wits' end.'

Viola put her head in her hands. 'I noticed I had more change in my purse than I thought. I'm always short of money but I found half a crown in there last night that I knew couldn't possibly be mine. Molly confessed she'd put it there to try and help out. Half a crown! Where would she get that kind of money? Any money at all? I thought she must have stolen it. Naturally I demanded to know where it had come from. God forgive me, Alice, but when she wouldn't say, I slapped her hard on her legs. She cried as if her heart would break. I held her in my arms until she quietened, and I begged her to tell me what was wrong and where the half-crown had come from.'

Behind them on the mantelpiece the clock chimed the hour. Alice held her breath.

'It all came out then. Oh, Alice, I don't know what to do. She told me that after school, on the way home, sometimes there's a man who walks with her.' Viola's voice broke and she dabbed at her eyes with a handkerchief. 'He started off just saying hello and giving her sweets. Georgie too. The children aren't used to getting treats. There's never enough money to buy them. So, they were delighted. At first, they were.' She began to cry again.

Alice moved round the table and sat beside her with her arm around Viola's shoulders.

'One day, he told Georgie to go on ahead. Molly wasn't

happy about that, but she wanted the sweeties...' She wiped her eyes. 'He told her how pretty she was, what a good girl. Said he'd seen her with Lottie Cutler, who was a bad girl. It was he who filled her head with all that rubbish about the orphanage and Lottie's mother being murdered.'

Alice could feel a rising tide of fury. 'Who is the man? Whereabouts did this happen?'

'On the track that leads to our cottage from the lane. He was taking her into the woods there. It's been happening for weeks.'

Alice's blood ran cold in her veins. 'Who, Viola? Tell me who?'

'That Mr Fitzwarren. The colonel's nephew from the big house up the hill.'

Alice dug her nails deep into her palms.

'He said if Molly told anyone she'd get into terrible trouble and be expelled from school and sent away to prison and the whole village would know she was a bad girl. She was terrified.'

'What did he do to her?' Alice bit her lip, not wanting to hear the details but knowing she must.

Viola fixed her eyes on the tabletop. Her voice was trembling. 'At first he made her sit on his knee and kissed her, then one day, he pulled down her knickers and looked at her, then... he... he touched her down there then made her touch him.' Her voice was barely a whisper. 'She was so ashamed and terrified. The poor child has been bottling all this up for weeks. It's why she took it out on Lottie. I think it's all been a cry for help. She thought everything he was doing to her was her fault. She couldn't bear to tell me.'

'Oh, Viola. I'm so sorry. Poor Molly. No wonder she did what she did. That man is a monster. An absolute perverted monster.'

It all fell into place. She'd always known the colonel's nephew was an unpleasant man with a bad character. He had long nursed a grudge against Alice, ever since she had rebuffed his drunken advances on their first meeting at his uncle's party. Before Alice's marriage, it had been Leonard Fitzwarren who had informed the gutter press that she, the daughter of a baron, was living out of wedlock with Edmund, a celebrated but married artist. It had been he who had schemed to bring about Edmund's earlier than necessary entry into the army. Now, it was Leonard Fitzwarren who had molested Viola's eight-year-old daughter.

'Oh, Lord, I wish Robert was here. He'd horsewhip the man.' Viola sobbed again. 'But what can I possibly do about it?'

Alice leant back and stared at the ceiling. 'He can't be allowed to get away with this.'

'But what can we do? The Fitzwarrens are so powerful round here. He has his uncle's protection. Who's going to believe a little girl?'

Alice knew the colonel would probably take his nephew's part. As a magistrate, chairman of the local Conservatives, as well as chair of the tribunal for conscientious objectors and enjoying a close friendship with Lord Kitchener himself, Colonel Fitzwarren was unassailable – and by the same token so was his nephew.

'We can't allow that despicable man to get away with this. If he's done this to Molly, he can do it to others.' Alice's jaw was set hard. She felt sick thinking about what Fitzwarren had done to an innocent child. 'Right,' she said at last. 'We women must stick together. I'm going to call a meeting of the Little Badgerton Suffrage Society. We haven't met since before the war, but if ever there was a reason to get the group together again this is it.'

'But I don't want the whole village to know what's happened to Molly. She'd be mortified.'

'That's exactly what Fitzwarren is hoping for. It's what every man who molests a child or tries to shame a woman relies upon. That we'll be too ashamed to reveal the truth. But the shame is all theirs. Molly has done nothing wrong. Leonard Fitzwarren on the other hand most certainly has. But I understand your wish to protect Molly, so we'll keep her identity secret.'

Within two hours, the women were gathered in the drawing room at the vicarage. As well as Alice and Viola, Miss Pendleton the parish organist, Mrs Collins the doctor's wife, Eleanor Hargreaves, Harriet Wallingford and half a dozen others. Miss Trimble the schoolmistress had been a stalwart of the group but was occupied with her teaching duties and unable to attend, as were a couple of the VADs at Bankstone.

Alice called the meeting to order and stood in front of the group. These women had been her friends and neighbours ever since she had come to the village back in 1908 and with Eleanor had established the women's group. Several, like her and Viola, had husbands or sons at the front and all had been involved in the war effort, even if it was only in knitting socks.

'Ladies, it's with a heavy heart I've gathered us all together. We have living among us a man who is what I can only describe as a predator. And not only a predator of women – for he is that, as I can attest – but it has now come to my knowledge – of little girls.'

There was a collective gasp.

'An innocent child has been molested by this man. He has not only terrified her but convinced her that she will be the object of shame and retribution if she speaks out against him. I'm not going to identify the child in question nor am I going to spell out the disgusting details of what he has done – suffice to say it was shameful and involved highly inappropriate touching.'

A murmur of horror went around the room.

'Who is this devil?' Mrs Collins spoke first.

'Mr Leonard Fitzwarren of Padgett Hall.'

'No. Surely not! The colonel's nephew. I refuse to believe it.' Miss Pendleton bristled and shook her head. 'He sings in the choir.'

Alice suppressed a groan. Sometimes Miss Pendleton was exceedingly stupid. 'You may not wish to believe it, but alas it's true. The man is without morals or principles.'

Miss Pendleton continued to tut her disapproval.

Harriet spoke next. 'As a newcomer, I have no acquaintance with the man in question, but I can speak for my friend here. Alice Cutler would never make such an accusation lightly and without evidence.'

Alice was grateful for her friend's intervention. Reluctantly, she decided she needed to reveal her own unpleasant encounter with Fitzwarren. 'I have personal experience that Mr Fitzwarren is a dishonourable man, having been the object of his unwelcome advances myself. I let him know in no uncertain terms that his behaviour was dishonourable and unacceptable. But I'm a grown woman capable of defending myself.' She'd been about to say 'defending her honour', but decided the word honour would be viewed as inappropriate by Miss Pendleton. The elderly spinster had frowned on the unconventional extra-marital relationship Alice had with Edmund until Dora's death permitted their marriage. Quickly, Alice added, 'It is quite another matter when his chosen victim is a small child.'

Harriet voiced her opinion again. 'As the mother of three small children, one of whom is a little girl, I for one will not sleep easy while that man is free to roam this village.' Two other young mothers added their agreement. Miss Pendleton had the sense not to object.

Alice wanted to keep the focus on action. 'So what are we to do, ladies? Go to the constable? Speak with the colonel?'

For the first time, Viola spoke up. 'The colonel will defend his nephew to the death. And what will the constable do?

Colonel Fitzwarren is a JP. There's no possibility the local bobby will have the courage to stand up to a magistrate.'

'True.' Eleanor clasped her hands. 'But the colonel may well listen to the vicar.'

Alice turned to look at her aunt. 'You think Walter would speak to him?'

'I'm sure he would. My husband will stand up for any innocent child in the face of such a predator.'

'But we're the women's suffrage group. Surely, we should find a way to handle this ourselves without turning to a man to fight our battles.' Miss Pendleton folded her arms.

'This isn't only a battle for women. This is on behalf of our children. We owe it to them to use whatever weapons we have at our disposal. The colonel is never going to listen to a group of women. Our cause is less important than keeping our children safe.' Alice sat down and looked around the assembled women.

'Alice is right,' said Mrs Collins at last. She turned to address Eleanor. 'Assuming you're willing, Mrs Hargreaves, I propose that you ask the vicar to intercede on our behalf. But if that fails, then I propose our next course of action is to get out the boards and paints again, make up some placards and we picket the magistrates' court next time it's in session.'

There was a spontaneous outbreak of applause and one of the young mothers said, 'Why don't we do that anyway? The man should be publicly shamed.'

'Leonard Fitzwarren should, I agree, but not his uncle.' Alice felt a sudden spurt of loyalty towards her former employer. 'Let's give the colonel the chance to do the right thing first.'

When the women had left, Alice remained with Eleanor in order to brief the vicar. Viola went to meet her children from school and Harriet offered to bring Lottie back to The Hawthorns for tea with the Wallingfords.

The Reverend Walter Hargreaves listened in silence as Alice briefed him on what had happened to Molly – without naming her. When she had finished, he put his head in his hands. 'The loathsome creature.' He got up. 'I'll drive over and see the colonel now.'

'I shall come with you,' Alice said firmly.

'Better not. You know what a misogynistic old curmudgeon he is.'

'But I know all the details of what he did.'

'Unless it was your own child, you've only heard them second hand from the mother.' Walter folded his arms.

'It wasn't Lottie. But I do have more details that the mother chose not to share widely. Besides, while the colonel doesn't like me, at least having been my employer for many years he knows I'm honest and will always tell the truth.'

Walter still looked doubtful, but his wife gave him a meaningful look and he relented. 'Very well, Alice, but don't be surprised if he's unpleasant towards you. That good-for-nothing nephew is the apple of his eye. And let me do most of the talking.'

At Padgett Hall they were shown by a maid into the large study-library so familiar to Alice. Entering the room, she gave an involuntary shudder as she remembered the days spent here at the little table under the window, deciphering the old man's spidery handwriting and transcribing his boring memoirs into a typewritten manuscript. He had subsequently paid a fortune to publish the work privately and it now stood in five fat, leather-bound volumes between a pair of ivory bookends on a shelf at the other end of the room.

The door opened and the colonel came in. The war and his

duties as the chairman of the tribunal which determined the fate of conscientious objectors had given him a new lease of life. His stride was spritely, his posture was more upright than of old and he was wearing uniform. When he saw Alice sitting beside her uncle, he stopped short and glared at her with cold grey eyes under heavily overgrown eyebrows. 'What the devil's this all about, Hargreaves?'

'Mrs Cutler is here on behalf of the women of the village who approached me on a very serious matter. It concerns your nephew, Mr Leonard Fitzwarren.'

'You mean *Captain* Fitzwarren? He's a ranking officer again. Doing a fine job too, recruiting across the county.'

Alice glanced at her uncle. As Walter had said, Leonard was the apple of his eye.

'What serious matter? If this is a complaint about their husbands and sons being conscripted then you're wasting your time, Vicar.'

'It's nothing to do with the war.' Walter placed his hands on his knees. 'I'm afraid Captain Fitzwarren has been accused of molesting a little girl.'

The colonel's face turned scarlet and the tangled hedgerows that were his eyebrows came together as his face contorted in rage. 'How dare you make such an accusation of my nephew. Leonard is doing a fine patriotic job and this is how the parish repays him?' He was out of his seat and pacing in front of the fireplace.

'I'm afraid they're serious allegations, Colonel. I was visited by a delegation of a dozen mothers. All with children at the village school and threatening to make a public protest. I think you need to listen to what I have to say.'

'My nephew needs to hear this himself. I won't have you sitting here accusing him when he can't defend himself.' He rang the bell and a maid appeared. 'Fetch Captain Fitzwarren immediately.'

The colonel, still red-faced, returned to his stiff-backed wing chair and sat waiting. There was an awkward silence punctuated only by the ticking of the carriage clock on the mantelpiece.

After a few minutes Leonard Fitzwarren entered the room. He stopped short as soon as he saw Alice and Walter. 'What's happened?' He looked between his uncle and the two visitors, his eyes blinking rapidly.

'Sit down,' the colonel barked.

Curling a lip at Alice, he took a seat opposite them. 'What's she doing here?'

Alice felt Walter's hand on her arm, anticipating her angry retaliation. 'Leave this to me,' he muttered. 'Colonel, it seems Mr Fitz... err... Captain Fitzwarren, has been regularly accosting a child on her way home from school.'

Leonard Fitzwarren went pale but denied it immediately. 'This is preposterous. Why would anyone believe anything coming from this adulterous woman who lived in sin with her married lover?'

'Who is the child who has accused my nephew? Is it your stepdaughter?' The colonel pointed a finger at Alice.

'No, it's not my child. The mother concerned has chosen not to reveal her daughter's identity to protect her, but she has given the details of what happened to the other mothers in the village.'

Alice glanced at her uncle, who gave her a reassuring smile and squeezed her hand. 'Go on, Alice.'

Ignoring the colonel's glares, Alice spoke calmly and set out what had happened to Molly Fuller. 'At first he coaxed her and won her trust with sweets, then after he'd interfered with her, he bought her silence with half a crown, and believed he'd ensured it with threats.'

Colonel Fitzwarren's face was red as a boiled lobster while

Leonard's was drained of all colour. 'Where's your evidence?' he snarled.

The vicar shook his head, his expression grave. Ignoring Leonard, he addressed the older man. 'Colonel, who in Little Badgerton can spare half a crown to give to a child? People are struggling. Most of the menfolk are at the front. I know you don't want to hear it but I'm as sure as I can be that it's true.'

The colonel got up and began pacing again. 'I simply can't believe that a member of my family would do such a despicable thing. It's the behaviour of an absolute cad.' He directed his angry gaze again at Alice.

She reached into her jacket pocket and pulled out a linen handkerchief. 'There's also this.' She handed the item to the colonel. 'You'll see the initials LGF embroidered on it.'

'Where did you get this?' Colonel Fitzwarren dropped the handkerchief on the side table beside him as though it was poisonous.

'I lost that handkerchief when I was out walking. The girl must have picked it up.'

Alice spoke again. 'The child told her mother your nephew dried her tears with it. He forgot to ask her to return it.'

Leonard Fitzwarren jumped to his feet, his face reddened with rage. 'That's a lie. I never went near the girl. She's made the whole thing up.' He halted, thinking, bottom lip protruding. 'Is it any wonder? She's the product of another immoral liaison. Remember that Fuller chap who tried to claim he was a conchie. You dismissed his claim. This is just a nasty act of revenge of the family's part.'

Walter leant forward, his hands on his knees. 'No one has named the child. At least no one other than you.' His tone was icy. 'I think you've just admitted your own guilt, Fitzwarren.'

'This is monstrous.' The colour drained from Leonard Fitzwarren's face. He looked at his uncle, his eyes wide with what appeared to be growing panic.

The colonel buried his head in his hands. Then with a suddenness that took them all by surprise he leapt from his seat, grabbed his swagger stick from where it lay on top of the nearby desk and swiped his nephew over the head and shoulders.

Leonard Fitzwarren wailed in pain and curled himself into a ball, drawing his knees up as his uncle set about him with the stick.

Walter was on his feet immediately and pulled the elderly colonel back.

Colonel Fitzwarren slumped into his chair. 'Who else knows about this, Vicar?'

Alice answered. 'So far only some of the women but I can't be sure they won't have gone home and alerted their menfolk. At least those who are not overseas. Understandably they feel no child is safe.'

Walter bent forward and looked straight at the colonel. 'I strongly urge you to do something about this before there's trouble. You don't want an angry mob marching on Padgett Hall.'

Colonel Fitzwarren collected himself. He smoothed a hand over his be-medalled jacket and stood. 'Pack your bags immediately. I'll no longer have you under my roof. Forget inheriting my estate. I'll have my will redrawn. This house and the money will all go to my old regiment. You'll not get a penny from me.'

Leonard, snivelling, picked up the handkerchief where it lay abandoned on the side table and wiped his nose and eyes. 'You can't believe her, Uncle. She's lying.'

'Get out, Leonard. I don't want to set eyes on you again. And consider yourself dismissed from your role. No more strings pulled for you by me. They can send you to the front for all I care. In fact that's what I'll be suggesting to HQ.'

'But I can't. My injury—'

'There is no injury, Leonard. No need to pretend anymore. That old polo accident healed long ago. You're a coward and a sham and I'm sorry I let sentimentality and family loyalty get in the path of my better judgement. Now get out.'

Later, back at the vicarage Alice and Walter told Eleanor what had happened.

'So he's leaving Little Badgerton altogether?' asked Eleanor. 'But that means sending the problem elsewhere. Shouldn't he be prosecuted?'

'The chances of that are nil, I'm afraid.' Walter crossed over to the sideboard and poured out three sherries, handing one each to the two women. 'Getting the police to prosecute something like this would be well-nigh impossible – especially in wartime – and there'd be no chance of proving the case without bringing the poor child into court. Something I imagine her mother would be loath to do.'

'That's true,' said Alice. 'She'd never allow her daughter to testify. Nor would I in her place. Besides, if the colonel means what he says, then he's hitting Leonard where it will hurt most – in the pocket.'

'Most definitely,' Walter agreed. 'And the man is out of his cosy sinecure too. If I know the colonel that young man will soon be in France. And I wouldn't rate his chances too highly there. All that nonsense about him being wounded out of the Indian Army when it was only a minor injury from playing polo.'

Eleanor savoured her sherry and said, 'I was walking behind him along Nightingale Lane the other day. He didn't see me. He had that walking stick he always hobbles along with. There he was, bold as brass, believing there was no one to see him, striding confidently with no apparent limp and using his stick to slash at the long grass in the verge.'

'He's a liar and a cheat as well as a child molester.' Alice drained her glass. 'Thank you both so much. I'll sleep soundly tonight knowing we'll hear no more of that horrible man.'

But as she walked home Alice felt bitter that Leonard Fitzwarren's disgrace had happened only now. Too late to have prevented Edmund from attesting. He would inevitably have been conscripted anyway, but in a war where every second could bring death, Alice begrudged every additional day she might have had Edmund at home. Every day he was gone, the pain intensified. If anything happened to him, how would she ever find the strength to carry on?

TWENTY-EIGHT

Victor was exhausted. Still plagued by pain from his shrapnel injuries, he was juggling a lot of balls in the air: The ministry, the brokerage, the Dalton estate, Harriet's finances, and the mysterious Madame Renard. All that, as well as coming to terms with the fact that he was head over heels in love with Maurice Kynaston and had to find a way to protect them both from the risk of scandal. As he thought of Maurice an idea occurred to him. Why didn't he offer Maurice a position at Dalton Hall, running the estate. It would solve two problems – giving them a reason to be living under the same roof, as well as easing the pressure of Victor's workload. The more he thought about it the more he liked the idea. He hoped Maurice would too.

He smiled to himself, then turned his attention back to the ministry investigation. If he were to figure out whether and how Herbert Cutler might have got hold of faulty ordnance and redirected it to the Western Front, he had to understand how the flow of materials in and out of the factories worked. Since he couldn't possibly visit them all, he'd have to select one and hope it was typical.

After reviewing the list of munitions production facilities, he consulted a map and selected a purpose-built one in the Midlands. He knew it would save time to choose one of the many in west London, but Victor was keen to escape the city and have some time to think.

He drove there in his Morris Oxford Bullnose. He'd missed driving since joining the army. Not as much as horse riding though. He thought of his horse, Connemara. Connie had accompanied him as far as Alexandria, but he'd been forced to say goodbye to her there. It had been decided that no more horses were to be shipped across to Turkey due to the unsuitable terrain and the fact that the Gallipoli mission had failed to penetrate beyond a narrow coastal strip, meaning there was no possibility of cavalry being deployed. Victor wondered if Connie was still alive. Had she been shipped back across the Mediterranean to France? Over to Salonica? Kept in Egypt? Or sent to Palestine or Mesopotamia? He hoped she was alive, and that whichever lucky officer had inherited her would love and care for her as much as he had.

The ordnance factory consisted of a series of ugly redbrick buildings, along with several warehouses and offices spaced widely apart and surrounded by barbed wire fencing. A siding from the mainline railway passed through the site, which was also served by a canal with a wharf. Victor presented his identification and was shown into an office building and told to wait.

The factory manager, a short dapper man, greeted him with ill-concealed irritation, clearly viewing this visit as an intrusion and a distraction from more pressing business. He looked briefly at Victor's credentials, noting with a flicker of approval the DSO which the ministry had insisted on including after his name.

'We have a rush on today. The quotas are up and one of the

belts broke yesterday. That's set us back a bit. I've asked the head foreman to show you around the place. He knows his stuff so you can ask him any questions.'

Victor followed the foreman into the enormous factory. It was a vast space supported by steel joists and pillars, like a cathedral, only in place of pews it was crammed with long aisles of machinery – heavy flywheels, with belts and pulleys rising above them into the roof space. The noise was deafening. Each of the lathes was operated by a man or to Victor's surprise more often by a woman. The operators stood in front of their machines, deftly operating their individual piece of equipment before the hot metal passed to the next operator for a further process. As the shifts were twelve hours long with only a couple of ten-minute breaks it must have been exhausting. Men, wearing brown cloth coats, presumably foremen or supervisors, patrolled up and down the aisles.

Over the racket from the machines, the foreman told Victor that in peacetime there had been a tendency for highly skilled operators to work through every stage of the production process on one machine, but in the interests of efficiency, and to allow the rapid employment of unskilled women, the process was now broken down into a series of easy-to-master stages with machines customised for each individual step.

They walked up and down the lines with Victor asking his questions and struggling to hear the responses over the roar of the machinery.

'These are the casing production lines.' The foreman competed with the thump and roar of the machinery. He explained that each cartridge consisted of a casing, with primer, gunpowder and the bullet head. 'We're making up to three million rounds a week, but they want us to get up to six million. We also fill the cartridges on site. That's done in a separate building. The propellants we use are highly explosive, so the propellant storage and filling sheds are some distance from here.

They're surrounded by earth bunds on three sides to contain any accidental explosion from the rest of the site.'

The man led him out of the far end of the facility, and they walked a short distance along a concreted pathway beside a narrow-gauge railway line to a smaller building.

'Storage and filling of explosives must be separate from the manufacturing of the casings. Filling must be done in what we call clean areas. Nothing that can spark. No matches, no metal of any description.' The foreman shook his head. 'We have to drum it into the women working on cartridge filling. No hair-pins or safety pins, no metal buttons – even covered ones. Anyone caught is out on their ear. There was a lass last year went to prison for it. Had to make an example.'

As they walked, Victor asked him about shell manufacture.

'We don't do shells here. We used to do some shrapnel shells at the beginning of the war – but never high explosive shells.' The man explained that the creation of shell casings was done in a specialist foundry then the shells were usually taken to separate filling factories to be filled with shrapnel and deto-nator fuses. Victor cursed to himself that he hadn't realised this was a specialist cartridge factory. If he wanted to find out about shell manufacture, he'd need a separate trip to another facility. 'I was hoping to find out more about shells today. About what causes so many duds. But it seems I'll need to visit another facility.'

'As it happens, I can answer that.' The foreman then went through a lengthy explanation of what made a dud shell – that the most common problem in faulty shells was faulty fuses. These delicate mechanisms could be prone to fault if not made to exacting specifications. 'At the beginning of the war there was enormous pressure on production and some of the factories couldn't cope. Now that there are more factories and the inspec-tions are more rigorous, things have got better.'

The foreman led him to a quieter part of the site, away from

the deafening din of the cartridge shop and the danger of the
explosive stores. The man was clearly pleased to have been
asked to host the visitor from the ministry – a welcome break
from his routine work overseeing the operatives. He explained
how since Lloyd George had created the Ministry of Munitions,
prior to becoming prime minister, the problem had been significantly reduced. 'Most of the dud detonators were traced to one
factory and it's all been sorted out now.' He went on to explain
that most of the fuses used were triggered on contact and when
they landed in soft mud they often failed to detonate. 'That's
been the trouble this summer on the Somme. On the other
hand, some of the buggers go off if the gunners jolt the shell
while they're loading. Poor bastards get blown up by their own
shells.'

Victor wanted a cigarette but even though they were some
distance from the explosives store he didn't want to risk it.
There was something unnerving about being in this enormous
site where a single spark could cause a massive conflagration.

As he drove back to London, he felt disheartened. Fasci-
nating though the tour of the factory had been, he was no nearer
to discovering any way that Herbert Cutler might have been
involved in nefarious dealing.

Two days later, Victor was sitting on the floor of his office at the
ministry, surrounded by sheets of paper. His focus that day was
on scrap and returns. Before the Shell Crisis led to David Lloyd
George's reorganisation of the production of ordnance and the
creation of the Ministry of Munitions, there appeared to have
been a variety of procedures in place among individual production sites to dispose of rejects and returns – by controlled deto-
nation – with scrap dealers sometimes handling the process.
Since the reorganisation, everything came under the control and
oversight of the ministry. At the same time, a more rigorous

quality control regime had been put in place across the factories leading to a significant reduction in the number of duds. Another blind alley.

Dispirited, he glanced at his watch, and started to gather the papers together. It was time to head for the City and Dalton Associates.

A name on one of the papers caught his eye. He was sure he'd come across that firm before somewhere. He reached for his notebook and scribbled the name in it. After returning the papers to their files and securing them in a locked filing cabinet, he left, locking the door to his office behind him.

Back at the brokerage, Victor dealt rapidly with the queries brought to him by the chief clerk, then turned his attention to Herbert Cutler's portfolio, which he was in the process of liqui-dating in line with Cutler's instructions. Something had been nagging at his brain. He shuffled the papers back and forth, pulled out ledgers and looked through the columns of figures.

There! The name that had given him pause back in the ministry that morning.

Fox & Co. A firm based in the northeast.

It appeared Herbert Cutler himself had owned the majority holding in the business. The remaining thirty per cent had been owned by a series of smaller shareholders, including Victor's late father, Lord Dalton. The firm had been sold in the middle of 1915, not long before Herbert Cutler's arrest, and the proceeds reinvested in a range of stocks.

Something else was puzzling Victor. He couldn't put his finger on exactly what. Then in a flash it struck him. He remem-bered what Harriet had said when she'd seen Madame Renard at the office. *Renard* was the French word for fox. Was there a connection? Victor's instincts told him there must be.

TWENTY-NINE

Alice looked up as the door to the studio opened. She put down her paintbrush and rushed to greet Maurice Kynaston, helping him off with his jacket and on with his apron.

'It's wonderful to have you back, Maurice. How did it go?' Alice thought he looked happier than she'd ever seen him. She couldn't help wondering how much this was due to her brother.

Maurice beamed. 'Thank you, Alice. I learnt a lot from Mr Whall – and from his daughter too. Veronica was my guardian angel while I was in Hammersmith. She's a fine craftswoman and was extremely helpful and patient as I struggled to get the hang of it at first.'

'I find it hard to believe you struggled!'

Maurice looked sheepish. 'I was rather in awe. It's an impressive operation there. The first morning I was so nervous I tripped and knocked a sheet of glass off the bench and shattered it.'

'Oh no! I'm so sorry.'

'Everyone was very kind, and I'm pleased to say that was the low point and everything picked up nicely after that.' He moved across to the worktable in the centre of the studio. 'How have you been getting on?'

'Almost finished. I've got some touching up to do on Bevis's face before the final firing of that piece. Otherwise, we're ready to start the leading. I'm looking to you to take charge of that now you've been so well trained.'

He smiled. 'I'll try not to let you down.'

Alice jerked her head in the direction of the kiln. 'As soon as it's hot enough can you get the next batch ready for firing. It's all laid out here.' She indicated a section of the floral border, to which she had been stippling and adding textural highlights. 'Then I think you can start the leading tomorrow.'

The two worked on in silence until mid-morning, when Alice made a pot of tea and they paused for a short break.

'I was very sorry about your father, Alice.'

'Thank you.'

'I was shocked when you telephoned and told me what had happened. I'd only seen Lord Dalton a few days earlier and he'd seemed in fine fettle.'

'You saw Papa?' Alice looked up at the captain and saw his face was flushing.

He looked away, clearly embarrassed. 'Your brother kindly invited me to luncheon at Dalton Hall.'

'I see.' Alice paused, searching for something to say to relieve the captain's evident discomfort. 'You and Victor have become good pals, haven't you?'

Maurice sipped his tea, avoiding Alice's eyes. 'While we were both at Bankstone, we found we have much in common. Not least our life-changing injuries.'

'Of course,' said Alice, anxious not to probe too much.

There was an awkward silence until Maurice broke it. 'I've been meaning to talk with you. Now that we've almost finished the Latchington window and the medical officer is happy that I'm ready for discharge, I need to think about my future.'

Alice bit her lip. 'I wish I had something to offer you here, but without Edmund, there's no new work. In fact, Matron has asked whether I can resume working part-time on the wards. Just during school hours when Lottie isn't around.'

'I completely understand. Indeed, once the MO discharges me, I'm thinking of moving to London.'

'I see. Do you think Mr Whall might take you on?'

'Not while the war continues. But perhaps there might be a role of some kind afterwards.'

Alice frowned. 'Oh dear. I should have thought of that. No one's commissioning work at the moment.' She paused. 'Perhaps, like Victor, you could find a position in the War Office?'

'Oh Lord, no! I'd hate it. He and I are very different in that respect.'

Alice realised from the speed of the response that it was something that had probably already been discussed between the two men.

'So, what will you do?' She put down her cup.

Again, the captain's face took on a flush. 'Er, Victor has suggested I assist him at Dalton Hall.'

Alice's jaw dropped in surprise. 'Doing what?'

'Some kind of estate management role.'

'I see,' she said, but she didn't really see at all. 'I thought you wanted to work with your hands?'

'Yes, I do. Victor mentioned it being a very physical role. There's a lot to be done around the home farm and the gardens. Carpentry, felling trees. That kind of thing. As well as keeping a watch over the estate in general.'

'Would you live there? At Dalton Hall?'

The colour of Maurice's face was deepening. 'Apparently there's a cottage behind the stables, that used to be occupied by the head groom who's no longer around. It was suggested I might stay there.'

'Like a servant? Really?' Alice remembered how Victor had

so scathingly described the little cottage she and Edmund lived in as a love nest, so it was ironic that he was contemplating establishing Maurice in a similar setting where they could spend time together safe from the scrutiny of Lady Dalton.

Maurice finished his tea, put the cup and saucer back on the tray and with the help of his crutch got up. 'As I said. It's just been mooted. There's still lots to discuss.'

Alice stretched out her hand and touched his sleeve. 'I'm sorry for subjecting you to an inquisition, Maurice. It's really none of my business. I just want to be sure that you'll be all right.'

'Thank you, Alice. That's most kind.' He turned and went over to check on the kiln.

When she got back to the cottage a letter from Victor awaited her. The date had at last been set for Herbert Cutler's trial. Alice was torn. The thought of sitting in court and seeing that man in the dock made her uncomfortable. If she never laid eyes on Cutler again it would be too soon. But she knew that were Edmund here he would attend. And Dora was Lottie's mother. Distasteful as the prospect of attending the trial was, Alice felt it was her duty to put in an appearance. Victor was planning to be there so she decided to join him.

Later that night, after Lottie was sleeping, Alice thought back to her conversation with Maurice. She was now certain there was more than friendship between him and her brother. Whatever her own feelings on the matter, she determined that she would not let them come between her and Victor as had happened nine years ago when she'd come upon him with Edmund's brother, Gilbert.

But it was hard not to worry. If her suspicions were correct, the two men were putting themselves at risk. And at Dalton Hall they'd have her mother to contend with. While Lady Dalton had brushed away Alice's distress about discovering Victor and Gilbert together, dismissing it as youthful horseplay, it would be quite a different matter were she to suspect something untoward between her son and his friend the captain. Back in 1908, Lady Dalton had been entirely focused on marrying off her daughter and chose to look no further than the planned engagement. But now, with Victor, a bachelor, employing his close friend as what Her Ladyship would doubtless regard as a servant, her tolerance would be tested, and her suspicions aroused.

Alice struggled to sleep as she pondered the problem. She had never thought of herself as a schemer but surely there was some way to protect Victor. Otherwise, he could be heading for trouble.

A few days later, Alice was walking with Harriet. Godfrey, Harriet's baby son, was asleep in the perambulator and it was a fine if cloudy day. The two friends walked slowly, ambling along, leaving the village behind them.

'How are you getting on?' Alice asked her friend. 'Aren't you finding Little Badgerton rather dull?'

'Not dull exactly. It's a lovely place and I've been made to feel so welcome by everyone. It's not so much Little Badgerton as me...'

'You?'

'I feel purposeless. A bit at a loss since the war started and the suffrage movement was put on pause. I miss having the cause to champion. I miss the meetings. All the tedious tasks which made me feel useful. Poor old Monty dying has made things worse. I may not have cared a great deal for the old buffer, but being his wife and running the London house gave me something to do. More than that – it gave me my identity. Now I feel rather pointless. I exist merely as the mother of my children. I know that ought to be enough but I'm afraid it isn't.' Harriet stopped and looked at her friend. 'Is that shocking?'

'No. Of course not. I understand.' Alice placed her hand over Harriet's where it gripped the handle of the perambulator. 'I'd feel the same way. I've almost finished the window Edmund and I started together, and I intend to go back to nursing at Bankstone. I couldn't bear simply being at home while Lottie's at school and Edmund's away.' She looked at the sleeping baby. 'Of course, you have the two little ones at home—'

Harriet interrupted. 'Oh, I adore the children, but being stuck with only them for company all day is not my idea of a purposeful life. In London the nanny spent more time with the little darlings than I did.'

'Have you thought of getting a nanny and joining me at Bankstone then? There's plenty to do there.'

'I'd be utterly useless at nursing. For a start I'm squeamish and run a mile at the sight of blood. I know it's a poor show in the face of all the sacrifices the men are making fighting for us all. Believe me, I'd rather be over there fighting the war than trying to play Florence Nightingale.' Harriet steered the pram around a puddle. 'You must think I'm awful.'

'I know you too well to think that. Your trouble, Harriet, is you're too honest. You say things others might think but never dare to utter. It's why I love you so dearly. You're an open book.' She stretched an arm around her friend. 'I'll have a think and see if I can come up with something to occupy you.'

'As long as it doesn't involve helping you with your stained-glass windows or emptying bedpans for wounded soldiers.' Harriet gave her an apologetic grin.

'I can ask Walter if there's anything he needs a hand with in the parish. Something that would use your organisational skills.'

They walked on in companionable silence. An idea began

to take shape in Alice's head. She decided to let it simmer for a few days before trying it out on Harriet.

After a few minutes, she changed the subject. 'I hear we're in for some hot weather.'

'Not before time.'

'I was speaking to one of the sisters who live in the cottage by the pond. They're both prodigious jam-makers. She told me this summer has been a disaster for fruit. We had all those cold nights in June and then nothing but rain. Lots of the strawberries were ruined. But apparently there's a heatwave coming in a day or so.' As Alice said this, she thought of Edmund. What would be worse for him out there in the trenches? Being mired in mud, with the constant threat of trench foot and the endless depressing rain? Or suffering in a heatwave, sweating in khaki and burning under an unrelenting sun?

'What's wrong?' Harriet must have sensed the change in her friend's mood. 'You suddenly look very sad. Are you thinking about Edmund?'

'I'm always thinking about him,' Alice said. She changed her tone to a brisk one. 'School will be out in ten minutes or so. We'd better get back.'

Alice, Maurice and Lady Lockwood stood side by side examining the finished window. Alice and Maurice, with the assistance of Lady Lockwood's groundsman, had just finished installing it in the memorial hall at Latchington. Alice felt a rush of pride that she'd not only finished the work but that it was beautiful. She was also hugely relieved that the window fitted into the *ferramenta* perfectly and the latter in turn fitted the embrasure. She wished Edmund could be here standing beside them looking at it. So often she'd doubted herself and despaired that she would be unable to do justice to the work without his guiding hand. Yet as she gazed at it now, she knew it was all she could have hoped for.

Lady Lockwood had said nothing, and Alice scarcely dared to breathe as she waited for the reaction from their patron. Then she realised the older woman was crying.

'Don't you like it?' Alice's throat constricted in fear. She had convinced Lady Lockwood to allow them to depart from the original brief of a simple visual of Latchington House with a coat of arms, Bevis's name and dates, and an inscription. Was Her Ladyship backtracking now?

Lady Lockwood reached out and took Alice's hand. 'My dear. Like it? I absolutely love it. I know you showed me the preliminary drawings, but nothing could have prepared me for the sheer beauty of this window. It's utterly breathtaking. I only wish my darling Bevis and my late husband could have seen it.' She wiped her eyes with a handkerchief. 'The colours are so vibrant. The power of the soaring eagle. And I can't believe how perfectly you have captured my son's likeness.'

She moved closer to the window and ran her finger over the inscription at the bottom. Lady Lockwood had chosen it herself – a quotation from Shakespeare's *Julius Caesar*: '*Cowards die many times before their deaths. The valiant never taste of death but once.*' Her finger moved on and traced the dates of Bevis's brief life.

Alice wanted to cry too. She thought about the quotation and hoped it didn't apply to Edmund. She didn't want him to be brave. She didn't want that one single and final death. But if Shakespeare had been right then the alternative was worse – living life in the constant fear of death as it slowly ate away one's soul.

As though sensing Alice's distress, Lady Lockwood wrapped an arm around her. 'As well as doing Bevis proud you've done yourself proud. I was quite right when I insisted you work on this window too. I knew you alone would understand what I wanted to convey. You have exceeded my hopes.' She pulled Alice closer. 'Now enough tears. It's time for a toast. I have a bottle of champagne on ice and I'd like us to raise a glass to Bevis and to all those who can't be with us today.' She turned to Maurice. 'You'll join us too, Captain?'

'I'd be honoured,' he said. 'Although my role has been small.'

'Small perhaps but according to Alice, significant.'

Later when they were leaving, Maurice walked on ahead to the waiting motorcar that Lady Lockwood had laid on to bring them. Alice turned to say goodbye to her friend and patron.

'I hope to see you at the official opening of the memorial hall. The captain too. I'll also be inviting your aunt and uncle. But I hope you'll forgive me, Alice, if I don't invite your mother. I'm afraid she and I had a falling out.'

Alice didn't know this. 'I thought you were close friends.'

'So did I. Until I saw how Lady Dalton behaved towards you when you lost your baby. I found that unforgivable. It also made me question lots of the things I had taken for granted before. Including my stance on women's rights. I've had to rethink that too. I've resigned from the Anti-Suffrage League. Since then, I've come to the conclusion that young women as plucky and capable as you, my dear, deserve the vote as much as any man does. More so in many cases. Once the war is over and the campaign starts up again, I intend to join the suffragists. I draw the line at acts of violence. There's been enough of those in this dreadful war to last any lifetime. But peaceful campaigning will suit me well and give me something to do in my dotage.'

'Your dotage is a long way off, Lady Lockwood. But I'm

delighted to hear you've decided to support the cause. Thank you!'

Lady Lockwood patted Alice's cheek. 'Don't thank *me*. It's I who needs to thank you. God bless you, Alice. And may your husband return safely soon. Once the war's over and word spreads about my wonderful window I think you'll both be extremely busy.'

THIRTY

Edmund's first experience of the battlefield was in support of his company when they were required to undertake a night operation. The objective was to capture an area of woodland occupied by the Germans. It was part of an ongoing series of attacks over the course of several days, in what became a rico-cheting back and forth of territory as it was captured, lost, and recaptured, in poorly coordinated efforts.

The attack was hampered by dense, heavy undergrowth which impeded the men's progress, tearing at their puttees and scratching their hands and arms. All the while they were moving forward, they were subject to constant shellfire – hazard enough anyway, but in this heavily wooded area there was the added risk of trees being blasted out of the ground and crushing men beneath them as they fell. Before long, the land was a scarred blight, strewn with fallen trees, tangled barbed wire, and dead men – both German and British.

Edmund was at the front of a stretcher, paired as usual with Johnny Ivans, with two other lads at the rear. He called back over his shoulder. 'I can't see a damn thing.'

Their training had been mainly on open ground where

they'd learnt to carry the stretchers up and down steep slopes and sand dunes, while keeping them level, but they'd had little or no experience of dealing with dense undergrowth. Most significantly they had always been able to see where they were heading. Here they were stumbling blind all over the place.

'I know,' gasped Johnny. 'I can't tell what's up and what's down.'

As they were speaking, a shell whistled past and exploded a matter of yards behind them, creating an enormous hole.

'Blimey! That was close!' The normally calm Johnny looked rattled. 'You all right back there?' he asked the patient.

Edmund looked back at the man lying half-conscious on the stretcher. A big lad, a miner in civilian life, he was one of the company sergeants. 'Don't worry, Sarge,' he said, aware that his words were lies. 'We're nearly there. Hang on and you'll soon be safe and sound.'

They moved forward again, trying to pick their way through the tangle of bracken, brambles, and barbed wire.

Visibility was a challenge too, thanks to the smoke from shellfire and burning vegetation, as well as the lack of a clear vista ahead due to the steep incline, the remaining tree cover and the darkness.

'Watch out!' Johnny called to the two men at the rear. 'Dead Jerries in the way. We'll have to go round them.' A frequent hazard for the bearers was the presence of dead bodies – most of them having lain there for many days, from the terrible first morning of the Somme. They picked their way around the pile of grey uniformed dead.

Inside the woods, there were still some German snipers and the noise from their machine-gun post, combined with the sound of artillery fire, made hearing the calls from the wounded difficult.

As the night progressed, they stumbled about, disorientated, trying to locate injured men, load them onto the stretcher and then find their way back to the aid post with them. Their hand-drawn maps were of limited use as the landscape bore little resemblance to what was illustrated. Edmund was soon to realise that the scenery the battalion fought through changed almost hourly, significantly hampering the movement of both the advancing troops and the returning bearers. Landmark buildings and signs no longer existed and the pattern of the treescape constantly changed, so that between one round trip and the next the whole picture was completely different.

After each carry, Edmund quickly sketched out a new version of the map to help guide them on the route back, only to find it had changed yet again. The confusion caused by this lack of bearings was intensified by the incessant din of gunfire and artillery barrages thumping away to the point of madness.

Edmund found that losing their way entirely was to be a frequent occurrence on the Somme. Out there in that devastated wasteland it was hard to believe they were inhabiting the earth rather than some strange nightmarish underworld of myth and legend.

Physical and mental exhaustion was exacerbated by the knowledge that all too often, wounded men who might otherwise have been saved, died from their injuries because their stretcher bearers lost their way and ran out of time. Edmund discovered that there was nothing more heartbreaking than carrying a man for hours only for him to expire when the dressing station was in sight.

All around them was ugly mud-brown earth, devoid of all the colours and features that usually signified life. Edmund remembered long ago reading *Macbeth* as a schoolboy. He would not have been surprised had the three ghostly witches themselves materialised before him here on the Somme. It felt as though they were trapped on that same 'blasted heath'.

As dawn was breaking, orders came for their unit to dig in and consolidate their capture of the wood. Although they had achieved the objective of capturing the territory from the enemy, there was little to show for the long night, other than a heavy increase in the toll of the dead, who lay scattered amid the fallen trees and churned-up mud of the once wooded hillside. The Germans they'd been attacking had retreated to form a new line of defence. Edmund knew it was likely there would be a counterattack before long.

It all seemed pointless – like an old-fashioned square-dance where the dancers stepped forward then turned and stepped back, covering the dance floor, back and forth until the music stopped. But here on the Somme the music was discordant, deafening and he doubted it would ever stop.

When the attack on the wood ended, the battle continued for Edmund, Johnny and the other bearers. After the fighting finished, they worked on, tramping back and forth from what was left of the shell-blasted wood to the aid post, long past the arrival of daylight. Their fighting colleagues now enjoyed some respite as they dug into new trenches and regrouped in what had once been the wood. But the bearers continued to retrieve the wounded and carry them to safety. The daylight improved visibility – but it also helped the German snipers so extra vigilance was needed to negotiate the furrowed field of battle while in view of the enemy and open to stray shellfire.

Edmund found the hardest part about being out on the battlefield was having to leave behind men who were dying. The stretcher bearers had been constantly drilled on the importance of carrying back to the aid posts only those men with a chance of survival. While he understood the logic of this and had no argument with it, nonetheless it was a wrench having to turn his back on a dying man to rescue one with a fighting chance of survival. Sometimes there was enough time to hold a hand, administer some morphine to ease the passage to death, whisper a few words of comfort, or light a cigarette and help the dying man to smoke a few puffs. But often there wasn't. Every time he had to turn his back and walk on to another man, he felt a shaft of guilt, powerlessness and shame.

All those men with outstretched hands desperate for their pain to end. The expressions of incomprehension on their faces. This wasn't the glorious chance to win the honour and victory they'd been promised when they'd signed up and taken the King's shilling. It was dirty, ugly, obscene. And for what?

Edmund knew that no matter how long he lived, he would never be able to eradicate the Somme from his head. But then, he reflected, he probably wouldn't need to. Increasingly, he and his comrades counted not only each day, but each hour or even minute they survived as an avoidance of death rather than the continuum of life. And in the depths of physical and mental exhaustion, he sometimes envied the dead. At least this hell was over for them. When would his time come?

While most of the injured men Edmund and Johnny carried were intensely grateful, there were some who were a trial to carry. There was a term used among the bearers for these – the wailing whingers – men who shouted and screamed so loudly – usually disproportionately to their level of injuries – telegraphing their presence to the enemy and making the bearers' progress more hazardous. Even more unpopular were those men who were quite evidently suffering from self-inflicted wounds. It angered the bearers that their efforts were diverted away from the more deserving. But tonight, as he and Johnny and their fellow bearers carried the wounded back to safety, all he saw around him was resilience, stoicism and supreme courage. Besides, who were they to condemn a man who was so terrified, so desperate, so close to mental collapse, that he'd fire a gun into his own hand or foot to escape?

By the time they concluded that there was no one left to rescue, Edmund was shattered. Bone tired. Exhausted to the point that he could barely keep himself upright. His shoulders felt as though they'd been crushed under a ton of concrete and the blisters on his hands had burst so that gripping the heavy stretcher with its precious load was sheer agony. The stretcher straps that went over the bearers' shoulders were backbreaking, cutting deep into the skin where it covered the bone with little to cushion the weight. But every time he'd wanted to give up there would be another man in worse pain, often with injuries so terrible that their agony was unimaginable.

At last, when they returned to the trench he crawled into the dugout. There, regardless of the lack of space, the water underfoot and the numerous rats fattened by feeding on the flesh of dead men, he collapsed into a deep and dreamless sleep.

The following evening when he finally awoke, Edmund was relieved to know that there was no action planned that night for their unit. He found Robert, who was scribbling something on a pad of paper.

'Writing home?' Edmund asked.

'No. Just random thoughts about last night.' He closed up the notepad and tucked it into his tunic pocket. 'I couldn't ever tell Viola what that was like.'

Edmund nodded. Telling Alice of the horrors he had been witnessing ever since they'd arrived on the Somme was unthinkable. He couldn't find words capable of summing up what he'd seen and even were he able to, it wouldn't be right to burden her with the worry and the horror.

Robert lit a cigarette and offered one to Edmund, who accepted gratefully. His own supply had been exhausted on dying and agonised men out there. Exhaling slowly, Robert said, 'I discovered last night why the Germans seem to be outgunning us.'

'Yes?'

'One of the lads ended up in a shell hole with me. His foot blown off. Your lads fetched him back to the aid post. Hope they manage to save the poor bastard.' He drew the cigarette smoke deep into his lungs. 'Anyway, he told me he and another lad in his unit had stumbled into an abandoned German trench. Said it was so deep it was no wonder they were impervious to our bombardment. Even had electricity and beds and solid floors. Like the blooming Ritz.' He sucked every last breath of his cigarette, then spat out the butt before it could burn his lips. 'And what's worse, the ground there was so much higher they could see into our trenches. We never stood a bloody chance. Meanwhile our generals are sitting safe behind the lines, making daft decisions from the comfort of their *chateaux*.'

'No point in being bitter about it. It will just eat us alive.' Edmund said the words but didn't mean them. He was very bitter. He'd never wanted to be here. Nor had Robert. They'd had no choice. But even the poor deluded bastards who'd happily volunteered did so without any knowledge of what they'd signed up for.

One of the hardest things Edmund found about life on the front was the lack of solitude. Everywhere he looked there were men. Hundreds and thousands of them. No escaping them. Yes, he valued the comradeship, the banter, the generosity and the support, but he also longed to be alone.

Ever since they'd left the camp near Gosport, solitude had been an impossibility. They were crowded together into lorries, trains, on the ship across the Channel, in the camp, on the route march to the front, and here, most of all, in the cramped conditions of the trench. Packed tightly into muddy holes in the ground, to freeze, to get drenched or to burn under a blazing sun.

He tried to imagine he was back in the studio at Bankstone, wrapped in blessed silence, with only the occasional birdsong, the crackle of the fire or the soft sound of Alice's skirt rustling as she moved between the workbench and the table.

He tried to imagine he was up on the Hangers, sitting on the fallen oak where he and Alice had first acknowledged their love, looking out over the valley below towards the distant coast.

He tried to recall the rich smell of damp leaf mould, of bluebells, of the scent of newly mown grass in the verges.

But it was impossible.

All around was the stench of the trenches. All around were men. Aimlessly chatting, half-heartedly telling jokes, playing the harmonica, reading, writing letters home.

But mostly men just sitting, staring into nothingness, waiting, waiting, waiting.

THIRTY-ONE

The courtroom at the Old Bailey was packed. Alice and Victor managed to get the last two seats in the public gallery. The press was out in force – a toff on trial for murder was a guaranteed success on the newsstands.

Alice looked down at the man in the dock. Herbert Cutler had lost weight during his months on remand. His face was gaunt – with its sharp pointed nose and prominent brow into which were etched wrinkles like deep ravines. Otherwise Cutler looked as smart as he always did – his greying hair was well-oiled and swept back and he still sported a glossy moustache. He was wearing an expensively tailored Savile Row suit with the chain of a large fob watch. Edmund's father managed to look both distinguished and formidable.

Alice shuddered involuntarily. It was more than seven years since she'd seen Herbert Cutler – at one of those interminable dinners she'd endured at Grosvenor Square with her parents, during the period between her brief engagement to Gilbert and the planned but aborted engagement to Edmund.

Victor had come today to provide her with moral support. Alice herself had turned up because she felt she owed it to

Edmund to witness the trial of his father. She wondered whether he would have come himself, had he been able. Although there was no love lost between father and son, she thought he probably would. After all, he had visited him in prison. One thing was clear. No matter how much animosity existed between them, Edmund would never have gloated about his father's fate.

But above all, Alice felt Dora deserved justice. It was important for Alice to understand why Cutler had taken her life and deprived Lottie of the mother she loved. One thing Edmund had always been clear about was that despite Dora's shortcomings as a wife she had been a devoted and loving parent.

The proceedings opened with a plea of not guilty from Cutler, which produced a shiver of excitement around the courtroom.

The prosecution barrister made his opening remarks briskly, claiming this was a clearcut case of murder. Herbert Cutler had been angry and had been overheard arguing heatedly with his daughter-in-law. There was a motive for the quarrel – a letter found at the scene of the crime demonstrated that Dora Cutler had defied her father-in-law's edict that his granddaughter was not to meet her father, Mr Edmund Cutler. The barrister added that Edmund was currently serving his country on the Western Front, as though to underline that denying him access to his only child was an act of cruelty. Finally, the deceased woman had a range of injuries – bruising to the front of her face consistent with a violent assault, a fractured skull and a severed jugular vein. The lawyer pointed out that the defence would try to claim that her extensive injuries were a result of her tripping over, hitting the marble fireplace and landing on broken glass already present in the hearth but it would stretch the margins of probability for the presence of three sets of injuries to different parts of the head and neck all to be accidental. Most damning was the fact that the defendant had done nothing to raise the alarm or attempt to assist the victim. It had fallen to the butler to run for help.

He concluded, 'The prosecution will today set out its case that Herbert Cyril Cutler, being of sound mind, did unlawfully kill his daughter-in-law, Mrs Edmund Cutler, formerly Miss Dora Fisher. We will demonstrate how this man violently attacked a defenceless woman in a chilling act of brutality that caused her death.'

The first witness called was Logan, Cutler's butler at Grosvenor Square. Logan outlined the events of that fateful evening, confirming that the defendant had returned from an outside engagement and had requested a sandwich in his study.

'What was your employer's frame of mind?'

The defence objected immediately that this called for supposition.

'Let me reframe my question. How did the defendant appear when you saw him that evening?'

Logan spoke confidently. 'When Mr Cutler returned from his club, there was nothing unusual about him or how he acted. He often had a simple supper alone in his study, if he was not entertaining guests.'

'After you brought the defendant his sandwich when did you see him again that night?'

'About half an hour later he rang for me to bring him another tumbler for his whisky.'

'Did you establish the reason for this request?'

'Mr Cutler merely said the glass was broken.'

'Broken? How?'

Logan coughed and glanced at the man in the dock. 'He didn't say. I could see the pieces in the hearth, so I presumed he'd thrown the tumbler there. I offered to clear the pieces up and pour him another whisky but he told me to go.'

'Who was with the defendant when this happened?'

'No one, sir. He was alone.'

'And his manner at that time?'

'He seemed angry. But that wasn't unusual. Mr Cutler can have quite a temper, sir. He asked me where Mrs Dora Cutler was and I told him she was visiting friends to express sympathy for the loss of their son over in Gallipoli. I enquired whether he needed anything else, but he told me that was all and I could go to bed.'

'And did you?'

'No. I joined Mrs Fairfax, the housekeeper, for a cup of cocoa in the kitchen. She then went up to bed, but I make it a rule never to retire until after Mr Cutler does.'

The examination continued, as the prosecution barrister established Dora's arrival, the raised voices behind the closed door of the study, laughter from the victim, followed by a scream.

'I went into the room and saw Mrs Cutler lying in the hearth. She was all bloodied round her face and there was blood in the grate.'

'What was the defendant doing?'

'He was standing near her.'

'Near her?'

'Over her I suppose.' Again, Logan glanced nervously at the dock.

'And was the lady alive at this point?' The barrister leaned on the wooden bench, keeping his voice calm and measured.

'As far as I could tell, she was. She was breathing. But she didn't look in a good state. I presumed she'd tripped and hit her head on the marble fireplace.'

'Kindly stick to the facts. The court is not interested in your suppositions, Mr Logan. What happened next?'

'I ran out into the square and alerted the bobby on his beat and asked him to summon a doctor. When I got back to the house, Mrs Cutler had stopped breathing. The doctor arrived a few minutes later and pronounced her dead.'

'What was Mr Cutler doing all this time?'

'He was sitting at his desk.'

'Sitting at his desk? Doing what?'

'Nothing. Just sitting there.'

The barrister raised his eyebrows and looked intently at the jury as he repeated the words with emphasis. 'Just sitting there. What happened next?'

'Mrs Fairfax, the housekeeper, appeared. She'd been in bed and heard the commotion. And the bobby used the telephone to call for more police. When they arrived, they took pictures of Mrs Cutler's body before it was taken away to the mortuary. They asked us all questions, one by one, and after that they took Mr Cutler away in handcuffs. I sent a telegram to Mr Edmund Cutler to tell him his wife was dead, and his father had been arrested.'

When the prosecution finished examining the witness, the defence barrister rose for his cross-examination.

'Mr Logan, you implied that Mr Cutler threw a whisky tumbler at the fireplace and caused it to smash. In other words, a deliberate act of anger?'

Logan hesitated. 'Yes, sir. That's what it sounded like.'

'Sounded? So, you were not able to *see* this act?'

'No, but—'

'Just answer the question. A yes or no will suffice.'

'No.'

'In fact, the door was shut at the time was it not?'

'Yes.'

And where exactly were you, Mr Logan, when you heard this noise?'

'In the butler's pantry.'

'Quite a substantial distance from Mr Cutler's study? According to the measurements in Exhibit One, a plan of the property, some thirty feet away with two doors between.'

He paused, allowing the gentlemen of the jury to absorb that piece of information.

'At what time that evening did Mrs Cutler return to the house in Grosvenor Square?'

'I can't recall the exact time. But it was after eleven.'

'You can't recall?' The barrister's voice was incredulous, as though underlining that Logan was a far from credible witness. 'How would you characterise your relationship with your employer?'

'I have been in Mr Cutler's employ for fifteen years.'

'Answer the question. How would you characterise your relationship?'

'Respectful.'

'You found him a congenial employer?'

'I suppose so. Yes.'

'Yet in your cross examination by my learned friend, you implied he was quick to anger and that you were unsurprised by hearing raised voices.'

'Yes.'

'I put it to you, Mr Logan, that you jumped to the conclusion that your employer had violently attacked his daughter-in-law and deliberately led the police to reach this conclusion too. The same daughter-in-law whom Mr Cutler had welcomed warmly into his home and supported financially after her husband had abandoned her.'

Alice gasped. She clenched her fists tightly and felt Victor's arm around her.

'All I said was that Mr Cutler had a bit of a temper.' Logan, clearly put out, ran his fingers between his shirt collar and his neck.

'Had you ever witnessed Mr Cutler arguing with the deceased woman before?'

'No.' The butler stood erect, staring at the wall beyond the barrister's head.

'Did you ever witness him striking the deceased?'

'No, but I did wonder whether he'd hit his late wife—'

The judge intervened. 'The witness must stick to answering only those questions put to him by Counsel and not to speculate on other matters. I direct the gentlemen of the jury to ignore the last remark.'

Logan's face was now red and he looked down as though he was wishing for his ordeal to be over.

The defence barrister continued. 'When you entered the room and saw the lady lying bleeding in the hearth did you try to assist her?'

'My instinct was to go at once for medical help. As I said before, she looked in a very bad way.'

'I repeat, did you try to offer any assistance to the injured woman?'

'No.'

'No further questions.'

By the time the court recessed for lunch, Alice felt as though she'd been wrung out like an item of laundry. She and Victor went into a tearoom near the court. She gripped his hand. 'The defence was clearly trying to discredit Logan. And the trouble is that in the absence of a witness in the room, it looks difficult to prove that Cutler did it.'

'It's early days yet. There's the coroner's report, and the police report on the scene of the crime. All the prosecution has to prove is that Cutler's actions were a substantial cause of Dora's death, not necessarily the only cause or even the main one. They don't even need to prove he had a motive or wanted to kill her, just to do her harm.'

Victor's tone was reassuring, but Alice couldn't help thinking he was trying to offer comfort rather than speaking with conviction.

'But is the fact that he raised his voice sufficient to prove that he meant her harm? As the butler pointed out, he often raised his voice in anger. Heavens, he did it often enough to Edmund. But it didn't mean he meant to kill him. Dora could still have slipped and hit her head.'

'A young healthy woman? She was hardly unsteady on her feet. And according to the autopsy she hadn't had a drop of alcohol. I can't conceive how she'd manage to fall accidentally and with sufficient force that she'd injure herself mortally.'

'Even if she fell on a sharp piece of glass?'

Victor shrugged. 'I don't know. But as the prosecution said, there were so many different injuries that it's hard to believe they were *all* accidental.'

Alice looked at her brother anxiously. 'I hope they can convince the jury of that.'

'The question is whether Cutler will opt to appear in the witness box himself?'

'Do you think he will testify?'

'Herbert knows juries don't like defendants who refuse to testify. They assume it's a sign of guilt.'

'Oh Lord!' Alice bit her lip. 'He can be very plausible when he chooses. Charming even.'

'Look, Alice, there's no point speculating. I don't think we should come to court again. At least not until the end of the trial. For a start I can't spare the time. I'm drowning in work. I completely underestimated how much would be involved in the job with the ministry and getting the brokerage into shape is a full-time job in itself. Not to mention sorting Papa's affairs. Have you given any more thought to coming back to Dalton Hall?'

Alice sucked in her lips. It was now or never. She'd been mulling her idea over in her head for several days and she had to find a way to suggest it to Victor without antagonising him.

'Maurice mentioned he might be going to work for you.'

'*With* me. I don't see him as an employee. He's my friend.'

Alice hesitated. Should she speak up, let Victor know she knew there was more than friendship between him and Maurice? She took a deep breath and said, 'I know how much he means to you. And I know that people may talk.'

She felt Victor flinch as she spoke. 'Please, let me finish what I have to say. I blame myself for Gilbert taking his life. It's something I'll have to live with forever. If I could do something, anything, to right that wrong I would do it. I have a suggestion that might help you and Maurice.'

Victor looked at her, his expression closed and stony. 'What do you mean? How can you possibly help me and Maurice?'

'Marry Harriet!'

'What?' He looked at her in bewilderment. 'How would that help us? And why do you imagine Harriet would agree?'

'You would have married Dora if you hadn't decided to take a commission. The reasons are just as valid now. Having a wife would protect you from gossip and divert attention from your relationship with Maurice.' She looked up at him but couldn't read her brother's expression.

'It's not only that though. It would give Harriet a sense of purpose. She's always been susceptible to status and being married to you would be infinitely preferable to being a lonely widow in Little Badgerton.' Alice saw him thinking, and pressed home the advantage. 'Harriet would be a huge asset to you. She loves entertaining and is frightfully good at it. She can give Mama a run for her money and wouldn't be cowed by her. She'd be able to help to run the house and the management of the estate.'

'She'd never agree. Why would she want to marry a man who can't be a true husband to her?'

'Harriet doesn't care about all that. She has her children. She's never been interested in the physical side of marriage.

And she adores you, Victor. I think it would be a perfect solution for both of you... for all three of you.'

Victor frowned but Alice knew him well enough to see that he was giving the proposal serious consideration.

'There's another reason.' She leant towards him.

'And what might that be?'

'Harriet's eldest, Crispin. He inherits his father's earldom, and she worries about the absence of a father to guide him and act as an example to him. You'd be perfect at that too, Victor.'

'Have you already discussed this with Harriet?'

'Of course not. I wouldn't do that without asking you first. But please think it over carefully. I'm sure it will be a wonderful solution for both of you.'

As the murder trial progressed, contrary to what he had told his sister, Victor occasionally slipped into the public gallery to observe proceedings.

One afternoon, he arrived in time to witness the defence questioning Herbert himself. Victor listened in horror as Cutler's apparent sincerity and evident grief over the demise of his daughter-in-law appeared to warm the jury to him. Seemingly close to tears in the witness box, he assured the jury that he had felt nothing but affection for his daughter-in-law.

Victor was relieved that Alice wasn't there to witness the nauseating theatrical performance.

'I harboured the hope and dream that my son, Edmund, would be reconciled with Dora and that he would return to the bosom of our family. I am broken hearted that after dear Dora's tragic death, my son immediately married his mistress. Far from wishing Dora dead, I desperately wanted the best for her and my beloved granddaughter. Dora's death and little Charlotte's loss of her mother has broken my heart. I didn't kill Dora. I would never have done her harm.' He made a sobbing noise and turned his head away.

Glancing down at the jury Victor could see sympathy in their faces where previously they had appeared impassive or even stern. Unable to bear any more, Victor left the court and went in search of a stiff drink.

In the gloomy saloon bar of a pub near the Old Bailey, Victor tried to push the spectacle of Cutler's theatrical performance from his head. He had some more thinking to do – about Alice's idea of him marrying Harriet. Already, the initial shock having subsided, he was beginning to see merit in the plan.

But, despite Alice's enthusiasm for the arrangement, Victor found it hard to believe that Harriet herself would entertain it. Why would she agree to a marriage they would never consummate? And what about Maurice? How would he feel about Victor taking a wife?

Why was life so complicated? If only he and Maurice were free to live the lives they wanted without fear.

THIRTY-TWO

About a week later, Victor was still chewing over Alice's suggestion.

As he walked towards the ministry building, he pondered the idea. As his sister had pointed out, he'd been willing enough to contemplate marrying Dora Cutler when Herbert had pressed him. A marriage to Harriet would be no different than to Dora – apart from the fact that he genuinely liked Harriet and enjoyed her company. It would also provide him with an heir to Dalton Hall – young Crispin Wallingford could inherit the estate. The Dalton barony itself would die with Victor. It couldn't pass to an adopted son. But Crispin was already in possession of an earldom, higher up the pecking order than a barony anyway – and Victor had long since known he would have no children of his own.

Were he to pursue this, Harriet would have to be made aware of the nature of his relationship with Maurice. That was only fair. Could he trust her? Victor thought that he probably could. Harriet was more worldly-wise than his sister and had always seemed to be tolerant and broad-minded. But Maurice?

How would he feel? Both Maurice and Harriet would have to approve the plan.

Thoughts of marriage left him as soon as Victor entered the ministry building. He gathered all the paperwork pertaining to Fox & Co. After locking the office door and pulling down the blind on the glass panel, Victor placed the relevant papers on the floor so he could get an overview of the operations of the company. He separated out orders, invoices and bills of lading, then began the laborious process of matching them.

It appeared that Fox & Co's operations had been focused on two shell production factories. For both, the company was responsible for the collection and safe disposal of rejected shells and detonators. Lost in the study of the documents he barely noticed the time passing, until the gloom in the office caused him to get up from the floor to switch on the electric lights. When he returned to his position, kneeling on the floor, he suddenly saw a pattern emerging in the documents before him. There was a clear discrepancy between the quantities of rejects shipped out of the factories and those disposed of by Fox & Co. An enormous discrepancy.

Where were the missing rejects going?

If they were being illegally shipped to the frontlines, there was no evidence here to prove it. Fox & Co appeared to be dedicated only to the disposal of scrap materials. There had to be another piece in this puzzle.

Victor collected the paperwork, filed it away then left the office. Outside, he crossed the gardens onto the Embankment and walked briskly to Somerset House, where Companies House was housed along with numerous other government offices. There he deposited the paperwork Cutler had signed regarding the brokerage, before showing his Ministry of Munitions identity card and requesting to see the files for Fox & Co.

The firm had been wound up the previous year but he was able to ascertain the names of its directors. He'd hoped to examine the accounts, but none had been filed. There were only three directors listed: Herbert Cutler, Camille Renard and Desmond Colin Troughton. Victor had never heard of Troughton and still didn't know whether Camille was the mysterious Madame Renard or her husband.

He needed to do another search, this time the other way around. He walked over to the counter and spoke to the clerk. 'I need to establish what other companies these three people hold directorships for. Is that possible?'

The clerk looked up. 'It's possible but it will take time. We're short staffed.' He took in Victor's uniform and said, 'As you'll know only too well, Captain, there's a war on.'

Victor bit back his frustration. 'What will it take to get the information and when? It's important. It's relevant to the war effort.'

'That may be, sir, but if I am to give this priority, you'll need to produce the necessary authorisation.'

'And what might that be?'

'Form D613-106.'

'Where do I get one of those?'

The clerk pushed out his bottom lip, evidently milking the small power he had. 'You don't, sir. I'm afraid they're issued only by the War Cabinet. You'll have to wait your turn. Could take days. Even weeks.'

'Right.' Victor was determined this petty official wasn't going to get the better of him. 'I'll be back within the hour with the form.'

'We close in fifty minutes.' The man was now preening.

Victor ran downstairs, through the Great Arch and out onto the Embankment where, wincing at the shafts of pain from his injured leg, he raced back to the ministry building.

He met Major Rothbury-Harris as the officer was leaving

the building. Victor, breathless, gasped out what he needed. To his great relief the officer told him to walk over to Whitehall with him, where he was due to meet Lloyd George himself and would procure the necessary consents.

'I hope you're getting somewhere with your investigation, Dalton. We need to hit this one for a six,' the major said as he strode along.

'I have some promising leads. I'll be able to tell you more when I've finished digging at Companies House.'

A signed Form D613-106 safely in his jacket pocket, Victor hailed a taxi and headed back to Somerset House, arriving just five minutes before the clerk closed for the day.

The man looked less than happy to be presented with the paperwork. 'You really do want this quickly, don't you? Come back tomorrow after two p.m. and it will be ready for you.'

The following afternoon, back at Companies House, Victor was seated at a long oak table when the same clerk presented him with just two folders.

'I searched for each name individually but apart from the record you saw yesterday for Fox & Co, there was just this one for Cutler & Son, stockbrokers, and this one here with all three names listed as directors.' The man paused, clearly interested to find out more.

Victor placed the files on the table and pulled out a chair. 'Thank you. I have all I need now.'

Disappointed, the clerk returned to his desk on the other side of the room, from where he surveyed Victor with curiosity, while chewing on a pencil. His claim that there was a staff shortage didn't appear to be impacting his productivity.

Leaving aside the papers relating to the brokerage, already

familiar to him, Victor pulled the second folder towards him. The company was Gilbert International Shipping Ltd. He remembered the name from invoices and bills of lading for numerous shipments from the shell factories. He turned the page and read the entry for directors. The managing director was Herbert Cutler. So it seemed he had named the company after his dead son. Victor felt a ripple of anger that Gilbert's name had been sullied in this way.

The other directors were listed as Desmond Colin Troughton of The Coach House, Wallingford Magna, and Camille Renard of The Dower House, Wallingford Magna.

Victor could barely breathe. Not only must Camille Renard indeed be the same woman whom Harriet and Alice had met at Lord Wallingford's funeral, but it was clear that Desmond Colin Troughton, whoever he was, hailed also from the late earl's estate. The name wasn't familiar to Victor – but why would it be? He had never visited Wallingford Hall and had barely known the late earl.

His suspicions were now aroused. Was there a link between this shipping company, Herbert Cutler and the sudden diminution of Monty Wallingford's fortunes?

Had Madame Renard used her role as the dowager countess's companion to gain inside knowledge of the earl's affairs? Was she the wife or mistress of this Desmond Colin Troughton? It was hard not to draw the conclusion that the pair of them must have been in league with Herbert Cutler and had probably played a significant part in depriving Harriet and the children of their rightful inheritance.

Victor copied out the details from the paperwork, thanked the clerk effusively and left Somerset House for the brokerage. There he extracted the file on Harriet Wallingford and went through it with mounting concern.

· · ·

When he'd finished examining the papers relating to Harriet's inheritance, Victor debated whether to travel to Norfolk and continue his investigations there, or to pass on what he had discovered so far to Major Rothbury-Harris and Mr Pointer. His deliberations were interrupted by the chief clerk.

'Excuse me, sir, but I thought you'd like to know that apparently the jury in Mr Cutler's trial have reached their verdict and are returning to court. You should be able to get to the Bailey in ten minutes. I've asked the office boy to hail you a cab.'

Victor pushed the files into his briefcase, thanked the clerk and rushed down the stairs and into the street.

The trial had been covered in detail in the newspapers and Victor had been following progress daily since he'd last attended. He'd felt no temptation to return and witness more of the proceedings, as he couldn't stomach it after Cutler's sham performance in the witness box and was keen to get his investigation completed before Cutler was sentenced.

Despite his employer's confidence of an acquittal, Victor couldn't believe that would be possible, even were the jurors now favourably disposed towards him. Dora was dead. If murder couldn't be proved, then surely there was enough evidence to convict him of manslaughter, a verdict likely to earn him several years' imprisonment with hard labour. Herbert Cutler seemed to think that if he threw enough money at any problem, it would go away. But Victor didn't believe the British justice system could be so easily subverted.

The press and public galleries were packed when he squeezed in at the back. The jury was assembled but to Victor's relief the judge had yet to return to the courtroom.

A moment later, the judge entered the court and a hush of anticipation descended.

The jury foreman got to his feet.

'Do you find the defendant guilty or not guilty of murder?'

'Not guilty.'

Victor, glad that his boss couldn't see him, looked to where Herbert sat in the dock. There was a smirk of satisfaction.

'To the charge of manslaughter, do you find the defendant guilty or not guilty?'

Victor held his breath.

'Guilty.'

Instantly the court erupted, and the judge banged his gavel to restore order.

'Herbert Cyril Cutler, you have been found guilty of the manslaughter of Dora Cutler. In view of your good standing as a citizen with no previous blemish on your character and your evident distress at the tragedy that has befallen your family, I hereby sentence you to three years' imprisonment reduced by ten months for the time you have already spent as a prisoner on remand.'

As the judge pronounced the sentence, Cutler yelled, 'I am an innocent man! I will appeal!' Two prison officers grabbed him by his arms and led him away as he continued shouting.

Victor let the verdict sink in. He hadn't expected a murder verdict – the absence of witnesses and Cutler's display of grief over Dora's death had ruled that out. Manslaughter was a reasonable verdict. But the sentencing was an outrage. The old boys' club looking after their own. Mr Justice Kingston, the judge, was not a client, and as far as Victor knew wasn't a member of the same club as Herbert. But Victor wouldn't be surprised if they'd played golf together. Had Herbert been a factory worker or a clerk he'd have got at least ten years with hard labour. If Cutler behaved himself in jail, he was likely to be released within a year.

Victor left the Old Bailey, summoned a cab to take him to Albany where he collected his motor and set off for Little Badgerton. The investigation into Fox & Co would have to wait.

But his determination to bring Cutler to justice for his munitions dealings was now even stronger. Cutler may have got away with murder, but Victor intended to turn over every stone to secure his conviction for his other crimes. He owed it to Dora, to Harriet and to all the victims of his treasonous arms dealing.

THIRTY-THREE

'I was worried sick he'd get away with it altogether.' Alice hugged her brother when he told her of the verdict in Cutler's trial. 'Finding him guilty of manslaughter means there's some justice for poor Dora.'

'I haven't told you the sentence yet.'

Alice paled. 'I thought you said manslaughter meant at least ten years with hard labour.'

'If he were a working man and not a member of the wealthy elite it would have been. However, the judge let him off with just three years' imprisonment less the ten months he's already served. If he behaves, he could be out in a year.' Victor's expression was grave. 'But he left the court shouting about injustice and his intention of appealing.'

Alice listened in disbelief. 'Are there grounds for an appeal?'

'I very much doubt it. The only reason the courts would allow an appeal was if there was evidence of a grave miscarriage of justice. As far as I can see the only miscarriage of justice was the over-lenient sentence.'

Alice slumped into a chair. 'At least it's over. After all the waiting and uncertainty. And he will always have a criminal record.' She wanted to put a positive light on the matter, but it was hard not to think Herbert Cutler had got away with murder.

'What will you tell the child?'

'I don't know. Lottie's so young.' Alice had been putting off thinking about this and now she felt weighed down with responsibility. 'Hearing that the court has decided her grandfather caused her mother's death will be hard for her to comprehend.' She pressed the heels of her hands against her forehead. 'What do you think, Victor?'

Victor considered. 'Does she ever ask you about Dora or Cutler?'

'From time to time she talks about her mother but never about the circumstances of her death and she hasn't mentioned her grandfather much since she left London.'

'Then say nothing. Wait until Edmund's home and let him decide.'

Alice thought of what Molly Fuller had said to Lottie. 'One of her school friends mentioned it before. I had a lot of reassuring to do. I don't want to raise it again if I don't have to.'

'Then don't. Why worry her unnecessarily? If she asks you, it's different.'

Alice decided to tell Victor of her real fear. 'If something were to happen to Edmund, Herbert Cutler will try again to take Lottie away from me as soon as he's out of prison.' She squeezed her hands into tight fists on her lap. 'He prevented Edmund, her own father, spending time with her. Why would he let me continue to care for her when I'm not her natural mother?'

'Even if he gets out of prison quickly there's a stain on his character. No court in the land is going to grant a man who was found guilty of manslaughter custody of his victim's child.'

'You have more faith in British justice than I do. And after the verdict today you've just acknowledged that he's been treated with more leniency than he deserves.' Alice felt dispirited.

Victor looked about to say something else but clearly thought better of it.

'What?' she said.

'Nothing. Don't lose sleep over something that hasn't happened. And don't fret about Lottie. I'm certain that man will never be let near her. Don't tell her anything. No point in worrying the child unnecessarily.'

After his conversation with Alice, Victor booked himself a room at the Frog and Whistle before going to The Hawthorns to see Harriet. He was now more determined than ever that Herbert Cutler would be shown to be the villain he was. Victor wanted to ensure he would receive his rightful punishment for one crime – even though he hadn't for another. He'd been within a hair's breadth of telling Alice about his investigation into Cutler, but he was bound by secrecy.

Harriet was upstairs reading the children bedtime stories, so he was shown by the housemaid into the drawing room. Restless, he prowled round the room like a stalking tiger, picking up objects and putting them back down. Already Harriet had made her mark on the place. There was an enormous vase of garden flowers, framed photographs of the children and several paintings she must have brought with her from Portman Square. Not Wallingford family portraits but contemporary paintings he suspected she had chosen herself. They were bold, vibrant, with a primitive feel. He decided he liked them.

When Harriet arrived, she greeted him warmly, planting a kiss on his cheek. 'What a delicious surprise! I'm delighted to welcome you into my new home, Victor.' She offered him a drink and he accepted a glass of chilled wine.

'So, tell me, what brings you to see me, Victor? I hope it's not bad news about my investments.'

'I need your help. Can I trust you to keep what I'm about to tell you entirely confidential?'

Harriet gave an uncharacteristic frown. 'Now I'm definitely worried.'

'It's about your late husband's estate.'

'I thought there was nothing left of it.'

'There isn't. But I may have found out something about how the earl lost so much, so quickly. I need your help to find out for sure. Firstly, do you know a man called Troughton?'

Harriet nodded. 'I know *of* him, but I've never met him. Monty's estate manager.'

Victor nodded. 'That makes sense.' He went on to explain about the connections he'd unearthed between Herbert Cutler, Madame Renard and Desmond Troughton. 'All I know is that they were all three co-directors of two companies that were involved in the scrap business and marine shipping.'

'What?' Harriet's mouth was open. 'Your boss Herbert Cutler? The man who's up on murder charges?'

Victor interjected. 'Guilty only of manslaughter and given only a token sentence today.'

'Good Lord. He's got away with it.' She shook her head. 'But what on earth connects him, that unpleasant French woman and the estate manager? It's too bizarre for words. Are you sure you aren't imagining this? And how on earth did you find out?'

'Look, I can't tell you all the details as it's related to aspects of the Defence of the Realm Act. I'm investigating something under those powers for the War Office and I stumbled on this. But I need more proof. If I'm right, the three of them are tangled up in some dirty business and I have a hunch that it includes some form of embezzlement of your late husband's money.'

Harriet gasped. 'Go on.'

'Perhaps not by Cutler – he had enough of his own – but by Renard and Troughton. Whatever happens, I doubt we can do anything to recover your inheritance. It's too late for that. But at least we can try and make sure they receive their rightful punishment.'

'How can I help?' She gave him a mock salute.

'Where are the earl's papers?' He hoped she wasn't going to tell him they'd been destroyed or were held by his mother at Wallingford Magna.

She groaned. 'I wanted to clear them out. They were in his study at Portman Square. But the solicitor told me we had to hold on to them for a fixed period in case there was any query about the probate.'

'Where are they now?'

'Upstairs. In the attic. In tea chests. But I haven't been through them to sort them.'

Victor grinned. 'Thank goodness you kept them. May I take them up to London with me tomorrow? You'll get everything back when I've been through it all.'

'There's a ton of the stuff. It's all mixed up with his old school reports and that kind of thing. You'll never fit it in the motorcar. I have a better idea. Why don't you and I go through it together here? We can commandeer the morning room. I never use it and there's a big table we can lay everything out on. Please, Victor. I'd love to help. It would give me something to do. I'm bored out of my mind.'

He held out his hand. 'It's a deal.'

'Then let's have another glass of wine and I'll tell Cook you're staying for supper.'

It took them two days to sort through the earl's papers. Harriet had been right that there was a lot of irrelevant memorabilia including ancient copies of *The Field, Horse & Hound* and *The Harrovian*. It seemed the late earl had been a hoarder where paperwork was concerned, retaining every receipt, no matter how trivial the purchase. This had not been a sign of astute financial management. Quite the reverse. Among the bills for his London club, for the household expenses at both Portman Square and Wallingford Hall, there were invoices for numerous transactions relating to the pig farming business, as well as bills of sale for livestock, land and machinery. It seemed that Lord Montague Wallingford had paid little or no attention to what was beginning to look to Victor like systematic embezzlement of his land and assets by Desmond Troughton.

'I can't believe he didn't see what was going on.' Harriet shook her head and her eyes welled. 'Poor old Monty. There was me thinking he'd gambled his son's inheritance away when all the time the poor chap was being squeezed like a lemon by Troughton.' She frowned. 'But how come no one was aware. The family solicitor? Her Ladyship?' She paused. 'Me?'

'It looks to me as though Troughton was careful. Built up the earl's trust over time so that when it came to signing mortgage deeds and bills of sale, your late husband merely signed on the dotted line without reading.'

'But if Monty hadn't died, surely Troughton would have been caught. Monty would have discovered he had nothing left and called the police in.' Her hand flew to her mouth. 'My goodness, you don't think they killed him?'

Victor shook his head. 'I very much doubt it. He was in London with you. What did the death certificate say?'

Harriet ruffled through some documents and took out a paper. '*Myocardial infarction.* The doctor said it was a massive heart attack.'

Victor took a sip of water. 'It's possible that he'd found out the estate was mortgaged to the hilt and the bank foreclosing. It could have been the shock of losing everything that brought on the heart attack.'

'Poor old thing. I feel desperately guilty now for being mean about him.'

'He should have acted more responsibly and kept a closer eye on his estate.' Victor folded his arms.

'Monty thought all that a frightful bore. He just wanted to hunt and ride. He used to say how lucky he was to have Troughton to take care of things. Too jolly trusting.'

'Well, it's time we took care of Troughton. We need to seek justice for your late husband. And for you and the children.'

'Do you think he still has the money?'

Harriet's expression was hopeful but Victor didn't want to raise her expectations when there was little chance her money would be restored. 'That's what I need to find out. But I suspect it's gone overseas.'

'What will you do?'

'First, I have to take my findings about the matters to my superiors at the ministry.'

'Gosh. But I don't see how what Troughton did has to do with the Defence of the Realm.'

Victor smiled apologetically. 'I'm sorry I can't tell you that. But the information you've unearthed here is going to be essential to the case.'

Harriet shrugged. 'That's a bit rotten but I'll just have to try and rein in my curiosity.'

'Thank you, Harriet. You've done a great service to me – and to the country.'

'What on earth have you and Harriet been up to?' Alice raised an eyebrow. 'Closeted away together at The Hawthorns.'

'Just going through some of her late husband's paperwork.

All very tedious.' Victor brushed a hand through his hair. Least said the better.

'You're both getting on so well. Does this mean you're seriously considering my suggestion?'

He raised his eye to meet hers. 'I've been giving some thought to it. I'm thinking it's not such a bad idea.'

Alice beamed at him. 'Victor, that's marvellous—'

He interrupted her. 'Steady on! I haven't said I'm ready to propose. I need to sound out Maurice and I was hoping you might do the same with Harriet.' He avoided Alice's gaze. 'If I were to spring it on her it could be desperately embarrassing for both of us. Since it's your bright idea and you know her better than anyone, I think you should sound her out first. But, Alice – be subtle. Don't come straight out with it.'

'Give me some credit!'

'But not yet. I need to finish off a project I'm doing for the ministry. And tidy up various details about Harriet's affairs. I'd rather have all that settled before complicating matters by proposing marriage.'

'You know she's always treated you as her almost-brother.'

'I can't marry her unless she understands it won't be a marriage in the physical sense.'

'I suspect that may be part of the appeal if I know Harriet. All you need now is to ask her.'

'There's Maurice too?'

'Go and tell him. He's bound to agree that it's the perfect solution.' Alice thought it touching that her brother wanted Maurice's approval when she herself thought Maurice was hardly in a position to object. It was all too apparent to her that he was as besotted with Victor as Victor was with him. Any plan that enabled the two men to be together without courting suspicion had to win Maurice's approval.

. . .

The meeting with Pointer and Rothbury-Harris took place the following day in the same room at the ministry where he'd met them when he'd been appointed. There was a third man present whom they introduced as Mr Hemmings but gave no indication of his role or rank, or why he was present in the meeting.

Victor took them through his graphs and charts illustrating the discrepancies between arms shipments, the involvement of Fox & Co, its sudden closure in 1915 and the identities of its directors. When he showed them the papers relating to Gilbert International Shipping Ltd. and its directors, he saw them exchange a knowing look.

'Excellent work, Lieutenant Cutler.' Mr Pointer's expression was as close to a smile as Victor had seen in him before.

Major Rothbury-Harris opened a file and extracted a newspaper cutting with a grainy image of a couple evidently on the occasion of their marriage. He slid it across the table to Victor. 'Do you recognise this woman?'

Victor studied it. There was a date in the top corner – around ten years earlier. The caption was written in French. 'Yes, that's her. Madame Renard. But I've no idea about the man.'

Mr Pointer answered. Victor reflected that in another life the two officials would make an excellent double act. 'He is Count Santiago Ruiz-Zorro. Do you understand Spanish, Lieutenant?'

Victor told him he didn't.

'The word *zorro* means fox.'

Victor gasped. 'You already knew?'

The major took over. 'We knew of a connection between the count and Herbert Cutler but had no idea his French wife and this Troughton chap were involved. And we had no evidence how it was done.'

'What was the connection between the Spaniard and Cutler?'

'It was with Count Ruiz-Zorro that Herbert Cutler met at his London club on the evening his daughter-in-law died.'

'That didn't come out in court.' Victor pushed against the edge of the table with his hands.

'We decided it was better it didn't. We couldn't have the prosecution summoning the count to court as a witness. Not before we'd untangled the web. Which now, thanks to you, Lieutenant, we can.' Another smile from Mr Pointer.

Until now the man called Hemmings had said nothing and maintained an inscrutable expression. Now he nodded to the other two men. It was as though they were looking to him for permission before proceeding.

The major leaned forward, elbows on the table. 'It seems Herbert Cutler was arranging arms sales to the Turks and Austrians using Count Ruiz-Zorro as his intermediary. Prior to that, thanks to your efforts, we now have confirmation that he was buying up defective weaponry and redirecting it to our own front.'

'You're saying that Herbert Cutler was a traitor?'

'Most definitely.'

Victor scratched his head. 'I'm surprised. I never had the impression he was a supporter of Germany.'

'He probably wasn't. But I think you'll agree that he's a supporter of free markets and money-making. Selling arms to the enemy was a profitable enterprise. And repurposing scrap to sell as bona fide arms even more so.'

'But what's the connection with Troughton?'

'That we need to establish.' The major rubbed his hands together with relish. 'But if I were a gambling man, which of course I'm not, I'd hazard a guess Camille Renard – or to give her married name, Señora Camille Ruiz-Zorro – embarked on an affair with Mr Troughton and persuaded him to embezzle the funds from her employer's son, the Earl of Wallingford. The money was poured into Cutler's scheme. From what you have told us, it is likely that it's sitting in the bank in Paris where she instructed you to send the additional funds from Herbert Cutler.'

'Oh Lord!' An icy chill ran through Victor. 'The funds will have gone. She asked me to arrange that they should be transferred by Monday – that was yesterday.' He cursed himself for not moving more quickly.

'Fear not, Lieutenant. Officers of Special Branch have been monitoring Cutler's own and your firm's bank accounts ever since we discovered the connection with the count. A block has been put on the transfer.'

Victor nodded to himself as he realised who the mysterious Hemmings must be – an officer from Special Branch.

Mr Pointer turned to Hemmings. 'Do you have any further questions of Lieutenant Dalton?'

The man shook his head, then spoke in a low voice to Pointer before leaving the room. Other than this whispered exchange, Hemmings hadn't spoken for the entire meeting.

Once he was gone, Pointer and Rothbury-Harris each closed the buff-coloured folders in front of them and stood. The major addressed Victor. 'Thank you for your excellent work, Lieutenant, your work here is now complete, and you are free to devote your attention to your civilian career. I will ensure a note of your service is added to your record.' With that he left the room.

Victor turned to Mr Pointer. 'But what happens now? What of Cutler and the others?'

'Rest assured Troughton and the lady will be arrested and incarcerated under the Defence of the Realm Act. As for Cutler, he will be transferred to a military prison and detained indefinitely.'

'Will I be required to testify in court?'

Mr Pointer chuckled. 'There will be no court. No public trial. The provisions of DORA include the suspension of *habeas corpus.* They'll all be shut away for the rest of the war. After the war it's likely that using your evidence Troughton will be tried for the embezzlement of the earl's property. The woman will doubtless be deported and left to the French to handle – where she'll likely suffer a far worse fate than she would have done here.'

'And Cutler?'

'Ah, Mr Cutler. I don't think he will be seeing the outside of prison for a very long time – if at all. It depends on whether it's decided he has committed treason. Men have been shot at the Tower for less.'

'He could be executed?' Victor tried to swallow but his mouth was dry. He told himself that it was no more than Cutler deserved for taking Dora's life, and betraying his country to line his own pocket.

'It's possible.'

'When will I know?'

'You probably won't. Top secret, Lieutenant. Wouldn't be good for national morale to have the public know that one of their fellow citizens has both sold arms to the enemy and sent shells to the front that might have blown up some of our own brave lads.' Pointer walked round the table and stood beside Victor's chair. 'Now I'll need to ask for your security card, and I remind you that the oath of secrecy you were placed under when you accepted this assignment applies for the rest of your life.'

Victor swallowed. 'What about the late earl's widow? Doesn't she have the right to know that the man who stole her son's inheritance has been apprehended?'

'She's aware of Troughton's actions?' Pointer frowned as Victor nodded.

'Well, what's done's done. I suggest you merely tell her that the pair of them have gone to jail for a very long time but sadly too late to recover her money.'

'And Cutler's money? The cash I transferred yesterday?'

'Forfeited. The Crown will want to seek recompense for what's been done.' He signalled towards the door, so Victor got up and followed him.

He shook hands with Mr Pointer and left the ministry for the last time.

No more digging through all those tables of data. He was now free to focus on building the brokerage business without interference from his erstwhile employer. There was also Dalton Hall and the accompanying estate to manage – but that would mostly be in the capable hands of Maurice.

Victor felt a weight lift from his shoulders. Time now to tell Harriet the good news about Troughton and Renard. And yes, time to broach the question of marriage.

THIRTY-FOUR

November 1916

It was a quiet wedding. The couple had discussed whether to conduct it in a register office, but Alice had urged them that a small church wedding was less likely to arouse curiosity. There was an air of furtiveness about register office weddings and Victor wanted there to be no shadow of suspicion around his nuptials.

It was held in St Margaret's in Little Badgerton, officiated by the Reverend Walter Hargreaves, with Alice and Captain Maurice Kynaston as the witnesses. The two bridesmaids were Lottie Cutler and little Poppy Wallingford.

The absence of a grand and extravagant ceremony was an obvious and understandable consequence of the war, as well as the bereavement of the bride just six months earlier.

To Alice's relief, her mother agreed to attend. Maybe it wasn't so surprising, since Lady Dalton had never had the radical falling out with Victor that she'd had with Alice. On the other hand, Alice suspected that her very practical mother had realised she was rapidly running out of allies, and it was time to repair relations with both her children, as well as her sister-in-law.

Sitting in the small parish church as the service began, Alice's gaze couldn't help drifting across to the stained-glass window Mrs Bowyer of Bankstone had commissioned to honour her late husband. Every piece of glass, every image, every piece of lead, and every paint stroke was weighted with meaning for Alice.

She remembered the first time she and Edmund had made love and how later she'd said to him that should they ever be parted, she now had a bank of memories to draw upon and would never truly feel alone again. How bittersweet that was. She had not expected war to tear them apart.

That first time, she'd asked him to always imagine her hand at work alongside his in every piece of glass he ever cut. What she hadn't expected then in that glorious summer before the war was that it would be other way round – that she, alone, would be cutting and painting the glass while thinking of him.

She tried to imagine what he was doing now. His letters spoke of the eternal boredom of life in the trenches, how days were indistinguishable from each other, and life was subsumed in a monotony of endless waiting. But Alice was glad it was dull and boring. Monotony and tedium were preferable to fear and pain and death.

His letters told her little of the fighting. She knew that as a stretcher bearer he wasn't involved, but that was little comfort when he could still be hit by shells, caught in gas attacks and explosions or singled out by a sniper despite the red cross sewn on his armband. Edmund's letters didn't mention much about the injured men either. Alice was all too aware that he wanted to protect her. But that must surely mean that what he was witnessing was too awful to put into words. The fact that he was bearing this suffering alone tore at her heart. Instead, his letters were filled with little drawings in the margins and filling the spaces where he must have struggled to find words. He drew ruined villages, skeletal trees, birds, men's faces, concentrating as they bent over a hand of cards, or walking en masse in crocodile files across barren countryside.

In one letter he'd told her of his own brief stay in the casualty clearing station after being buried in a blast from shellfire. He'd tried to make light of it, described it as an almost humorous incident but she had barely slept the night she read it, imagining the horror of being engulfed and trapped. That night she had woken from a dream where she was buried alive and no matter how loudly she shouted no one could hear her.

Alice pushed these macabre thoughts away, dragged her eyes from the window and focused instead on her brother and her dear friend standing side-by-side in front of the altar, making their vows. Were other people to know the truth behind this marriage they would doubtless judge Victor and Harriet harshly. But Harriet's smiling face defied judgement or cynicism. Besides – was a marriage without physical relations so unusual? Alice thought of her own parents, who had slept in separate rooms as long as Alice could remember. And Harriet and Victor respected and cared for each other in a way her own parents had never done. No, she decided, there was no cause to condemn this marriage.

Maurice Kynaston was standing next to Victor as his best man. Both men wore their uniform and medals, and Maurice was wearing his prosthetic limb. Harriet, as a widow remarrying, had chosen not to wear white. Her simple gown was of soft green crepe marocain, under a long matching jacket with a black brocade collar. A black velvet hat completed the outfit, with a large silk bow in the same soft green as the dress. Alice thought her friend had never looked more lovely.

Miss Pendleton as usual was playing the organ. Alice found herself fighting back her tears as the congregation sang 'Dear

Lord and Father of Mankind'. When she tried to sing the last lines, she felt her voice start to break.

Speak through the earthquake, wind, and fire,
O still, small voice of calm.

A desire to run out of the church and keep running swept over her. Then Alice felt a steadying hand upon her sleeve and to her surprise she realised it was her mother. She turned to look at her, as her mother gave her a look that was close to tenderness. Alice gulped.

Lady Dalton patted her arm and whispered, 'He will come home to you, Alice. I'm sure of it.'

Alice watched the rest of the ceremony through a veil of tears.

THIRTY-FIVE

The weather on the Somme during the first two months of 1917 was brutally cold. The men shivered inside their army great-coats, desperate for some warmth. They tried lighting fires, but the smoke got trapped inside the walls of the trench and choked them. They layered up socks, gloves and balaclavas and constantly rubbed their hands and stamped their feet, hoping to stave off frostbite. Edmund wasn't sure which was worse, this biting cold that penetrated bones to the marrow, or the unending days of torrential rain they'd endured the previous year which turned the narrow trenches into rivers.

He tried to trick his brain and nervous system to feel warm, by imagining he was lying on sun-dried grass by the little stream at the end of the meadow at Bankstone, feeling the burning heat of the sun on his skin and its blinding light in his eyes as he swatted a fly away, made slow and drowsy by a long hot summer. No flies in the trenches now. Too cold. But the rats were still there. When that image failed to work on his constricted blood vessels, he pictured himself in bed with Alice, their naked bodies entwined, skin warmed and glowing from making love. But that was too painful. Would he ever get to experience that again? To hold her body hard against his, to lose himself in pleasure and to know that she was lost too.

'Penny for your thoughts?' Robert Fuller had a tin of boiled sweets and offered one to Edmund.

Edmund didn't want to reveal what he was really thinking about. Even though he imagined there were similar thoughts in the heads of men all along these trenches and in the enemy ones as well. No, he didn't want to talk about Alice in this godforsaken place. 'When we get out of here do you think you'll go back to doing what you did before? All the travelling? The writing?' He studied Robert's face as his friend leant against the fire step, sucking on his sweet.

'Since we've been here, home has taken on an allure it never held for me before.' Robert gave him a wry smile. 'Viola may get her way in the end and have me spending most of my time in Little Badgerton. If the Huns or the cold don't get me first. What about you?'

'I can't wait to get back into my workshop. To bring an idea to life. To make art again.'

Robert hugged his elbows, massaging his upper arms, while trying to bounce up and down to get warm. 'If – and it's a very big if – I do get out of this hellhole alive I might enter politics. Do everything I can to make sure a war like this never happens again. Try to bring some justice into this rotten stinking world. I'm joining the Labour Party when I get back. Then maybe I'll see if they'll take me on as a candidate.'

'You'd get my vote.'

Fuller laughed. 'What? A toff like you voting Labour?'

'I'm no toff. And anyone who's prepared to speak out to stop a war like this from happening again must be worth voting for.' Edmund frowned. 'Why do you call me a toff?'

Robert grinned. 'You went to a posh school. You're married to a woman whose father's a peer. You used to live in a big house in Grosvenor Square.' Robert swept his hands out in a wide gesture, palms up, as if to say, case proved.

'I turned my back on all that though. Didn't I? As did Alice.'

They shivered, teeth almost rattling in their jaws as they waited, knowing that as soon as darkness fell, they'd be going over the top again and facing what could be their final moments. Robert and the infantry first. Then Edmund and the bearers would follow behind, picking up the wounded and carrying them back behind the lines. Waiting now, colder than he'd ever been in his life, Edmund couldn't wait to climb up that ladder and face whatever he might encounter up there as it would mean moving, and the possibility of that movement bringing some warmth to his frozen bloodstream.

As the dusk settled, Edmund went back to wait with the other stretcher bearers. They were positioned behind the forward trenches until the signal came for them to advance, ready behind the fighting men. He stood, tense, nervous, as was always the case before an advance. Eventually the call came, 'Bearers up!'

He tried to swallow, his mouth dry, his throat almost closed. He and Johnny Ivans looked at each other, knowing this was the last call before the order to attack. Whistles shrieked simultaneously along the lines and the infantrymen rushed forward, scrambling up the trench ladders and going over the top.

Edmund and his fellow bearers wait for their own signal, then follow close behind. Their armed comrades rush forward, blindly, dodging shellfire and bullets, relentlessly racing towards the enemy, guns primed and bayonets at the ready. But the bearers must walk forward slowly, unarmed through that hail of lead, to seek out the injured among the fallen.

Slipping, slithering and sliding through mud. Blinking, squinting, straining to see through smoke and flashes of blinding light. Balancing like tightrope walkers as the earth shifts and rocks beneath them and shell craters open like the maws of hell.

Shoulders strain and leather straps cut into their flesh as a stretcher snags on unseen barbed wire. Bodies that breathed and moved moments ago litter the ground like fallen leaves. He trips over one, goes back to check. Dead. Move on.

Time is distorted. Hours or seconds? It stretches and shrinks, assumes a different dimension in this world where up is now down, where the sky seems to collapse and the ground to rise up.

How many men has he carried today? One face blurs into the next. No time for niceties. A man they carry is dead. They gently tip him off the stretcher and step forward to load the next one. On and on. Back and forth. Trapped in the endless production line of hell.

Then boom.

The sky is white, cut with plumes of grey smoke. Little bursts of vivid orange and gold shower earthward from distant shell explosions. Tiny spots of crimson poppies growing around the edges of abandoned shell craters. Faint traces of green from the few trees still standing beyond the reach of the battlefield. Chalk-white of ruined walls glowing like ghost buildings in the sudden stark light of the shellfire. The warm glow of fire, then blackness, with the darker shadows of burnt timber. Ochre soil becomes dark brown, then near-black mud. Drab khaki uniforms. Splashes of scarlet blood staining that drab khaki as the men in front tumble and fall like skittles. Small figures, dwarfed by the destruction around them, holding guns aloft as they stagger forward to certain death, boyish faces illuminated by the glowing embers and flashes of fire.

These little spots of colour contrast with the unrelenting expanse of dereliction and destruction. A portal to Hades. But above it all, a single shaft of pale golden light emerges through the white clouded expanse of sky to guide Edmund to whatever awaits him when he knows it may all end within the next few moments.

There's no sign of Johnny Ivans. No sign of any of the bearers. Edmund is alone.

He moves forward, the mud and heavy clay dragging down his boots, making progress slow. Everything around him has slowed as if time has moved into a new dimension, stretching, contracting, distorting, just as the slab glass does when it's blown. He can no longer hear the boom and crash of shellfire, the scream of bullets, the anguished cries of men as they die. Just an eerie silence, a hollow space inside his head between ears that no longer function.

Edmund isn't thinking of the war anymore. He looks ahead at the stained-glass window this ravaged scenery has become to him. He will recreate this scenery with slab glass, its imperfections and convexity refracting the natural light across this devastated landscape.

He knows it will be the finest work of his entire life. Stark, bold, uncompromising. A panorama to reveal the folly of mankind with its pointless wars and hearts filled with hatred. A monument to the sacrifice of so many innocent men. A focal point for the widows, mothers and children left behind to gaze on and understand something of what these men have endured.

Yes, he can see it clearly now. His hands move the brush across the glass as he strokes the acid in soft sweeping lines to etch away the colour and create the exact effect he seeks. It will be his finest window ever.

Outlined against the flaming sky is Alice, bathed in a shaft of light that's breaking through the clouds and sulphurous smoke. He looks up and moves forward to meet her.

THIRTY-SIX

February 1917

Alice watched the boy as he cycled along the lane from the village towards Bankstone, wobbling as he avoided the puddles from a heavy shower that morning.

Keep moving. Turn in at the big house. Or cycle up the hill towards Steep. Please don't turn in here.

The boy got off his bike and let it fall on its side on the grass. He walked across the meadow, moving steadily towards where she was standing in the doorway of the cottage.

She willed him to turn back, to check the address on the envelope in his hand and realise his mistake. But he moved forward, covering the ground all too quickly. Alice knew him. The postman's youngest son, he had been working as the telegraph boy since the war broke out. He pushed a hand back, took off his cap to scratch his head before replacing it. He adjusted the brim of the cap to protect his eyes from the sunlight.

The boy looked up, saw her in the doorway and speeded up. *Slow down. Please slow down.* It was as if every micro-second of not knowing must be prolonged, as once she opened that envelope there would be no returning. Her world would be changed forever. No matter what torture this moment was, there was still a grain of hope, so she wanted to stay, poised in this limbo of not knowing for as long as she could.

He looked at her then looked away immediately, embarrassed. He must have known the content of the envelope. Alice knew too. She'd been expecting this every day since she'd last heard from Edmund. He wrote all the time. But days had gone by with not a word. The boy, unsmiling, passed her the envelope. He didn't ask if she wanted him to wait for a reply. She knew he knew there wouldn't be one.

Holding the envelope, she stood in the doorway, watching the boy hurry back across the meadow, following the well-worn path. As he clambered back on his bicycle and disappeared up the lane, she went inside, propped the envelope against the jug of winter jasmine Lottie had picked for her yesterday, and put on the kettle to make a pot of tea. She told herself again that until she'd read what was inside that brown envelope nothing had changed.

The kettle whistled, but Alice realised she didn't want any tea. She looked again at the buff-coloured envelope. She snatched it up, wrapped a blanket around her shoulders and went outside to sit on the wooden bench where she and Edmund often drank tea together, talking about their work, listening to the birds singing, exchanging aimless conversation, simply enjoying each other's company and basking in the proximity of each other's presence.

She slipped a finger under the flap and slid it to tear the envelope open. It wasn't a telegram. This paper was buff not pink. She unfolded it. Printed at the top were the words Army Form B104-83.

Dear Sir or Madam

I regret to have to inform you that a report has been received from the War Office to the effect that number 199872 *rank* Private *name* Cutler EB

The words swam before her. She tried to focus, reading it over and over again, checking that there was no mistake. Instead of what she'd expected to read – *killed in action* – there was one word – *missing*, and the date.

Alice's heart lurched. She clung to the filigree of hope that he might be alive. She read on:

The report that he is missing does not necessarily mean that he has been killed, as he may be a prisoner of war or temporarily separated from his regiment.

Official reports that men are prisoners of war take some time to reach this country and if he has been captured by the enemy it is possible that unofficial news will reach you first. In that case I am to ask you to forward any letter received at once to this Office and it will be returned to you as soon as possible.

She folded the letter and put it back in the envelope, then sat, staring up at the rain clouds forming and darkening the sky. How many women in the village had received such a letter only for it to be followed a day or two later with one confirming death? The likelihood was that they had failed to identify and recover his body – so many men killed at once that there was no one to witness the moment he fell.

Her breathing turned jagged. What if he was out there somewhere, badly wounded, lying at the bottom of a shell hole, dying slowly? In agony? Or already dead but buried under earth from explosions? Alice knew the odds were more heavily weighted that he was dead than alive. Even if he'd been captured by the enemy what were his chances of survival? Slim, if the reports from rare successful POW escapees were correct. Maltreatment, disease, starvation, exhaustion from forced hard labour, vicious punishments and reprisals.

It was worse than a letter confirming he was killed in action. The uncertainty. The delayed confirmation. The desire to hope but the stronger fear that there was little reason to do so.

Alice couldn't even cry. To think of Edmund as dead would be a betrayal of him, of the hope he needed to stay alive. But to hope is to indefinitely postpone pain. A kind of slow torture.

Above her head she heard a lark singing. A song of yearning? Or of mockery? She was numb. Alice dug her fingernails into the palms of her hands but could feel no pain. She looked at the little sharp indentations, watching as the flesh slowly sprang back. It was like being underwater. Everything was blurred. She couldn't breathe.

Someone was coming. Alice looked up and saw Maurice Kynaston crossing the field. He had his prosthetic leg on. He'd been wearing it more often lately. She wondered why he was in Little Badgerton then remembered he had been due to see the medical officer to finalise his army discharge. Strange how all these inconsequential things went through her mind as she avoided thinking about the words she'd just read.

It was too late for her to hide inside the cottage and pretend to be out. She waited, wishing Maurice would turn around and go away.

'I saw the postboy,' he said, his eyes full of concern. 'Bad news?' His voice was soft, kindly. It made her want to cry when until now she hadn't been able to.

She looked away but handed him the letter.

He read then looked up. 'I'm sorry, Alice.'

'It means he's dead, doesn't it?'

Maurice stared into the distance. 'Probably,' he said at last. 'I won't lie to you. But don't give up hope yet. I was in a shell hole for days wounded with dead men piled all around me until by a miracle someone found me. That could happen to Edmund too.'

'You were lucky.'

'I was. Although that's not how it felt at the time.'

'When will I know for sure?'

He shook his head. 'I can't answer that.' He put an arm around her, and she was grateful for the bulk of his warm body and the shoulder where she laid her head.

Eventually Maurice said, 'If they get no word within four weeks, they'll declare him as Missing Presumed Dead.'

'I see. Thank you.'

'Don't thank me. When did you last hear from him?'

'Five days ago. At first, I thought there must be an advance and he was too busy or too exhausted to write. But I think inside I knew. I had a sense that something wasn't right.'

Maurice took her hand and squeezed it. 'There's nothing I can say to comfort you, Alice. The pain must be unimaginable. All I can say is that I'm sorry. I know you and Edmund loved each other very much.'

His kindness was more than she could bear. She wanted to hide. To crawl away and curl up into a tight ball to shut out the world.

'I'm going to lie down for a while. Lottie will be home from school in a couple of hours, and I'll need to think about how I'm going to tell her.' It was the thought of Lottie that broke her – Alice felt the tears run down her cheeks. 'Can you let Victor know, please. And my aunt.'

'Of course. Right away. I'll ask your aunt if she'll take Lottie for her tea, as I imagine you'd like some time on your own.'

'Thank you. That would be kind.' Then she reached for his arm. 'Victor will try to persuade me to return to Dalton Hall. But I can't do it, Maurice. Please make him understand that this is my home now. It will always be my home. Our home. Mine and Edmund's. I can't leave. It would be like leaving him.

Leaving all our memories. Everything about this place reminds me of him. I can't possibly go. Please make my brother understand.'

Maurice nodded. 'I promise, Alice.'

Alice rose from the bench and walked inside the cottage. Only when she knew the captain had gone did she finally allow herself to weep freely.

EPILOGUE

Late January 1919

From the day she got the fateful report that Edmund was missing presumed dead, Alice was able to function only because of the need to love and care for Lottie. Now, almost three months after the end of the war, the pain of loss was as acute as it had been that first day.

She'd worked at Bankstone, throwing herself into the care and rehabilitation of the wounded officers there. Only by keeping busy could she stem the terrible emptiness, the void in the core of her that could never now be filled. But at night, when Lottie slept, Alice's loneliness was overwhelming. Everywhere she looked there was something that reminded her of Edmund's absence.

Sometimes she would go into the adjacent studio, hoping that she might feel inspired to work. She would run a finger over a sheet of glass and remember his words about why he had selected it and for what piece of a particular window. She would pick up his tools and remember holding them as his hand had closed over hers guiding her along a cutting line, when he first instructed her. She would sit in front of the fire remembering how they would sit there side-by-side sharing a sandwich and an apple prepared for them by the cook at Bankstone in those early days before they became a couple.

And in their bed at night she had to stop herself crying out his name in despair, loneliness and longing, that she mustn't let Lottie hear.

Edmund's loss had brought her and Lottie closer. She was the only family the little girl had left now and every day when grief threatened to fell her, Alice forced herself to find the strength to keep going for her daughter's sake. Lottie had become her only reason for living.

Harriet and Victor had begged her to move to Dalton Hall, stressing that it would be good for Lottie too. She had sometimes been tempted but in the end she couldn't tear herself away from the cottage at Bankstone, beyond spending the occasional weekend there with Lottie – who loved to be reunited with the Wallingford children. It would have been like turning her back on Edmund and the happiness they had once shared. In Little Badgerton she also had the support and friendship of Eleanor and Walter, who she loved as if they were her parents.

When Robert Fuller was demobilised and returned to Little Badgerton in December 1918, he called on Alice immediately after seeing his wife.

He held her hand, talked to her for hours about his friend. They both cried. Alice was surprised at the generosity and love in Robert and the all too evident pain he shared with her at the loss of Edmund.

'I'm blessed to have known him, Alice. I'll be honest, when I first met Edmund, I couldn't see past the posh accent and the public school. But as soon as we talked, I knew I'd found a friend for life. A man of intelligence, sensitivity, warmth. He was the truest friend a man could hope for.' His voice broke. 'I would never have made it through without him, Alice. That's no comfort to you. But it's the truth. I bloody loved him.'

Alice smiled. 'It is a comfort, Robert. A great comfort to know that until the day he went missing, he had you there beside him. I know from his letters how much you supported each other.'

Robert gave a half laugh. 'I'm meant to be comforting you and here you are trying to make me feel better. No wonder he adored you, Alice. The one thing that was most certain about that quiet, enigmatic man was that he loved the very bones of you. You were the joy of his life. His reason for living.'

Alice closed her eyes. She wasn't going to let herself cry. She'd done enough already and had promised herself not to cry anymore. For Lottie's sake in particular. She needed to be strong. Positive. Brave. But most of all because she knew what Edmund would want was for her to go on living, bringing up his little girl, carrying on their artistic endeavours, trying desperately to make his sacrifice worthwhile.

The bells of St Margaret's were ringing for the Sunday service.

Alice hated the sound. It reminded her of the Armistice, when the bells had rung out all over the country in a jubilant celebration of the end of the war. It had torn her heart open again, the joy of others in sharp contrast to her own loss and pain. Of course, she was glad the war was over, happy for those who were reunited with loved ones. It would be graceless not to be. She tried not to begrudge the joy of Viola Fuller at the return of Robert. She tried not to wallow in self-pity.

At her low points she told herself that Edmund would have hated her to be maudlin and miserable. But every night, alone in their bed she longed for him. *Where are you, Edmund? Where are you?*

The church bells stopped ringing as she climbed up the escarpment through the trees. Lottie was in Sunday school and Alice herself could no longer bear attending church, in spite of her affection and loyalty to her uncle the vicar. Every Sunday, she did this same walk as a ritual, up through the copper beech trees, following the well-worn path to the summit where once she'd heard the faint thunder of guns on the Western Front.

The fat, old fallen tree trunk was still there in the clearing, its bark worn away by the passage of time. Alice sat, as she had sat every Sunday morning since Edmund had left for the training camp in Gosport. She always felt close to him here – the spot where they had first come together and acknowledged their love.

Now she gazed out towards the Channel. The only sounds were of birdsong and the slight breeze rippling through the leaves. No more guns.

She was about to get up and walk back down the hill to meet her aunt, uncle and stepdaughter at the vicarage when she heard the snap of a twig. Her arms tingled. An electric shiver ran through her as it had once before in this very spot. She turned, just as she had on that other morning, almost five years earlier. There he stood, gazing at her, eyes full of love, threadbare greatcoat now looking too big for him.

'I went to the cottage first,' he said. 'But I knew I'd find you here.'

He opened his arms, and she ran into them.

A LETTER FROM THE AUTHOR

Huge thanks for reading *The Artist's War*; I hope you enjoyed following the trials and tribulations of Alice, Edmund and Victor. If you want to join other readers in hearing all about my Storm new releases and bonus content, you can sign up for my newsletter:

www.stormpublishing.co/clare-flynn

And if you want to keep up to date with all my other publications, you can sign up to my mailing list:

www.subscribepage.com/r4w1u5

If you enjoyed this book and could spare a few moments to leave a review, it would be hugely appreciated. Even a short review can make all the difference in encouraging a reader to discover my books for the first time. Thank you so much!

When I decided to follow Edmund to the Western Front in 1916 and to the Battle of the Somme, I knew I didn't want him to be one of those poor unfortunates who surged up the ladders and walked slowly into an onslaught of gunfire on that terrible first day. Nor did I want him to be the average infantryman marching forward with a bayonet on the end of his rifle. Eventually, I made him a member of the Royal Army Medical Corps (RAMC) like my own grandfather. William Flynn joined up in Liverpool in 1914 as one of the Pals and served on the Western

Front for the duration of the war, until demobbed from his last posting in Prussia in January 1919. I have no idea whether he was a stretcher bearer, an orderly or possibly an ambulance driver – in civilian life he was a clerk in the Liverpool Education Office, not a medical man. As I researched the RAMC my respect for the grandfather I never met increased dramatically. I'd always thought being in a non-combat role might have been a cushy number, but by the time I'd finished my research I decided stretcher bearers were some of the bravest men at the front. I hope that comes across in Edmund's story.

Thanks again for being part of this amazing journey with me and I hope you'll stay in touch – I have so many more stories and ideas to entertain you with!

Clare Flynn

clareflynn.co.uk

facebook.com/authorclare!ynn
x.com/clarefly
instagram.com/clarefly

ACKNOWLEDGEMENTS

One of the inspirations for Edmund's experiences on the Western Front was my own paternal grandfather. I never had the chance to meet him as he died when my father was just thirteen. My granny believed his experiences during his years on the Western Front contributed to his early demise.

William (Bill) Flynn joined as an infantryman in September 1914 along with colleagues from the Liverpool Education Office. Soon after joining up, he was attached to the RAMC, serving as a private and eventually as a sergeant. He was twenty-four when he volunteered and engaged to be married to my granny, a nurse. They married immediately after he was demobbed in January 1919. While I have many of his letters to his younger brother (also in the RAMC but serving at Salonika in the Balkans) only one, dated December 1918 from Prussia, is from his time as an enlisted man, so I have no information at all about what he did. His post-war letters reveal a man desperate to be a published author. He did a lot of public speaking, had strong political views and taught English Language at night school – a stickler for grammar and punctuation. While I have a few of his short stories, he never had any accepted. Evidently achieving publication was as tough back in the 1920s and 30s as it is today! I hope he'd be chuffed that one of his grandchildren has sixteen novels published in three languages. I can't begin to imagine how hard those years on the Western Front must have been for him. Apart from one rather whimsical short story set in Belgium, none of his work relates to his war experience. Most of the stories are humorous – no doubt a way of coping with the horrors he must have witnessed.

There are so many people who contribute to bringing a book to publication. I am hugely grateful to Vicky Blunden, my editor, who is a joy to work with – as well as to the whole Storm team who make the process of publishing and marketing a book as smooth and easy as possible.

My writer friends in the Sanctuary help keep me sane. Their support, humour and advice has been a real boon over the years. We don't have enough opportunities to get together but when we do, it reinforces how fortunate I am to have their friendship.

My friend Margaret Kaine, here in Eastbourne, has been a massive help as I wrote this book. Margaret supplied encouragement and helpful feedback, chapter by chapter, and generally helped keep up my motivation.

I consulted a lot of books in researching and writing *The Artist's War*. Notable amongst these was the moving and informative *Wounded* by Emily Mayhew – a godsend in helping me understand the roles of all the medical corps on the Western Front. It's a terrific read.

The book also gave me the excuse to continue my fascination with stained glass. I took the opportunity to see as many windows as possible including a trip to The Stained Glass Museum at Ely Cathedral – I highly recommend a visit.

Last, but not least, my thanks to Clare O'Brien, Hilary Bruffell and Anne Caborn, aka my former MIAMI pals – always ready to buck me up with a good dose of laughter when things don't go so well. Your friendship has helped keep me sane!

Printed in Great Britain
by Amazon